SERENA

Also by Ron Rash

NOVELS

One Foot in Eden

Saints at the River

The World Made Straight

SHORT STORIES

The Night the New Jesus Fell to Earth

Casualties

Chemistry and Other Stories

POETRY

Eureka Mill

Among the Believers

Raising the Dead

SERENA

RON RASH

CANONGATE

Edinburgh · London · New York · Melbourne

This paperback edition published in 2010 by Canongate Books

5

First published in the United States in 2008 by Ecco, an imprint of HarperCollins Publishers, 10 East 53rd Street, New York, NY 10022

First published in Great Britain in 2009 by Canongate Books Ltd, 14 High Street, Edinburgh EH1 1TE

www.meetatthegate.com

British Library Cataloguing-in-Publication Data
A catalogue record for this book is available on request from the British Library

ISBN 978 1 84767 488 3

Designed by Jessica Shatan Heslin / Studio Shatan, Inc.

Printed and bound in Great Britain by Clays Ltd, St Ives plc

For my brother, Thomas Rash

A hand, that with a grasp may grip the worlde.

—Christopher Marlowe

PART I

One

When Pemberton returned to the North Carolina mountains after three months in Boston settling his father's estate, among those waiting on the train platform was a young woman pregnant with Pemberton's child. She was accompanied by her father, who carried beneath his shabby frock coat a bowie knife sharpened with great attentiveness earlier that morning so it would plunge as deep as possible into Pemberton's heart.

The conductor shouted "Waynesville" as the train shuddered to a halt. Pemberton looked out the window and saw his partners on the platform, both dressed in suits to meet his bride of two days, an unexpected bonus from his time in Boston. Buchanan, ever the dandy, had waxed his mustache and oiled his hair. His polished bluchers gleamed, the white cotton dress shirt fresh-pressed. Wilkie wore a gray fedora, as he often did to protect his bald pate from the sun. A Princeton Phi Beta Kappa key glinted on the older man's watch fob, a blue silk handkerchief tucked in his breast pocket.

Pemberton opened the gold shell of his watch and found the train on time to the exact minute. He turned to his bride, who'd been napping. Serena's dreams had been especially troubling last night. Twice he'd been waked by her thrashing, her fierce latching onto him until she'd fallen back asleep. He kissed her lightly on the lips and she awoke.

"Not the best place for a honeymoon."

"It suits us well enough," Serena said, leaning into his shoulder. "We're here together, which is all that matters."

Pemberton inhaled the bright aroma of Tre Jur talcum and remembered how he'd not just smelled but tasted its vividness on her skin earlier that morning. A porter strolled up the aisle, whistling a song Pemberton didn't recognize. His gaze returned to the window.

Next to the ticket booth Harmon and his daughter waited, Harmon slouching against the chestnut board wall. It struck Pemberton that males in these mountains rarely stood upright. Instead, they leaned into some tree or wall whenever possible. If none was available they squatted, buttocks against the backs of their heels. Harmon held a pint jar in his hand, what remained of its contents barely covering the bottom. The daughter sat on the bench, her posture upright to better reveal her condition. Pemberton could not recall her first name. He wasn't surprised to see them or that the girl was with child. *His child,* Pemberton had learned the night before Pemberton and Serena left Boston. Abe Harmon is down here saying he has business to settle with you, business about his daughter, Buchanan had said when he called. It could be just drunken bluster, but I thought you ought to know.

"Our welcoming party includes some of the locals," Pemberton said to his bride.

"As we were led to expect," Serena said.

She placed her right hand on his wrist for a moment, and Pemberton felt the calluses on her upper palm, the plain gold wedding band she wore in lieu of a diamond. The ring was like his in every detail except width. Pemberton stood and retrieved two grips from the overhead compartment. He handed them to the porter, who stepped back and followed as Pemberton led his bride down the aisle and the steps to the platform. There was a gap of two feet between the steel and wood. Serena did not reach for his hand as she stepped onto the planks.

Buchanan caught Pemberton's eye first, gave him a warning nod toward Harmon and his daughter before acknowledging Serena with a stiff formal bow. Wilkie took off his fedora. At five-nine, Serena stood taller than either man, but Pemberton knew other aspects of Serena's appearance helped foster Buchanan and Wilkie's obvious surprise—pants and boots instead of a dress and cloche hat, sun-bronzed skin that belied Serena's social class, lips and cheeks untinted by rouge, hair blonde and thick but cut short in a bob, distinctly feminine yet also austere.

Serena went up to the older man and held out her hand. Though he was, at seventy, over twice her age, Wilkie stared at Serena like a smitten schoolboy, the fedora pressed against his sternum as if to conceal a heart already captured.

"Wilkie, I assume."

"Yes, yes, I am," Wilkie stammered.

"Serena Pemberton," she said, her hand still extended.

Wilkie fumbled with his hat a moment before freeing his right hand and shaking Serena's.

"And Buchanan," Serena said, turning to the other partner. "Correct?"

"Yes."

Buchanan took her proffered hand and cupped it awkwardly in his.

Serena smiled. "Don't you know how to properly shake hands, Mr. Buchanan?"

Pemberton watched with amusement as Buchanan corrected his grip quickly withdrew his hand. In the year that Boston Lumber Compar had operated in these mountains, Buchanan's wife had come only on arriving in a pink taffeta gown that was soiled before she'd cro

Waynesville's one street and entered her husband's house. She'd spent one night and left on the morning train. Now Buchanan and his wife met once a month for a weekend in Richmond, as far south as Mrs. Buchanan would travel. Wilkie's wife had never left Boston.

Pemberton's partners appeared incapable of further speech. Their eyes shifted to the leather chaps Serena wore, the beige oxford shirt and black jodhpurs. Serena's proper diction and erect carriage confirmed that she'd attended finishing school in New England, as had their wives. But Serena had been born in Colorado and lived there until sixteen, child of a timber man who'd taught his daughter to shake hands firmly and look men in the eye as well as ride and shoot. She'd come east only after her parents' deaths.

The porter laid the grips on the platform and walked back toward the baggage car that held Serena's Saratoga trunk and Pemberton's smaller steamer trunk.

"I assume Campbell got the Arabian to camp," Pemberton said.

"Yes," Buchanan said, "though it nearly killed young Vaughn. That horse isn't just big but quite spirited, 'cut proud' as they say."

"What news of the camp?" Pemberton asked.

"No serious problems," Buchanan said. "A worker found bobcat tracks on Laurel Creek and thought they were a mountain lion's. A couple of crews refused to go back up there until Galloway checked it out."

"Mountain lions," Serena said, "are they common here?"

"Not at all, Mrs. Pemberton," Wilkie answered reassuringly. "The last one killed in this state was in 1920, I'm glad to say."

"Yet the locals persist in believing one remains," Buchanan said. "There's quite a bit of lore about it, which the workers are all aware of, not only about its great size but its color, which evolves from tawny to jet-black. I'm quite content to have it remain folklore, but your husband desires otherwise. He's hoping the creature is real so he can hunt it."

"That was before his nuptials," Wilkie noted. "Now that Pemberton's married man I'm sure he'll give up hunting panthers for less dangerous rsions."

"I hope he'll pursue his panther and would be disappointed if he were to do otherwise," Serena said, turning so she addressed Pemberton as much as his partners. "Pemberton's a man unafraid of challenges, which is why I married him."

Serena paused, a slight smile creasing her face.

"And why he married me."

The porter set the second trunk on the platform. Pemberton gave the man a quarter and dismissed him. Serena looked over at the father and daughter, who now sat on the bench together, watchful and silent as actors awaiting their cues.

"I don't know you," Serena said.

The daughter continued to stare sullenly at Serena. It was the father who spoke, his voice slurred.

"My business ain't with you. It's with him standing there beside you."

"His business is mine," Serena said, "just as mine is his."

Harmon nodded at his daughter's belly, then turned back to Serena.

"Not this business. It was done before you got here."

"You're implying she's carrying my husband's child."

"I ain't *implying* nothing," Harmon said.

"You're a lucky man then," Serena said to Harmon. "You'll not find a better sire to breed her with. The size of her belly attests to that."

Serena turned her gaze and words to the daughter.

"But that's the only one you'll have of his. I'm here now. Any other children he has will be with me."

Harmon pushed himself fully upright, and Pemberton glimpsed the white-pearl handle of a bowie knife before the coat settled over it. He wondered how a man like Harmon could possess such a fine weapon. Perhaps booty in a poker game or an heirloom passed down from a more prosperous ancestor. The depot master's face appeared behind the glass partition, lingered a moment, and vanished. A group of gangly mountaineers, all Boston Lumber employees, watched expressionless from an adjacent livestock barn.

Among them was an overseer named Campbell, whose many duties included serving as a liaison between the workers and owners. Campbell always wore gray chambray shirts and corduroy pants at camp, but this afternoon he wore overalls same as the other men. *It's Sunday*, Pemberton realized, and felt momentarily disoriented. He couldn't recall the last time he'd glanced at a calendar. In Boston with Serena, time had seemed caught within the sweeping circle of watch and clock hands—passing hours and minutes unable to break free to become passing days. But the days and months had passed, as the Harmon girl's swelling belly made clear.

Harmon's large freckled hands grasped the bench edge, and he leaned slightly forward. His blue eyes glared at Pemberton.

"Let's go home, Daddy," Harmon's daughter said, and placed her hand on his.

He swatted the hand away as if a bothersome fly and stood up, wavered a moment.

"God damn the both of you," Harmon said, taking a step toward the Pembertons.

He opened the frock coat and freed the bowie knife from its leather sheath. The blade caught the late afternoon sun, and for that brief moment it appeared Harmon held a glistening flame in his hand. Pemberton looked at Harmon's daughter, her hands covering her stomach as if to shield the unborn child from what was occurring.

"Take your father home," Pemberton told her.

"Daddy, please," the daughter said.

"Go get Sheriff McDowell," Buchanan yelled at the men watching from the livestock barn.

A crew foreman named Snipes did as commanded, walking rapidly not toward the courthouse but to the boarding house where the sheriff resided. The other men stayed where they were. Buchanan moved to step between the two men, but Harmon waved him away with the knife.

"We're settling this now," Harmon shouted.

"He's right," Serena said. "Get your knife and settle it now, Pemberton."

Harmon stepped forward, wavering slightly as he narrowed the distance between them.

"You best listen to her," Harmon said, taking another step forward, "because one of us is leaving here with his toes pointed up."

Pemberton leaned and unclasped his calfskin grip, grabbled among its contents for the wedding present Serena had given him. He slipped the hunting knife from its sheath, settled the elk-bone handle deeper in his palm, its roughness all the better for clasping. For a lingering moment, Pemberton allowed himself to appreciate the feel of a weapon well made, the knife's balance and solidity, its blade, hilt and handle precisely calibrated as the épées he'd fenced with at Harvard. He took off his coat and laid it across the grip.

Harmon took another step forward, and they were less than a yard apart. He kept the knife held high and pointed toward the sky, and Pemberton knew that Harmon, drunk or sober, had done little fighting with a blade. Harmon slashed the air between them. The man's tobacco-yellowed teeth were clenched, the veins in his neck taut as guy wires. Pemberton kept his knife low and close to his side. He smelled the moonshine on Harmon's breath, a harsh greasy odor, like coal-oil.

Harmon lunged forward and Pemberton raised his left arm. The bowie knife swept the air but its arc stopped when Harmon's forearm hit Pemberton's. Harmon jerked down and the bowie knife raked across Pemberton's flesh. Pemberton took one final step, the hunting knife's blade flat as he slipped it inside Harmon's coat and plunged the steel through shirt cloth and into the soft flesh above the older man's right hip bone. He grabbed Harmon's shoulder with his free hand for leverage and quickly opened a thin smile across the man's stomach. A cedarwood button popped free from Harmon's soiled white shirt, hit the plank floor, spun a moment, and settled. Then a soft sucking sound as Pemberton withdrew the blade. For a few moments there was no blood.

Harmon's bowie knife fell clattering onto the platform. Like a m attempting to rescind the steps that had led to this outcome, the h lander placed both hands to his stomach and slowly walked back then sagged onto the bench. He lifted his hands to assess the damage, and his intestines spilled onto his lap in loose gray ropes. Harmon studied the inner workings of his body as if for some further verification of his fate. He raised his head one last time and leaned it back against the depot's boards. Pemberton looked away as Harmon's blue eyes dimmed.

Serena stood beside him now.

"Your arm," she said.

Pemberton saw that his poplin shirt was slashed below the elbow, the blue cloth darkened by blood. Serena unclasped a silver cuff link and rolled up the shirtsleeve, examined the cut across his forearm.

"It won't need stitches," she said, "just iodine and a dressing."

Pemberton nodded. Adrenaline surged through him and when Buchanan's concerned face loomed closer, his partner's features—the clipped black hedge of moustache between the pointed narrow nose and small mouth, the round pale-green eyes that always looked slightly surprised—seemed at once both vivid and remote. Pemberton took deep measured breaths, wanting to compose himself before speaking to anyone.

Serena picked up the bowie knife and carried it to Harmon's daughter, who leaned over her father, hands cradling the blank face close to hers as if something might yet be conveyed to him. Tears flowed down the young woman's cheeks, but she made no sound.

"Here," Serena said, holding the knife by the blade. "By all rights it belongs to my husband. It's a fine knife, and you can get a good price for it if you demand one. And I would," she added. "Sell it, I mean. That money will help when the child is born. It's all you'll ever get from my husband and me."

Harmon's daughter stared at Serena now, but she did not raise a hand to take the knife. Serena set the bowie knife on the bench and walked across the platform to stand beside Pemberton. Except for Campbell, who was walking toward the platform, the men leaning against the live-stock barn's railing had not moved. Pemberton was glad they were there, because at least some good might come from what had happened. The workers already understood Pemberton was as physically strong as any of them, had learned that last spring when they'd put down the train tracks. Now they knew he could kill a man, had seen it with their own eyes. They'd respect him, and Serena, even more. He turned and met Serena's gray eyes.

"Let's go to the camp," Pemberton said.

He placed his hand on Serena's elbow, turning her toward the steps Campbell had just ascended. Campbell's long angular face was typically enigmatic, and he altered his path so as not to walk directly by the Pembertons—done so casually someone watching would assume it wasn't deliberate.

Pemberton and Serena stepped off the platform and followed the track to where Wilkie and Buchanan waited. Cinders crunched under their feet, made gray wisps like snuffed matches. Pemberton gave a backward glance and saw Campbell leaning over Harmon's daughter, his hand on her shoulder as he spoke to her. Sheriff McDowell, dressed in his Sunday finery, stood beside the bench as well. He and Campbell helped the girl to her feet and led her into the depot.

"Is my Packard here?" Pemberton asked Buchanan.

Buchanan nodded and Pemberton addressed the baggage boy, who was still on the platform.

"Get the grips and put them in the back seat, then tie the smaller trunk onto the rack. The train can bring the bigger one later."

"Don't you think you'd better speak to the sheriff?" Buchanan asked after he handed Pemberton the Packard's key.

"Why should I explain anything to that son-of-a-bitch?" Pemberton said. "You saw what happened."

He and Serena were getting in the Packard when McDowell walked up briskly behind them. When he turned, Pemberton saw that despite the Sunday finery the sheriff wore his holster. Like so many of the highlanders, the sheriff's age was hard to estimate. Pemberton supposed near fifty, though the sheriff's jet-black hair and taut body befitted younger man.

"We're going to my office," McDowell said.

"Why?" Pemberton asked. "It was self-defense. A dozen men will verify that."

"I'm charging you with disorderly conduct. That's a ten-dollar fine or a week in jail."

Pemberton pulled out his billfold and handed McDowell two fives.

"We're still going to my office," McDowell said. "You're not leaving Waynesville until you write out a statement attesting you acted in self-defense."

They stood less than a yard apart, neither man stepping back. Pemberton decided a fight wasn't worth it.

"Do you need a statement from me as well?" Serena said.

McDowell looked at Serena as if he hadn't noticed her until now. "No."

"I would offer you my hand, Sheriff," Serena said, "but from what my husband has told me you probably wouldn't take it."

"He's right," McDowell replied.

"I'll wait for you in the car," Serena told Pemberton.

When Pemberton returned, he got in the Packard and turned the key. He pressed the starter button and released the hand brake, and they began the six-mile drive to the camp. Outside Waynesville, Pemberton slowed as they approached the saw mill's five-acre splash pond, its surface hidden by logs bunched and intertwined like kindling. Pemberton braked and slipped the Packard out of gear but kept the engine running.

"Wilkie wanted the saw mill close to town," Pemberton said. "It wouldn't have been my choice, but it's worked out well enough."

They looked past the splash pond's stalled flotilla of logs awaiting dawn when they'd be untangled and poled onto the log buggy and sawn. Serena gave the mill a cursory look, as well as the small A-frame building Wilkie and Buchanan used as an office. Pemberton pointed to an immense tree rising out of the woods behind the saw mill. An orange growth -rred the bark, and the upper branches were withered, unleafed.

"Chestnut blight."

"Good that it takes them years to die completely," Serena said. "That gives us all the time we need, but also a reason to prefer mahogany."

Pemberton let his hand settle on the hard rubber ball topping the gear shift. He put the car into gear and they drove on.

"I'm surprised the roads are paved," Serena said.

"Not many are. This one is, at least for a few miles. The road to Asheville as well. The train would get us to camp quicker, even at fifteen miles an hour, but I can show you our holdings this way."

They were soon out of Waynesville, the land increasingly mountainous, less inhabited, the occasional slant of pasture like green felt woven to a rougher fabric. Almost full summer now, Pemberton realized, the dogwood's white blossoms withered on the ground, the hardwood's branches thickened green. They passed a cabin, in the side yard a woman drawing water from a well. She wore no shoes and the towheaded child beside her wore pants cinched tight by twine.

"These highlanders," Serena said as she looked out the window. "I've read they've been so isolated that their speech harks back to Elizabethan times."

"Buchanan believes so," Pemberton said. "He keeps a journal of such words and phrases."

The land began a steep ascent, and soon there were no more farms. Pressure built in Pemberton's ears and he swallowed. He turned off the blacktop onto a dirt road that curved upward almost a mile before making a final sharp rise. Pemberton stopped the car and they got out. A granite outcrop leaned over the road's right side, water trickling down the rock face. To the left only a long falling away, that and a pale round moon impatient for the night.

Pemberton reached for Serena's hand and they walked to the dropoff's edge. Below, Cove Creek Valley pressed back the mountains, opening a square mile of level land. At the valley's center was the camp, surrounded by a wasteland of stumps and branches. To the left, Half Acre Ridge had been cut bare as well. On the right, the razed lowe quarter of Noland Mountain. As it crossed the valley, the railroad track appeared sewn into the lowland like stitches.

"Nine months' work," Pemberton said.

"We'd have done this much in six out west," Serena replied.

"We get four times the amount of rain here. Plus we had to lay down track into the valley."

"That would make a difference," Serena acknowledged. "How far do our holdings go?"

Pemberton pointed north. "The mountain beyond where we're logging now."

"And west."

"Balsam Mountain," Pemberton said, pointing it out as well. "Horse Pen Ridge to the south, and you can see where we quit cutting to the east."

"Thirty-four thousand acres."

"There were seven thousand more east of Waynesville that we've already logged."

"And to the west, Champion Paper owns that?"

"All the way to the Tennessee line," Pemberton said.

"That's the land they're after for the park?"

Pemberton nodded. "And if Champion sells, they'll be coming after our land next."

"But we'll not let them have it," Serena said.

"No, at least not until we're done with it. Harris, our local copper and kaolin magnate, was at the meeting I told you about, and he made clear he's against this national park scheme as much as we are. Not a bad thing to have the wealthiest man in the county on our side."

"Or as a future partner," Serena added.

"You'll like him," Pemberton said. "He's shrewd and he doesn't suffer fools."

Serena touched his shoulder above the wound.

"We need to go and dress your arm."

"A kiss first," Pemberton said, moving their joined hands to the small of Serena's back and pulling her closer.

Serena raised her lips to Pemberton's and pressed them firm against his. Her free hand clutched the back of his head to bring him nearer, a soft exaltation of her breath into his mouth as she unpursed her lips and kissed fiercer, her teeth and tongue touching his. Serena pressed her body fully into his. Incapable of coyness, as always, even the first time they'd met. Pemberton felt again what he'd never known with another woman—a sense of being unshackled into some limitless possibility, limitless though at the same time somehow contained within the two of them.

They got in the Packard and descended into the valley. The road became rockier, the gullies and washouts more pronounced. They drove through a creek clogged with silt, then more woods until the woods were gone and they were driving across the valley floor. There was no road now, just a wide sprawl of mud and dirt. They passed a stable and a shotgun frame building whose front room served as the payroll office, the back room a bar and dining area. To the right were the workers' dining hall and the commissary. They crossed over the railroad track, passing the line of flat cars waiting for morning. A caboose that served as a doctor's office sat next to the track, its rusting wheels sunk into the valley floor.

They passed below a row of three dozen stringhouses set precariously on Bent Knob Ridge, their foundations propped by ragged locust poles. The stringhouses resembled cheap wooden boxcars, not just in size and appearance but also in the way cable connected each in the line to the other. On top of every one was an iron rung. Axes had gouged splintery holes through the wood to serve as windows.

"The workers' housing, I assume," Serena said.

"Yes, as soon as we're finished here we can set them on flat cars and haul them to our new site. The workers don't even have to move their belongings."

"Very efficient." Serena said, nodding as she spoke. "How much is the rent?"

"Eight dollars a month."

"And their pay."

"Two dollars a day right now, but Buchanan wants to raise it to two-ten."

"Why?"

"He claims we'll lose good men to other camps," Pemberton said as he pulled up in front of their house. "I say these government land grabs mean a surplus of workers, especially if Champion sells out."

"What does Wilkie think?"

"Wilkie agrees with me," Pemberton said. "He says the one good thing about this stock market crash is cheaper labor."

"I agree with you and Wilkie," Serena said.

A youth named Joel Vaughn waited on the front steps, beside him a cardboard box, in it meat and bread and cheese, a bottle of red wine. As Pemberton and Serena got out of the Packard, Vaughn stood and doffed his wool golf cap, revealing a thatch of carrot-colored hair. A mind equally bright, Campbell had quickly realized, and trusted Vaughn with responsibilities usually given to much older workers, including, as evidenced by the scraped forearms and purple swelling on his freckled left cheekbone, tussles with a horse as spirited as it was valuable. Vaughn retrieved the grips from the car and followed Pemberton and his bride onto the porch. Pemberton opened the door and nodded for the youth to enter first.

"I'd carry you over the threshold," Pemberton said, "but for the arm."

Serena smiled. "Don't worry, Pemberton. I can manage."

She stepped inside and he followed. Serena examined the light switch a moment as if skeptical it would work. Then she turned it on.

In the front room were two Coxwell chairs set in front of the fireplace, off to the left a small kitchen with its Homestead stove and ice box. A poplar table with four cane-bottom chairs stood beside the front room's one window. Serena nodded and walked down the hall, glanced at the bathroom before entering the back room. She turned on the bedside lamp and sat on the wrought iron bed, tested the mattress's firmness and seemed satisfied. Vaughn appeared at the doorway with the steamer trunk, which had belonged to Pemberton's father.

"Put it in the hall closet," Pemberton said.

Vaughn did as he was told and went out, came back with the food and wine.

"Mr. Buchanan thought you might be needful of something to eat."

"Put it on the table," Pemberton said. "Then go get iodine and gauze from the caboose."

The youth paused, his eyes on Pemberton's blood-soaked sleeve.

"You wanting me to get Doctor Cheney?"

"No," Serena said. "I'll dress it for him."

After Vaughn left, Serena stepped closer to the bedroom window and peered out at the stringhouses.

"Do the workers have electricity?"

"Just in the dining hall."

"It's best that way," Serena said, stepping back into the room's center. "Not just the money saved but for the men. They'll work harder if they live like Spartans."

Pemberton raised an open palm toward the room's bare rough-board walls.

"This is rather Spartan as well."

"Money freed to buy more timber tracts," Serena said. "If we'd wished our wealth spent otherwise we'd have stayed in Boston."

"True enough."

"Who lives next door?"

"Campbell. He's as valuable as any man in this camp. He can book keep, repair anything, and uses a Gunter's chain as well as any of the surveyors."

"And the last house?"

"Doctor Cheney."

"The wag from Wild Hog Gap."

"The only doctor we could get to live out here. Even to get him we had to offer a house and an automobile."

Serena opened the room's chifforobe and looked inside, perused the closet as well.

"And what of my wedding present, Pemberton?"

"In the stable."

"I've never seen a white Arabian."

"It's an impressive horse," Pemberton said.

"I'll take him for a ride first thing tomorrow."

When Vaughn had delivered the iodine and gauze, Serena sat on the bed and unbuttoned Pemberton's shirt, removed the weapon wedged behind his belt. She took the knife from the sheath, examined the dried blood on the blade before placing it on the bedside table. Serena opened the bottle of iodine.

"How does it feel, fighting a man like that? With a knife I mean. Is it like fencing or . . . more intimate."

Pemberton tried to think of how what he'd felt could be put in words.

"I don't know," he finally said, "except it feels utterly real and utterly unreal at the same time."

Serena gripped his arm harder but her voice softened.

"This will sting," she said, and slowly poured the auburn-colored liquid into the wound. "The cause of your notoriety in Boston, did that knife fight feel the same as the one today?"

"Actually, it was a beer stein in Boston," Pemberton replied. "More of an accident during a bar room brawl."

"The story that I heard involved a knife," Serena said, "and made the victim's demise sound anything but accidental."

As Serena paused to dab iodine leaking from the wound, Pemberton wondered if he detected a slight disappointment in Serena's tone or only imagined it.

"But this one, hardly an accident," Serena noted. *"Myself will grip the sword—yea, though I die."*

"I'm afraid I don't recognize the quote," Pemberton said. "I'm not the scholar you are."

"No matter. It's a maxim best learned the way you did, not from a book."

As Serena loosed gauze from its wooden spool, Pemberton smiled.

"Who knows?" he said lightly. "In a place this primitive I suspect knife-wielding is not the purview of one sex. You may do battle with some snuff-breathed harridan and learn the same way I have."

"I would do it," Serena said, her voice measured as she spoke, "if for no other reason than to share what you felt today. That's what I want, everything a part of you also a part of me."

Pemberton watched the cloth thicken as Serena wrapped it around his forearm, iodine soaking through the first layers, then blotted by the dressing. He remembered the Back Bay dinner party of a month ago when Mrs. Lowell, the hostess, came up to him. *There's a woman here who wishes to be introduced to you, Mr. Pemberton,* the matron had said. *I should caution you, though. She has frightened off every other bachelor in Boston.* Pemberton recalled how he'd assured the matron he was not a man easily frightened, that perhaps the woman in question might need to be cautioned about him as well. Mrs. Lowell had noted the justness of Pemberton's comment, matching his smile as she took his forearm. *Let us go meet her then. Just remember you were warned, just as I've warned her.*

"There," Serena said when she'd finished. "Three days and it should be healed."

Serena picked up the knife and took it into the kitchen, cleaned the blade with water and a cloth. She dried the knife and returned to the back room.

"I'll take a whetstone to the blade tomorrow," Serena said, setting the knife on the bedside table. "It's a weapon worthy of a man like you, and built to last a lifetime."

"To extend a lifetime as well," Pemberton noted, "as it has so fortuitously shown."

"Perhaps it shall again, so keep it close."

"I'll keep it in the office," Pemberton promised.

Serena sat down in a ladderback chair opposite the bed and pulled off her jodhpurs. She undressed, not looking at what she unfastened and let fall to the floor. All the while her eyes were fixed upon Pemberton. She took off her underclothing and stood before him. The women he'd known before Serena had been shy with their bodies, waiting for a room to darken or sheets to be pulled up, but that wasn't Serena's way.

Except for her eyes and hair, she was not conventionally beautiful, her breasts and hips small and legs long for her torso. Serena's narrow shoulders, thin nose and high cheekbones honed her body to a severe keenness. Her feet were small, and considering all other aspects of her features, oddly delicate, vulnerable looking. Their bodies were well matched, Serena's lithe form fitting his larger frame and more muscular build. Sometimes at night they cleaved so fiercely the bed buckled and leaped beneath them. Pemberton would hear their quick breaths and not know which were Serena's and which his. *A kind of annihilation*, that was what Serena called their coupling, and though Pemberton would never have thought to describe it that way, he knew her words had named the thing exactly.

Serena did not come to him immediately, and a sensual languor settled over Pemberton. He gazed at her body, into the eyes that had entranced him the first time he'd met her, irises the color of burnished pewter. Hard and dense like pewter too, the gold flecks not so much within the gray as floating motelike on the surface. Eyes that did not close when their flesh came together, pulling him inside her with her gaze as much as her body.

Serena opened the curtains so the moon spread its light across the bed. She turned from the window and looked around the room, as if for a few moments she'd forgotten where she was.

"This will do quite well for us," she finally said, returning her gaze to Pemberton as she stepped toward the bed.

Two

THE FOLLOWING MORNING PEMBERTON INTRO-duced his bride to the camp's hundred workers. As he spoke, Serena stood beside him, dressed in black riding breeches and a blue denim shirt. Her jodphurs were different from the ones the day before, European made, the leather scuffed and worn, toes rimmed with tarnished silver. Serena held the gelding's reins, the Arabian's whiteness so intense as to appear almost translucent in the day's first light. The saddle weighting the horse's back was made of German leather with wool-flocked gusseted panels, its cost more than a logger earned in a year. Several men made soft-spoken observations about the stirrups, which weren't paired on the left side.

Wilkie and Buchanan stood on the porch, cups of coffee in their hands. Both were dressed in suits and ties, their one concession to the environment knee-high leather boots, pants cuffs tucked inside so as not to get muddied. It was clothing Pemberton, whose gray tiger cloth pants and plaid workshirts differed little from the workers' attire, found faintly ridiculous in such an environment, now even more so in light of Serena's attire.

"Mrs. Pemberton's father owned the Vulcan Lumber Company in Colorado," Pemberton said to the workers. "He taught her well. She's the equal of any man here, and you'll soon find the truth of it. Her orders are to be followed the same as you'd follow mine."

Among the gathered loggers was a thick-bearded cutting crew foreman named Bilded. He hocked loudly and spit a gob of yellow phlegm on the ground. At six-two and over two hundred pounds, Bilded was one of the few men in camp big as Pemberton.

Serena opened the saddle bag and removed a Waterman pen and a leather-bound notepad. She spoke to the horse quietly, then handed the reins to Pemberton and walked over to Bilded and stood where he'd spit. She pointed beside the office at a cane ash tree, which had been left standing for its shade.

"I'll make a wager with you," Serena said to Bilded. "We both estimate total board feet of that cane ash. Then we'll write our estimates on a piece of paper and see who's closest."

Bilded stared at Serena a few moments, then at the tree as if already measuring its height and width. He looked not at Serena but at the cane ash when he spoke.

"How we going to know who's closest?"

"I'll have it cut down and taken to the saw mill," Pemberton said. "We'll know who won by this evening."

Doctor Cheney had now come on the porch to watch as well. He raked a match head across the railing to light his after-breakfast cigar, the sound audible enough that several workers turned to find its source. Pemberton looked also, and noted how morning accentuated the doctor's unhealthy pallor, making the corpulent face appear gray and malleable, like dirty bread dough. An effect the wattled neck and pouchy cheeks further emphasized.

"How much we wagering?" Bilded asked.

"Two weeks' pay."

The amount gave Bilded pause.

"There ain't no trick to it? I win I get two weeks' extra pay."

"Yes," Serena said, "and if you lose you work two weeks free."

She offered the pad and pen to Bilded, but he didn't raise a hand to take it. A worker behind him snickered.

"Perhaps you want me to go first then?" Serena said.

"Yeah," Bilded said after a few moments.

Serena turned toward the tree and studied it a full minute before she raised the pen in her left hand and wrote a number. She tore the page from the pad and folded it.

"Your turn," she said and handed the pen and notepad to Bilded.

Bilded walked up to the cane ash to better judge its girth, then came back and examined the tree a while longer before writing his own number. Serena turned to Pemberton.

"Who's a man we and the workers both trust to hold our estimates?"

"Campbell," Pemberton said, nodding toward the overseer, who watched from the office doorway. "You all right with that, Bilded?"

"Yeah," Bilded said.

Serena rode out behind the cutting crews as they followed the train tracks toward the south face of Noland Mountain, passing through acres of stumps that, from a distance, resembled grave markers in a recently vacated battlefield. The loggers soon left the main train line that went over the right side of the mountain and instead followed the spur, their lunches in tote sacks and paper bags, metal milk pails and metal boxes shaped like bread loaves. Some of the men wore bib overalls, others flannel shirts and pants. Most wore Chippawah boots and a few wore shoes of canvas or leather. The signal boys went barefoot. The loggers passed the Shay train engine they called a sidewinder and the two coach cars that brought and returned workers who lived in Waynesville, then the six flat cars for timber and the McGiffert loader and finally at the spur's end the hi-lead skidder already hissing and smoking, the boom's lon steel cables spooling off the drums and stretching a half mile upward to where the tail block looped around a massive hickory stump. From a distance, the boom resembled a huge rod and reel, the cables like cast lines. The boom angled toward the mountain, and the cables were so taut it looked as if the whole mountain was hooked and ready to be dragged down the tracks to Waynesville. Logs cut late on Saturday yet dangled from the cables, and men passed heedfully under them as they might clouds packed with dynamite. All the while, the air grew thinner as the workers made their way up the steep incline toward tools hidden under leaves, hung on tree branches like the harps of the old Hebrews. Not just axes but eight-foot cross-cut saws and steel wedges and blocks and pike poles, the nine-pound hammers called go-devils and the six-pound hammers called grab skips. Some of these implements had initials burned in their handles, and some were given names as might be allowed a horse or rifle. All but the newest had their handles worn slick by flesh much in the manner of stones smoothed by water.

As the men made their way through the stumps and brush they called slash, their eyes considered where they stepped, for though snakes rarely stirred until the sun fell full on the slopes, the yellow jackets and hornets offered no such respite. Nor did the mountain itself, which could send a man tumbling, especially on a day such as this when recent rains made the ground slick and yielding to feet and grasping hands. Most of the loggers were still exhausted from last week's six eleven-hour shifts. Some were hung over and some were injured. As they made their way up the mountain, the men had already drunk four or five cups of coffee, and all carried with them cigarettes and chewing tobacco. Some used cocaine to keep going and stay alert, because once the cutting began a man had to watch for axe blades glancing off trees and saw teeth grabbing a knee and the tongs on the cable swinging free or the cable snapping. Most of all the sharded limbs called widow makers that waited minutes or hours or even days before falling earthward like javelins.

Pemberton stood on the porch as Serena followed the crews into the woods. Even at a distance he could see the sway of her hips and arched back. Though they'd coupled that morning as well as last night, Pemberton felt desire quicken his pulse, summon the image of the first time he'd watched her ride at the New England Hunt Club. That morning he'd sat on the clubhouse veranda and watched Serena and her horse leap the hedges and railings. He'd never been a man easily awed, but that was the only word for what he'd felt as Serena and the horse lifted and then hung aloft for what seemed seconds before falling on the barriers' far sides. He'd felt incredibly lucky they'd found one another, though Serena had already told him their meeting wasn't mere good fortune but inevitability.

That morning at the club two women had come out on the veranda and sat nearby, dressed, unlike Serena, in red swallowtail hunting blazers and black derbies, hot tea set before them to ward against the morning's chill. *I suppose she imagines riding without a coat and cap de rigueur,* the younger of the women had said, to which the other replied that it probably was in Colorado. *My brother's wife attended Miss Porter's with her,* the older woman said. *She just showed up one day, an orphan from the western hinterlands. A wealthy orphan albeit, better educated than you'd imagine, but even Sarah Porter had no luck teaching her any social graces. Rather too proud, my sister-in-law claims, even for that haughty bunch. A couple of the girls pitied her enough to invite her home with them for the holidays and she not only refused but in a very ungracious manner. She stayed there with those old school marms instead.* The younger woman had noticed Pemberton listening and had turned to him. *Do you know her?* she'd asked. *Yes,* he'd replied. *She's my fiancée.* The younger woman had blushed, but her companion had turned to Pemberton with a smile. *Well,* she'd said frostily, *she at least deems you worthy of her company.*

Except for Mrs. Lowell's brief comment about previous suitors, that morning had been the only time he'd heard Serena's past spoken of by anyone besides Serena. She'd volunteered little herself. When Pemberton asked about her time in Colorado or New England, Serena's answe were almost always cursory, telling him that she and Pemberton neec the past no more than it needed them.

Yet Serena's bad dreams continued. She never spoke of them, even when Pemberton asked, even in those moments he pulled her thrashing body out of them as if pulling her from a treacherous surf. Something to do with what had happened to her family back in Colorado, he was sure of that. Sure also that others who knew her would have been astonished at how childlike Serena appeared in those moments, the way she clung so fiercely to him until she whimpered back into sleep.

The kitchen door slammed as a worker came out and hurled a washtub of gray dishwater into a ditch reeking of grease and food scraps. The last logger had disappeared into the woods. Soon Pemberton heard the axes as the lead choppers began notching trees, a sound like rifle shots ricocheting across the valley as workers sawed and chopped another few acres of wilderness out of Haywood County.

By this time the crew chosen to fell the cane ash had returned to camp with their tools. The three men squatted before the tree as they would a campfire, talking among themselves about how best to commence. Campbell joined them, answering the loggers' questions with words arranged to sound more like suggestions than orders. After a few minutes Campbell rose. He turned toward the porch, giving Pemberton a nod, allowing his gaze to linger long enough to confirm nothing more was required of him. Campbell's hazel eyes were almond-shaped, like a cat's. Pemberton had found their wideness appropriate for a man so aware of things on the periphery, aware and also cautious, reasons Campbell had lasted into his late thirties in an occupation where inattentiveness was rarely forgiven. Pemberton nodded and Campbell walked up the track to talk to the train's engineer. Pemberton watched him go, noting that even a man cautious as Campbell had a missing ring finger. If you could gather up all the severed body parts and sew them together, you'd gain an extra worker every month, Doctor Cheney had once joked.

The cutting crew quickly showed why Campbell picked them. The ad chopper took up his ax and with two expert strokes made an under- a foot from the ground. The two sawyers got down on one knee and ped the hickory handles with both hands and began, wedges of bark crackling and breaking against the steel teeth. The men gained their rhythm, and soon sawdust mounded at their feet like time sieving through an hourglass. Pemberton knew the workers who used them called the cross-cut saws "misery whips" because of the effort demanded, but watching these men it appeared effortless, as if they slid the blade between two smooth-sanded planks. When the saw began to pinch, the lead chopper used the go devil to drive in a wedge. In fifteen minutes the tree lay on the ground.

Pemberton went inside and worked on invoices, occasionally looking out the window toward Noland Mountain. He and Serena hadn't been apart for more than a few minutes since the marriage ceremony. Her absence made the paperwork more tedious, the room emptier. Pemberton remembered how she'd waked him that morning with a kiss on his eyelids, a hand settled lightly on his shoulder. Serena had been drowsy as well, and when she'd brought Pemberton ever so languidly into her arms, it was as if he'd left his own dream and together they'd entered a better richer one.

Serena was gone all morning, getting familiar with the landscape, learning the names of workers, ridges and creeks.

The Franklin clock on the credenza chimed noon when Harris' Studebaker pulled up beside the office. Pemberton set the in voices on the desk and walked out to meet him. Like Pemberton, Harris dressed little better than his workers, the only sign of his wealth a thick gold ring on his right hand, in the setting a sapphire sharp and bright-blue as its owner's eyes. Seventy years old, Pemberton knew, but the vigorous silver hair and shiny gold tooth fillings were congruent for a man anything but rusty.

"So where is she?" Harris asked as he stepped onto the office porch. "A woman as impressive as you claim shouldn't be hidden away."

Harris paused and smiled as he turned his head slightly, his right eye focused on Pemberton as if to better sight a target.

"Though on second thought, maybe you should hide her away. If she is all you say."

"You'll see," Pemberton said. "She's over on Noland. We can get horses and ride up there."

"I don't have time for that," Harris said. "Much as I'd enjoy meeting your bride, this park nonsense takes precedent. Our esteemed Secretary of the Interior got Rockefeller to donate five million. Now Albright is sure he can buy out Champion."

"Do you think they'll sell?"

"I don't know," Harris said, "but just the fact that Champion's listening to offers encourages not only Secretary Albright but the rest of them, here and in Washington. They're already starting to run farmers off their land in Tennessee."

"This needs to be settled once and for all," Pemberton said.

"Goddamn right it needs to be settled. I'm tired as you are of lining the pockets of those Raleigh pettifoggers."

Harris pulled a watch from his pocket and checked the time.

"Later than I thought," he said.

"Have you had a chance to look at the Glencoe Ridge tract?" Pemberton asked.

"Come by the office Saturday morning and we'll go see it together. Bring your bride along too," Harris said, and paused to nod approvingly at the valley's stumps and slash. "You've done well here, even with those two fops you have for partners."

Pemberton did not go back into the office after Harris left but instead rode out to Noland Mountain. He found Serena eating lunch with two foremen. Between bites of sandwiches, they discussed whether buying a second hi-lead skidder would be worth the extra cost. Pemberton got off his horse and joined them.

"The cane ash is at the saw mill," Pemberton said as he sat down beside her, "so Campbell will have the board feet by five-thirty."

"Any of the other men make side bets with you?"

"No."

"Would either of you care to wager?" Serena said to the foremen.

"No ma'am," the older worker replied. "I don't have a hankering to bet against you on anything concerning lumber. I might have before this morning, but not now, especially after you showed us that trick with the choker."

The younger worker merely shook his head.

The two men finished eating and gathered their crews. Soon the sounds of axes and cross-cut saws filled the nearby woods. The Arabian snorted and Serena walked over and placed her hand on the horse's mane. She spoke to the horse softly and the gelding calmed.

"Harris came by," Pemberton said. "He wants the three of us to go look at the Glencoe Ridge tract Saturday."

"Will he be looking for anything other than kaolin and copper?"

"I doubt it," Pemberton said, "though some gold has been panned from creeks in the county. There are ruby and sapphire mines near Franklin, but that's forty miles from here."

"I hope he finds something," Serena said, stepping closer to take Pemberton's hand. "It will be another beginning for us, our first real partnership."

Pemberton smiled. "Plus Harris."

"For now," Serena said.

As Pemberton rode back to camp, he thought of an afternoon back in Boston when he and Serena were lying in bed, the sheets damp and tangled. The third, maybe the fourth day he'd been with her. Serena's head had lain on his shoulder, her left hand on his chest.

"After Carolina, where to next?"

"I haven't thought that far ahead," Pemberton had replied.

"'I'?" she'd said. "Why not 'we'?"

"Well since it's 'we', Pemberton had replied playfully, "I'll defer to you."

Serena had lifted her head and met his eyes.

"Brazil. I've researched it. Virgin forests of mahogany and no law but nature's law."

"Very well," Pemberton had said. "Now the only decision 'we' have worry about is where to have dinner. Since you've decided everything for us, am I allowed to choose?"

She had not answered his question. Instead, she'd pressed her hand more firmly against his chest, let her palm stay there as she measured the beat of his blood.

"I'd heard you had a strong heart, fearless," she'd said, "and so it is."

"So you research men as well as potential logging sights?" Pemberton had asked.

"Of course," Serena had said.

AT six, every worker in camp gathered in front of the office. Though most cutting crews consisted of three men, a crew that lost a man often attached to another, an arrangement that wasn't always temporary. A man named Snipes acted as leader for such a crew since the other foreman, Stewart, was a diligent worker but of dubious intelligence. Stewart was relieved as anyone by this arrangement.

Among Snipes' crew was an illiterate lay preacher named McIntyre, who was much given to vigorous pronouncements on the imminent apocalypse. McIntyre sought any opportunity to espouse his views, especially to Reverend Bolick, a Presbyterian cleric who held services at the camp on Wednesday nights and Sunday mornings. Reverend Bolick considered his fellow theologian not only obnoxious but demented and went out of his way to avoid McIntyre, as did most men at the camp. McIntyre had been absent all morning with a bout of the flux but had come to work at noon. When he saw Serena standing on the office porch in pants, he choked on the peppermint he sucked to ease his stomach.

"There she is," McIntyre sputtered, "the whore of Babylon in the very flesh."

Dunbar, the youngest member of the crew at nineteen, looked toward the porch incomprehensively. He turned to McIntyre, who was dressed his black preacher's hat and frayed black dress coat he wore even on hottest days as a sign of his true calling.

"Where?" Dunbar asked.

ight there on that porch, standing there brazen as Jezebel."

Stewart, who along with McIntyre's wife and sister comprised the whole of the lay preacher's congregation, turned to his minister and spoke.

"Why are you of a mind to say such a thing as that, Preacher?"

"Them pants," McIntyre proclaimed. "It's in the Revelations. Says the whore of Babylon will come forth in the last days wearing pants."

Ross, a dour man not kindly disposed to McIntyre's rants, stared at the lay preacher as he might a chimpanzee that had wandered into camp and begun chattering.

"I've read Revelation many a time, McIntyre," Ross said, "and somehow missed that verse."

"It ain't in the King James," McIntyre said. "It's in the original Greek."

"Read Greek, do you?" Ross said. "That's ever amazing for a man who can't even read English."

"Well, no," McIntyre said slowly. "I don't read Greek, but I've heard from them what does."

"Them what does," Ross said, and shook his head.

The crew foreman, Snipes, removed a briar pipe from his mouth to speak. His overalls were so worn and patched that the original denim seemed an afterthought, but there'd been no attempt to blend new colors with old. Instead, the crew foreman's overalls were mended with a conflagration of yellow, green, red, and orange cloth. Snipes considered himself a learned man and argued that, since colors bright and various were known in nature to warn other creatures of danger, such patches would deter not only varmints both large and small but might in the same manner also deter falling limbs and lightning strikes. Snipes held the pipe out before him, contemplated it a moment, then raised his head and spoke.

"They's differences in every language in the world," Snipes said sagely, and appeared ready to expound on this point when Ross raised an open palm.

"Here comes the tally," Ross said. "Get ready to have your pockets lightened, Dunbar."

Campbell stood on the ash tree's stump and took a pad from his coat pocket. The men grew silent. Campbell looked at neither the men nor the owners. His gaze remained on the pad as he spoke, as if to belie any favoritism even as he rendered the verdict.

"Mrs. Pemberton the winner by thirty board feet," Campbell said, and he stepped down without further comment.

The men began to disperse, those who had bet and won, such as Ross, stepping more lightly than the losers. Soon only those who'd watched from the porch remained.

"Cause for a celebratory drink of our best scotch," Buchanan announced.

He and Wilkie followed Doctor Cheney and the Pembertons into the office. They passed through the front room and entered a smaller room with a bar on one wall and a fourteen-foot dining table in the center, around it a dozen well-padded captain's chairs. The room had a creek-stone fireplace and a single window. Buchanan stepped behind the bar and set a bottle of Glenlivet and soda water on the lacquered wood. He lifted five Steuben tumblers from under the bar and filled a silver canister with chips from the ice box.

"I call this the Recovery Room," Doctor Cheney said to Serena. "You see it is well stocked with all manner of alcohol. I find it quite sufficient for my own medicinal needs."

"Doctor Cheney has no need for a recovery room elsewhere, because the good doctor's patients rarely recover," Buchanan said from behind the bar. "I know these rogues' preferences, but what is yours, Mrs. Pemberton?"

"The same."

Everyone sat except Buchanan. Serena studied the table, let the fingers of her left hand trail across its surface.

"A single piece of chestnut," Serena said appreciatively. "Was the tree cut nearby?"

"In this very valley," Buchanan said. "It measured one-hundred-and-twelve feet. We've yet to find a bigger one."

Serena raised her eyes from the table and looked around the room.

"I'm afraid this room is quite austere, Mrs. Pemberton," Wilkie said, "but comfortable, even cozy in its way, especially during winter. We hope you'll take your evening meals here, as the four of us have done before the pleasure of your arrival."

Still apprising the room, Serena nodded.

"Excellent," Doctor Cheney said. "A woman's beauty would do much to brighten these drab surroundings."

Buchanan spoke as he handed Serena her drink.

"Pemberton has told me of your parents' unfortunate demise in the 1918 flu epidemic, but do you have siblings?"

"I had a brother and two sisters. They died as well."

"All in the epidemic?" Wilkie asked.

"Yes."

Wilkie's moustache quivered slightly, and his rheumy eyes saddened.

"How old were you, my dear?"

"Sixteen."

"I lost a sibling as well in that epidemic, my youngest sister," Wilkie said to Serena, "but to lose your whole family, and at such a young age. I just can't imagine."

"I too am sorry for your losses, but your good fortune is now our good fortune," Doctor Cheney quipped.

"It was more than good fortune," Serena replied. "The doctor said so himself."

"What then did my fellow healer ascribe your survival to?"

Serena looked steadily at Cheney, her eyes as inexpressive as her tone.

"He said I simply refused to die."

Doctor Cheney slowly tilted his head, as if peering around a corner. The physician stared at Serena curiously, his thick eyebrows raised a few moments, then relaxed. Buchanan brought the other drinks to the table and sat down. Pemberton raised his drink, offered a smile as well t lighten the moment.

"A toast to another victory for management over labor," he said.

"I toast you as well, Mrs. Pemberton," Doctor Cheney said. "The nature of the fairer sex is to lack the male's analytical skills, but, at least in this instance, you have somehow compensated for that weakness."

Serena's features tightened, but the irritation vanished as quickly as it had appeared, swept clear from her face like a lock of unruly hair.

"My husband tells me that you are from these very mountains, a place called Wild Hog Gap," Serena said to Cheney. "Obviously, your views on my sex were formed by the slatterns you grew up with, but I assure you the natures of women are more various than your limited experience allows."

As if tugged upward by fishhooks, the sides of Doctor Cheney's mouth creased into a mirthless smile.

"By God you married a saucy one," Wilkie chortled, raising his tumbler to Pemberton. "This camp is going to be lively now."

Buchanan retrieved the bottle of scotch and placed it on the table.

"Have you ever been to these parts before, Mrs. Pemberton?" he asked.

"No, I haven't."

"As you've seen, we are somewhat isolated here."

"Somewhat?" Wilkie exclaimed. "At times I feel I've been banished to the moon."

"Asheville is only fifty miles away," Buchanan said. "It has its village charms."

"Indeed," Doctor Cheney interjected, "including several T.B. sanatoriums."

"Yet you've no doubt heard of George Vanderbilt's estate," Buchanan continued, "which is there as well."

"Biltmore is indeed impressive," Wilkie conceded, "an actual French castle, Mrs. Pemberton. Olmsted himself came down from Brookline to design the grounds. Vanderbilt's daughter Cornelia lives there now, with er husband, a Brit named Cecil. I've been their guest on occasion. Very cious people."

Wilkie paused to empty his tumbler and set it on the table. His cheeks were rosy from the alcohol, but Pemberton knew it was Serena's presence that made him even more loquacious than usual.

"I heard a phrase today worthy of your journal, Buchanan," Wilkie continued. "Two workers at the splash pond were discussing a fight and spoke of how one combatant 'feathered into' the other. It apparently means to inflict great damage."

Buchanan retrieved a fountain pen and black leather notebook from his coat's inner pocket. Buchanan placed the pen on the notebook's rag paper and wrote *feathered into,* behind it a question mark. He blew on the ink and closed the notebook.

"I doubt that it goes back to the British Isles," Buchanan said. "Perhaps instead a colloquialism to do with cockfighting."

"Kephart would no doubt know," Wilkie said. "Have you heard of him, Mrs. Pemberton, our local Thoreau? Buchanan here is quite an admirer of his work, despite Kephart's being behind this national park nonsense."

"I've seen his books in the window at Grolier's," Serena said. "As you may imagine, they were quite taken with a Harvard man turned Natty Bumpo."

"As well as being a former librarian in Saint Louis," Wilkie noted.

"A librarian and an author," Serena said, "yet he'd stop us from harvesting the very thing books are made of."

Pemberton drained his second dram of scotch, felt the alcohol's smooth slide down his throat, its warm glow deepening his contentment. He felt an overwhelming wonder that this woman, whom he'd not even known existed when he'd left this valley three months earlier, was now his wife. Pemberton settled his right hand on Serena's knee, unsurprised when her left hand settled on his knee as well. She leaned toward him and for a few seconds let her head nestle in the space between his neck and shoulder. Pemberton tried to imagine how this moment could be better. He could think of nothing other than that he and Serena were alone.

At seven o'clock, two kitchen workers set the table with Spode bone china and silver cutlery and linen napkins. They left and returned pushing a cart laden with wicker baskets of buttered biscuits and a silver platter draping with beef, large bowls of Steuben crystal brimmed with potatoes and carrots and squash, various jams and relishes.

They were midway through their meal when Campbell, who'd been bent over the adding machine in the front room, appeared at the door.

"I need to know if you and Mrs. Pemberton are holding Bilded to the bet," Campbell said. "For the payroll."

"Is there a reason we shouldn't?" Pemberton asked.

"He has a wife and three children."

The words were delivered with no inflection, and Campbell's face was an absolute blank. Pemberton wondered, not for the first time, what it would be like to play poker against this man.

"All for the better," Serena said. "It will make a more effective lesson for the other workers."

"Will he still be a foreman?" Campbell asked.

"Yes, for the next two weeks," Serena said, looking not at Campbell but Pemberton.

"And then?"

"He'll be fired," Pemberton told the overseer. "Another lesson for the men."

Campbell nodded and stepped back into the office, closing the door behind him. The clacking, ratchet and pause of the adding machine resumed.

Buchanan appeared about to speak, but didn't.

"A problem, Buchanan?" Pemberton asked.

"No," Buchanan said after a few moments. "The wager did not involve me."

"Did you note how Campbell attempted to sway you, Pemberton,"

Doctor Cheney said, "yet without doing so outright. He's quite intelligent that way, don't you think?"

"Yes," Pemberton agreed. "Had his circumstances been such, he could have matriculated at Harvard. Perhaps, unlike me, he would have graduated."

"Yet without your experiences in the taverns of Boston," Wilkie said, "you might have fallen prey to Abe Harmon and his bowie knife.

"True enough," said Pemberton, "but my year of fencing at Harvard contributed to that education as well."

Serena raised her hand to Pemberton's face and let her index finger trace the thin white scar on his cheek.

"A Fechtwunde is more impressive than a piece of sheepskin," she said.

The kitchen workers came in with raspberries and cream. Beside Wilkie's bowl, one of the women placed a water glass and bottles containing bitters and iron tonics, a tin of sulpher lozenges, potions for Wilkie's contrary stomach and tired blood. The workers poured the cups of coffee and departed.

"Yet you are a woman of obvious learning, Mrs. Pemberton," Wilkie said. "Your husband says you are exceedingly well read in the arts and philosophy."

"My father brought tutors to the camp. They were all British, Oxford educated."

"Which explains the British inflection and cadence of your speech," Wilkie noted approvingly.

"And no doubt also explains a certain coldness in the tone," Doctor Cheney added as he stirred cream in his coffee, "which only the unenlightened would view as a lack of feeling towards others, even your own family."

Wilkie's nose twitched in annoyance.

"Worse than unenlightened to think such a thing," Wilkie said, "cruel as well."

"Surely," Doctor Cheney said, his plump lips rounding contemplatively. "I speak only as one who hasn't had the advantages of British tutors."

"Your father sounds like a most remarkable man," Wilkie said, returning his gaze to Serena. "I would enjoy hearing more about him."

"Why?" Serena said, as if puzzled. "He's dead now and of no use to any of us."

Three

DEW DARKENED THE HEM OF HER GINGHAM dress as Rachel Harmon walked out of the yard, the grass cool and slick against her bare feet and ankles. Jacob nestled in the crook of her left arm, in her right hand the tote sack. He'd grown so much in only six weeks. His features transformed as well, the hair not just thicker but darker, the eyes that had been blue at birth now brown as chestnuts. She'd not known an infant's eyes could do such a thing and it unsettled her, a reminder of eyes last seen at the train depot. Rachel looked down the road to where Widow Jenkins' farmhouse stood, found the purl of smoke rising from the chimney that confirmed the old woman was up and about. The child squirmed inside the blanket she'd covered him in against the morning chill.

"You've got a full belly and fresh swaddlings," she whispered, "so you've no cause to be fussy."

Rachel tucked the blanket tighter. She ran her index finger across the ridge of his gums, Jacob's mouth closing around the finger to suckle. She wondered when his teeth would come in, something else to ask the widow.

Rachel followed the road as it began its long curve toward the river. On the edges, Queen Anne's lace still held beaded blossoms of dew. A big yellow and black writing spider hung in its web's center, and Rachel remembered how her father had claimed seeing your initial sewn into the web meant you'd soon die. She did not look closely at the web, instead glanced at the sky to make sure no clouds gathered in the west over Clingman's Dome. She stepped onto the Widow's porch and knocked.

"It ain't bolted," the old woman said, and Rachel stepped inside. The greasy odor of fry pan lard filled the cabin, a scrim of smoke eddying around the room's borders. Widow Jenkins rose slowly from a caneback chair pulled close to the hearth.

"Let me hold that chap."

Rachel bent her knees and laid down her tote sack. She shifted the child in her arms and handed him over.

"He's acting fussy this morning," Rachel said. "I'm of a mind he might be starting to teethe."

"Child, a baby don't teethe till six months," Widow Jenkins scoffed. "It could be the colic or the rash or the ragweed. There's many a thing to make a young one like this feel out of sorts, but it ain't his teeth."

The Widow raised Jacob and peered into the child's face. Gold-wire spectacles made her eyes bulge as if loosed from their sockets.

"I told your daddy to marry again so you'd have a momma, but he wouldn't listen," Widow Jenkins said to Rachel. "If he had you'd know some things about babies, maybe enough to where you'd not have let the first man who gave you a wink and a smile lead you into a fool's paradise. You're still a child and don't know nothing of the world yet, girl."

Rachel stared at the puncheon floor and listened, the way she'd done for two months now. Folks at her Daddy's funeral had told her much the same, as had the granny woman who'd delivered Jacob and women in town who'd never given Rachel any notice before. Telling her for her own good, they all claimed, because they cared about her. Some of them like Widow Jenkins did care, but Rachel knew some just did it for spite. She'd watch their lips turn downward, trying to look sad and serious, but a mean kind of smile would be in their eyes.

Widow Jenkins sat back down in her chair and laid Jacob in her lap.

"A child ought to carry his daddy's name," she said, still speaking like Rachel was five instead of almost seventeen. "That way he'll have a last name and not have to go through his life explaining why he don't."

"He's got a last name, Mrs. Jenkins," Rachel said, lifting her gaze from the floor to meet the older woman's eyes, "and Harmon is as good a one as I know."

For a few moments there was no sound but the fire. A hiss and crackle, then the gray shell of a log collapsing in on itself, spilling a slush of spark and ash beneath the andirons. When Widow Jenkins spoke again, her voice was softer.

"You're right. Harmon is a good name, and an old woman ought not have to be reminded of that."

Rachel took the sugar teat and fresh swaddlings from the tote sack, the glass bottle of milk she'd drawn earlier. She laid them on the table.

"I'll be back soon as I can."

"You having to sell that horse and cow just to get by, and him that's the cause of it richer than a king," Widow Jenkins said sadly. "It's a hard place this world can be. No wonder a baby cries coming into it. Tears from the very start."

Rachel walked back up the road to the barn and took a step inside. She paused and let her gaze scan the loft and rafters, remembering, as she always did, the bat that had so frightened her years ago. She heard the chickens in the far back clucking in their nesting boxes and reminded herself to gather the eggs soon as she returned. Her eyes adjusted to the barn's darkness, and objects slowly gained form and solidity—a rusting milk can, the sack of lice powder to dust the chickens with, a rotting wagon wheel. She looked up a final time and stepped all the way inside, lifted the saddle and its pad off the rack and went to the middle stall. The draft horse was asleep, his weight shifted so the right hoof was at an angle. Rachel patted his rear haunches to let him know she was there before placing the cabbage sack in the pack. She tethered the mattock to the saddle as well.

"We got us a trip to make Dan," she told the horse.

Rachel didn't take the road past Widow Jenkins' house but instead followed Rudisell Creek down the mountain to where it entered the Pigeon River, the path narrowed by sprawling poke stalks that drooped under the weight of their purple berries and goldenrod bright as caught sunshine. Enough dew yet remained on the leaves to dampen her legs and dress. Rachel knew in the deeper woods the ginseng leaves would soon begin to show their brightness as well. The prettiest time of year, she'd always believed, prettier than fall or even spring when the dogwood branches swayed and brightened as if harboring clouds of white butterflies.

Dan moved with care down the trail, gentle and watchful with Rachel as he'd always been. Her father had bought the horse a year before Rachel was born. Even when he'd been at his drunkest or angriest, her father had never mistreated the animal, never kicked or cursed it, never forgotten to give it feed or water. Selling the horse was another lost link to her father.

She and Dan came to the dirt road and followed the river south toward Waynesville, the sun rising over her right shoulder. A few minutes later Rachel heard an automobile in the distance, her heart stammering when she glanced up and saw the vehicle coming toward her was green. It wasn't the Packard, and she felt ashamed that a part of herself, even now, could have wished it was Mr. Pemberton coming to Colt Ridge to somehow set things right. The same as when she'd gone to the camp's church service the last two Sundays, dawdling outside the dining hall with Jacob in her arms, hoping Mr. Pemberton would walk by.

The automobile sputtered past, leaving its wake of gray dust. Soon she passed a stone farmhouse, hearth smoke wisping from the chimney, in the fields plump heads of cabbage and corn stalks taller than she was, closer to the road pumpkins and squash brightening a smother of weeds. All of which promised the kind of harvest they might have had on Colt Ridge come fall if her father had lived long enough to tend his crops. A wagon came the other direction, two children dangling their legs off the back. They stared at Rachel gravely, as if sensing all that had befallen her in the last months. The road leveled and nudged close to the Pigeon River. In the morning's slanted light, the river gleamed like a vein of flowing gold. Fool's gold, she thought.

Rachel remembered the previous August, how at noon-dinner time she'd take a meal to Mr. Pemberton's house and Joel Vaughn, who'd grown up with her on Colt Ridge, would be waiting on the porch. Joel's job was to make sure no one interrupted her and Mr. Pemberton, and though Joel never said a word there'd always be a troubled look on his face when he opened the front door. Mr. Pemberton was always in the back room, and as Rachel walked through the house she looked around at the electric lights and the ice box and fancy table and cushioned chairs. Being in a place so wondrous, even for just a half hour, made her feel the same way as when she pored over the Sears wish book. Only better, because it wasn't a picture or description but the very things themselves. But that wasn't what had brought her to Mr. Pemberton's bed. He'd made notice of her, chosen Rachel over the other girls in the camp, including her friends Bonny and Rebecca, who were young like her. Rachel had believed she was in love, though since he'd been the first man she'd ever kissed, much less lain down with, how could she know. Rachel thought how maybe the Widow was right. If she'd had a mother who'd not left when Rachel was five, maybe she would have known better.

But maybe not, Rachel told herself. After all, she'd ignored the warning looks of not only Joel but also Mr. Campbell, who'd shook his head *No* at Rachel when he saw her going to the house with the tray one noon. Rachel had just smiled back at the hard stares the older women in the kitchen gave her each time she returned. When one of the men who cooked said something smart to her like *don't look like he had much of an appetite today, for food at least,* she'd blush and lower her eyes, but even then a part of her felt proud all the same. It was no different than when Bonny or Rebecca whispered *Your hair's mussed up,* and the three of them giggled like they were back in grammar school and a boy had tried to kiss one of them.

One day Mr. Pemberton had fallen asleep before she left his bed. Rachel had gotten up slowly so as not to wake him, then walked room by room through the house, touching what she passed—the bedroom's gold-gilded oval mirror, a silver pitcher and basin in the bathroom, the Marvel water heater in the hallway, the ice box and oak-front shelf clock. What had struck her most was how such wonders appeared placed around the rooms with so little thought. That was the amazing thing, Rachel had thought, how what seemed treasures to her could be hardly noticed by someone else. She'd sat in one of the Coxwell chairs and settled the plush velvet against her hips and back. It had been like sitting on a plump cloud.

When her flow stopped, she'd kept believing it was something else, not telling Mr. Pemberton or Bonny or Rebecca, even when one month became three months and then four. It'll come any day now, she'd told herself, even after the mornings she'd thrown up and her dress tightened at the waist. By the sixth month, Mr. Pemberton had gone back to Boston. Soon enough she didn't have to tell anyone because despite the loose apron her belly showed the truth of it, not only to everyone in the camp but also to her father.

Outside of Waynesville the dirt road merged with the old Asheville Toll Road. Rachel dismounted. She took the horse by the reins and led it into town. As she passed the courthouse, two women stood outside Scott's General Store. They stopped talking and watched Rachel, their eyes stern and disapproving. She tethered Dan in front of Donaldson's Feed and Seed and went in to tell the storekeeper she'd take his offer for the horse and cow.

"And you won't pick them up till this weekend, right?"

The storekeeper nodded but didn't open his cash register.

"I was hoping you could pay me now," Rachel said.

Mr. Donaldson took three ten-dollar bills from his cash register and handed them to her.

"Just make sure you don't lame that horse before I get up there."

Rachel took a snap purse from her dress pocket, placed the money in it.

"You want to buy the saddle?"

"I've got no need for a saddle," the storekeeper said brusquely.

Rachel walked across the street to Mr. Scott's store. When he produced the bill, it was more than she'd expected, though what exactly Rachel expected she could not say. She placed the remaining two dollar bills and two dimes in her snap purse and went next door to Merritt's Apothecary. When Rachel came out, she had only the dimes left.

Rachel untethered Dan and she and the horse walked on by Dodson's Café and then two smaller storefronts. She was passing the courthouse when someone called her name. Sheriff McDowell stepped out of his office door, not dressed in Sunday finery like three months ago but in his uniform, a silver badge pinned to his khaki shirt. As he walked toward her, Rachel remembered how he'd put his arm around her that day and helped her off the bench and into the depot, how later he'd driven her back up to Colt Ridge and though the day wasn't cold, he'd built a small fire in the hearth. They'd sat there together by the fire, not talking, until Widow Jenkins arrived to spend the night with her.

The sheriff tipped his hat when he caught up to her.

"I don't mean to hold you up," he said, "just wanted to check and see how you and your child were doing."

Rachel met the sheriff's eyes, noting again their unusual hue. Honey-colored, but not glowy like that of bees fed on clover, but instead the darker amber of basswood honey. A warm comforting color. She looked for the least hint of judgment in the sheriff's gaze and saw none.

"We're doing okay," Rachel said, though there being only two dimes in her snap purse argued otherwise.

A Model T rattled past, causing the horse to shy toward the sidewalk.

Sheriff McDowell and Rachel stood together in the street a few moments more, neither speaking until McDowell touched the brim of his hat again.

"Well, like I said, I just wanted to see how you're doing. If I can help you, in any way, you let me know."

"Thank you," Rachel said and paused for a moment. "That day Daddy was killed, I appreciate what you did, especially staying with me."

Sheriff McDowell nodded. "I was glad to do it."

The sheriff walked back toward his office as Rachel tugged Dan's reins and led him on past the courthouse.

At the end of the street Rachel came to a wooden frame building, in its narrow yard a dozen blank marble tombstones of varying sizes and hues. Inside she heard the tap tap tap of a hammer and chisel. Rachel tethered the horse to the closest hitching post and crossed the marble-stobbed yard. She paused at the open door above which was written LUDLOW SURRATT—STONE MASON.

An air presser and air hammer lay next to the entrance, in the room's center a work bench, on it mallets and chisels, a compass saw and a slate board chalked with words and numbers. Some of the stones lining the four walls had names and dates. Others were blank but for lambs and crosses and volutes. The air smelled chalky, the room's earthen floor whitened as if with a fine snow. Surratt sat in a low wooden chair, a stone leaning against the work bench before him. He wore a hat and an apron, and as he worked he leaned close to the marble, the hammer and chisel inches from his face.

Rachel knocked and he turned, his clothes and hands and eyelashes whitened by the marble dust. He laid the hammer and chisel on the bench and without a word went to the back of the shop. He lifted the sixteen- by fourteen-inch marble tablet Rachel had commissioned the week after her father had died. Before she could say anything, he'd set it beside the doorway. Surratt stepped back and stood beside her. They looked at the tablet, the name Abraham Harmon etched in the marble, above it the fylfot Rachel had chosen from the sketch pad.

"I think it come out all right," the stone mason said. "You satisfied?"

"Yes sir. It looks fine," Rachel said, then hesitated. "The rest of your money. I thought I'd have it, but I don't."

Surratt did not look especially surprised at this news, and Rachel supposed there were others who had come to him with similar stories.

"That saddle," Rachel said, nodding toward the horse. "You could have it for what I owe."

"I knew your daddy. Some found him too bristly but I liked him," Surratt said. "We'll work something else out. You'll need that saddle."

"No sir, I won't. I sold my horse to Mr. Donaldson. After this weekend I'll not need it."

"This weekend?"

"Yes sir," Rachel said. "That's when he's coming to pick up the horse and cow both."

The stone mason mulled this information over.

"I'll take the saddle then, and we'll call it square between us. Have Donaldson bring it back with him," Surratt said, pausing as another Model T sputtered past. "Who have you hired to haul the stone up there?"

Rachel lifted the burlap cabbage sack from the saddle pack.

"I figured to do it."

"That stone weighs more than it looks, near fifty pounds," Surratt said. "It'll bust right through a sack that thin. Besides, once you get up there you still got to plant it."

"I got a mattock with me," Rachel said. "If you help me tie the stone to the saddle horn I can manage."

Surratt took a red handkerchief from his back pocket, winced and rubbed the cloth across his forehead. He stuffed the handkerchief back in his pocket as his eyes resettled on Rachel.

"How old are you?"

"Almost seventeen."

"Almost."

"Yes sir."

Rachel expected the stone mason to tell her what Widow Jenkins had said, how she was just a girl and knew nothing. He'd be right to tell her so, Rachel supposed. How could she argue otherwise when all morning she'd figured wrong on everything from a baby's teething time to what things cost.

Surratt leaned over the tombstone and blew a limn of white dust from one of the chiseled letters. He let his hand linger on the stone a moment, as if to verify its solidity a final time. He stood and untied his leather apron.

"I ain't that busy," he said. "I'll put the stone in my truck and take it on up there right now. I'll plant it for you too."

"Thank you," Rachel said. "That's a considerable kindness."

She rode back through Waynesville and north on the old toll road, but quickly left it for a different trail than the one she'd come on. The land soon turned steeper, rockier, the mattock's steel head clanking against the stirrup. The horse breathed harder as the air thinned, its soft nostrils rising with each pull of air. They sloshed through a creek, the water low and clear. Leathery rhododendron leaves rubbed against Rachel's dress.

She traveled another half hour, moving up the highest ridge. The woods drew back briefly and revealed an abandoned homestead. The front door yawned open, on the porch a spill of pans and plates and moldering quilts that bespoke a hasty exodus. Above the farmhouse's front door a rusty horseshoe upturned to catch what good luck might fall the occupant's way. Clearly not enough, Rachel thought, knowing before too long her place might look the same if she didn't have a good harvest of ginseng.

The mountains and woods quickly reclosed around her. The trees were all hardwoods now. Light seeped through their foliage as through layers of gauze. No birds sang and no deer or rabbit bolted in front of her. The only things growing along the trail were mushrooms and toadstools, the only sound acorns crackling and popping beneath Dan's iron hooves. The woods smelled like it had just rained.

The trail rose a last time and ended at the road. On the other side stood a deserted white clapboard church. The wide front door had a padlock on it, and the white paint had grayed and begun peeling. So many people lived in the timber camp now that Reverend Bolick held his services in the camp's dining hall instead of the church. Mr. Surratt's truck was not parked by the cemetery gate, but Rachel saw the stone was set in the ground. She tied Dan to the gate and walked inside. She moved through the grave markers, some just creek rocks with no names or dates, others soapstone and granite, a few marble. What names there were were familiar—Jenkins and Candler and McDowell and Pressley, Harmon. She was almost to her father's grave when she heard howling down the ridge below the cemetery, a lonesome sound like a whippoorwill or a far-off train. A pack of wild dogs made their way across a clearing, the one who'd raised his throat to the sky now running to catch up with the others. Rachel remembered the mattock strapped to the saddle and thought about getting it in case the dogs veered up the ridge, but they soon disappeared into the woods. Then there was only silence.

She stood by the tombstone, dirt the stone mason had displaced darkening the grave. Her father had been a hard man to live with, awkward in his affection, never saying much. His temper like a kitchen match waiting to be struck, especially if he'd been drinking. One of Rachel's clearest memories of her mother was lying on her parents' bed on a hot day. She'd told her mother that the blue bedspread felt cool and smooth despite the summer heat, like it'd feel if you could sleep on top of a creek pool. *Because it's satin,* her mother said, and Rachel had thought even the word was cool and smooth, whispery like the sound of a creek. She remembered the day her father took the bedspread and threw it into the hearth. It was the morning after her mother left, and as her father stuffed the satin bedspread deeper into the flames, he'd told Rachel to never mention her mother again, if Rachel did he'd slap her mouth. Whether he would have or not, she had never risked finding out. Rachel heard an older woman at the funeral claim her father had been a different man before her mother left, less prone to anger and bitterness. Never bad to drink. Rachel couldn't remember that man.

Yet he'd raised a child by himself, a girl child, and Rachel figured he'd done it as well as any man could have alone. She'd never gone wanting for food and clothing. There were plenty of things he hadn't taught her, maybe couldn't teach her, but she'd learned about crops and plants and animals, how to mend a fence and chink a cabin. He'd had her do these things herself while he watched. Making sure she knew how, Rachel now realized, when he'd not be around to do it for her. What was that, if not a kind of love.

She touched the tombstone and felt its sturdiness and solidity. It made her think of the cradle her father had built two weeks before he died. He'd brought it in and set it by her bed, not speaking a single word acknowledging he'd made it for the child. But she could see the care in the making of it, how he'd built it out of hickory, the hardest and most lasting wood there was. Made not just to last but to look pretty, for he'd sanded the cradle and then varnished it with linseed oil.

Rachel removed her hand from a stone she knew would outlast her lifetime, and that meant it would outlast her grief. I've gotten him buried in Godly ground and I've burned the clothes he died in, Rachel told herself. I've signed the death certificate and now his grave stone's up. I've done all I can do. As she told herself this, Rachel felt the grief inside grow so wide and deep it felt like a dark fathomless pool she'd never emerge from. Because there was nothing left to do now, nothing except endure it.

Think of something happy, she told herself, something he did for you. A small thing. For a few moments nothing came. Then something did, something that had happened about this time of year. After supper her father had gone to the barn while Rachel went to the garden. In the waning light she'd gathered ripe pole beans whose dark pods nestled up to the rows of sweet corn she'd planted as trellis. Her father called from the barn mouth, and she'd set the wash pan between two rows, thinking he needed her to carry the milk pail to the springhouse.

"Pretty, isn't it," he'd said as she entered the barn.

Her father pointed to a large silver-green moth. For a few minutes the chores were put off as the two of them just stood there. The barn's stripes of light grew dimmer, and the moth seemed to brighten, as if the slow open and close of its wings gathered up the evening's last light. Then the creature rose. As the moth fluttered out into the night, her father had lifted his large strong hand and settled it on Rachel's shoulder a moment, not turning to her as he did so. A moth at twilight, a touch of a hand on her back. Something, Rachel thought.

As she rode back down the trail, she remembered the days after the funeral, how the house's silence was a palpable thing and she couldn't endure a day without visiting Widow Jenkins for something borrowed or returned. Then one morning she'd begun to feel her sorrow easing, like something jagged that had cut into her so long it had finally dulled its edges, worn itself down. That same day Rachel couldn't remember which side her father had parted his hair on, and she'd realized again what she'd learned at five when her mother left—that what made losing someone you loved bearable was not remembering but forgetting. Forgetting small things first, the smell of the soap her mother had bathed with, the color of the dress she'd worn to church, then after a while the sound of her mother's voice, the color of her hair. It amazed Rachel how much you could forget, and everything you forgot made that person less alive inside you until you could finally endure it. After more time passed you could let yourself remember, even want to remember. But even then what you felt those first days could return and remind you the grief was still there, like old barbed wire embedded in a tree's heartwood.

And now this brown-eyed child. Don't love it, Rachel told herself. Don't love anything that can be taken away.

Four

WHEN THEY'D LAID THE TRAIN TRACK THE PREvious September, Pemberton worked alongside the three dozen men hired for the job. He was as broad shouldered and thick armed as any of the highlanders, but Pemberton knew his fine clothes and Boston accent counted against him. So he'd taken off his black tweed coat, stripped to his waist and joined them, first working with the lead crews as they used picks and shovels and wheelbarrows to move earth and remove stumps, make the fills and cuts and ditching. Pemberton cut trees for crossties and set them on the proper gradient, unloaded flat cars stacked with rails and angle bars and switch gear, laid down relay rails and hammered spikes and never took a break unless the other men did. They worked eleven hour days, six days a week, moving across the valley floor in a fixed line. What obstacles not dug up or filled in were leveled with dynamite or trestles.

When a new piece of track was set down, the Shay engine lurched forward immediately to cover it, as though the wilderness might seize the rails if they weren't gripped and held by the iron wheels. From a distance, train and men appeared a single bustling entity, the steel rails left in their passing like a narrow gleaming wake.

He'd enjoyed the challenge of working with the men, the way they'd watched for a first sign of weakness, for Pemberton to linger by the water pail or lean too long on a shovel or sledge hammer. To see how soon he joined Buchanan and Wilkie on the porch of the newly built office. When a month had passed and all but the spur lines were built, Pemberton put his shirt back on and went to the office where he'd spend most of his time from that point on. By then he'd gained more than just the workers' respect. He'd found among them a capable lieutenant in Campbell, and Pemberton knew first-hand which men to keep and which to let go when Boston Lumber Company hired the actual cutting crews.

Among those Pemberton insisted be retained was an older man named Galloway. Already in his forties, Galloway was at an age when most loggers were too worn down and damaged to do the job, but despite his graying hair, small stature and wiry build, he outworked men half his age. He was also an expert tracker and woodsman who knew the region's forests and ridges as well as anyone in the county. A man who could track a grasshopper across caprock, workers claimed, as Pemberton himself had learned when he'd used Galloway as a hunting guide. But Galloway had spent five years in prison for killing two men during a card-game dispute. Other workers, many with violent tendencies of their own, gave Galloway a wary respect, as they did his mother, who shared a stringhouse with her son. When Pemberton had suggested they make Galloway a crew boss, Buchanan had been against the idea. He's a convicted murderer, Buchanan had protested. We shouldn't even have him in camp, much less leading a crew.

Now, a year later, Pemberton again suggested Galloway be made a foreman, this time as Bilded's replacement.

"It's the most undisciplined crew in the camp," Pemberton said between bites of his steak. "We need someone they'll be afraid to buck."

"What if he tries to buck us instead?" Buchanan asked. "Besides being a convicted murderer, he's surly and disrespectful."

"A crew won't be laggards for a foreman they're afraid of," Serena said. "I would argue that's more important than his lack of social graces."

Buchanan was about to continue the argument when Wilkie raised a hand to silence him.

"Sorry, Buchanan," Wilkie said, "but I'm siding with the Pembertons this time."

"It appears Mr. and Mrs. Pemberton rule the day," Doctor Cheney said, his tone becoming manneredly casual. "Your wife, Buchanan, I assume she plans to summer again in Concord?"

"Yes," Buchanan said tersely.

"Perhaps you have similar plans to return to Colorado for the summer, Mrs. Pemberton?" Cheney asked. "I'm sure the family manse is much grander than your present abode."

"No, I don't," Serena said. "Once I left Colorado I've never returned."

"But who looks after your parents' house and estate?" Wilkie asked.

"I had the house burned down before I left."

"Burned," Wilkie exclaimed in astonishment.

"Fire is indeed an excellent purifier after contagion," Doctor Cheney said, "but I suspect burning the bed sheets would have sufficed."

"What of your family's timber holdings?" Wilkie asked. "I certainly hope you didn't burn those as well."

"I sold them," Serena said. "It's money better used here in North Carolina."

"No doubt in a venture with Mr. Harris," Doctor Cheney said, setting down his fork. "Despite his bluster he's a crafty old fox, as I'm sure you ascertained when you met him."

"I suspect Mrs. Pemberton can hold her own against Harris," Wilkie said, and nodded at Pemberton. "And Pemberton too. I for one wish them well in any new ventures, whether it's with Boston Lumber Company or anyone else. We need people with confidence right now, else we'll never get out of this depression."

Wilkie turned his attention back to Serena, and smiled widely, smitten as Harris had been when he'd met her. Unlike the swains in Boston, these older men seemed unintimidated by Serena. Their withered genitals made her charms less daunting, Pemberton suspected, kept at an untouchable distance.

"I'm sure you feel the same, Buchanan," Doctor Cheney said, "in regard to the Pembertons' possible partnership with Harris."

Buchanan nodded, his eyes not on the physician or the Pembertons but the table's center.

"Yes, as long as our own present partnership is not neglected."

Except for the clink of silverware, the rest of the main course was eaten in silence. Pemberton did not wait for dessert and coffee but set his napkin on the table and stood up.

"Campbell's left for the night so I'll go tell Galloway of his promotion. That way he'll be ready come morning," Pemberton said, and turned to Serena. "I'll meet you back at the house. I won't be long."

As he came into the office, Pemberton saw Campbell had left two letters on the desk, a Boston postmark on each.

Pemberton stepped off the porch into the summer evening. Fireflies winked as the sun settled behind Balsam Mountain. In the distance a whippoorwill called. Next to the dining hall a rusty fifty-gallon drum smoldered with supper's detritus. Pemberton dropped the unopened letters into its fire and walked on. He stepped onto the train rails he'd help lay and followed them toward the last stringhouse where Galloway lived with his mother. She was granted great deference by all in the camp, and Pemberton had assumed it was because Galloway was her son. He'd noted as much to Campbell one afternoon as they watched the old woman, whose eyes were misted by cataracts, being helped up the commissary steps by two large bearded workers.

"It's more than that," Campbell said. "She can see things other folks can't."

Pemberton had snorted. "That old crone's so blind she couldn't even see herself in a mirror."

For the only time they'd worked together, Campbell had spoken to Pemberton without deference, his reply acerbic and condescending.

"It ain't that kind of seeing," Campbell had said, "and it ain't nothing to be made light of either."

Galloway met him at the door. The older man wore no shirt, revealing a span of pale skin stretched taut over shoulders and ribs, paired knots of stomach muscle. Veins on his neck and arms rippled blue and varicose, as if Galloway's flesh could not fully contain the surge of blood within it. A body seemingly incapable of repose.

"I've come to tell you I've fired Bilded. You're the new crew foreman."

"I figured as much," Galloway replied.

Pemberton wondered if Campbell had come by and mentioned the promotion. He looked past Galloway into a room completely dark except for the glow of a coal-oil lamp on the table. The thick lamp glass made the light appear not just encased but fluid, as though submerged in water. Galloway's mother sat before the lamp, eyes only inches from the flame. Her white hair was clinched in a tight bun, and she wore a black front-buttoned dress Pemberton suspected had been sewn in the previous century. Galloway's mother raised her eyes and stared directly at him. *Looking at the direction of my voice,* Pemberton told himself, but it was somehow more than that.

"Anyway," Pemberton said, taking a step back, "I wanted you to know before morning."

As Pemberton walked back to the house, he passed a group of kitchen workers gathered on the dining hall steps. Most still wore their aprons. A cook named Beason strummed a battered Gibson guitar, beside him a woman nestling a steel-stringed wooden instrument in her lap. She bent over the instrument, long tangled hair obscuring her face. While her right hand strummed, the middle and index fingers on her left hand made rapid presses around the narrow neck as if probing for some obscure pulse, all the while singing of murder and retribution on the shores of a Scottish loch. Border ballads were what Buchanan called such songs, and claimed the mountaineers had brought them from Albion.

The Harmon girl had once sat out on these steps after supper as well, but he'd not paid her much attention until the evening Pemberton helped haul a maimed logger off Half Acre Ridge. It was full dark by the time they'd gotten the man to camp, and he'd been so tired and dirty he'd told Campbell to have his meal brought to the house. The Harmon girl had brought the food, and something had caught Pemberton's attention. Perhaps a glimpse of bosom when she laid the tray on the table, or a shapely ankle exposed as she turned to leave. Something he could no longer remember.

Pemberton walked on, the music fading behind him as he mused on the chain of events that had led to noon trysts, later a gutted man dying on a train depot bench, a child that surely had been born by now. How far back could you trace the links in such a chain, he wondered—past the Harmon girl being chosen that night to bring his food, past the tree shattering a man's backbone due to a badly notched trunk, past that to an axe unsharpened because a man drank too much the night before, past that to why the man had gotten drunk in the first place? Was it something you never found the end to? Or was there no chain at all, just a moment when you did or didn't step close to a young woman and let your fingers brush a fall of blonde hair behind her ears, did or didn't lean to that uncovered ear and tell her that you found her quite fetching.

Pemberton smiled at himself. Dwelling on the past, the very thing Serena had shown him he, and they, had no need of. And yet, the child. As he mounted the porch steps, Pemberton forced his mind to a Baltimore furniture factory's delinquent account.

THE following afternoon a worker on Noland Mountain was struck on the thigh by a timber rattlesnake. His leg swelled so rapidly that a crew foreman had to first cut free the denim pant with a hawkbill, then slash an X into each puncture. By the time the crew got the man to camp, his pulse was no more than a felt whisper. The leg below the knee swelled black and big around as a hearth log, and the man's gums bled profusely. Doctor Cheney didn't bother to take him into his office. He told the workers to set him in a chair on the commissary porch, where the man soon gave a last violent shudder and died.

"How many men have been bitten since the camp opened?" Serena said that evening as they ate supper.

"Five before today," Wilkie replied. "Only one of them died, but the other four had to be let go."

"A timber rattlesnake's venom destroys blood vessels and tissue," Doctor Cheney said to Serena. "Even if the victim is fortunate enough to survive the initial bite, lasting damage is incurred."

"I'm aware of what happens when someone is bitten by a rattlesnake, Doctor," Serena replied. "Out west we have diamondbacks, which reach six feet in length."

Cheney gave a brief half bow in Serena's direction.

"Pardon me," he said. "I should never have doubted your knowledge of venom."

"Their coloration varies here," Buchanan said. "Sometimes they are the yellowish complexion of copperheads, but they can also be much darker. Those called satinbacks are a purplish black, and believed much deadlier. I've seen one, a surprisingly graceful creature, in its own way quite beautiful."

Doctor Cheney smiled. "Another of nature's paradoxes, the most beautiful creatures are so often the most injurious. The tiger, for instance, or black widow spider."

"I would argue that's part of their beauty," Serena said.

"The rattlesnakes cost us money," Wilkie complained, "and not just when a crew is halted by a bite. The men get overcautious so progress is slowed."

"Yes," Serena agreed. "They should be killed off, especially in the slash."

Wilkie frowned. "Yet that is the hardest place to see them, Mrs. Pemberton. They blend in so well as to be nearly invisible."

"Better eyes are needed then," Serena said.

"Cold weather will be here soon and send them up to the rock cliffs," Pemberton said. "Galloway says that after the first frost they never venture far from their dens."

"Until spring," Wilkie fretted. "Then they'll be back, every bit as bad as before."

"Perhaps not," Serena said.

Five

Winter came early. One Saturday morning men awoke in their stringhouses to find a half-foot of snow on the ground. Wool union suits and quilts were pulled from beneath beds, the makeshift windows boarded up with oilcloths, scraps of wood and tin, the splayed hides of bear and deer, other pelts including the tattered remains of a wolverine. Smaller gaps were bunged with rags and newspaper, daubs of tobacco and mud. Before stepping outside, the workers donned coats and jackets that had sagged on nails for six months. They walked down to the dining hall tugging at sleeves and re-forming collars. Most wore mackinaws, though others wore wide-pocketed hunting jackets, black frocks or leather jerkins. Some donned what they'd once worn in more prosperous or martial times—lined submarine coats and Chesterfields, moleskin suit tops, coats from the Great War. Some wore what had been passed down from their forbearers, frayed work coats of pre-twentieth-century vintage, including ones made of raccoon and buckskin, even older cloaks whose butternut and blue colors bespoke long-ago divisions in the county.

Snipes' crew worked the crest of Noland Mountain where snow lay deepest and the wind surged across the ridge, bending the upper halves of the biggest hardwoods. Dunbar lost his stetson when a gust sent it sailing off the mountain toward Tennessee, the hat spinning and turning, falling then rising like a wounded bird.

"I should have tied it to my head," Dunbar said glumly. "That hat cost me two dollars."

"Best that you didn't," Ross said. "You might have gone sailing off with it and not touched ground till Knoxville."

The crew ate lunch around a brush pile they'd cleared snow off and set fire to. The men huddled close, not just for warmth but to protect the flames from gusts of snowdrift that stung their faces like sand. They shed their gloves and held their numbed hands toward the fire as if surrendering to it.

"Listen to that wind howl," Dunbar said. "For the sound of it you'd think it could lift this whole mountain."

"Barely October and snow already on the ground," Ross said. "A hard winter's coming."

"My daddy said the wooly worms was wearing a thicker coat all summer and we're sure enough seeing the truth of it," Stewart said. "Daddy allowed that wasn't the only sign. He said the hornets was building their nests close to the ground."

"Them's pagan believings, Stewart," McIntyre said to his congregant, "and you best stay clear of them."

"There's some science in it," Snipes said. "Those wooly worms was growing thicker hair for to stand a hard winter. There ain't no pagan in that. Wooly worms is just using the knowledge God give them. The hornets the same."

"The only signs you need to follow is in the Bible," McIntyre said.

"What about that sign that says No Smoking on the dynamite shed," Ross noted. "You saying we don't need to follow that one?"

"You can make sport of it," McIntyre said to Ross, "but this unnatural weather is a certain sign we're in the last days. *The sun will be darkened and the moon shall not give her light.*"

McIntyre looked up at the gray-slate sky as if it were some Gnostic text only he was capable of deciphering. He tipped his black preacher's hat heavenward, seemingly satisfied at what he'd seen.

"There will be famines and pestilences coming after that," McIntyre proclaimed. "There'll be nary a plant sprout out of the ground but thorns and you'll have grasshoppers big as rabbits eating everything else, even the wood on your house, and snakes and scorpions and all such terrible things falling out of the sky."

"And you think all this is going to happen any day now?" Ross asked.

"Yes, I do," McIntyre replied. "I'm certain of it as old Noah himself was when he built that boat."

"Then I reckon we better start bringing umbrellas with us to work," Ross said.

"Ain't no *we* to it," McIntyre said. "I'll be raptured up the day before it starts. It'll be you and the other infidels has to deal with it."

The men watched the fire for a few moments, then Dunbar looked down the south slope at the valley. Snow hid the stumps, but slash piles raised white humps across the landscape like burial mounds.

"Ain't as many critter tracks as you'd think."

"They've hightailed on over to Tennessee," Ross said. "That's the direction we're herding them and they've give up fighting it."

"Maybe they got word of the new park over that way," Snipes said, "figured they'd be left alone there since all the two-legged critters have near been run out."

"They run my uncle off his place last week," Dunbar said. "Said it was eminent domain."

"What does eminent domain mean?" Stewart asked.

"It means you're shit out of luck," Ross said.

"What's the name of the hermit fellow down in Deep Creek," Dunbar asked, "the one who writes the books?"

"Kephart," Ross said.

"Yeah," Dunbar said, "him and that newspaperman in Asheville is hep on this land for the park too. Got some big bugs up in Washington on their side."

"They'll need them," Ross said. "You can count on Harris and the Pembertons fattening every wallet from the county courthouse up to the governor's mansion."

"Not Sheriff McDowell's pocket," Dunbar argued. "He never kowtowed to them from the very start. I helped lay the track, so I was here the morning Sheriff McDowell come and arrested Pemberton for driving too fast through town."

"I never knew you to have witnessed that," Stewart said. "He really threatened to handcuff him?"

"You're damn right he did," Dunbar said. "He was going to haul Pemberton off in his police car too but for Buchanan saying he'd drive him."

"I heard he kept Pemberton in that cell overnight," Snipes said.

"Not overnight," Dunbar replied. "No more than a hour before the magistrate got him out. But he put him in there, and there's not another in this county would of done that."

The flames began to wither, so Ross and Snipes got up and found more wood. They shook free the snow and gently placed the limbs crosswise on what lingered. The fire slowly revived, climbing the wood webbing like a plant ascending a trellis, flames coiling, coming forth then retreating, finally holding fast on one limb, then one more. The men watched the orange blossoming, not moving or speaking until all the branches had caught. McIntyre stared especially intently, as though awaiting another prophecy.

The snow came in thicker flakes, whitening Dunbar's bare head. He raked his fingers through his hair, held out to the others what flakes clung to his hand.

"It'd be a good day to see that panther's tracks with snow thick and soft as this," Dunbar said.

"If there's really a panther left up here," Ross said. "Nobody's killed one in nine year."

"But folks claims to see it right regular," Stewart noted.

"Revelations says they'll be lions here when the judgment day comes," McIntyre said, still staring into the flames. "Leastways their heads will be. The yonder half of them will have legs no different than human people like us."

"Will they be wearing pants?" Ross asked. "Or is that just the whore of Babylon?"

Stewart stepped away from the fire, making sure the wind was at his back before freeing the copper buttons on his overalls.

"Be careful there, Stewart," Snipes said, "or you'll piss on Dunbar's hat."

Stewart shifted his stream slightly eastward. He buttoned his overalls and sat back down.

"What about you, Snipes?" Dunbar asked. "You think there to be mountain lions up here or is it just folks' imaginings?"

Snipes pondered the question a few moments before speaking.

"They's many a man of science would claim there ain't because you got no irredeemable evidence like panther scat or fur or tooth or tail. In other words, some part of the animal in question. Or better yet having the actual critter itself, the whole thing kit and caboodle head to tail, which all your men of science argue is the best proof of all a thing exists, whether it be a panther, or a bird, or even a dinosaur."

Snipes paused to gauge the level of comprehension among his audience and decided further explanation was necessary.

"To put it another way, if you was to stub your toe and tell the man of science what happened he'd not believe a word of it less he could see how it'd stoved up or was bleeding. But your philosophers and theologians and such say there's things in the world that's every bit as real even though you can't see them."

"Like what?" Dunbar asked.

"Well," Snipes said. "They's love, that's one. And courage. You can't see neither of them, but they're real. And air, of course. That's one of your most important examples. You wouldn't be alive a minute if there wasn't air, but nobody's ever seen a single speck of it."

"And chiggers," Stewart said helpfully. "You'll never see one but you get into a mess of them and you'll be itching for a week."

"So you're saying you believe there's still a panther around," Dunbar said.

"I'm not certain of such a thing," Snipes said. "All I'm saying is there is a lot more to this old world than meets the eye."

The crew foreman paused and stretched his open palms closer to the fire.

"And darkness. You can't see it no more than you can see air, but when it's all around you sure enough know it."

Six

By late Sunday morning the snow had stopped, and Buchanan and the Pembertons decided to go hunting a mile southwest of camp, a five-acre meadow Galloway had baited for a month. Wilkie, whose sporting life consisted of nothing more than an occasional poker game, stayed in Waynesville. Young Vaughn packed the Studebaker farm wagon with provisions, the gray wool golf cap pulled down over his red hair. Galloway had procured a farmer's pack of Plotts and Redbones considered the finest in the county. Galloway sat on the wagon's springboard seat with Vaughn, between them Shakes, the farmer's prize Plott hound, the rest of the dogs piled in back with the provisions. The Pembertons and Buchanan followed on horseback, crossing Balsam Mountain before veering east to enter a V-shaped gorge the mountaineers called a shut-in.

"Galloway's baited the meadow with corn and apples," Pemberton said. "That'll bring deer, maybe a bear."

"Perhaps even your panther," Serena said, "following the deer."

"The deer carcass the men found on Noland last week," Buchanan asked Galloway. "How did you know a mountain lion didn't kill it?"

Galloway turned, his left eye narrowing. His lips veered rightward, as though trying to slide the smile off his face.

"Because its chest wasn't tore open. There's cats will eat the tongue and ears before anything else, but not a panther. It eats the heart first."

They followed the wagon as it swayed and bumped into the gorge, rock cliffs pressing closer on both sides as they descended. They went single file now, the horses' pastern joints deftly negotiating the narrowing slantland. Halfway down, Galloway stopped the wagon and examined an oak tree whose lower branches were broken off.

"At least one bear in this shut-in," Galloway said, "and goodly-sized to skin up a tree like this one done."

They soon passed directly under a cliff, spears of ice hanging from the rocks. At the tightest point, Vaughn and Galloway stopped and lifted the iron-rimmed left wheels one at a time over a rock jut, in the process spilling out three hounds and a larder filled with sandwiches. Pemberton paused to tighten his saddle's girth. After he finished, he looked up the trail and saw Serena thirty yards ahead, the Arabian blending so well with the snow that for a moment she appeared to ride the air itself. Pemberton smiled and wished a crew of loggers could have seen the illusion. Since her initial triumph over Bilded, the men ascribed all sorts of powers to Serena, some bordering on the otherworldly.

Finally the shut-in widened again, and they came to a bald where the trail ended. Galloway jumped into the back of the wagon and leashed the dogs.

"The brindled ones," Serena said. "What breed are they?"

"They're called Plotts, a local variety," Pemberton explained. "They're bred specifically for boar and bear."

"The broad chest is impressive. Is their courage?"

"Equally impressive," Pemberton said.

They took what was needed from the wagon and moved into the thickening woods, Galloway and Vaughn and the dogs well behind. The Pembertons and Buchanan progressed on foot now, the horses' reins in one hand, rifles in the other.

"Quite a few poplars and oaks," Serena noted, nodding at the surrounding trees.

"Some of our best acreage," Pemberton said. "Campbell's found a stand of tulip poplars where the smallest is eighty feet high."

Buchanan walked beside Pemberton now.

"This stock market collapse, Pemberton. I wonder about its long-term effects for us."

"We'll be better off than most businesses," Pemberton replied. "The worst for us is less building being done."

"Perhaps the need for coffins will offset that," Serena said. "There's evidently quite a demand for them on Wall Street."

Buchanan paused, grasped Pemberton's coat by the elbow and leaned closer. Pemberton smelled Bay Rum aftershave and Woodbury hair tonic, which bespoke coifed hair and smooth cheeks as part of Buchanan's hunt preparation.

"So the Secretary of the Interior's interest in this land. You still say we shouldn't consider it?"

Serena was a few steps farther ahead and turned to speak, but Buchanan raised his palm.

"I'm asking your husband's opinion, Mrs. Pemberton, not yours."

Serena stared at Buchanan a few moments. The gold flecks in her irises seemed to absorb more light even as the pupils receded into some deeper part of her. Then she turned and walked on.

"My opinion is the same as my wife's," Pemberton said. "We don't sell unless we make a good profit."

They walked another furlong before the land briefly rose, then began falling at a sharper grade. Soon the meadow's white leveling emerged through the trees. Galloway had brought a tote sack of corn the previous day, and a dozen deer placidly ate the last of it. Fresh snow muffled the hunters' footsteps, and no deer raised its head as the Pembertons and Buchanan tethered their horses, walked on through the remaining woods and took positions at the meadow's edge.

They each picked out a deer and raised their rifles. Pemberton said *now* and they fired. Two deer fell to the ground and did not move, but Buchanan's ran crashing into the brush and trees on the other side. It fell, got up, then disappeared into the deeper woods.

Galloway soon joined the Pembertons and Buchanan, the Plotts and Redbones gusting Galloway in different directions as if the leashes were attached to low-flying kites. Once in the meadow, Galloway freed the strike dog and then the others. The hounds ran in a yelping rush toward the far woods where the wounded deer had gone. Galloway listened to the pack for a few moments before turning to Buchanan and the Pembertons.

"This shut-in ain't got but one way out. If you flank this meadow and put one of you in the center, there ain't nothing on four legs getting by."

Galloway crouched on one knee and listened, his left hand touching the snow as if he might feel the vibration of the dogs running in the woods below. The hounds' cries grew dim, then began steadily rising.

"You best get them fancy guns of yours ready," Galloway said. "They're coming this way."

BY late afternoon the Pembertons and Buchanan had killed a dozen deer. Galloway made a mound of the carcasses in the meadow's center, and blood streaked the snow red. Buchanan had wearied of the shooting after his third deer and sat down with his rifle propped against a tree, content to let the Pembertons make the last kills. Midday there had been the sound of ice unshackling from limbs, the woods popping and crackling as if arthritic, but now the temperature had dropped, the woods silent but for the clamor of the hounds.

What sun the day's gray sky had allowed was settling atop Balsam

Mountain when the hollow cries of the Plotts and Redbones quickened into rapid barks. Galloway and Vaughn stood at the woods' edge, not far from where Pemberton waited, rifle in hand. The barks grew more resonant, urgent, almost a sobbing.

"Struck them a bear, a damn big one from the fuss they're allowing it," Galloway said, his breath whitened by the cold. "Mama told me we'd have some good hunting today."

As the hounds' barks lengthened and deepened into bays, Pemberton thought of Galloway's mother, how her eyes were the color of pockets of morning fog the workers called bluejon, like mist filling two inward-probing cavities. Pemberton remembered how those eyes had turned in his direction and lingered. A way to stupefy the credulous, he knew, but done damn well.

"You best be ready, for that bear's coming and once he hits this meadow he won't be dawdling," Galloway said, and turned to Serena and winked. "He won't care if you're man nor woman neither."

Buchanan picked up his rifle and positioned himself on the clearing's left, Serena in the center, Pemberton on the right. Galloway moved behind Serena, his eyes closed as he listened. The hounds were frantically baying now, yelping as well when the bear turned and swatted at its pursuers. Then Pemberton heard the bear itself, crashing through the woods with the torrent of dogs in pursuit.

It came into the meadow between Serena and Pemberton. The bear paused a moment and swatted the largest Plott off its hind leg, the bear's claws raking the dog's flank. The big Plott lay on the snow a moment before rising and attacking again. The bear's paw caught the dog on the same flank, only lower this time, the Plott sent tumbling into the air. It landed yards away, the hide on the dog's right side shred thin as shoestrings.

The bear rushed onward, straight towards Pemberton, only twenty yards away when it saw the man and swerved left just as Pemberton pulled the trigger. The bullet hit between shoulder and chest, enough to make the animal fall sideways as its left front leg buckled. The hounds leaped upon the bear, draping the creature's midquarters. The bear rose onto its back legs, and the dogs rose with it like pelts hung around the bear's belly.

The animal fell forward, steadied itself for a moment before charging toward Pemberton, whose second shot clipped a Plott's ear before entering the bear's stomach. There was no time for a third shot. The bear rose and pressed its bulk against Pemberton, and he felt himself swallowed within a vast weighted shadow. His rifle slipped from his hand as the bear clutched him. Instinct pushed Pemberton deeper into the bear's grasp, so close the creature's claws could do no more than rake the back of his duckcloth hunting jacket. The dogs leaped upon them, lunging and snapping at Pemberton as if believing him now part of the bear. Pemberton's head pressed deep against the bear's chest. Pemberton felt the creature's fur and flesh and the breastbone beneath and the quickened beat of the heart and the heat stoked by that heart. He smelled the bear, the musk of its fur, its spilling blood, smelled the forest itself in the earthy linger of acorn each time the bear exhaled. Everything, even the cries of the dogs, became slower, more distinct and heightened. He felt the whole of the bear's bulk as it teetered slightly, regained balance, felt also the bear's front right limb batting his shoulder as it slashed at the hounds. The bear growled and Pemberton heard the sound gather deep in the bear's chest before rumbling upward into the throat and out the mouth.

The Plotts circled and leaped, holding onto the bear with teeth and claw a few moments before falling away only to circle and leap again, the Redbones yelping and darting in to snap at the legs. Then Pemberton felt the barrel of a rifle against his side, felt its reverberation as the weapon fired. The bear staggered two steps backward. As Pemberton fell, he turned and saw Serena place a second shot just above the bear's eyes. The creature wavered a moment, then toppled to the ground and disappeared under a moiling quilt of dogs.

Pemberton lay on the ground as well, unsure if he'd been shoved by the bear or simply fallen. He didn't move until the side of his face pressed into the snow began to numb. With the help of his forearm, Pemberton raised his head. For a few moments, he watched Galloway as the highlander stood amid the squabbling pack, leashing the hounds so Vaughn could drag them off the bear one at a time. Footsteps crunched toward Pemberton, then stopped. Serena kneeled beside him, her face keen as she brushed snow off his face and shoulders. After the sheer physicality of the bear's embrace, he felt a kind of lightness, as if his body had been set gently upon the calmest water.

Serena helped him to a sitting position, and Pemberton's head swirled for a few moments, left a residue of grogginess. Blood covered the snow, and Pemberton wondered if any of it was his. Serena pulled off his hunting jacket and lifted the wool shirt and flannel undershirt. She ran her hand across his back and stomach before pulling the clothing back down.

"I was sure it had gutted you," Serena said as she helped him put his jacket back on.

Pemberton watched tears well up in Serena's eyes. She turned and wiped her coat sleeve across her face. Seconds passed before she turned back to him. When she did, her eyes were dry, and Pemberton wondered if his muddledness had caused him to imagine the tears.

Buchanan was also beside them now. He lifted Pemberton's rifle out of the snow but seemed unsure what to do with it.

"You need me to help you get him standing?" Buchanan asked.

"No," Serena replied.

"What about his gun?"

Serena nodded to where her rifle leaned against a redbud sapling.

"Put it over there beside mine."

In a few minutes Galloway had tied the last hound to a tree. Vaughn kneeled beside the injured dog, one hand stroking the Plott's head while the other probed the wounds. Galloway walked over to the bear, kicked its massive haunches with his boot toe to verify the creature was indeed dead.

"This is a quality black bear," he said. "I'd bet him to go five hundred."

Galloway turned his gaze from the bear to Serena, letting his eyes slowly lift to take in Serena's boots and breeches and hunting jacket, finally her face, even then appearing to look not only at Serena but beyond her into the woods.

"I've never seen a woman shoot a bear before," he said, "and I've known but a couple of men with the sand to have gone right at him the way you done."

"Pemberton would have done the same for me," Serena said.

"You sure of that, are you?" Galloway said, a grin slicing his face as he watched Serena help Pemberton to his feet. "A bear's more to handle than a drunk like Harmon."

Vaughn held the injured Plott in his arms. The youth stepped closer to the bear, showing the dog the bear was dead.

"I know a feller up on Colt Ridge who could mount that bear's head for you, Mrs. Pemberton," Vaughn said, "or tan the hide if you notioned that."

"No, leave it with the deer," Serena said, and turned to Galloway. "Carcasses are used out west to draw mountain lions. I assume it would work here as well."

"Maybe," Galloway said, looking at Pemberton though he spoke to Serena. "Like I told your Mister when he first come to these mountains, if there's one still around it's big and smart. It could end up tracking *him*. Let it get close as that bear did, and he'll get more than a hug."

"If you find that mountain lion and get me one shot at it I'll give you a twenty-dollar gold piece," Pemberton said, glaring at Galloway before turning to Vaughn. "Or anyone else who can lead me to it."

They reloaded the farm wagon and started toward camp. Galloway drove while Vaughn cradled the injured dog in his arms. The rusty springs beneath the buckboard squeaked rhythmically as they rose and fell, and the swaying motion made it appear Vaughn was rocking the hound to sleep. In the wagon bed, the other dogs huddled against the cold. The land slanted upward, and thick trunks of oaks and poplars quickly filled in the white expanse behind them.

Once they got to the ridge crest, Pemberton and Serena let the others ride on ahead. Pemberton's pulse still beat quick, and he knew Serena's did as well. The trail soon became only a space between trees in the day's last light. Cold seeped in through sleeves and collars. They rode close together, and Serena reached out and clasped Pemberton's hand with hers. He felt the coldness of it.

"You should have worn gloves," he said.

"I like to feel the cold," Serena said. "I always have, even as a child. My father used to walk me through the camp on days the loggers claimed it was too cold to work. I shamed them out of their shacks and into the woods."

"Too bad you didn't at least save a photograph of that," Pemberton said, recalling how he'd once asked about family photographs and Serena had answered that they'd burned with the house. "It might stop some of our workers griping about the weather."

They rode on, not speaking again until they crossed the last rise and descended onto the valley floor. Camp lights blazed in the distance. No tree unsmoothed the landscape, and the snow was tinged blue. Pemberton noted how the faint light gave the illusion they traversed a shallow sea.

"I liked the way we killed the bear together," Serena said.

"You had more to do with killing it than I did."

"No, it was gut shot. I merely finished it off."

A few flurries swirled around them, sifted from a sky the color of indigo. The only sound was the crunch of snow under the horses' hooves. In the quiet darkening Pemberton and Serena seemed to have entered a depthless space only they inhabited. Not so different from when they cleaved in the night, Pemberton realized.

"Too bad Harris couldn't come along today," Serena said.

"He assured me he'll come next time."

"Has he said anything about the Glencoe tract?"

"No, all he wants to talk about is this national park boondoggle and how we have to band together to keep it from happening."

"I assume that *we* also includes our partners."

"They have as much to lose as you and I do."

"They're timid men, especially Buchanan," Serena said. "Wilkie's just gotten old, but it's Buchanan's nature. The sooner you and I are shed of them the better."

"We'll still need partners though."

"Then men like Harris, and, as soon as we can, partnerships where we have a controlling interest," Serena said as they moved through the snow-capped stumps. "I'm going to hire a Pinkerton and find out what's really going on in Tennessee with this park. I'll have him check out Kephart as well. See if he's as stellar a citizen as John Muir."

The woods no longer sheltered them from the wind, and cold air worked its way through jacket tears the bear had made. Pemberton imagined Serena in her father's timber camp, rousing the workers on days colder than this one.

"What you told Galloway is the truth," Pemberton said as they entered the camp. "If the bear had attacked you instead of me, I would have done the same for you."

"I know," Serena said, clasping Pemberton's hand tighter. "I've known it since the night we met."

Seven

When Rachel went to the barn to get a cabbage sack for the ginseng, she found, for the third morning in a row, that no eggs warmed under the two bantams or the Rhode Island Red. A fox or weasel or dog would have killed the chickens as well, she knew, so figured it a possum or a raccoon, maybe a black snake come to fatten up for the winter. Rachel found the cabbage sack and left the barn. She thought about going ahead and getting the fishing pole and searching out a guinea egg. The sky was jay-bird blue, the day warmer than any in a week, but the chimney smoke wasn't rising but blowing down, so a change in the weather was coming, maybe by afternoon. Another snow would make the ginseng hard to find, and she couldn't risk that, so Rachel fetched the mattock from the shed but left the fishing pole. Something else I'll have to do when I get back, Rachel thought.

She wrapped Jacob in his bundlings, and they crossed a pasture whose barbed wire now kept nothing in, empty for the first time in her life. Rachel saw the trees they walked toward had all their fall colors now, their canopy bright and various as a button jar. Before long the land slanted up the north face of Colt Ridge. They entered a stand of silver birch and hemlock, which Rachel passed through without slowing down. Far off toward Waynesville, she heard a whistle and wondered if it was the lumber company train. She thought about Bonny and Rebecca, the two girls she'd worked with in the kitchen, and how much she missed being around them. And how she missed Joel Vaughn too, who could be a smart aleck, but had always been nice to her, not just in the camp but as kids on Colt Ridge when they'd been in elementary school together. He'd even given her a valentine in the sixth grade. She remembered how, after her belly showed and other folks in the camp shunned her, Joel hadn't.

The land's angle became more severe, the light waning, streaked as if cut with scissors and braided to the ridge piece by piece. Soon poplars and hickories replaced the softwoods. Rachel saw a witch hazel shrub and paused to pull off some leaves, their pungent smell evoking memories of chest salves and days sick in bed. Moss furred the granite outcrops a dark plush green. She walked slowly, looking not just for the four-pronged yellow leaves but bloodroot and cinnamon ferns and other plants her father had taught her signaled places where ginseng grew.

Rachel found the bloodroot first, under a shaded outcrop where a spring head seeped. She tugged the plants carefully from the ground and placed them in her sack. When she accidentally broke a stem, the red juice used for a tonic stained her fingers. A squirrel began chattering in a tree farther up the ridge and was soon answered.

Rachel stepped carefully across the boggy ground. An orange salamander scuttled out from beneath a matting of soggy oak leaves. She remembered how her father once told her never to bother salamanders in a spring because they kept the water pure. On the other side of the outcrop, she found more bloodroot and a thick growth of cinnamon ferns. The ferns felt like peacock feathers as she moved through them. They made a whispery sound against her dress, and the sound seemed to soothe Jacob because his eyes closed.

She entered another stand of hardwoods and there it was, the yellow leaves shimmering against the gloamy woods. Jacob was now asleep so she laid him down, loosening the bundling so she could fold some of the cloth back to cradle his head. Rachel dug a good six inches around the ginseng plant to insure she didn't cut the root. Then she pulled her dress up above her knees and kneeled in front of the plant, held the mattock's handle inches from the blade as she raked dirt from around the stem and tugged free a pale root shaped like a veiny carrot. She separated the berries from the ginseng plants and placed them in the broken soil, covered them up and moved on to the next plant.

They stayed in the woods until dark clouds began forming above the ridge crest. By then she'd searched out all the ginseng that could be found and gathered what other plants she'd wanted as well. As she and Jacob made their way out of the woods, Rachel's back already ached, and she knew it'd be sorer come morning. But the cabbage sack was a quarter filled, at least two pounds worth of roots she'd sell to Mr. Scott after they'd dried a month in the barn. Jacob was wide awake now, worming inside of the bundling, making it harder to hold the sack and mattock with her left hand.

"It ain't far now," she said, as much to herself as the child. "We'll put the mattock in the shed and take the Widow this bloodroot."

As they entered the pasture, Rachel heard dogs barking somewhere in the far woods and wondered if they were the same ones she'd seen at the cemetery. She walked faster, remembering a story she'd heard about wild dogs carrying off a child set down at a field edge. The child had never been found, only the bloody tatters of its blanket. Rachel watched the tree line until they were out of the pasture. She leaned the mattock against the shed, and they walked on to the Widow's cabin.

"I brought you some bloodroot," Rachel said, "for keeping Jacob the other day."

"That's sweet of you," Widow Jenkins said, accepting the handful of plants and placing them in the sink.

"I've got witch hazel too if you've got need of it."

"No, I've got a gracious plenty of witch hazel," the older woman said. "Did you dig up much sang?"

Rachel opened the sack and showed her the roots.

"How much you figure it worth when it dries?"

"I'd reckon Scott to give you ten dollars," Widow Jenkins said. "Maybe twelve if his lumbago ain't acting up."

"I was thinking it would be more than that," Rachel said.

"Before that stock market busted up north it might have been, but cash money's rare these days as sang."

Rachel stared at the hearth a few moments. The Widow always put some apple wood on the fire, not because it burned good but for the rosy color it gave off. A fire with apple wood in it is pretty to look at as any painting, the Widow claimed. Rachel felt the weight of Jacob in her arms and compared it to the cabbage sack's lightness. The weariness of carrying the child across the pasture and ridge, hardly noticed before, overwhelmed her. She set Jacob on the floor.

"That'll barely get us to spring," Rachel said. "As soon as I wean Jacob, I'll have to go back to work at the camp."

"I don't think you ought to do that," Widow Jenkins said. "I don't even like it that you go down there for Sunday church."

"I've sold the cow and horse and the saddle," Rachel said, "and now some varmint's stealing my eggs. There's nothing else I can do."

"What makes you think you can get your job back when there's folks lined up for every job in that camp."

"I done good work when I was there," Rachel replied. "They'll remember that."

Widow Jenkins leaned over, grunted softly as she lifted Jacob from the floor. She sat down in the cane back chair she kept by the hearth and settled the child in her lap. The fire's hue reflected in the old woman's spectacles, wavering in the glass like rose petals.

"You think that man is going to help you and this young one out," Widow Jenkins said, speaking in a soft flat way so it wasn't like a question or opinion but something that was simply the truth.

"Even if I was to think that, it don't matter as far as me going back," Rachel said. "I got to have some money to live on. That camp's the only place I know where there might be a job."

Widow Jenkins sighed and shifted Jacob deeper into her lap. She stared at the fire, her chapped lips pressed tight as she gave the slightest nod.

"So you'll keep Jacob if they'll hire me?" Rachel said, then paused. "If you don't, I'll find someone else to."

"I helped raise you so I can help with this one too," Widow Jenkins said, "but only if you wait till this boy's a year old. That way he'll be proper weaned. I won't take no pay for keeping him either."

"I wouldn't feel right if you didn't take some pay," Rachel said.

"Well, we'll worry about that when the time comes, if it comes. Maybe things will get better before then."

Widow Jenkins jostled Jacob with her knees. The child giggled, raised his arms outward as if balancing himself.

"But if it comes to that, this chap won't be no bother," Widow Jenkins said. "Me and him will get along fine."

When Rachel got back to the cabin, she spread the ginseng out on the cabbage sack so it could dry. The crows had settled into the trees and the squirrels tucked deep in their nests. The woods were hushed and attentive, the trees seeming to huddle themselves closer together, as if awaiting not just the rain but some story about to be told.

"We best find that guinea egg before the rain comes," she told Jacob. "We can check on the bees too."

They went into the woods behind the house, pausing first at the white bee box set at the wood's edge. Unlike during warm weather, Rachel had to lean close to hear them, their shifting huddle soft as a drowsy wind. The bee box's paint was chipped and fading, and she'd have to fix that by spring because white soothed the bees almost as much as smoke.

You have to tell the bees he died. They'll leave if you don't, Widow Jenkins had told Rachel the day of her father's funeral. It was something the old folks believed, and though Rachel wasn't sure if it was true or not she'd done it. She'd taken off her dark mourning clothes and put on a worn linen dress, then walked out to the shed to find the cheesecloth veil. It was white as well, made of muslin. By then almost all of the bees had returned for the night, only a few coming and going as she'd approached the box. Rachel remembered how she'd slowly opened the super, especially how clear and clean the smell had been, like moss on a creek bank. She'd spoken to the bees calmly, her voice merging with their own slurry voices. Afterward, as she'd walked back to the house in that late-June twilight, it had struck Rachel that someone at a distance might see her and easily mistake her for a bride. She'd also thought how, if that distance had been one of months instead of furlongs, taking her back to those winter middays she'd spent in Pemberton's bed, she could have imagined the same herself.

Jacob whined and Rachel felt the first drops of a cold drizzle.

"We better get that egg," she told the child.

It took a few minutes, because the guinea was good at hiding them, but Rachel finally found an egg in a wither of honeysuckle vines. Rachel pulled the bundling over Jacob's head, because the drizzle had quickened, tinged with ice that stung her face. She walked into the barn and set Jacob on a bed of gathered straw. The whispery sound of the drizzle hitting the tin roof made the barn feel snug, as if its broad-beamed shoulders had shrugged closer together.

Rachel went to the shed and unwound the hook and line from the fishing pole and returned to the barn. With the fish hook's barb, she chipped a small hole in the egg, then guided the hook's barb and shank into the yolk until no metal showed. Rachel delicately placed the egg back on the straw and tied the six feet of fishing line to a nail head. All this trouble because she was living so close to the bone a few pennies mattered, Rachel told herself bitterly. She and her father had had hard times before. When Rachel was seven they'd lost a milk cow that had eaten cherry leaves, and when she was twelve a hail storm had destroyed the corn crop. But even in the leanest times there'd always been a few dollars left in the coffee can stowed on the pantry's top shelf, a cow or horse in the pasture yet to be sold.

Sell it, it'll fetch a good price, Mrs. Pemberton had said when she'd handed Rachel the bowie knife. And it probably would, perhaps even as much as the ginseng, but Rachel couldn't abide doing what Mrs. Pemberton had commanded her to do. She'd sell the shoes off her feet before taking the knife out of the box trunk and selling it. Widow Jenkins would say Rachel was just being prideful, and maybe Preacher Bolick would agree, but she'd had enough proud shucked off her the last few months to believe God wouldn't begrudge her keeping just a little.

THE next morning Rachel found a raccoon crouched in the stall's corner, the fishing line tugging one side of the creature's mouth. Its pink tongue was panting. The raccoon's head did not turn when she opened the stall door. Only the black-masked eyes shifted. It wasn't the eyes but the front paws that made her hesitate. They looked like hands shriveled and blackened by fire, but human hands nevertheless. A year ago her father would have done this, done what he'd done when a big cur had come into the yard and killed a rooster, done what he did when a colt was born lame. What you had to do on a farm.

Let him go and he'll be back, Rachel told herself, and you won't catch him again because a coon's too smart to be fooled twice. It'll look for the line and hook and stay clear of that one while it takes every other egg in the barn. I don't even have a choice. Rachel thought how that was pretty much true of everything now, that you got one choice at the beginning but if you didn't choose right, and she hadn't, things got narrow real quick. Like trying to wade a river, she thought. You take a wrong step and set your foot on a wobbly rock or in a drop-off and you're swept away, and all you can do then is try to survive.

It ought not be like that, Rachel told herself, and she knew that for a few folks it wasn't. They could make a wrong choice and be on their way with no more bother than a cow swishing a fly with its tail. That wasn't right either. Her anger made it easier to go to the shed and get the axe.

When Rachel stepped into the stall, the raccoon didn't move. She remembered her father saying a bobcat's skull was so thin you could crush it with your hands. She wondered if a raccoon's skull was the same. She tried to decide if it was best done with the axe head or the blade. Rachel lifted the axe a few inches off the ground, thinking how if she didn't swing true with the sharp end she could slice the line.

She turned the handle so that the blunt end was what she'd strike with. She aimed and swung and heard a crack. The raccoon quivered a moment and grew still. Rachel kneeled and worried the fish hook free from the raccoon's mouth. She looked at the fur, knowing if the raccoon had come a few months later cold weather would have thickened the pelt enough to sell to Mr. Scott. She picked the raccoon up by the tail and took it out behind the cabin and flung it into the woods.

Eight

THE EAGLE ARRIVED IN DECEMBER. SERENA HAD notified the depot master it would be coming and must be brought immediately to camp, and so it was, the six-foot wooden-slat crate and its inhabitant placed on a flat car with two youths in attendance, the train making its slow ascent from Waynesville as if bringing a visiting dignitary.

With the eagle came two small leather bags. In one was a thick gauntlet of goat skin to cover the forearm from wrist to elbow, in the other the leather hood and jesses and swivels and the leash, that and a single piece of rag paper that may have been instructions or a bill or even a warning but written in a language the depot master had never seen before but suspected was Comanche. The conductor of the train that brought the bird to Waynesville disagreed, telling of the strange man who'd accompanied the bird from Charleston to Asheville.

Hair black as a crow's feather and wearing a dress so bright blue it hurt your eyeballs to look at it long, the conductor told the men at the depot, and a pointy fur hat. Plus a sword on his belt nigh tall as he was that give a fellow pause about making sport of the dress he wore. No sirrie, the conductor declared, that wasn't one of *our* Indians.

The bird's arrival was an immediate source of rumor and speculation, especially among Snipes and his crew. The men had come out of the dining hall to watch the two boys lift their charge off the flatcar, the youths solemn and ceremonious as they carried the crate to the stable. Dunbar believed the creature would be used as a messenger in the manner of a homing pigeon. McIntyre cited a verse from Revelations while Stewart suggested the Pembertons planned to fatten up the bird and eat it. Ross suggested the eagle had been brought in to peck out the eyes of any worker who closed them on the job. Snipes uncharacteristically ventured no theory about the creature's purpose, though he did give a lengthy discourse on whether or not men could fly if they had feathers on their arms.

Serena had the youths place the eagle in the back stall where Campbell had built a block perch of wood and steel and sisal rope. Serena then dismissed the two boys, and they walked out of the stable side by side, each matching his stride to his fellow's. They marched back to the waiting train and climbed onto the flat car and sat with legs crossed and faces shorn of expression, much in the manner of the Buddha. Several workers gathered around the car, inquiring of the eagle and its purpose. The youths ignored all imprecations. Only when the wheels turned beneath them did the two boys allow themselves condescending smiles aimed at lesser mortals who would never be entrusted as the guardians of things original and rare.

Serena and Pemberton remained in the stable, observing the eagle from outside the stall door. The bird's head was covered with the leather hood, and its immense yellow talons gripped the block perch inside the crate, the six-foot wingspan pressed tight to the body. Motionless. But Pemberton sensed the eagle's power as he might an unsprung coil of wrought iron, especially in the talons, which stabbed deep into the perch block's hemp.

"Those talons look very powerful," Pemberton noted, "especially the longer one at the back of the foot."

"That's the hallux talon," Serena said. "It's strong enough to pierce a human skull, or, as more often occurs, the bones of a human forearm."

Serena did not raise her eyes from the eagle as she reached out and took Pemberton's hand, but even in the barn's dim light he could see the intensity of her gaze. Serena's thin eyebrows arched as if to allow her vision to take in as much of the eagle as possible.

"This is what we want," she said, her voice deepening, the emotion so often controlled fully unbridled now. "To be like this always. No past or future, pure enough to live totally in the present."

Serena's shoulders shuddered, as if to cast off an unwanted cloak. Her face reassumed its look of measured placidity, the intensity not drained from her body but spread to a wider surface. They did not speak again until the Arabian shifted in the front stall and stamped its foot.

"Remind me to tell Vaughn to move the Arabian into the stall next to this one," Serena said. "The bird needs to get used to the horse."

"When you train the eagle," Pemberton asked, "you starve her, then what?"

"She weakens enough to take food from my glove. But it's when she bows and bares her neck that matters."

"Why?" Pemberton asked, "because it shows the bird has surrendered?"

"No, that's where she's most vulnerable. It means she trusts me with her life."

"How long will that take?"

"Two, perhaps three days."

"When will you start?" Pemberton asked.

"This evening."

Serena slept all afternoon, and at dinner she ate until her stomach swelled visibly. Afterward, she sent Vaughn to the commissary, and he returned with a chamber pot and a gallon bucket filled with water. When Pemberton asked about food or quilts, Serena told him she'd not eat or sleep again until the eagle did.

For two nights and a day Serena did not leave the stall. It was late morning of the second day when she came to the office. Dark half-moons lined the underside of Serena's eyes, her hair matted and straw-strewn.

"Come and see," she told Pemberton, and they walked out to the stable, Serena's gray eyes set in a heavy-lidded wince against the unaccustomed light. A heavy snow had fallen the day before and Serena slipped, would have fallen if Pemberton had not grabbed her arm and righted her.

"We should go on to the house," Pemberton said. "You're exhausted."

"No," Serena answered. "I need to show you."

To the west, gray clouds thickened, but the sun held sway in the center sky, the snow so bright-dazzling that as Serena and Pemberton entered the barn the day's light broke off as if cleaved. Pemberton still held Serena's elbow, but it was her eyes more than his that led them across the barn's earthen floor to the back stall. As Serena unhinged the stall door, the eagle's form slowly separated itself from less substantial darkness. The bird did not seem even to be breathing until it heard Serena's voice. Then its hooded head swiveled in her direction. Serena stepped inside the stall and removed the hood, placed a piece of red meat on her gauntlet and held out her arm. The eagle stepped onto Serena's forearm, gripping the goatskin as the head bowed to tear and swallow the meat between its talons. As the bird ate, Serena stroked the raptor's neck with her index finger.

"It's so beautiful," she said, gazing at the eagle. "It's no wonder it takes not just the earth but the sky to contain it."

Serena's tone of dreamy wonder was as disturbing to Pemberton as her feebleness. He told her again they should go to the house, but she didn't seem to hear him. Serena gave the bird the last hank of meat and settled it back on the block perch. Her hands trembled as they placed the hood back on. She turned and stared directly at Pemberton, her gray eyes glassy as marbles.

"I've never told you about going to our house after it burned down," Serena said. "I'd only been out of the hospital three days. My father's foreman, the man I was staying with, I'd told him to burn the house with everything left inside, everything. He hadn't wanted to do that, and even after saying he had I needed to make sure. He'd figured on that so he hid my boots and clothes, but I took one of his horses while he was gone, wearing just a robe and overcoat. The house had been burned, burned to the ground. The ashes were still warm when I stepped on them. When I got on the horse, I looked down at my footprints. They were black at first and then gray and then white, growing lighter, less visible with each step. It looked like something had moved through the snow before slowly rising. For a few seconds, I felt that I wasn't on the horse but actually . . ."

"We're going to the house," Pemberton said, taking a step into the stall.

"I didn't sleep when I was with the eagle," Serena said, as much to herself as to Pemberton. "I didn't dream."

Pemberton took her hand in his. He felt a limpness as if its last strength had been used to feed the eagle.

"All we'll ever need is within each other," Serena said, her voice barely more than a whisper. "Even when we have our child, it will only be an image of what we already are."

"You need to eat." Pemberton said.

"I'm not hungry anymore. The second day I was, but after that . . ."

Serena lost her train of thought. She looked around as if the thought might have drifted into one of the stall's corners.

"Come with me," Pemberton said, and led her by the hand.

Vaughn was outside the dining hall, and Pemberton motioned him over. He told the youth to get food and coffee from the kitchen. They walked slowly up to the house. Vaughn soon came with a silver platter normally used to hold a ham or turkey. Heaped on it were thick slabs of beef and venison, green beans and squash and sweet potatoes drenched in butter. Buttermilk biscuits and a bowl of honey. A coffee pot and two cups. Pemberton helped Serena to the kitchen table, placed the platter and silverware before her. Serena stared at the food as if unsure what to do with it. Pemberton took the knife and fork and cut a small piece of beef. He molded his hand around hers.

"Here," he said, and raised the fork and meat to her mouth.

She chewed methodically while Pemberton poured the coffee. He cut more pieces of beef for her and lifted the tin cup to her mouth so she could sip, allow the coffee's dense warmth to settle inside her. Serena did not try to talk, as if it took all her concentration to chew and swallow.

Afterwards, Pemberton drew her bath and helped Serena undress. As he helped her into the tub, he felt the terraced ribs and pinched stomach. Pemberton sat on the bathtub's rim and used soap and a washcloth to cleanse the reek of manure and livestock off Serena's skin. The thick tips of his fingers kneaded soap into her matted hair and quickly raised a lather so thick it gloved his hands white. A sterling silver pitcher and basin sat on the washstand, a wedding gift from the Buchanans. He rinsed Serena's hair with water poured from the pitcher. Yellow splinters of straw floated on the water's dingy surface. Outside, the sun had vanished and sleet had begun to fall. Pemberton helped Serena from the porcelain tub, dried her with a towel and helped her into her peignoir. She walked by herself to the back room, lay down and quickly fell asleep. Pemberton sat in the chair opposite the bed and watched her. He listened to the tapping of the sleet on the tin roof, soft but insistent, like something wanting in.

Nine

WHEN THE SICKNESS CAME UPON THEM RACHEL thought it was something picked up at the camp's church service, because it was a Tuesday when Jacob first glowed with fever. He fussed and his brow slickened with sweat. Rachel was no better off herself, fever sopping her dress and hair, the world off plumb and whirling like a spin-top. She laid cold poultices on the child's forehead and fed him clabber. She wet a paper and placed it around an onion and set it in the embers to bake, took the juice and mixed it with sugar and fed it to Jacob with a spoon. She used the witch hazel as well, hoping at least to clear his lungs. Rachel remembered how her father claimed a fever always broke on the third evening. Just wait it out, she told herself. But by late afternoon of the third day they both shivered as if palsied. She placed another log on the fire and made a pallet before the hearth, lay down with Jacob and waited for evening. They slept as dusk ambered the day's last light.

It was full dark when Rachel awoke, shivering though her calico dress was sweat-soaked. She changed Jacob's swaddlings and warmed a bottle of milk, but his appetite was so puny he did little more than gum the rubber nipple. Rachel pressed her hand to his brow, and it was just as hot as before. If it don't break soon I'll have to get him to the doctor, she said, talking aloud. The fire was almost out, and she laid a thick white oak log on the andirons, nestled kindling around it to make sure the log caught. She stirred the embers beneath with the poker, and sparks flew up the chimney like swarming fireflies.

The kindling finally caught and the room slowly emerged. Shadows scattered and reformed on the cabin walls. Rachel discerned shapes in them, first cornstalks and trees and then scarecrows and finally swaying human forms that steadily became more corporal. She lay back down on the pallet with Jacob, shivered and sweated and slept some more.

When Rachel woke, the fire had dimmed to a few pink embers. She pressed her palm to Jacob's brow, felt the heat against her skin. She lifted the barn lantern off the fireboard and lit it. We got to go to town, she told the child, and lifted him into the crook of her arm as her free hand clutched the lantern's tin handle.

She was feather-legged before they'd hardly left the yard, the lantern heavy as a brimming milk pail. The lantern spread a shallow circle of light, and Rachel tried to imagine the light was a raft and she wasn't on a road but on the river. Not even walking, just floating along as the current carried her towards town. She came to Widow Jenkins' house, and there was no light in its windows. She wondered why, then remembered the Widow had gone to spend New Year's week with her sister. Rachel thought about resting by Widow Jenkins's porch steps a few minutes but was afraid if she did she'd not get up.

For the first time since she'd left the house, Rachel looked at the sky. The stars were out, so many she'd have needed a bushel basket to gather them all. Plenty enough light to get her and Jacob to town, she decided, and set the lantern among the chicory and broom sedge bordering the Widow's pasture. Rachel felt Jacob's brow again and there was still no change. She shifted the child's weight closer so his head rested as much on her neck as her shoulder and they walked on.

The road followed the river now. A bat squeaked over the water, and Rachel remembered the shadowy barn loft, what she'd thought a rag draped over a cross beam. She'd brushed against the rag, and it had suddenly flapped alive and become tangled in her hair, a clawed flurry of wings trying to tear free, one leathery wing touching her face as it loosed itself and rose. Rachel had fallen to the loft floor, still screaming and raking at her hair even after her father had come and the creature had flown out the barn mouth.

The road curved closer to the river. Rachel could hear the water rubbing against the bank, smell the fresh soil loosened by recent rain. Another bat squeaked, nearer this time. The road narrowed and darkened, a granite cliff pressing close on the left side. On the right, willows lined the river, their branches leaning low overhead. The road slanted downward and the stars vanished.

Rachel stopped walking, too fevered to be sure where she was. It came to her that she'd taken a wrong turn and entered a covered wooden bridge, though she didn't understand how there could be a wrong turn if there was only one road. She felt something brush against her hair, then again. She couldn't see her feet, and she suddenly had a different notion, that the road had been washed out without her knowing it, the wooden bridge a detour that led back to the road. But that didn't make sense either. Maybe I just forgot there's always been one here, she told herself.

The sweat poured off her even more now that she'd stopped walking, not a good sweat like she'd get from hoeing in a field, but slimy feeling, like touching a snail. Rachel wiped sweat off her brow with the back of her forearm. A wooden bridge this long and dark would have bats, she knew, not just a few but hundreds of them clinging from the walls and ceilings, and if she touched the wall she would startle one and to startle one would startle them all and bring them flapping about her and Jacob in a rush of wind and wings. Something stirred her hair again. The breeze, it's just the breeze, she told herself. Rachel shifted Jacob lower in her arms, placed her free hand over his head.

The thought came to her again that this was a road she'd never been on, and she knew it could lead her anywhere. I've got to keep going, she told herself, but she was too afraid. Think of someplace good this road could take you, she told herself, someplace where you've never been. Think of that place and that you're going there, and that way maybe you won't be so afraid. She tried to imagine the map in Miss Stephens' classroom but all the map's colors blurred into one another, and after a few moments Rachel realized it wouldn't be marked on the map anyway. She imagined instead a woman standing in her front yard, who would see Rachel coming down the road and despite all the years would recognize her and call her name, come running to help her.

Walk a straight line, Rachel told herself. She took small slow steps, the same way she'd do in a cornfield with her feet following the tight furrows. Rachel imagined her mother clad in a white dress bright as a dogwood blossom, a dress whose buttons sparkled like jewels to help guide her and Jacob through the dark.

After a few yards the sky returned, widening overhead as the road made a sharp ascent, and Rachel saw she was on the right road after all. Rachel stopped to catch her breath and took a handkerchief from her skirt pocket to wipe the sweat off her brow, the tears flowing down her cheeks. She looked at the stars and they brightened and dimmed in accord with her breathing, as if one hard puff might blow the whole lot of them out like candles. She began walking again, and each step was like pushing through knee-high sand. Rachel told herself not to think about resting because if she did her body would take that thought and bull-rag it until she listened. Just a ways and you'll crest this hill, she told herself. She took one step and then another and finally the road leveled.

Rachel could see town lights now. For a moment the lights from the town and the lights from the stars merged, and Rachel had the sensation she and Jacob had come untethered from the earth. She clutched the child harder and closed her eyes. When Rachel opened them, she stared at her feet. She was barefoot, something she hadn't realized until that moment, but glad of it, because she could feel the pebbly dust sifted over the packed dirt, feel how it anchored her to the world.

Rachel let her eyes rise slowly, taking in the road ahead a few yards at a time, as if her gaze were a lever lifting the road and world back into proper alignment. She began walking again. The stars bobbed back up into the sky, and the town lights drifted down and reattached themselves to the earth. The bridge's shadowy outline became visible. Jacob woke and started fussing, though he was so puny as to sound like no more than a mewling kitten. We got to keep going, she told him, just one more hill and we'll be there.

Rachel moved downward toward the bridge, one that, unlike the covered bridge, she recognized. The trees crowding the bottomland grew taller, their branches narrowing the horizon, dimming the weathered planks and railing. They were only yards from the river when Rachel saw movement on the bridge, swirls like wisps of fog only more solid. Rachel took another step closer and saw it was three wild dogs snapping and snarling as they fought over a bloody white shirt. Two of the dogs each grabbed a sleeve and the cloth unfurled, and Rachel saw the shirt was her father's.

Rachel took two slow steps backward, then did not move. Jacob whined and she leaned to his ear and tried to shush him with soft words. When Rachel looked up, the dogs had quit fighting over the shirt. They watched her and Jacob, shoulder to shoulder, necks hackled and teeth bared. They ain't real, she said, and waited for her words to make it so. But the dogs didn't disappear.

Rachel edged over to the roadside, wondering if she might be able to wade across the river. Larger pieces of quartz and granite shoaled on the road's edge, made her wince as she looked for a breech in the trees. But there was no path down to the water, only more trees and a deeper dark where she'd be unable to find her way. She remembered the lantern, but it was too far back to fetch. The arm that held Jacob began to cramp, so she switched sides. Rachel felt the rocks underfoot and that gave her an idea. She stepped off the road edge and let her foot probe the thistles and broom sedge, finally find a fist-sized rock. She leaned and picked it up, then walked back toward the bridge.

"Git on now," she said and threw the rock, but the dogs still did not move.

She felt Jacob's forehead and the fever burned unabated. They ain't real, and even if they was I got no choice but to get past them, she told herself. Just watch your feet and don't look up and don't be afraid because a dog can smell the fear on you. Rachel took a step and paused, then took another, the pebbles and dirt sifting under her feet. Four more steps and her right foot landed on a plank. Feel how solid this bridge is, she told herself. Them dogs ain't real but this is, and it will get me and this young one to town.

Rachel took another step and both feet were on the grainy wood. She did not lift her eyes. The dogs remained silent, the only sound the river rushing beneath the planks. She closed her eyes a few moments, imagined not her and Jacob on a raft as she had before but the dogs adrift, the river carrying them farther and farther away. She opened her eyes and took more steps, and then she was back on a dirt surface and the road rose.

Rachel did not look up until she'd crested the last hill and was on Waynesville's main street. She stopped at the first house to ask where Doctor Harbin lived. The man who answered the door took one look at her and Jacob and helped them inside. The man's wife took Jacob into her arms while her husband telephoned the doctor. Lay down here on the couch, the woman told her, and Rachel was too weary to do otherwise. The room swayed and then blurred. Rachel closed her eyes. The dark behind her eyelids lightened a second, then darkened again, as if something had been unveiled but only for a moment.

WHEN Rachel came to it was morning. She did not know where she was at first, only that she'd never been tireder even after hoeing a field all day.

A man sat in a chair beside the couch, the face slowly unblurring to become Doctor Harbin's.

"Where's Jacob?" Rachel asked.

"In the back bedroom," Doctor Harbin said as he stood. "His fever's broken."

"So he'll be ok?"

"Yes."

Doctor Harbin came over and laid his hand on her brow a few moments.

"But you still have a fever. Mr. and Mrs. Suttles said you can stay here today. I'll check on you again this afternoon. If you're better, Mr. Suttles will take you back home."

"I don't have the money to pay you," Rachel said, "at least not right now."

"I'm not worried about that. We'll settle up later."

The doctor nodded at Rachel's feet, and she saw they had been bandaged.

"You cut up your feet pretty good, but nothing deep enough to need stitches. That was almost a mile walk and you sick as him, and barefoot to boot. I don't know how you did it. You must love that child dear as life."

"I tried not to," Rachel said. "I just couldn't find a way to stop myself."

PART II

Ten

THE LINGERING COLD DEFIED ANY CALENDAR. From October until May, snow and ice clung to the ridges. Several men died when they slipped trying to avoid falling trees or limbs. Another tumbled off a cliff edge and one impaled himself on his own axe and still another was beheaded by a snapped cable. A cutting crew lost its way during a snowstorm in January and was found days later, their palms peeling off when searchers pried the axe handles from their frozen hands. Fingers or toes lost to frostbite were among the season's lesser hazards.

The harshness of the winter was many-storied among the workers who survived it. One man who'd wintered in Alaska argued this one worse, took off his work boot to show five blackened nubs as proof. Owls frozen on tree limbs, the moon wrapping itself in clouds for warmth, the ground itself shivering—all manner of tall tales were spoken and nearly believed. Several workers argued the denuded forests had allowed winter to settle deeper into the valley, so deep it had gotten trapped in the same way as an animal caught in a rabbit gum or dead-fall trap. Men searched the sky night and day for signs of the season's end, a laying down moon, geese headed north, creasy greens on the stream banks.

The surest sign came at the end of May when Campbell killed a timber rattlesnake while surveying on Shanty Mountain. When Serena heard, she ordered every dead rattlesnake placed in an old applecart next to the stable entrance. No one knew why. One logger claimed from personal experience that rattlesnake meat was eaten in Colorado, and though it was not to his taste others had considered it a delicacy. Another worker suspected the snakes were fed to the eagle because they were a part of the bird's natural diet back in Mongolia. When a crew foreman asked Doctor Cheney what Mrs. Pemberton would want the snakes for, the physician replied that she milked the fangs and coated her tongue with the poison.

Each dawn in the following weeks, Serena walked into the stable's back stall and freed the eagle from the block perch. She and the bird spent an hour each morning alone below Half Acre Ridge where Boston Lumber had done its first cutting. For the first four days Serena rode out with the eagle behind her in the applecart, a blanket draped over the cage. By the fifth day the bird perched on Serena's right forearm, its head black-hooded like an executioner, the five-foot leash tied to Serena's upper right elbow and the leather bracelets around the raptor's feet. Campbell constructed an armrest out of a Y-shaped white oak branch and affixed it to the saddle pommel. From a certain angle, the eagle itself appeared mounted on the saddle. At a distance, horse, eagle and human appeared to blend into one being, as though transmogrified into some winged six-legged creature from the old myths.

It was mid-July when Serena freed the eagle from the block perch and rode west to Fork Ridge where Galloway and his crew worked on the near slope. The day was hot and many of the men worked shirtless. They did not cover themselves when Serena appeared, for they'd learned she didn't care.

Serena loosed the leather laces and removed the eagle's hood, then freed the leash from the bracelets. She raised her right arm. As if performing some violent salute, Serena thrust her forearm and the eagle upward. The bird ascended and began a dihedral circle over the twenty acres of stumps behind Galloway's crew. On the third circle the eagle stopped. For a moment the bird hung poised in the sky, seemingly outside the world's slow turning. Then it appeared not so much to fall but to slice open the air, its body vee'd like an axe head as it propelled downward. Once on the ground among the stumps and slash, the eagle opened its wings like a flourished cape. The bird wobbled forward, paused, and moved forward again, the yellow talons sparring with some creature hidden in the detritus. In another minute the eagle's head dipped, then rose with a hank of stringy pink flesh in its beak.

Serena opened her saddlebag and removed a metal whistle and a lariat. Fastened to one end of the hemp was a piece of bloody beef. She blew the whistle and the bird's neck whirled in her direction as Serena swung the lure overhead.

They Lord God, a worker said as the eagle rose, for in its talons was a three-foot-long rattlesnake. The bird flew toward the ridge crest then arced back, drifting down toward Serena and Galloway's crew. Except for Galloway, the men scattered as if dynamite had been lit, stumbling and tripping over stumps and slash as they fled. The eagle settled on the ground with an elegant awkwardness, the serpent still writhing but its movements only a memory of when it had been alive. Serena dismounted and offered the gobbet of meat. The bird released the snake and pounced on the beef. When it finished eating, Serena placed the hood back over the eagle's head.

"Can I have the skin and rattles?" Galloway asked.

"Yes," Serena said, "but the meat belongs to the bird."

Galloway set his boot heel on the serpent's head and detached the body with a quick sweep of his barlow knife. By the time the other men returned, Galloway had eviscerated the snake, its skin and rattles tucked inside his lunch pail.

By month's end the eagle had killed seven rattlesnakes, including a huge satinback that panicked Snipes' crew when it slipped from the bird's grasp mid-flight and fell earthward. The men hadn't seen the eagle overhead, and the serpent fell among them like some last remnant of Satan's rebellion cast from heaven. The snake landed closest to McIntyre and had just enough life left to slither a few inches and rest its head on the lay preacher's boot toe, causing McIntyre to fall backward in a dead faint.

Dunbar quickly finished off the snake with an axe while Stewart brought his spiritual mentor to consciousness by filling McIntyre's wide-brimmed preacher's hat with creek water, then dousing the unconscious man. Several wagers were made and then settled when Snipes' tape measure reached sixty-three inches from the triangle-shaped head to the last of the snake's twelve buttons.

"That eagle won't likely fetch her one bigger," Ross, the bet's winner, argued.

"Not less it flaps off to them jungles in South America and totes back a anaconder," Snipes interjected before pocketing the tape measure and wire-rimmed glasses that, though lacking lenses, the crew foreman nevertheless insisted worked because the oval frames better focused his vision.

"I'm wondering if she's of a mind to train up a whole flock of them?" Dunbar asked.

"If she done it them snakes would be clearing out like Saint Patrick himself was after them," Snipes said.

"It would sure enough be a blessing," Dunbar said, "not to have to hold your breath every time you picked up a log or limb."

Ross stashed the handful of coins he collected into his pocket.

"If I had my rathers I'd take them rattlesnakes where the Good Lord put them," he said. "At least then you'd not have the worry of them dripping out of the sky onto you."

Stewart and Dunbar looked uneasily upward.

"You're disturbing the natural order of things is what you're doing," Snipes added. "Same as Pemberton offering his gold doubloon for the feller who flushes that panther out. If that thing really is around, all it's done up to now is put the skeer in a few folks, but you start bothering a critter like that it's untelling the trouble you're stirring up."

"Still," Dunbar said wistfully as his gaze lowered to take in the mountains of east Tennessee. "If I was to be the one to find that panther, a twenty-dollar gold piece would buy me a new hat, a sure enough spiffy one with a bright-yallar hatband and feather to boot. Money left over to get me a good sparking outfit too."

"If you was still around to wear it," Ross noted. "It might end up being your burying clothes."

McIntyre, now conscious but still sprawled on the ground, looked up as well. Some frightening new thought appeared to come to him. He attempted to speak but only a few inarticulate sounds came from his throat before his eyes rolled into the back of his head and he passed out again.

"I heard Campbell built that eagle a perch in the stable," Dunbar said.

"I seen it," Snipes said, shaking his head with admiration. "He made it with a lead pipe and metal soldered off an old boxcar. Used that and a big block of hickory, put some sisal rope on top for the eagle to settle its claws in. I believe Campbell could make you a flashlight out of a tin can and a lightning bug. That bird sets there on that perch like a big old rooster. Don't blink nor nothing. It's partial to the darksomeness of that stable. Keeps it calm like the hood she puts over its head."

McIntyre moaned and opened his eyes briefly before closing them again. Stewart fetched more water, then seemed to think better of pouring it on the lay preacher so instead set the pail down. He took off his stricken mentor's coat and unbuttoned the top buttons of his shirt, then dipped a soiled handkerchief in the water and pressed it to McIntyre's forehead as if a poultice. The other men watched as McIntyre's eyes flickered a few moments and opened. This time he did not attempt to speak. Instead, McIntyre solemnly removed a kerchief that had been around his neck and tied it around his head, covering his eyes.

"He ain't never been in such a way as this," Stewart said worriedly, and helped McIntyre to his feet. "I'm taking him back to camp so Doctor Cheney can look at him."

Stewart helped McIntyre down the slope, moving slow and all the while holding his mentor's upper arm firmly, as if leading a fellow soldier newly blinded in battle.

"I reckon you'd argue the snake didn't land on you because of that get-up you're wearing," Ross said to Snipes.

"I don't have to argue it," Snipes said. "You seen well as I did where it landed."

"Well," Dunbar said, appraising the drabness of his own outfit. "I got me a shirt red as a mule-team tomato but I still ain't wearing it out here. I need me one thing pretty to catch a gal's eye."

The men paused to watch as Stewart led McIntyre down the ridge, pausing every few steps to nervously check the sky.

"That bird, it ain't from this country," Snipes said, pausing to tamp some tobacco into his pipe. "It's from Asia, a Mongoloid, and it's worth five hundred dollars so you best not be taking no pot shots at it. It's the same kind of eagle ole Kubla Khan used to hunt with, that's what Campbell says."

"That conversing you had with Campbell must have been the most he's said at one time in his life," Dunbar noted. "He's ever one to keep thoughts to his own self."

"A wise man always keeps his counsel," Snipes said.

"We've noticed," Ross said.

"One of the cooks claimed he seen Mrs. Pemberton training that bird one day," Dunbar said. "Dragged a dead snake around on a rope and ever time that bird tore off after the snake she'd give it a piece of prime-cut beef."

Ross had unpacked his lunch and stared dubiously at his sandwich.

He slowly peeled back a soggy piece of white bread in the same manner he might a scab, revealing a gray slab of meat that appeared coated with mucus. For a few moments he simply stared at the fatback.

"I'd near about chase a dead snake around my ownself for a hunk of steak," Ross said wistfully. "It's been ever so long since I had a piece of prime cow meat."

"Put it betwixt a big yallar-butter biscuit and I'd near give up the promise of heaven," Dunbar said.

A raven flew overhead, wing shadow passing over the men like a dark thought. Dunbar flinched when he saw the bird's shadow, looked upward.

"I believe you're right, Ross," Dunbar said, still staring at the sky. "It's trouble coming from every direction now."

The men watched the raven disappear over Balsum Mountain.

"Her putting that eagle in the stable all night," Dunbar said. "Ain't she afeared of some fox or other varmint getting it?"

Ross looked up from his sandwich and nodded at the dead snake.

"If it can handle a boss rattler like that one it can handle anything on four legs or even two if it come to that. I'd no more strut up and tangle with that eagle than I'd tangle with the one what can tame such a critter," Ross concluded.

Eleven

IT WAS CAMPBELL WHO TOLD PEMBERTON THAT the Harmon girl had returned to the camp.

"She's waiting over at the dining hall," he said. "She wants her old job in the kitchen back."

"Where's she been all this time?" Pemberton asked.

"Living up at her daddy's place on Colt Ridge."

"Does she have the child with her?"

"No."

"Who's going to care for the child while she's working?"

"A widow-woman who lives near her. She said she'd still live up there and take the train to camp." Campbell paused. "She was a good worker before she left last summer."

"You think I owe her a job, don't you?" Pemberton said, meeting Campbell's eyes.

"All I'm saying is she's a good worker. Even if we

don't need her right now, one of our dishwashers is leaving end of the month."

Pemberton looked down at his desk. The note to himself to call Harris, which he'd done earlier, lay crumpled on the foolscap showing Serena's plans for a new spur line. Pemberton stared at the charcoal etching's precise rendering of topography, the carefully calibrated degrees of ascent, all done by Serena's hand.

"I'll have to talk with Mrs. Pemberton first," he told Campbell. "I'll be back in an hour."

Pemberton got his horse and left camp. He crossed Rough Fork Creek and wove his way up the ridge through the stumps and slash. He found Serena on a down slope giving instructions to a cutting crew. The men slumped in various attitudes of repose, but all were attentive. After the foreman asked a final question, the lead chopper began notching a looming tulip poplar, the only uncut hardwood left on the ridge. Serena watched until the sawyers began their work, then rode over to where Pemberton waited.

"What brings you out this morning, Pemberton?"

"I talked with Harris. Secretary Albright called over the weekend and wants to set up a meeting. Harris says he's willing to come here."

"When?"

"Albright's willing to accommodate us on that as well. He said anytime between now and September."

"September then," Serena said. "However this turns out, the more time we have to keep logging the better."

Serena nodded, her eyes rising beyond the tulip poplar to the ridge where crews had gained a first foothold above Henley Creek.

"We've made good progress in the last six months, even with the bad weather."

"Yes we have," Pemberton agreed. "We could be finished here in eighteen months."

"I think less than that," Serena said.

The gelding snorted and stamped its foot. Serena leaned slightly forward, her left hand stroking the Arabian's neck.

"I'd better go and check the other crews."

"There's one more thing," Pemberton said. "Campbell says the Harmon girl's in camp. She wants her old job in the kitchen back."

"Does Campbell think we should hire her?"

"Yes."

Serena continued to stroke the Arabian's neck, but she looked at Pemberton now.

"What I said at the depot, about her getting nothing else from us."

"Her wages will be the same as before," Pemberton said, "and like before she won't be living in camp."

"While she's at work, who cares for the child?"

"A neighbor will keep him."

"'Him,'" Serena said. "So it's a male."

The sawing paused for a few moments as the lead chopper placed another wedge behind the blade. Serena raised her left hand and settled it over the saddle pommel. Her right hand, which held the reins, settled over the pommel as well.

"You be the one to tell her that she's hired," Serena said. "Just make it clear she has no claim on us. Her child either."

The cross-cut saw resumed, the blade's rapid back-and-forth like inhalations and exhalations, a sound as if the tree itself were panting. The Arabian stamped the ground again and Serena tightened her fist around the reins, preparing to turn the gelding's head in the direction of the cutting crew.

"One other thing," Serena said. "Make sure she's not allowed around our food."

Horse and rider made their way back through drifts of snow toward the deeper woods. Serena upright, her posture impeccable, the gelding's hooves set down almost disdainfully on the whitened earth. Cut proud, Pemberton thought.

When Pemberton returned to camp, he went into the dining hall where Rachel Harmon waited alone at a table. She wore a pair of polished but well-worn black oxford shoes and a faded blue and white calico dress Pemberton suspected was the nicest clothing she owned. When he'd had his say, Pemberton asked if she understood.

"Yes sir," she said.

"And what happened with your father. You saw it yourself, so you know I was defending myself."

A few moments of silence passed between them. She finally nodded, not meeting his eyes. Pemberton tried to remember what had attracted him to her in the first place. Perhaps her blue eyes and blonde hair. Perhaps that she'd been almost the only female at the camp who wasn't already haggard. Aging in these mountains, especially among the women, happened early. Pemberton had seen women of twenty-five here who would pass for fifty in Boston.

She kept her head slightly bowed as Pemberton surveyed her mouth and chin, her bosom and waist and the white length of ankle showing below her threadbare dress. Whatever had attracted him was now gone. Attraction to any woman besides Serena, he realized, unable to remember the last time he'd thought of a past consort, or watched a young beauty in Waynesville and imagined what her body would be like joined to his. He knew such constancy was rare, and before meeting Serena would have believed it impossible for a man such as himself. Now it seemed inevitable, wondrous but also disconcerting in its finality.

"You can start the first of December," Pemberton said.

She got up to leave and was almost to the door when he stopped her.

"The child, what's his name?"

"Jacob. It comes from the Bible."

The name's Old Testament derivation did not surprise him. Campbell's first name was Ezra, and there was an Absalom and a Solomon in the camp. But no Lukes or Matthews, which Buchanan had once noted, telling Pemberton that from his research the highlanders tended to live more by the Old Testament than the New.

"Does he have a middle name?"

"Magill, it's a family name."

The girl let her eyes glance his a moment.

"If you was to want to see him . . ."

Her voice trailed off. A kitchen worker came into the hall, a mop and bucket in her hands.

"You can start first of next month," Pemberton said, and went into the kitchen to have the cook make him a late lunch.

Twelve

IN THE FOLLOWING WEEKS, MOST OF NOLAND Mountain had been logged and crews had worked north to Bunk Ridge before turning west, following a spur across Davidson Branch and into the wide expanse between Campbell Fork and upper Indian Creek. The men worked faster now that full summer had come, in part because there hadn't been a single rattlesnake bite since the eagle's arrival. As the crews moved forward, they left behind an ever-widening wasteland of stumps and slash, brown clogged creeks awash with dead trout. Even the more resilient knottyheads and shiners eventually succumbed, some flopping onto banks as if even the ungillable air offered greater hope of survival. As the woods fell away, sightings of the panther grew more frequent, fueled in part by hopes of earning Pemberton's gold piece. No man could show a convincing track or scrap of fur, but all had their stories, including Dunbar, who claimed during an afternoon break that something large and black had just streaked through the nearby trees.

"Where?" Stewart asked, picking up his axe as he and the rest of Snipes' crew perused the nearby woods.

"Over there," Dunbar said, pointing to his left.

Ross went to where Dunbar pointed and skeptically studied ground still damp from a morning shower. Ross came back and sat on a log beside Snipes, who'd returned to perusing his newspaper.

"Maybe it was that eagle," Ross said, "because there's nary a sign of a track. You're just hoping for that flashy hat."

"Well, I thought I saw it," Dunbar said gloomily. "I guess sometimes you've got the hope-fors so much it makes you imagine all sorts of things."

Ross turned to Snipes, expecting Dunbar's comment to provoke a philosophical treatise, but the crew foreman was immersed in his newspaper.

"What's in your paper that's got you so squinch eyed, Snipes?"

"They've got a big-to-do meeting about that park in two weeks," Snipes said from behind his veil of newsprint. "According to Editor Webb here, the Secretary of the Interior of the whole U S of A will be there. Bringing John D. Rockefeller's own personal pettifogger with him too. Says they're coming to make Boston Lumber and Harris Mineral Company sell their land or face eviction."

"Think they'll be able to do that?" Dunbar asked.

"It'll be a battle royal," Snipes said, "not a smidgen of doubt about that."

"They won't beat them," Ross said. "If it was just Buchanan and Wilkie they might, but not Harris and Pemberton, and especially not her."

"We better hope that's the way of it," Dunbar said. "If this camp gets shut down we'll be in the worst kind of fix. We'll be riding the boxcars sure enough."

"JUST Albright and Rockefeller's lawyer," Pemberton replied that evening as he and Serena prepared for bed. "Albright wanted no state politicians at the meeting. He said even with Webb and Kephart there we'll still have a five to four advantage."

"Good, we'll get this settled, once and for all," Serena said, her eyes settling on the Saratoga trunk at the foot of the bed, a trunk whose contents Pemberton had yet to see. "It jeopardizes more important matters."

Serena took off her jodphurs and placed them in the chifforobe. Overhead, a few tentative taps announced the hard rain promised all afternoon by clouds draped low across Noland Mountain. The rain steadily picked up pace, soon galloping on the tin roof. Pemberton began to undress, reminded himself to get his hunting boots from the hall closet. Don't fret none if it rains tonight, Galloway had told him that afternoon. Momma says it'll clear up by morning. She's counting on that as much as we are.

Serena turned from the chifforobe.

"What's the bard of Appalachia like, in person?"

"Stubborn and cranky as his buddy Sheriff McDowell," Pemberton said. "Kephart told me at the first meeting how it pleased him to know I'd die and eventually my coffin would rot, and how then I'd be nourishing the earth instead of destroying it."

"Which is one more thing he's wrong about," Serena said. "I'll make sure of that, for both of us. What else?"

"He's also overly fond of the bottle, not nearly the saint the newspapers and politicians make of him."

"Though they have to make him appear so," Serena said. "He's their new Muir."

"Galloway says we'll be going right past Kephart's cabin tomorrow, so you could see the great man himself."

"I'll meet him soon enough," Serena said. "Besides, Campbell and I are putting down the stobs for the new spur line."

Serena stepped out of her undergarments. As Pemberton gazed at her, he wondered if it was possible that a time would come when he'd look at her naked and not be stunned. He couldn't imagine such a moment, believed instead that Serena's beauty was like certain laws of math and physics, fixed and immutable. *She walks in beauty.* Words recited years ago in a voice dry as the chalk dust choking the classroom's air, part of a poem Pemberton had paid attention to only so he might laugh at its sentiment. But now he knew the truth of the words, for Serena's beauty was like that—something the world opened a guarded space around so it could go forth unsullied.

After they'd coupled, Pemberton listened to Serena's soft breaths mingle with the rain hitting the roof. She slept well now, in a deepness beyond dreams, she claimed. It had been that way since she'd stayed in the stable with the eagle, as though the nightmares had come those two sleepless nights and, with no dream to enter, gone elsewhere, the way ghosts might who find a house they've haunted suddenly vacated.

The rain stopped during the night, the sky blue and cloudless by midday. Scouting, not hunting, Galloway had called their trip, searching for tracks and scat, a fresh-killed deer carcass with its heart ripped out, but Pemberton took his rifle from the hall closet, just in case.

When Pemberton walked down to the office, he found not only Galloway on the porch but also Galloway's mother. She wore the same austere dress as last summer and a black satin bonnet that made her face recede as if peering from a cave mouth. The old woman's shoes were cobbled out of a reddish wood that looked to be cedar. Comical looking, but something else as well, Pemberton realized, a disconcerting *otherness* that was part of these mountains and would always be inexplicable to him.

"She likes to get out on a pretty day like this," Galloway explained. "Says it warms her bones and gets her blood to flowing good."

Pemberton assumed getting out meant the office porch, but when he walked over to the Packard, the old woman shuffled toward the car as well.

"Surely she's not going with us?"

"Not on the traipsing part," Galloway said, "just the riding."

Galloway did not give Pemberton a chance to argue with the arrangement. He opened the Packard's back passenger door and helped his mother in before seating himself beside Pemberton.

They drove toward Waynesville a few miles before turning west. The old woman pressed her face close to the window, but Pemberton couldn't imagine what her blighted eyes could possibly see. They shared the road with families returning from church, most walking, some in wagons. As Pemberton passed these highlanders, they characteristically lowered their eyes so as not to meet his, a seeming act of deference belied by their refusal to sidle to the road's shoulder so he might get around them easier. When they drove into Bryson City, Galloway pointed at a storefront, SHULER DRUGSTORE AND APOTHECARY lettered red on the window.

"We got to stop here a minute," he said.

Galloway came out of the store with a small paper bag, which he gave to his mother. The old woman clutched the folded top of the bag with both hands, as if the bag's contents might attempt to escape.

"She's a fool for horehound candy," Galloway said as Pemberton shifted the car into gear.

"Does your mother ever speak?"

"Only if she's got something worth listening to," Galloway said. "She can tell your future if you want. Tell you what your dreams mean too."

"No thanks," Pemberton said.

They drove another few miles, passing small farms, a good number inhabited only by what creatures sheltered inside the broken windows and sagging roofs, foreclosure notices nailed on doors and porch beams. In the yard or field always some remnant left behind—a rusty harrow or washtub, a child's frayed rope swing, some last forlorn claim on the place. Pemberton turned where a leaning road sign said Deep Creek, traversing what might have been a dry river bed for all its swerves and rocks and washouts. When Pemberton got to where the road ended, he saw that a car was already parked in the small clearing.

"Kephart's?" Pemberton asked.

"He ain't got no car," Galloway said, and nodded at a tan lawman's hat set on the dash. "Looks to be the high sheriff's. Him and that old man is probably out looking for pretty bugs or flowers or some such. The sheriff's near hep on naturing as Kephart is."

Galloway and Pemberton got out of the car, and Galloway opened the back door. The old woman was motionless except for her cheeks creasing and uncreasing like bellows with each suck of the candy. Galloway went around and opened the other back door as well.

"That way she can get her a nice breeze," Galloway said. "That's what she's been craving. You don't get no breeze in them stringhouses."

They walked down the path a hundred yards before the trees fell away to reveal a small cabin. Sheriff McDowell and Kephart sat in cane chairs on the porch. A ten-gallon hoop barrel squatted between them, on it a tattered topographical map draped over the barrel like a tablecloth. McDowell watched intently while Kephart marked the map with a carpenter's pencil. Pemberton placed a boot on the porch step, saw that the map encompassed the surrounding mountains and eastern Tennessee. Gray and red markings covered the map, some overlapping, some partially erased, as if a palimpsest.

"Planning a trip?" Pemberton asked.

"No," Kephart replied, acknowledging Pemberton for the first time since he'd stepped into the clearing. "A national park."

Kephart laid the pencil on the barrel. He took off his reading glasses and set them down as well.

"What are you doing on my land?"

"Your land?" Pemberton said. "I assumed you'd already donated it to this park you're wanting so bad. Or is it just other people's property that the park gets?"

"The park will get any land I own," Kephart said. "I've already taken care of that in my will, but until then you're trespassing."

"We're just passing through," Galloway said, beside Pemberton now. "Heard a panther might be roaming around here. We're just helping to protect you."

McDowell stared at the rifle in Pemberton's hands. Pemberton motioned at the map with the gun's barrel.

"You for that park, too, Sheriff?"

"Yes," McDowell said.

"I wonder why that doesn't surprise me," Pemberton said.

"Move on, or I'll arrest you for trespassing," McDowell said. "And if I hear that gun go off, I'll arrest you for hunting out of season."

Galloway grinned and was about to say something, but Pemberton spoke first.

"Let's go."

They walked around the cabin, then passed a woodshed, behind which a rusty window screen lay atop two sawhorses. On the screen were arrowheads and spear points, other stones various in size and hue, including some little more than pebbles. Galloway paused to inspect these, lifting one into the light to reveal its murky red color.

"I wonder where he found you," Galloway mused.

"What is it?" Pemberton asked.

"Ruby. These ain't big enough to be worth anything, but if you was to find a bigger one, you'd have something that sure enough would get your pockets jingling."

"Do you think Kephart found them around here?"

"Doubt it," Galloway said, tossing the stone back on the screen. "Probably found them over near Franklin. Still, I'll keep my eyes open while we're sauntering around the creek. Might be something hiding around here besides a panther."

They walked on past the woodshed and followed the trail into the forest. Few hardwoods rose around them, and those that did were small. After a while Pemberton heard the stream, then saw it through the trees, larger than he'd imagined, more a small river than a creek. Galloway's eyes focused intently on the sand and mud. He pointed to a small set of tracks on a sand bar.

"Mink. I'll be back to trap him this winter when his fur thickens up."

They moved upstream, Galloway stopping to peruse tracks, sometimes kneeling to trace their indentions with his index finger. They came to a deep pool, above it a boggy swath of mud printed with tracks larger than any they'd yet seen.

"Cat?" Pemberton asked.

"Yeah, it's a cat."

"I'd have thought there'd be claw marks."

"No," Galloway said. "Them claws don't come out until it's time to do some killing."

Galloway grunted as he settled himself on one knee. He placed a finger to the side of a track, pressed into the mud so water drained from the print.

"Bobcat," Galloway said after a few more moments. "A damn big one, though."

"You're sure it can't be a mountain lion?"

Galloway looked up, something of both irritation and amusement on his face.

"I reckon you could stick a tail on it and claim it for a panther," Galloway snorted. "There's fools that'd not know the difference."

The highlander stood up and stared at the sun to gauge the time.

"Time to go," he said, and stepped onto the bank. "Too bad Mama's with us or we could stay longer. If that panther's really around, come the nightfall we might hear him."

"What do they sound like?" Pemberton asked.

"Just like a baby crying," Galloway said, "except after a few seconds it shuts off of a sudden like something that's had its throat slashed. You'll have need to hear it only once to know what it is. It'll make the back of your neck bristle up like a porcupine."

They made their way back up the ridge, the sound of the stream's fall and rush dimming behind them. In a few minutes, Kephart's cabin came into view.

"Want to find out if that sheriff has some real sand in him or is just talk?" Galloway asked.

"Another time," Pemberton said.

"All right," Galloway said, veering right and crossing a small creek. "This way then. But I'm getting some water out of that springhouse. Mamai will be thirsty after sucking on that candy."

When they came to the springhouse, Galloway took a tobacco tin from his back pocket and poured out what crumbs remained in it. As Galloway filled the tin, Pemberton looked through the trees at the cabin. A chess board had replaced the map, and Kephart and McDowell stared at it intently. One of Pemberton's fencing partners at Harvard had introduced him to the game, claiming it was fencing with the mind instead of the body, but Pemberton had found the slow pace and lack of physical movement tedious.

The match was nearing its end, fewer than a dozen pieces left on the board. McDowell placed his finger and thumb on his remaining knight and made his move, its forward-left motion angling not only toward Kephart's king but also into the path of his rook. Pemberton thought the sheriff had made a mistake, but Kephart saw something Pemberton didn't. The older man resignedly took the knight with his rook. The sheriff moved his queen across the board, and Pemberton saw it then. Kephart made a final move and the match was over.

"Let's go," Galloway said, holding the tin so as not to slosh out the water. "I got better things to do than watch grown men play tiddlywinks."

They walked on, finding Galloway's mother just as they'd left her. The only sign that she'd made the slightest movement was the wadded paper bag on the floorboard.

"Brought you some cold spring water, Mama," Galloway said and lifted the tobacco tin to his mother's cracked purplish lips.

The old woman made sucking sounds as her son slowly tilted the container, pulled it back so she could swallow before pressing it to her lips again. Doing this several times until all the water had been drunk.

As they drove back to camp, Galloway looked out the window toward the Smokies.

"Don't worry," he said. "We'll get you a panther yet."

They rode the rest of the way in silence, following the blacktop as it made a convoluted circuit through the landscape's see-saws and swerves. Outside Bryson City, the mountains swelled upward as if taking a last deep breath before slowly exhaling toward Cove Creek Valley.

As they drove into camp, Pemberton saw a green pickup parked beside the commissary. Shakily affixed to its flatbed was a wooden building, steep-pitched and wide-doored, resembling a very large doghouse or very small church. On the sides in black letters R.L. FRIZZELL—PHOTOGRAPHER. Pemberton watched as the vehicle's owner lifted his tripod and camera from the truck's work shed, set up the equipment with the swift deftness of one long practiced in his trade. The photographer looked to be in his sixties, and he wore a wrinkled black suit and wide somber tie. A loupe dangled from the silver chain around his neck, the instrument worn with the same authority a doctor might wear a stethoscope.

"What's going on over there?" Pemberton asked.

"Ledbetter, the sawyer that got killed yesterday," Galloway said. "They're taking his picture for a remembering."

Pemberton understood then. Another local custom that fascinated Buchanan—taking a picture of the deceased, the photograph a keepsake for the bereaved to place on a wall or fireboard. Campbell stood behind the photographer, though for what reason, if any, Pemberton could not discern.

"Put this in the office," Pemberton said, and handed Galloway the rifle before walking toward the commissary to stand with Campbell.

An unlidded pine coffin leaned against the commissary's back wall, the deceased propped up inside. A placard bearing the words REST IN PEACE had been placed on the coffin's squared head, but the corpse's tight-shouldered rigidity belied the notion, as if even in death Ledbetter anticipated another falling tree. Frizzell squeezed the shutter release. On one side of the coffin was a haggard woman Pemberton assumed was Ledbetter's wife, beside her a boy of six or seven. As soon as a click confirmed the picture taken, two sawyers came forward and placed the lid on the coffin, entombing Ledbetter in the very thing that had killed him.

"Where's my wife?" Pemberton asked Campbell.

Campbell nodded toward Noland Mountain.

"She's up there with the eagle."

The photographer emerged from beneath the cloth, eyes blinking in the mid-afternoon light. He slid the negative into its protective metal sleeve, then went to his truck and took out a wicker fishing creel he slung over his shoulder before procuring another plate. Frizzell inserted the new plate before lifting the camera and tripod into his arms and making awkward sidling movements toward the dining hall where Reverend Bolick's congregation had taken advantage of the warm day and brought tables from the dining hall for an after-service meal. The food had been eaten and the tables cleared, but many of the congregants lingered. The women wore cheap cotton-print dresses, the men rumpled white dress shirts and trousers, a few in threadbare coats. The children were arrayed in everything from cheap bright dresses to jumpers fashioned out of burlap potato sacks.

Frizzell set up his camera, aiming at a child wearing a blue gingham smock. The photographer disappeared under the black cloth, attempting to hold the child's attention with all manner of gee-gaws brought forth from the wicker creel. After a toy bluebird, rattle and whirligig had failed, Frizzell rose from beneath the cloth and demanded the child be made to sit still. Rachel Harmon emerged from behind the other churchgoers. Pemberton had not seen her until that moment. She spoke to the boy quietly. Still hunched over, she backed slowly away as if afraid any sudden movement might startle the child back into activity. Pemberton stared at the child, searching for a feeling, a thought, that could encompass what lay before him.

When Campbell made a motion to leave, Pemberton grabbed him by the arm.

"Stay here a minute."

The photographer disappeared under the cloth again. The child did not move. Nor did Pemberton. He tried to make out the boy's features, but the distance was too great even to tell eye color. A flash of light and the picture was done. Rachel Harmon lifted the child in her arms. Turning and seeing Pemberton, she did not avert her eyes. She shifted the child so it gazed in Pemberton's direction. Her free hand brushed the child's hair behind its ears. Then an older woman came and the child turned away, the three of them heading toward the train that would take them to Waynesville.

"Pemberton took out his billfold and handed Campbell a five-dollar bill, then told him what he wanted.

That night Pemberton dreamed he and Serena had been hunting in the same meadow where they'd killed the bear. Something hidden in the far woods made a crying sound. Pemberton thought it was a panther, but Serena said no, that it was a baby. When Pemberton asked if they should go get it, Serena had smiled at him. That's Galloway's baby, not ours, she had said.

Thirteen

SHE HAD FORGOTTEN HOW MUCH LOGGERS COULD eat, how it was like stoking a huge fire that burned wood faster than you could throw it on. Rachel worked the early shift, the hardest because breakfast was the camp's biggest meal. She lit the lantern and took Jacob to Widow Jenkins each morning and then walked down to the depot and rode the train to camp, arriving at 5:30 to help fill the long tables, setting out first the tin forks and spoons and coffee cups, thick kaolin plates and bowls soon to be heaped with food. All the while the fire boxes roared, their mouths opened and stuffed with hickory, their heat passing through the thin pig-iron partitions into the twin thousand-pound Burton grange stoves. Inside the oven doors, puddles of bread dough rose and browned while on the stove eyes pots rattled and steamed like overheated engines. The kitchen thickened with smoke and heat, soon hotter and more humid than the worst July afternoon. Sweat beaded the workers' skin with an oily sheen as they came and went. Then the food itself was brought forth from the yard-wide oven racks, ladled and poured from the five- and ten-gallon pots, slid and peeled off black skillets big around as harrow discs. Gallon bowls were filled with stewed apples and fried potatoes and grits and oatmeal, straw bread baskets stuffed with cat-head biscuits, heaped platters of hotcakes and fatback, thick wedges of butter and quart mason jars of blackberry jam. Last the coffee, the steaming pots set on plates, cups of cream and sugar as well though nearly all the men drank it black.

For a few moments everything waited—the kitchen workers, the long wooden benches, the plates and forks and cups. Then the head cook took his gut-hammer and clanged the three-foot length of train track hung outside the main door. The timber crews came in, and for fifteen minutes the men hardly spoke to one another, much less to Rachel and the other kitchen workers. They raised their hands and pointed to empty bowls and platters, their mouths still working as they did so. After fifteen minutes passed, the work bell rang. The men left so quickly their cast-down forks and spoons seemed to retain a slight vibration, like pond water rippling after a splash.

The tables were cleared immediately, but the dishwashing and preparation for the next meal were put off until after the kitchen staff themselves ate. Rachel had always found these moments the best in the workday. The chance to catch a breath after the rush of feeding the men, to talk to some of the folks who worked with her, it was something she'd looked forward to after months hardly speaking to an adult besides Widow Jenkins. But Bonny had gotten married and moved to South Carolina, and Rebecca had been fired. The older women hadn't had much to do with her before and even less so now. Rebecca's replacement, a woman named Cora Pinson from Grassy Bald, hadn't been especially friendly either, but she was younger than the other women and a new hire. After three weeks of eating alone, Rachel set her plate down where Cora and Mabel Sorrels had a table to themselves.

"Would you mind if I was to sit with you?" Rachel asked.

Mrs. Sorrels just stared at her as if she wasn't worth the bother of replying to. It was Cora Pinson who spoke.

"I don't sit with whores."

The two women lifted up their plates and turned their backs to Rachel as they moved to another table.

Rachel sat down and looked at her plate. She could hear several of the other women talking about her, not bothering to whisper. Go ahead and eat like it don't bother you, she told herself. She took a bite of biscuit, chewed and swallowed it though it went down like sawdust. Rachel set her fork in a piece of stewed apple, but she didn't raise it to her mouth, merely stared at it. She didn't even see Joel Vaughn until he set his plate opposite her. He took off his blue and black mackinaw and draped it on an empty seat.

"Don't pay no mind to them old snuff mouths," Joel said as he pulled back a chair and sat down. "I see them every morning out back sneaking them a dip. Don't want Preacher Bolick to see that nasty tobacco juice dripping down their chins like brown slobber."

Joel said his words loud enough for the women to hear them. Rachel lowered her head, but a smile creased her lips. Cora Pinson and Mabel Sorrels got up in a huff and went to the kitchen with their trays.

Joel took off his gray cap, revealing the thatch of curly bright-orange hair that had been an uncombable tangle ever since Rachel had known him.

"That young one of yours is sprouting up like June corn," Joel said. "When I seen him Sunday at church I'd have not known who it was if you hadn't been holding him. I didn't know babies grew so fast, but I reckon us boys don't know much about such things."

"I didn't know it either," Rachel said. "I don't seem to know much about babies at all."

"He's stout and healthy, so I'd say that shows you know enough," Joel said, nodding at Rachel's plate as he reached for his fork. "You best be eating too."

He lowered his eyes and ate with the same fixed attentiveness as all the other men. Rachel looked at him, and it surprised her how much he had changed but not changed. As a child, Joel had been smaller than most of the boys, but he'd caught up in his teens, not just taller but wider-shouldered, more muscled. A man now, even a thin mustache over his lip. But his face was the same, freckled and easy to grin, a boy you knew had mischief in him. Smart as a whip, and kind, a kindness you could see in his green eyes as well as his words. Joel set the fork down and raised the coffee cup to his lips, took a swallow and then another.

"You've been doing good for yourself," Rachel said. "From what folks say you'll be an overseer like Mr. Campbell before too long. There's no surprise in that though. You always had the most smarts of any of us at school."

Joel's face reddened into a blush. Even his freckles appeared to darken.

"I just fill in where they need me. Besides, soon as I can find another job I'm leaving here."

"Why do you want to leave?" Rachel asked.

Joel met her eyes.

"Because I don't like them," he said, and turned back to his food.

Rachel looked at the clock by the doorway and saw it was time for her to get back to work. She could already hear the clatter of crockery and metal being washed and rinsed in the fifty-gallon hoop barrels, but she didn't want to get up. It had been so long since she'd talked to someone her own age. Rachel remembered how growing up she'd thought living on a farm with just a father was as lonely as you could be.

"We had some good times at that school," she said as Joel finished the last bit on his plate. "I didn't know how good those times was till I left, but I guess that's the way of it."

"We did have some fun," Joel said, "even if Miss Stephens was a grumpy old sow."

"I remember the time she asked where in the United States we'd want to go, and you said far as you could get from her and the schoolhouse. That really got her out of sorts."

The dining hall suddenly grew quiet as Galloway opened the side door and took a step inside, his head cocked slightly to the right as he scanned the room. He found Joel and jerked his head toward the office.

"I better go and see what old flop arm wants," Joel said, and got up.

Rachel got up as well, speaking softly across the table as she did so. "Have you ever heard Mr. or Mrs. Pemberton say anything about me?"

"No," Joel said, his face clouding.

Joel looked like he wanted to say something more, and whatever that something more was it wouldn't be said in a playful tone or with a smile on his face. But he didn't. He put on his cap and mackinaw.

"Thanks for sitting with me," Rachel said.

Joel nodded.

As Joel went out the door, Rachel saw Mrs. Pemberton through the dining hall's wide window. Horse and rider moved briskly through the last crews walking toward the woods. Rachel watched until Mrs. Pemberton and the horse began their ascent onto the ridge. She raised herself from the chair, her eyes about to turn away from the window when Rachel saw her own reflection. She did not bend to pick up her plate but let her gaze linger. Despite the apron and her hair tied back in a bun, Rachel saw that she was still pretty. Her hands were chapped and wrinkled by the kitchen work, but her face was unlined and smooth. Her body hadn't yet acquired the sagging shapelessness of the other women in the kitchen. Even the soiled apron could not conceal that.

You're too pretty to stay covered up, Mr. Pemberton had told her more than once when Rachel waited until she was in bed to take off her dress and step-ins. She remembered how after the first few times there'd been pleasure in the loving for her as well as him, and she'd had to bite her lip to not be embarrassed. She remembered the day she'd walked through the house while he slept, touching the ice box and the chairs and the gilded mirror, Rachel also recalling what hadn't been there—no picture of a sweetheart hung on the wall or set on a bureau, just as there'd been no woman come down from Boston like Mrs. Buchanan had once. At least not one until Serena.

Someone called Rachel's name from the kitchen, but she did not move from the window. She remembered again the afternoon at the train station when Serena Pemberton held the bowie knife by its blade, offering the pearl handle to her. Rachel thought how easily she might have grasped the bowie knife's handle, the blade that had just killed her father pointed at the other woman's heart. As Rachel continued to stare at her reflection, she suddenly wondered if she'd been wrong about having had only one real choice in her life, that in that moment at the depot Serena Pemberton had offered her a second choice, one that could have made laying down in bed with Mr. Pemberton the right choice after all, even at the cost of her father. *Don't think a thing that terrible,* Rachel told herself.

Rachel turned and walked into the kitchen, setting her plate and fork on the oak stacking table before settling herself beside the hoop barrel closest to the back door. She picked up the scrub brush in her right hand and the slab of Octagon soap in the left, dipped her hands in the gray water and scuffed the wood bristles against the tan-colored soap to make her lather. As Rachel took up her first plate to clean, one of the other kitchen workers shouldered open the back door. In her hands was a tin tub filled with breakfast dishes and silverware from the office.

"Mr. Pemberton wants more coffee brought to his office," the woman said to Beason, the head cook.

Beason looked around the kitchen, his eyes passing over Rachel before settling on Cora Pinson.

"Take a pot of coffee over there," Beason said to her.

As Cora Pinson went out the back door, Rachel thought of Mrs. Pemberton astride the great horse, erect and square-shouldered, not looking anywhere but straight ahead. Not needing to, because she didn't have to care if someone stepped in front of her and the horse. She and that gelding would go right over whoever got in their way and not give the least notice they'd trampled someone into the dirt.

Smart of her, Rachel thought, not to allow me near her food.

Fourteen

THE MEETING WITH THE PARK DELEGATION WAS set for eleven on Monday morning, but by ten o'clock Pemberton, Buchanan and Wilkie had already gathered in the office's back room, smoking cigars and discussing the payroll. Harris also sat at the table, reading the morning's *Asheville Citizen* with visible ire. Campbell stood in the corner until Pemberton checked his watch and nodded it was time to get Serena.

"They're early," Buchanan said minutes later when the office door opened, but it was Doctor Cheney and Reverend Bolick instead. They came into the back room, and Cheney settled into the closest chair. Bolick held his black preacher's hat in his hand, but he sat down without being asked and placed his hat on the table. Pemberton couldn't help but admire the man's brazenness.

"Reverend Bolick wishes to have a word with you," Doctor Cheney said. "I told him we were busy but he was insistent."

The morning was warm and the preacher dabbed his forehead and right temple with a cotton handkerchief, not touching the left side of his face where the skin was withered and grainy, thinner seeming, as if once shaved with a planer. Caused by a house fire during his childhood, Pemberton had heard. Bolick placed the handkerchief in his coat pocket and set his clasped hands before him.

"As you have guests arriving soon, I'll be brief," Reverend Bolick said, addressing them all but looking specifically at Wilkie. "It's about the pay raise we've discussed. Even half a dollar more a week would make a huge difference, especially for the workers with families."

"Have you not seen all those men on the commissary steps?" Wilkie said, his voice quickly shifting from annoyance to anger. "Be grateful your congregation has work when so many don't. Save your proselytizing for your congregation, Reverend, and remember you serve here at our indulgence."

Bolick glared at Wilkie. The fire-scarred side of the preacher's face appeared to glow with some lingering of that long-ago violence.

"I serve only at God's indulgence," he said, reaching for his hat.

Pemberton had been looking out the window and now he spoke.

"Here comes my wife," he said, and the others turned and looked out the window as well.

Serena paused at the ridge crest before her descent. Lingering fog laid a thick mist on the ground and the ridge, but the morning's brightness broke full on the summit. Threads of sunlight appeared to have woven themselves into Serena's cropped hair, giving it the appearance of shone brass. She sat upright on the gelding, the eagle perched on the leather gauntlet as if grafted to her arm. As Bolick pushed back his chair to rise, Wilkie turned his gaze from the window and met Bolick's eyes.

"There's a true manifestation of the godly," Wilkie said admiringly. "Such an image gave the Greeks and Romans their deities. Gaze upon her, Reverend. She'll never be crucified by the rabble."

For a few moments no one spoke. They watched Serena descend into the swirling fog and vanish.

"I'll listen to no more of this blasphemy," Bolick said.

The preacher put on his hat and quickly walked out of the room. Doctor Cheney remained seated until Pemberton told him his services were no longer needed.

"Of course," Cheney said dryly as he got up to leave. "I forgot my input is needed only in matters of life and death."

Pemberton went to the bar and brought a bottle of cognac to the table, went back and got the crystal tumblers. Buchanan looked at the bottle and frowned.

"What?" Pemberton asked.

"The liquor. It could be perceived as a provocation."

Harris looked up from his newspaper.

"I was under the impression we were meeting the Secretary of the Interior, not Eliot Ness."

THE park delegation was twenty minutes late, by which time Wilkie had gone to the commissary for a bromide. Everyone shook hands, the visitors unsurprised when Serena offered hers. Pemberton surmised they'd been told she was not a woman of deference, and that it might help their cause to acknowledge as much. Except for Kephart, who was dressed in a clean flannel shirt and dark wool pants, the visitors wore dark suits and ties, lending the meeting a formal air despite the room's rusticity. Albright and Pemberton sat at opposing ends of the table. Davis, Rockefeller's lawyer, seated himself to the right of Albright, Kephart and Webb near the table's center. Cuban cigars and cognac were passed around. Several of the late arrivals took a cigar, but all in the visiting contingent politely declined the alcohol except Kephart, who filled his tumbler. Gunmetal-blue streams of cigar smoke soon rose, raveled into a diaphanous cloud above the table's center.

Harris folded the newspaper and laid it on the table.

"I see you've folded the paper to my most recent editorial, Mr. Harris," Webb said.

"Yes, and as soon as my constitution allows, I plan to wipe my ass with it."

Webb smiled. "I plan to write enough articles on this park to keep you well supplied, Mr. Harris. And I won't be alone. Secretary Albright informs me a *New York Times* reporter will arrive this weekend to write about what land has already been purchased, as well as complete a profile on Kephart's role in the park's creation."

"Perhaps the article will discuss Mr. Kephart's desertion of his family," Serena said, turning to Kephart. "How many children were left in Saint Louis for your wife to raise alone, was it four or five?"

"This is not really relevant," Albright said, looking at the table as if for a gavel.

"It's very relevant," Serena said. "My experience has been that altruism is invariably a means to conceal one's personal failures."

"Whatever my personal failings, I'm not doing this for myself," Kephart said to Serena. "I'm doing it for the future."

"What future? Where is it?" Serena said sarcastically, looking around the room. "All I see is the here and now."

"With all respect, Mrs. Pemberton," Albright said. "We are here to discuss a reality, the creation of a national park, not engage in sophistry."

"The sophistry is on your side," Harris said. "Even with the land you've bought, this park is still nothing more than a fairy dream on a goat hill."

"Rockefeller's five million dollars is real enough," Webb countered. "This country's eminent domain law is real enough also."

"So the threats begin," Harris said.

The door opened and Wilkie entered. He apologized profusely to all though Pemberton noted the old man's eyes were on Secretary Albright as he spoke. Albright stood and offered his hand.

"No need to apologize, Mr. Wilkie," Albright said as they shook. "It's good to finally meet you in person. Henry Stimson speaks highly of you as both a businessman and a gentleman."

"That's kind of him to say," Wilkie replied. "Henry and I go back many years, all the way to Princeton."

"I'm a Princeton man myself, Mr. Wilkie," Davis said, offering his hand as well.

Pemberton spoke before Wilkie could respond.

"We are very busy, gentlemen, so please tell us about your proposition."

"Very well, then," Albright said, as Wilkie took his seat. "The initial price we offered Boston Lumber Company for its 34,000 acres was, I admit, too low, and with the generous help of Mr. Rockefeller we can make a far more substantial offer."

"How much?" Pemberton asked.

"Six hundred and eighty thousand."

"Our price is eight hundred thousand," Pemberton said.

"But the land has been appraised at six hundred and eighty thousand," Davis objected. "This country is in a potentially long-term depression. In this market our offer's more than fair."

"What about my eighteen thousand acres?" Harris asked.

"Thirty-six thousand, Mr. Harris," Davis said. "That's two dollars an acre, and, as with Boston Lumber, a substantial increase on our initial offer."

"Not nearly good enough," Harris replied.

"But think how much you already have profited here," Webb said with exasperation. "Can't you give something back to the people of this region?"

Serena raised her index finger to her chin, held it there a moment as if bemused.

"Why is this pretense necessary, gentlemen?" she said. "We know what's going on with these land grabs. You've already run two thousand farmers off their land, that's according to your own census. We can't make people work for us and we can't buy their land unless they want to sell it, yet you force them from their livelihood and their homes."

Davis was about to speak but Albright raised his hand. The Secretary's visage achieved a profound solemnity Pemberton suspected was an innate talent of undertakers as well as career diplomats.

"An unfortunate aspect of what has to be done," Albright said. "But like Mr. Webb, I believe it's ultimately for the common good of all people in these mountains."

"And therefore all should sacrifice equally, correct?" Serena said.

"Certainly," Albright agreed, and as he did so Davis grimaced.

Serena took a sheaf of papers from her pocket and placed them on the table.

"This is part of the bill passed by the Tennessee legislature. In it are provisions stating that a number of wealthy landowners will be exempt from eminent domain. They get to keep their land, even though it's inside your proposed park. Perhaps your *New York Times* reporter can do an article about that."

"We had to have their support at that time," Davis replied. "If we hadn't, the park would have been doomed from the start. That was 1927, not today."

"We expect nothing more than to be treated like other wealthy landowners," Serena said.

"That just can't be done now," Davis said, shaking his head.

"Can't or won't?" Harris jeered.

"We'll get this land either way," Davis said, his voice now strident, "and if it's by eminent domain you'll be lucky to get half what we're offering now."

Albright gave a deep sigh and leaned back.

"No final answer is needed today," he said, looking at Buchanan and Wilkie, who'd been silent during the exchange. "Discuss it among yourselves. And consider the fact that Mr. Rockefeller is a businessman like all of you, yet he has given five million dollars. Think about how little in comparison we're asking of Boston Lumber Company."

Buchanan nodded. "We'll certainly discuss the matter."

"Yes," Wilkie said. "We appreciate your coming all this way to talk to us personally."

"My pleasure," Albright said and raised his hands, palms open in a gesture of mollification. "As I said, nothing need be decided today. We'll be in Tennessee this weekend but back in Asheville Monday. We're beginning negotiations with your fellow timberman, Colonel Townsend. His Elkmont tract has more virgin hardwoods than any land in the Smokies, yet we're offering you the same price per acre as him."

"He's taking your offer seriously?" Serena said.

"Very much so," Davis said. "He's smart enough to know a small profit is better than a big loss."

Secretary Albright stood and the rest of the delegation rose as well. Wilkie and Buchanan accompanied them as they walked back to the train.

"A total waste of time," Harris complained on the office porch.

"I disagree, Mr. Harris," Serena said. "We may have learned about a tract we can invest in together."

"Ah," the older man said, his smile broadening enough to show glints of gold. "That would be something, wouldn't it? Buying Townsend's land out from under them would really throw a monkey wrench in this park business."

Harris paused and watched as the train pulled out and headed back to Waynesville. He took out his car keys, jangled them loosely in his palm before enclosing them in his fist, mimicking a throw of the dice.

"Let's get it in touch with Townsend. They've mined copper on that tract. I don't know how much, but I can find out. This could be a boon for both of us, virgin hardwoods for you and copper for me."

Harris walked out to his Studebaker and drove off. As Pemberton and Serena walked toward the stable, Pemberton saw Buchanan and Wilkie lingered beside the tracks though the train had disappeared over McClure Ridge.

"I believe Buchanan's wavering."

"No, he's not wavering" Serena said. "He's already decided."

"How do you know?"

"His eyes. He wouldn't look our way, not once." Serena smiled. "You men notice so little, Pemberton. Physical strength is your gender's sole advantage."

Pemberton and Serena stepped inside the stable, pausing a moment to let their eyes adjust. The Arabian stamped his foot impatiently at Serena's approach. She unlatched the wooden door and led the gelding out.

"Wilkie wasn't as resolute as he usually is either," Pemberton said.

"Hardly," Serena said. "They stroked him like a housecat and he purred."

She paused and lifted the saddle, placed it below the horse's withers.

"So if Buchanan sides against us," Pemberton said, "you believe Wilkie could be swayed as well?"

"Yes."

"So what should we do?"

Serena led the Arabian to the mounting block and handed the reins to Pemberton.

"We'll rid ourselves of Buchanan."

She strapped the gauntlet on her right forearm and opened the adjacent stall where the eagle waited quiet and unmoving as a soldier at attention. It's a Berkute, Serena had told Pemberton the week after the creature arrived, much like the golden eagles she and her father hunted with in Colorado, only bigger and stronger, more fierce. The Kazakhs hunted wolves with them, and Serena had claimed Berkutes attacked even snow leopards given the opportunity. Looking at the eagle's huge talons and muscled keel, Pemberton believed it possible.

Serena emerged from the stall, the bird on her arm. She stepped onto the mounting block, then slipped her left foot in the stirrup and swung onto the saddle. Serena's legs and hips clinched the horses saddled midsection as she balanced herself. It was a deft maneuver, equal parts strength and agility. The eagle raised its wings a moment, resettled them as if also balancing itself.

"Are you still hunting with Harris Sunday?" Serena asked.

"Yes."

"Ask Buchanan to come along as well. Tell him it'll give the two of you a chance to discuss the Secretary's offer. On the way out there, talk to Harris some more about the Townsend land, maybe also mention the Jackson Country tract Luckadoo called you about. You probably won't have a chance to talk afterward."

Because? Pemberton almost said, but then understood. Serena stared fixedly at Pemberton, her pupils waxing in the barn's muted light.

"I need to get that second skidder up and running Sunday morning, but I could join you in the afternoon. I can do it, if you want me to."

"No. I'll do it."

"Another time for me, then," Serena said.

Fifteen

THE PARTY GATHERED SUNDAY MORNING IN FRONT of the commissary. Galloway suggested they hunt an abandoned homestead at the headwaters of Cook Creek, an apple orchard that had drawn game all winter. Fresh tracks showed plenty of deer yet lingered. Enough to draw any panther that might be around, Galloway had added, and told Pemberton to carry the twenty-dollar gold piece in his front pocket, just in case. Vaughn and Galloway and the hounds rode in the wagon while the other men followed on horseback.

The hunting party crossed Noland Mountain and then Indian Ridge, moving beyond the last timbered land. Buchanan and Harris rode side by side. Pemberton followed. Woods soon surrounded them, newly fallen leaves softening the trail. A few large hardwoods caught Pemberton's eye, but much of what they passed through was white pine and fir, near a creek a stand of river birch. Pemberton noted as much to Buchanan, who only nodded in response, his gaze fixed ahead of him. They began their descent into the gorge. The trail followed a creek, and Harris' eyes scanned the bedding of the exposed rock.

"Think there might be something of value here?" Pemberton asked.

"Up top there was granite, maybe enough for a quarry, but this is more interesting."

Harris tethered his horse to a sycamore and stepped across the creek. He ran his finger across the lighter color streaking an outcrop.

"Copper," Harris said, "though impossible to say how much without some blasting and sediment samples."

"But not coal?" Pemberton asked.

"Wrong side of the Appalachians," Harris said. "The Allegheny plateau, that's where the coal is. You have to go to Pennsylvania to find any on the eastern slopes."

Harris kneeled on the creek bank and used his fingers to sift through sand and silt. He picked out a few small stones, examined each a moment before flicking it into the water.

"Looking for something special?" Pemberton asked.

"No," Harris replied, and stood up, brushing wet sand off his corduroy breeches.

"I talked to Colonial Townsend last night," Pemberton said as the older man remounted. "He's as willing to sell to us as to Albright."

"Good," Harris said. "I know a geologist who's worked for Townsend. I'll have him send me a report."

"We also found nine thousand acres in Jackson County that looks promising, a recent foreclosure."

"Promising for *who*," Harris said brusquely. "That Glencoe Ridge tract was 'promising' as well, but only for you and your wife."

They rode on. The trail narrowed and they traveled single file behind the wagon, Buchanan first, then Pemberton. Harris trailed, still studying the landscape's geology. Buchanan wore a black split-tailed fox hunting coat ordered from London, and as they passed through the narrowest portion of the trail Pemberton kept his eyes on Buchanan's coat, using its dark cloth to better summon forth a picture of the past.

Buchanan's wedding had been at Saint Marks in downtown Boston. Unlike the Pembertons' civil ceremony, it had been a large and elegant affair, Buchanan and the groomsmen and the bride's father in tuxedos, the reception afterward at the Hotel Touraine. Buchanan and his bride had stood at the head of the receiving line as guests entered the ballroom. Pemberton had shaken his partner's hand and hugged Elizabeth. Pemberton recalled how small her waist had been as they embraced, an hourglass figure a recent photograph in Buchanan's office showed she'd retained.

Pemberton closed his eyes a moment, trying to raise an image of who'd been next in the receiving line. Buchanan's parents were dead, so it had to have been Elizabeth's parents. A dim face surfaced and then receded, nothing more than white hair and spectacles. Of the mother he could remember nothing, nor of Buchanan's siblings. Their lack of any lasting impression boded well, Pemberton realized. He'd always believed himself good at recognizing formidability in others.

"Your siblings, Buchanan," Pemberton said. "A brother and sister?"

Buchanan switched the reins to his right hand and turned.

"Two brothers," he said.

"And their occupations?"

"One teaches history at Dartmouth. The other is studying architecture in Scotland."

"And Mrs. Buchanan's father?" Pemberton asked. "What's his occupation?"

Buchanan did not answer. Instead he looked at Pemberton with a mixture of curiosity and suspicion. Harris listened as well and entered the conversation.

"Such reticence must mean he's a bootlegger or bawdy house owner, Pemberton. Whichever it is, I'll make every effort to sample his product the next time I'm in Boston."

"I'm sure it's nothing unseemly," Pemberton suggested. "I thought perhaps a banker or lawyer."

"He's a physician," Buchanan said tersely, not bothering to turn around as he spoke.

Pemberton nodded. The coming negotiations would be easier than expected, good news he'd soon enough share with Serena. He'd call Lawyer Covington tonight and have him prepare the necessary documents to make an offer for Buchanan's third interest. His right hand felt the rifle holstered to the saddle. One well-aimed shot. Then it would be just Serena and him.

Soon the trees fell away and the men entered an old pasture. Locust fence posts still stood, draping brown tendrils of barbed wire. Milking traces were faint but visible, indenting the slantland like the wide steps of some Aztec ruin. Though wisps of fog held fast to the coves and valleys, sunlight leaned into the pasture. The air was bracing, more reminiscent of fall than spring.

"A good day for a hunt," Harris said, glancing skyward. "I was afraid it might start raining again, but from the looks of it we'll be able to stay out until evening."

Pemberton agreed, though he knew they wouldn't be gone that long. He would be back with Serena by early afternoon. *Do this one thing,* he told himself, reciting the words like a mantra, as he'd done since he'd awakened at first light.

They splashed through Cook Creek and soon came to the homestead. No deer grazed the orchards, so Galloway and Vaughn unleashed the dogs and they moved in a swaying wave across the orchard, quickly into the deeper gorge. Vaughn unloaded the wagon and gathered wood for a cooking fire.

"We'll give Harris the upper orchard," Pemberton told Buchanan. "You and I can take the lower."

Pemberton and Buchanan walked to where the orchard ended at a sagging farmhouse, beside it a barn and well. The well bucket dangled from a rotting rope, a rusty dipper beside the well mouth. Pemberton dropped the dipper into the darkness, unsurprised when he heard no splash.

"You take this side," Pemberton said. "I'll be near the barn."

Pemberton walked a few paces, then stopped and turned.

"I almost forgot, Buchanan. Mrs. Pemberton wanted me to tell you that you are wrong about the origin of 'feathered into.'"

"How so?" Buchanan asked.

"She says the phrase is indeed from Britain. The feathers referred to are the fletching of an arrow. If you've feathered into your opponent, the arrow's so deep the feather itself has entered the body."

Buchanan gave a slight nod.

Pemberton walked on toward the barn, the smell of hay and manure yet lingering inside the gray wood. The front had collapsed but the back portion's spine remained level. From the side, the barn resembled the petrified remains of an immense kneeling animal. As Pemberton got closer, he saw something on the barn's back wall. Little more than withered rags of skin and fur held by rotting nails, but Pemberton knew what it was. He touched a tawny boll of fur.

Half an hour passed before the Redbones' long-spaced howls quickened. Shortly thereafter a deer came into Harris' shooting alley. He fired twice and a few moments later a buck staggered through the orchard's center row toward Pemberton and Buchanan. The animal was shot in the hindquarters, and when it fell Pemberton knew it would not get up. Buchanan stepped into the orchard.

"Save your bullet," Pemberton said. "The dogs will finish it off."

"I can afford the damn bullet," Buchanan said, pausing to glare at Pemberton.

Pemberton released his safety, the click so audible in the crisp morning air that for a moment he thought Buchanan might have heard. But Buchanan's eyes stayed on the deer. The buck's head lifted, dark eyes rolling. Its forelegs treaded the air, the torso flinging blood as the animal tried vainly to rise. Buchanan aimed but the deer's writhing allowed no clean head shot. He took off the fine English hunting jacket and set it behind him. Laid on the grass but nevertheless neatly folded, Pemberton noted, a man of propriety to the very end. Something about Buchanan's fastidiousness extinguished Pemberton's last misgiving.

Buchanan placed the barrel against the buck's skull, pressed hard enough to hold the deer's head still. Pemberton stepped into the apple orchard and aimed his rifle as well.

VAUGHN had gone ahead of the party, racing back to camp on Buchanan's horse although Doctor Cheney would only be able to confirm what Vaughn and the rest of the hunting party already knew. It was early afternoon when the wagon crested the last ridge and rolled into camp. The scene appeared almost Egyptian, Buchanan wrapped inside an oilcloth, the Plotts and Redbones gathered around the corpse like the animals of old pharaohs accompanying their master into the afterlife. Pemberton and Harris followed the wagon, Buchanan's black hunting jacket tied to the hitch-gate's top slat like a banner of mourning. The wagon halted in front of the office.

The procession had barely come to a stop when Frizzell's green pickup jolted up beside the commissary. Pemberton suspected the photographer had heard there'd been an accident and assumed the dead man a highlander. Doctor Cheney and Wilkie stepped off the office porch. Sheriff McDowell, who'd been sitting on the cane ash stump, got up and walked over to the wagon as well.

For a few moments the three men did nothing but stare at the shrouded body. Galloway came around and lifted the hitch-gate from its tracks and shooed the Plotts and Redbones off the wagon. When the last dog was out, Doctor Cheney climbed aboard. He unwrapped Buchanan's corpse so it lay face upward on the planked bed, then probed where the bullet had passed through the heart before shattering the spine. *Rifle,* Cheney said softly, as much to himself as McDowell. Doctor Cheney picked up something from the wagon bed, rubbed the blood from its oval shape to reveal a dull whiteness. Sheriff McDowell placed his hands on the wagon's sideboard and leaned forward.

"Is that a button?"

"No," Doctor Cheney said, "a piece of vertebrae."

Wilkie's face paled. Sheriff McDowell turned to Pemberton and Harris, who were still on their horses.

"Who shot him?"

"I did," Pemberton said. "He was in the orchard. He was supposed to be farther away, over by the barn. I wouldn't have shot otherwise."

"Anybody else with you?" Sheriff McDowell asked.

"No."

McDowell looked at the dead man.

"Interesting how your shot hit dead center in the heart. I'd call that a rather amazing accident."

"I would call it an especially unfortunate accident," Pemberton said.

The sheriff raised his eyes, looking not at Pemberton but at Serena, who watched from the Pembertons' porch, a boot she was polishing in her right hand, a rag dabbed black in the other.

"Mrs. Pemberton doesn't seem particularly distressed by the loss of your partner."

"It's not her nature to make outward shows of emotion," Pemberton said.

"What about you, Wilkie?" McDowell asked. "Any suspicions as to why your partner might be shot, other than an accident."

"None at all," Wilkie quickly said, then walked toward the office, stepping through a mud hole he seemed not to notice until his right pant cuff got soaked.

Sheriff McDowell pulled the oilcloth over Buchanan's head and torso, the legs alone visible. Several loggers had wandered over to look into the wagon. They stared at Buchanan's corpse impassively.

"Put his body on the train," McDowell told the loggers. "I'm going to have an autopsy done."

As the men lifted the corpse out of the wagon, the sheriff looked over at Galloway, who stood amid the hounds.

"You got anything to add?"

"It was an accident," Galloway said.

"How do you know that?" McDowell asked.

Galloway nodded at Pemberton, baring a grin toothless but for a few nubs of brown and yellow.

"He ain't a good enough shot to do it on purpose."

McDowell turned to Vaughn, who had not moved from the buckboard. The youth looked frightened.

"What about you, Joel?"

"No sir," Vaughn said, looking at the floorboard when he spoke. "I stayed with the horses and wagon."

"Anything else, Sheriff?" Pemberton asked.

McDowell did not acknowledge the comment, but in a few moments he got in his car and left. Galloway herded the dogs back into the wagon bed. He took the reins from Vaughn and followed the police car's dusty wake out of the camp. Doctor Cheney lingered a few more moments, then walked toward his house. As Pemberton turned to join Wilkie on the porch, he saw the photographer's truck had left as well.

Wilkie sat in a ladderback chair. He dabbed his forehead with a blue silk handkerchief that was usually no more than an ornament. Pemberton joined Wilkie on the porch, pulling up a chair in front of his partner.

"It must give you pause to see someone three decades younger die so suddenly," Pemberton said. "As a matter of fact, I'd think it would persuade you to sell your third interest and go back to Boston, live out what time you have left in comfort instead of in these inhospitable mountains."

Pemberton shifted the chair closer, their knees touching now. Pemberton could smell the shaving cream mailed from Boston each month, see a small razor nick just below Wilkie's left ear lobe.

"Perhaps you were already thinking something similar when the politicians were courting you Thursday morning."

Wilkie looked not at Pemberton but at the silk handkerchief in his lap. The old man's gnarly fingers rubbed the cloth as if fascinated with its texture. It was an oddly childlike gesture, and Pemberton wondered if Wilkie was succumbing to dotage at that very moment.

"Mrs. Pemberton and I will pay half of what the park service offered for your share."

"Half?" Wilkie said, the proposal's unjustness rousing him to meet Pemberton's eyes.

"It's more than enough to live out your remaining years in comfort. Think of it as a kind of eminent domain."

"But half," Wilkie said, his voice teetering between dismay and anger.

The old man looked past Pemberton at a cur come down from one of the stringhouses. The dog hunched where the wagon had been, its long tongue licking dust moistened by Buchanan's blood. Another cur came, sniffed the ground and began licking as well.

"All right," Wilkie said bitterly.

"We'll draw the papers up this evening," Pemberton said. "Doctor Cheney is a notary and Campbell can be a witness. I'll have Campbell take the papers to Lawyer Covington tonight. We can have the complete transaction done at Covington's office tomorrow. And a handshake, of course. We are, after all gentlemen, even here in this forsaken landscape."

Pemberton offered his hand. Wilkie raised his also, but very slowly, as if lifting some invisible weight. The old man's palm was moist, and he made no effort to match Pemberton's confident grip.

Pemberton left Wilkie on the porch. He walked across the yard to the house and went inside. He found Serena looking out the back room's window at the stumps and slash that covered a quarter-mile before rising upwards to the ridge crest. Her boots dried in the corner on a piece of newspaper. The gray cotton stockings she wore were pulled off as well. In the muted light, Serena's feet and ankles shown pale as alabaster.

Pemberton came and stood behind her, placed his arms around her waist, his head leaned close to hers. Serena did not turn but eased back into him. He felt the curve of her hips against his groin, and desire seemed to fill not only his body but the whole room. The air felt charged with some small but discernable electrical current. What light slanted through the window gave the room a honeyed tinge.

"So it's done," Serena said, her right hand taking his and pressing it to her thigh.

"Yes."

"And the sheriff?"

"Suspicious, but he has no proof or witness to show it wasn't an accident."

"And our senior partner's agreed to sell his share?"

Pemberton nodded.

"What did you learn about Buchanan's siblings?"

"One's a student, the other a professor."

"Good news all around," Serena said, staring out the window. "You'll have to spend more time at the saw mill, at least at first, but we'll promote a foreman and hire a few new men. From what I've heard, it's the foremen who have run the day-to-day operation, even when Wilkie and Buchanan were there. Campbell can help eventually, but first he needs to walk the Jackson County land, Townsend's tract as well."

Serena's hand slid down a few inches, her fingers molding his to the curve of her thigh. Serena's gold band settled over Pemberton's. The current he'd felt since entering the room intensified, as if the touching gold provided a conduit for the energy to flow directly through Serena into him. Part of Pemberton ached to move his hand so he could lead her to the bed, but another part did not want to move, even slightly, lest the touching bands separated and the current became more diffuse. Serena seemed to feel the same energy, because her hand remained where it was. She shifted slightly, pressed her body deeper into his.

"You didn't shoot him in the back, did you?"

"No," Pemberton said.

"I knew you wouldn't. But concerns like that don't matter. We're beyond them, Pemberton."

"He's dead," Pemberton replied. "That's all that matters. It's over and done with and we've got all we wanted."

"At least for today," Serena said. "A start, a true beginning."

Pemberton bowed his head, smelled the French cologne he'd ordered at Christmas, which Serena wore only after her evening bath and only at his behest. He let its smell, the touch of his lips against her neck, overwhelm everything else.

Serena lifted her hand from Pemberton's and stepped out of his embrace. She began to undress, letting her clothes fall to the floor. When Serena was completely naked, she turned and pressed her body full against his. The pants he wore were still damp from helping carry Buchanan to the wagon, and when Serena stepped back Pemberton saw a thin smear of red on her lower stomach. Serena saw it as well but did not go to the bathroom for a washcloth.

Pemberton sat on the bed and took off his boots and clothes. He reached to open the lamp table's drawer for a condom, but Serena grasped his wrist, settled his hand firm against her hip.

"It's time to make our heir," Serena said.

Sixteen

THE PREVIOUS DECEMBER, BUCHANAN HAD suggested all the workers be given Christmas presents. If for no other reason a matter of morale, he'd argued to Pemberton and Wilkie, so Campbell, who'd been put in charge of the buying, went to Waynesville on Christmas Eve, taking Vaughn with him. This Christmas, on his own volition, Campbell did the same. He and Vaughn loaded a flat car with all manner of gifts from Scott's General Store, stopping at the saw mill to retrieve items purchased earlier. Once the train returned to camp, the flat car's bounty filled makeshift shelves on the commissary porch. Campbell and Vaughn unloaded and arranged the gifts, finishing well after midnight. Come morning, the camp's employees ascended the commissary porch. Campbell had chosen the gifts with a wide sympathy of taste and imagination, ordering what he could not find in Scott's General Store from the Sears, Roebuck catalogue and a Soco Gap moonshiner, so the workers had much to choose from with their fifty-cent allowance. Those with children came up first. Because Campbell wouldn't allow it otherwise, these men spent at least half their portion lightening the shelf that held licorice whips and oranges, another shelf of dolls and teddy bears and pop guns, bright-metal toy cars and toy train engines. While Vaughn checked off names, Campbell tabulated each worker's allotment in his head.

The rest of the workers came next and chose from fishing lines and fish hooks, hats more rakish than pragmatic, cigarette papers and pipes and jackknives and, placed discretely on a bottom shelf, pint jars of moonshine. On another set of shelves, items for wives and girlfriends and the women in the kitchen—lengths of calico and lace, scarves and perfume, hair braids and bracelets. Strewn among these more traditional offerings were Campbell's more esoteric choices. These gifts were singular in nature, a teakwood flute, a pair of red-and-green baseball stockings, a jigsaw puzzle of the United States. Though the workers could, not one ventured into the commissary itself, lest they be tempted to use their fifty cents in trade to acquire something more utilitarian, such as gloves or step-ins, a new axe head or wool socks. They instead wandered the porch, lifting one item, possessing it a moment, and then setting it aside to pick up another. An occasional quarter was flipped in the air, caught, and slapped on the back of the hand, leaving the final decision to some other power.

By mid-morning the shelves were half empty, yet there was a steady traffic up and down the porch steps, among them workers brought by train from Waynesville, occupants of the stringhouses who decided a few rare hours of extra sleep worth a more desirous gift. Snipes and his crew had been among the early arrivals. Except for Stewart, who'd left to eat a Christmas meal at Preacher McIntyre's house, the crew remained, watching the comings and goings from the dining hall's porch steps. Their gifts were already on display. Snipes' red-and-green baseball stockings sprouted out of his brogans to cover his overalls up to his knees. Dunbar donned his felt hat that, though a dusty brown, had a rakish tilt to its brim. Ross had chosen the moonshine, most of which now smoldered in his stomach.

Ross raised his pint jar and took another swallow. His eyes watered and his lips made a fleshy O as he vigorously exhaled a plume of white breath.

"I'm ever amazed Santy Claus had the grit to come to this camp," he said, "especially after what happened to Buchanan."

"He wouldn't have if it hadn't been for Campbell just up and doing it without asking," Snipes said.

"They'd of fired any other man but him for that," Dunbar noted, "buying them gifts without asking, I mean."

"He knows they need him more than ever with Buchanan and Wilkie gone," Ross said. "Campbell's a good man but he's nobody's fool, and he's going to look after his own hide when it starts getting scorched."

"Still," Dunbar said, "there's not many a overseer would have done this for us."

"I'd not argue against that," Ross conceded.

The men turned their gazes to the commissary porch, where Rachel Harmon was setting her gifts before Campbell.

"Looks to be she picked nothing but denim cloth and a play-pretty for her young one," Snipes said. "I remember last year she got good-smelling soap and a fancy hair-bow."

"She was giggling and acting silly with them other kitchen girls all the while," Dunbar said, "but she don't look to be giggling much these days."

"Having a child and no daddy tends to take the giggle out of a gal," Ross said.

"You'd think Pemberton would own up to it and help her out some," Dunbar said. "I don't see how a man can do something like that and not tote a lot of guilt."

"I'd say maybe his missus has some say in that," Ross surmised.

"There's one fellow that / treats her good, though," Dunbar said, as Joel Vaughn came up the steps.

The crew watched as Vaughn spoke to Rachel Harmon a moment

before giving her a toy train engine, its bright metal catching the late-morning light. Vaughn and the Harmon girl talked a little longer before she left, the toy train engine placed in the poke with what she'd selected. For a few minutes, the commissary porch was vacant but for Campbell and Vaughn. Dunbar turned to the dining hall's wide window and apprised himself in his new haberdashery.

"This one's got some pert to it," he said, "but I still wish it had a bright-yallar hatband."

"If it did, Snipes might have snatched it up," Ross said. "That's all you got left needing brightening now, ain't it, Snipes, your head?"

"That and my brogans."

Dunbar tilted the brim a little more and sat back down.

"What do you reckon Galloway got from Santy Claus?" Dunbar asked. "A set of fangs to go with them rattles he's wearing atop his head?"

"Maybe some rat poison for to season his victuals," Snipes suggested.

"That's what I probably ought to have got instead of this hat," Dunbar said. "Since the cold's settled in the rats has pretty much laid claim to my stringhouse. You'd think they was having a revival the way they're packing in."

"Wouldn't do no good," Ross said. "I used some of that Paris Green in my stringhouse and it's the stoutest poison going. Them rats ate it like it was no more than salt on popcorn."

"What about them traps at the commissary you bait with cheese?" Dunbar asked. "You all tried them?"

"These is some bully rats," Ross said. "They'd likely haul the traps down to the commissary and turn them back in for a rebate, same as you would a sody bottle."

"The thing to kill them is snakes," Snipes said, examining his boots as he spoke, "but that eagle has done upset what the Orientals call the yen and the yang."

"What does that mean?" Dunbar asked.

"The way things is balanced. Everything in the world has its natural place, and if you take something out or put something in that ought not be out or in, everything gets lopsided and out of sorts."

"Kindly like not having different seasons," Dunbar said.

"Exactly. If you was to have just winter all year round we'd freeze, and if it was summer all year the water would dry up and your crops die."

"I wouldn't mind spring all year round," Dunbar said. "It's warm but there's rain, and everything's sprouting and feeling alive, the birds all a-singing."

"That'd be the problem," Snipes said. "You'd have too much aliveness. Everything would be sprouting all the time, and pretty soon there'd be trees and vines and grass covering every inch of the earth. You'd need your axe every morning just to whittle you out a place to stand up."

Ross finished the last of his moonshine and raised his gaze to take in the gray and brown valley floor, the scalped ridges of Noland Mountain.

"So what happens when there ain't nothing left alive at all?" he asked.

THE next morning the camp returned to its normal work schedule. Some men were rested and some were hungover and some a bit of both. Serena went out with a crew working on Indian Ridge. She was pregnant, though none in the camp other than Pemberton knew it. When he'd asked if she should risk riding a horse, she'd smiled and told him any child of theirs could stand a little jostling.

Harris called the office in the early afternoon. He'd been out of state for two weeks and returned to find a telegram from Albright chastising Harris and the Pembertons for pursuing the Townsend tract, especially since the park was inevitable, as was eminent domain for those unwilling to sell.

"He's given up being a diplomat," Harris seethed. "Thinks if he bares his teeth we'll roll over and show our belly the same way Champion did. Luckadoo at the Savings and Loan had a message for me too. He said Webb and Kephart have been over there inquiring about that Jackson

County tract you like. God knows what that's about, but it can't be good."

After Harris hung up, Pemberton went to the stable and rode east toward Indian Ridge. As he rode through the camp, Pemberton saw a few wreaths yet adorned the stringhouses. Some of the highlanders considered the true Christmas to be on January fourteenth. Old Christmas, they called it, believing it was the day the magi visited the Christ child. Another tidbit Buchanan had written in his notebook. Remembering the notebook brought with it a memory of the man, but only for a few moments before Pemberton turned his thoughts to Serena and the life she held within her.

He found her with a crew helping to build a new spur line, the four of them contemplating a massive white oak that blocked the rail path. Serena made a final suggestion and rode over to Pemberton. Pemberton told her about the telegram.

"If the park's inevitable, Albright wouldn't bother," Serena said. "Townsend's tract must be more valuable to them than they want us to know, probably because of those virgin hardwoods. They'll use them to sway the public the same way Muir used his redwoods in Yosemite. Let them keep blustering and we'll keep cutting."

A momentary silence fell over the nearby woods as the lead cutter finished his notching and stepped away. The two sawyers kneeled on the frozen ground where yesterday's snow lingered, between them the twelve-foot cross-cut saw used only on the biggest trees. As they lifted the saw to slide into the notching, the afternoon sun fell full upon the polished blade, and it appeared the steel was being forged anew to confront the white oak. Serena and Pemberton watched as the men gained their rhythm after a few slips and catches. The crew foreman raised his hand and signaled to Serena that whatever problem had confounded the crew had been surmounted.

"Webb and Kephart came by the Savings and Loan," Pemberton said. "Luckadoo told Harris they were inquiring about the Jackson County tract. For more park land, Harris thinks. Harris said they're starting to believe they can do anything."

Serena had been watching the sawyers, but she turned to Pemberton now.

"But that makes no sense when all the other park land's at least twenty miles away."

"Let them do what they like over there," Pemberton said. "Campbell claims Townsend's land is the better buy for us. Anyway, Harris is so flummoxed about this park that he may be completely wrong about Webb and Kephart's inquiry."

"But they are growing more confident," Serena said, watching the cross-cut's blade work its way into the heartwood. "Harris is right about that."

Seventeen

ON THE FIRST SUNDAY OF THE NEW YEAR, THE Pembertons and Harris drove east toward Jackson County to look at the land Waynesville Savings and Loan had repossessed six months before, land Harris suddenly insisted on seeing before committing to the Townsend tract. Harris sat in the backseat, using a wool overcoat and a flask of whiskey to keep himself warm. Sleet had fallen the day before, and though now only drizzle smudged the windshield, scabs of ice lingered on bridges and curves where cliff hangs shaded the blacktop. Pemberton drove cautiously, staying in the road's center whenever possible, all the while wishing Serena hadn't insisted on coming.

Harris leaned forward and offered the flask but the Pembertons declined. Harris slipped the flask back into his pocket and took out the Wednesday edition of the *Asheville Citizen*, began to read aloud.

"While our attention to the creation of a national park is crucial to our region's future, we must also act as a state to secure our own immense but threatened natural beauty. The recent foreclosure on 9,000 acres of farmland in the Caney Creek region of Jackson County, while tragic for those who owned that land, offers a rare opportunity to buy a tract as pristine as any in our region and at a very reasonable price. This hidden jewel is rich in hardwoods and sparkling streams, as well as a profusion of plant and animal life. Mr. Horace Kephart, our region's leading authority on these matters, believes the acreage is as rich in natural resources as any he's seen in southern Appalachia. Nevertheless, Mr. Kephart argues that the time to act is now. Because of the land's proximity to Franklin, the property is beginning to receive interest from speculators who have no concern for western North Carolina other than lining their own pocketbooks. Since North Carolina, like the rest of this country, has its monetary resources stretched to the limit, now is the time for our state's wealthier inhabitants to take the lead and contribute to a legacy not only for themselves but for all North Carolinians."

Harris folded the paper and slapped it against the seat.

"I knew those bastards were up to something like this. Webb and Kephart came back to the Savings and Loan Friday. They were being damn coy about it, but Luckadoo thinks someone around here is interested in helping them, someone with a lot of money."

"Who could that be?" Pemberton asked.

"I think it's Cornelia Vanderbilt and that English fop husband of hers Cecil," Harris said. "Her fool mother gave 5,000 acres for that Pisgah Forest, so this kind of silliness runs in the family. Plus, they're friends with Rockefeller."

Harris paused long enough to sip from the flask, his ire mounting.

"It's got to be them," he fumed. "No one else has that kind of money. Why can't they just play king and queen in their goddamn castle and keep out of other people's business. All of them, from Webb to Rockefeller, they're nothing but Bolsheviks. They won't be satisfied until the government owns every acre in these mountains."

"When people finally realize it comes down to jobs or a pretty view, they'll come around," Pemberton said.

"Jobs or a pretty view," Harris said. "I like that. We can suggest that as a caption for Webb's next editorial. I assume you saw his so-called open letter to Colonel Townsend?"

"We saw it," Serena said, "but Townsend's a smart enough businessman not to be swayed by Webb's doggerel or Albright's threats."

"I should have stopped this park nonsense in 1926 when it started," Harris said. "If I didn't have so much money tied up in new machinery, I'd buy both of these tracts, just to spite all of them."

"Despite Webb's flowery description, I doubt this land can beat Townsend's," Pemberton said.

"Perhaps," Harris said, "but it's worth a couple of hours to check it, especially if some folks in Franklin are nosing around. They tend to have little interest in anything this far north."

Harris sipped again from the flask and stuffed it back in his coat pocket. The sun broke through the low clouds. Only for a little while, Pemberton suspected, but maybe enough to melt some of the ice on the blacktop, make the return trip easier. After a while, they came to a crossroads. Pemberton braked and checked a hand-drawn map Luckadoo had given him months before. He gave the map to Serena and turned right. The road made a wide curve, and soon the Tuckaseegee River appeared on the left. The water looked smooth and slow moving, as if the cold made the river sluggish. The river began to bend toward the road, and a metal one-lane bridge appeared before them. Another automobile came toward the bridge from the opposite direction. As they got closer, Pemberton saw the car was a Pierce-Arrow.

"That's that son-of-a-bitch Webb's car," Harris spat. "If we meet on the bridge, bump it into the water."

The two vehicles appeared about to arrive on the bridge simultaneously when the Pierce-Arrow braked. The bridge's iron frame shuddered as the Packard drove on across.

"Stop," Harris told Pemberton.

Pemberton eased up beside the Pierce-Arrow. Webb was not alone. Kephart sat beside the newspaperman, looking badly hungover, his eyes bloodshot, hair uncombed. He huddled inside a frayed mackinaw, a pair of soggy boots in his lap. Kephart stared straight ahead, no doubt envying his companion's expensive wool Ulster overcoat. Harris rolled down his window and Webb did the same.

"Didn't expect to see anyone else out on the road today," Webb said. "What brings you and your confederates to Jackson County?"

"Just checking out a tip on some good land," Harris said. "Not that it's any of your goddamn business."

"I'd argue it's the people of North Carolina's business," Webb replied.

"We are North Carolina business, you dumb shit," Harris said. "When people in this state are grubbing up roots in your parks to keep from starving, they'll realize it too and start using those trees of yours for hangings. You can pass that on to your friends as well, tell them they'd better get a moat and a drawbridge to go with their castle."

"I have no idea what you're talking about," Webb said.

"No, of course you don't. Just as I'm sure there's no reason you happen to be in Jackson County this morning."

"There's a reason," Webb replied, and lifted a Hawkeye camera from the seat. "Kephart knew where an especially impressive waterfall was, so he took some photographs. I'm putting one on the front page tomorrow."

"Looks like he got wet doing it," Harris said, nodding at Kephart's boots. "Too bad he didn't fall and drown."

"Nice to stop and chat," Webb said, already rolling his window up, "but we've got a busy week ahead."

Webb released his hand brake and the Pierce-Arrow clattered on across the bridge.

"Waterfalls," Harris muttered.

They passed a thick stand of hickory and ash, then a pasture where a single birch tree rose in the center, its silver bark peeling from the trunk like papyrus. Beside the tree, a salt lick and wooden trough. The road came to an abrupt end at the farmhouse and they got out. A foreclosure notice was nailed to the front door. *Hoover can go to Hell* scrawled across it in what looked to be charcoal. A sense of recent habitation lingered—stacked poplar in the woodpile, on the porch a cloth sack of pumpkin seeds, a cane pole with line and hook. A dipper hung in a branch over the creek, reflecting the midday light like a crow-scat.

"They were up here," Harris said, pointing to a set of fresh tire prints.

Harris reached down and lifted a couple of stones from beside the tire's indention, examined them a moment and tossed them back on the ground. He picked up a smaller stone and looked at it more carefully.

"Looks like it could have some copper in it," he said, and placed it in his pocket.

Serena ascended the porch steps and peered through a window.

"It looks like solid oak all the way through," she said approvingly. "If we knocked down some walls, this could be used for a dining hall."

"Meet back here at five?" Harris asked.

"Fine," Pemberton said. "Just make sure you don't lose track of time contemplating the beauty of Kephart's waterfall."

"I'll make sure I don't," Harris said grimly, "though I may piss in it."

Harris tucked his pant cuffs into his boots and walked up the creek, quickly disappeared inside a green tangle of rhododendron. Pemberton and Serena followed a trail up the ridge. The mid-afternoon sun was out, spreading cold light across the slope. Last week's snow lingered beneath the bigger trees, and a springhead they stepped over was cauled by ice. Pemberton walked slowly and made Serena do the same. At the top they could see the entire tract, including a section where several towering chestnuts rose.

"Campbell's right," Pemberton said. "A good deal at twenty an acre."

"But still not as good as Townsend's price," Serena said, "especially with the expense of building a trestle over the river. That's slow work as well, and you always lose some men."

"I hadn't thought of that."

Serena placed a hand on her coat where the wool cloth covered her stomach. Pemberton nodded at a boulder smooth and flat as a bench.

"Sit down and rest."

"Only if you do as well," Serena said.

They sat and gazed out at the vast unfold of mountains, some razed but many more yet uncut. The Tuckaseegee flowed to the west, low drifts of fog obscuring the banks. To the far north, Mount Mitchell pressed against a low graying sky that promised snow. A skein of blue smoke rose from nearer woods, probably a hunter's campfire.

Pemberton reached out, placed his hand inside Serena's coat and laid his palm lightly on her stomach, held it there a few moments. Serena gave him a wry smile but did not remove his hand, instead placed her hand on top of his, her words whitened by the cold as she spoke.

"The world lies all before us, Pemberton."

"Yes," Pemberton agreed, looking out on the vista. "As far as we can see."

"Farther," Serena said. "Brazil. Mahogany forests the same quality as Cuba's, except we'll have them all to ourselves. There's not a single timber company in operation there, just rubber plantations."

It was the first time Serena had spoken in any detail about Brazil since they'd left Boston, and Pemberton now, as then, responded to Serena's fancy with good-humored irony.

"Amazing how no one else has ever thought of harvesting those trees."

"They have," Serena said, "but they're too timid. There are no roads. Miles that miles that never have been mapped. A country big as the United States, and it will be ours."

"We have to finish what we've started here first," Pemberton said.

"Investors' money we raise for Brazil can help us finish quicker here as well."

Pemberton said nothing more. They waited a while longer, silent as they watched the afternoon wane before them, then slowly walked down the ridge, Pemberton stepping ahead of Serena where the ground was icy, holding her arm. It was almost five when they got to the farmhouse, but Harris was still off scouring the creek and outcrops.

"His being gone this long," Serena said as they waited on the porch steps. "Surely that's a sign he's found something."

As though summoned by Serena's words, Harris emerged from the rhododendron. His boots were clotted with mud, and cuts on his hand showed he'd fallen. But as he stepped across the creek an enigmatic smile rose beneath his clipped moustache.

"So what do you think, Harris?" Pemberton asked as they drove back to camp.

"For my interests this tract's better," Harris replied. "Not by much, but enough to sway me. There's definitely more kaolin here. Maybe some copper as well."

Serena turned toward the back seat.

"I wish we could say the same about this tract, but Campbell's right. There's some good lumber but not nearly the hardwoods Townsend's has."

"Maybe we can get Luckadoo to lower the Saving and Loan's price to fifteen an acre," Harris said, "especially if we offer to close quickly."

"Maybe," Serena said, "but ten an acre would be better."

"I'll talk to him tomorrow," Harris said. "I suspect we can get the price down."

It was after seven when they got back to camp. Pemberton pulled in front of the office where Harris had parked his Studebaker. The older man departed the back seat slowly, due more to the empty flask than his age.

"Want to eat something before you go back to Waynesville?" Pemberton asked.

"Hell yes," Harris said. "All the scampering up and down that creek has given me the appetite of a horse."

Pemberton looked at Serena and saw that her eyes were heavy lidded.

"Why don't you go on to the house and rest. I'll get Harris fed, then bring our dinner."

Serena nodded and left. Though it was seven, the lights were on in the dining hall. From inside the building's walls, a ragged choir sang "Thy Might Set Fast the Mountains."

"We let Bolick hold evening services around Christmas and New Year's," Pemberton said. "I find it worth a few dollars of electricity to keep the workers Godly, though I will get a less bothersome camp preacher next time."

Harris nodded. "A great business investment, religion. I'll take it over government bonds anytime."

Pemberton and Harris stepped onto the side porch and opened the door. The kitchen was deserted, despite pots left on the grange stove, soiled dishes piled beside the fifty-gallon hoop barrels filled with gray water. Pemberton nodded toward the main hall's doorway, where Bolick's sonorous voice had replaced the singing.

"I'm going to get a cook and server."

"I'll go with you," Harris said. "Get my yearly dose of religion."

The men went into the back of the hall, their boot steps resonant on the puncheon floor. Workers and their families filled the benches set before the long wooden tables, women and children in front, men in the rear. Reverend Bolick stood behind two nailed-together vegetable crates that raised a rickety altar. Laid upon it was a huge leather-bound Bible, wide pages sprawling off both sides of the wood.

Pemberton scanned the closest benches and found his cook, stepped into the makeshift aisle and motioned to the man. Pemberton moved past more tables and finally found a server, but the woman was so rapt that Pemberton was almost beside Bolick before he got her attention. The woman left her seat and made her way slowly through a bumpy aisle of knees and rumps. But Pemberton no longer looked at her.

The boy sat in his mother's lap, clothed in a gray bundling. He held a toy train engine in his hand, rolling the steel wheels up and down his leg with a solemn deliberateness. Pemberton studied the child's features intently. He'd grown immensely since the day of the photograph, but that was the least of it. More striking to Pemberton was how the face had become thinner, more defined, what had been wisps of hair now thick. Most of all the eyes dark as mahogany. Pemberton's eyes. Reverend Bolick stopped speaking and the dining hall became silent. The child quit rolling the train and looked up at the preacher, then at the larger man who stood close by. For a few moments the child stared directly at Pemberton.

The congregation shifted uneasily on the benches, many of their eyes on Pemberton as Reverend Bolick turned the Bible's wide pages in search of a passage. When Pemberton realized he was being watched, he made his way to the back of the hall where Harris and the kitchen workers waited.

"I thought for a minute you were about to go on up and deliver the sermon yourself," Harris said.

The cook and server went into the kitchen, but Harris and Pemberton lingered a few more moments. Bolick found the passage he'd been searching for and settled his eyes on Pemberton. For a few seconds the only sound was a spring-back knife's soft click as a worker prepared to pare his nails.

"From the book of Obadiah," Reverend Bolick said, and began reading. *The pride of thine heart hath deceived thee, thou that dwellest in the cleft of the rock, whose habitation is high, that saith in his heart, who shall bring me down.*

Harris smiled. "I believe the right reverend is addressing us."

"Come on," Pemberton said, and took a step toward the kitchen as Bolick continued to read.

Harris grasped Pemberton's arm.

"Don't you think we should hear the fellow out, Pemberton?"

"Serena's waiting for her dinner," Pemberton said tersely and pulled free from Harris' grip as Bolick finished the passage.

The preacher closed the Bible with a slow and profound delicacy as if the ink on the onionskin were susceptible to smearing.

"The word of the Lord," Reverend Bolick concluded.

After Harris had eaten and left, Pemberton went to the house with his and Serena's dinner. He set the dishes on the table and went to the back room. Serena was asleep and Pemberton did not wake her. Instead, he softly closed the bedroom door. Pemberton didn't go to the kitchen and eat but instead went to the hall closet and opened his father's steamer trunk. He rummaged through the stocks and bonds and various other legal documents until he found the cowhide-covered photograph album his aunt insisted he pack as well. He shut the trunk softly and walked down to the office.

Campbell was in the front room, working on the payroll. He left without a word when Pemberton said he wished to be alone. Orange and yellow embers glowed in the hearth, and he set kindling and a hefty ash log on the andirons. Pemberton felt the heat strengthen against his back as he took Jacob's photograph from the bottom drawer. The fire's rosy glow heightened and soon spilled over the desk's surface. Pemberton turned off the lamp's bunched electric light, thought for the first time in years of a parlor and its wide fireplace. His earliest memory was of that hearth, its warmth enclosing him like an invisible blanket, light flickering on the fireboard's marble fonts where strange men with wooly legs played flutes while long-haired women in swaying dresses danced. Whenever Pemberton had watched them long enough, the figures had begun to move in the wavering flames and shadows. As Pemberton carefully opened the photograph album, he had the sensation of entering an attic on a rainy day. The desiccated binding creaked with each turned cardboard page, releasing the smell of things long stashed away. When Pemberton found a photograph of himself as a two-year-old, he stopped turning.

Eighteen

SLEET FELL AGAIN IN THE MIDDLE OF THE night, but by morning the sky rose blue and unclouded. Ice clung to Noland Mountain's remaining hardwoods like brittle sleeves, a marvel of shifting hues when the sun shone full on them. Most of the workers shaded their eyes as they trudged into the upland, but a few held their gaze until their eyes burned from the glare, such was the beauty of it. By the time the last man made his ascent to the ridge, the warming ice had begun to slip free from the branches. Smaller pieces at first, tinkling like bells as they hit the frozen ground. Then came water-clear downfalls that quickly covered the understory, crackled and snapped beneath every footstep. Men walked through them as they would the remnants of a vast shattered mirror.

Pemberton had just set his coffee on the office desk when Harris called, his voice even more brusque than usual.

"Webb and Kephart made an offer on the Jackson County land," Harris said. "They came in soon as Luckadoo opened up, and they're willing to pay him full price."

"Were the Cecils with them?"

"Hell no. You think they'd deign to come down from their castle for something like this. They'll wait till it's over, have that goddamn waterfall named after them."

"But you still believe it's the Cecils behind all this?"

"It doesn't matter a dog's turd who is backing them," Harris shouted. "That son-of-a-bitch Luckadoo thinks Webb and Kephart have the money. He gave me a *courtesy* call."

"How far along with this are they?"

"They've co-signed everything for the down payment. All that's left is the transfer deed." Harris paused. "Damn it, I knew I should have called Luckadoo last night."

"It's a good tract but so is Townsend's," Pemberton said. "You said as much yourself yesterday."

"This is the tract I want."

Pemberton started to speak, then hesitated, unsure if he wanted to risk Harris' wrath being turned on him, but it was a question he and Serena needed answered.

"Are you sure you're not just wanting to spite Webb and Kephart?"

For a few moments Harris didn't respond. Pemberton could hear the older man's breath slow. When Harris spoke, his words were more measured but just as belligerent.

"If we don't do this deal, Pemberton, we never do one, and that includes Townsend's acreage."

"But if the transaction's gone this far . . ."

"We can still get the land if we pay off Luckadoo. That's the only reason he called me in the first place. It's just going to cost more."

"How much more?"

"Five hundred," Harris said. "Luckadoo's giving us an hour to make up our minds. Like I said, we do this deal or we never do another one. That's the way of it, so make up your mind."

"I'll have to talk to Serena first."

"Talk to her then," Harris said, lowering his voice for a moment. "She's smart enough to know what's best in your long-term interest."

"I'll call you back as soon as I can."

"You do that," Harris said. "And make damn sure *soon* is within an hour."

Pemberton hung up and walked to the stable. Serena was in the back stall with the eagle, her fingers reddened from the raw meat she fed the bird. He told her about the phone call. She fed the eagle a last piece of meat and placed the hood back over its head.

"We need Harris' money," Serena said. "We'll have to humor him, this time, but have Lawyer Covington put in the contract that Harris can't begin any mining operations until the site's timber is cut. Harris has found something up there besides kaolin and some copper, something he doesn't want us to know about. We'll hire our own geologist and find out what it is, then refuse to cut the timber until Harris gives us a percentage, a good percentage."

Serena stepped out of the stall. She handed Pemberton the tin plate and lifted the wooden latch, closed the stall door. A few stringy remnants remained on the plate. Many of the workers claimed that Serena fed the eagle the hearts of animals as well, to make the bird fiercer, but Pemberton had never seen her do such a thing and believed it just one more bit of the camp's lore about Serena.

"I'd better go call Harris."

"Call Covington as well," Serena said. "I want him there when Harris talks to Luckadoo."

"Our having to pass on Townsend's land will doubtless delight

Albright," Pemberton said, "but at least this will take care of Webb and Kephart on one front."

"I'm not so sure about that," Serena said.

WITH the purchase of a second skidder, the men now worked on two fronts. By the first Monday in April the northern crews had crossed Davidson Branch and made their way to Shanty Mountain, while the crews to the south followed Straight Creek west. Recent rains had slowed progress, not just forcing men to slog through mud but causing more accidents as well. Snipes' crews worked the west end of Shanty. Since McIntyre hadn't recovered from the falling snake incident, a man named Henryson had been hired as his replacement. Henryson and Ross were second cousins who'd grown up together in Bearpen Cove. Both men viewed the world and its inhabitants with a sharp and pessimistic wit. This shared dourness Snipes had duly noted, and hinted it would be the subject of some future philosophic discourse.

A cold rain had fallen all day, and by mid-morning the workers resembled half-formed Adams dredged from the mud, not yet molded to human. When Snipes signaled for a break, the men didn't bother to seek what shelter thicker trees might afford them. They merely dropped their tools where they stood and sat down on the boggy earth. They looked as one toward the camp and its day's-end promise of warmth and dryness with longing and a seeming degree of skepticism, as if unsure the camp's existence wasn't some phasma conjured in their waterlogged heads.

Ross took out his tobacco and rolling papers but found them too wet to hold fire even in the unlikely event he could find a dry match.

"I got enough mud daubed on my ass to grow a peck of corn," Ross said miserably.

"I got enough just in my hair to chink a cabin," Henryson said.

"Makes me wish I was a big boar hog, cause at least then I'd enjoy slopping around in it," Stewart sighed. "There can't be a worser job in the world."

Dunbar nodded toward the camp where several job seekers sat on the commissary porch steps, enduring the rain in hopes of proving their fortitude as potential hires.

"Yet there's folks wanting them."

"And more coming every day," Henryson said. "They's jumping off them boxcars passing through Waynesville like fleas off a hound."

"Coming from far and near too," Ross said. "I used to think hard times rooted best in these hills, but this depression seems to have laid a fair crop of them most everywhere."

The men did not speak for a few minutes. Ross continued to stare sullenly at his drowned cigarette while Snipes scraped mud off his overalls, trying to reveal some remnants of brightness amid the muck. Stewart took out the pocket Bible he'd wrapped in a square of oilcloth, shielded the book from the rain with the cloth. He mouthed the words as he read.

"Is McIntyre doing any better?" Dunbar asked when Stewart put the Bible back in his pocket.

"Not a lick," Stewart said. "His missus took him back over to the nervous hospital and for a while they was favoring electrocuting him."

"Electrocuting him?" Dunbar exclaimed.

Stewart nodded. "That's what them doctors said. Claimed it for a new thing they been talking up big in Boston and New York. They get some cables same as you'd spark a car battery off with and pinch them on his ears and run lectricity all up and down through him."

"Lord have mercy," Dunbar said, "they figure McIntyre for a man or a light bulb."

"His missus don't like the idea one bit neither, and I'm with her," Stewart said. "How could you argue such a thing would do anybody good?"

"They's a scientific principle involved in it," Snipes said, speaking for the first time since the men had stopped work. "Your body needs a certain amount of electricity to keep going, same as a radio or a telephone or even the universe itself. A man like McIntyre, it's like he's got a low battery and needs sparked back up. Electricity, like the dog, is one of man's best friends."

Stewart pondered Snipes' words a few moments.

"Then how come they use it down there in Raleigh to kill them murderers and such?"

Snipes looked at Stewart and shook his head, much in the manner of a teacher who knows his fate is to always have a Stewart in his class.

"Electricity is like most everything else in nature, Stewart. They's two kinds of humans, your good and bad, just like you got two kinds of weather, your good and bad, right?"

"What about days it rains and that's good for a man's bean crop but bad because the feller was wanting to go fishing?" Ross interjected.

"That ain't relevant to this particular discussion," Snipes retorted, turning back to Stewart.

"So you understand what I'm a getting at, there being the good and the bad in all manner of things."

Stewart nodded.

"Well," Snipes said. "That's your scientific principle in action. Anyways, what they'd use on McIntyre is the good kind of electricity because it just goes into you and gets everything back to flowing good. What they use on them criminals fries your brains and innards up. Now that's the bad kind."

THE rain had not lessened by afternoon, but despite Pemberton's protests Serena mounted the Arabian and rode to check the southern front where Galloway's crew cut on the sloping land above Straight Creek. The angled ground would have made footing tenuous on a sunny day, but in the rain the workers labored with the slipfootedness of seamen. To make matters more difficult, Galloway's crew had a new lead chopper, a boy of seventeen stout enough but inexperienced. Galloway was showing where to make the undercut on a barrel-thick white oak when the youth's knee buckled as the axe swung forward.

The blade's entry made a soft fleshy sound as Galloway and his left hand parted. The hand fell first, hitting the ground palm down, fingers curling inward like the legs of a dying spider. Galloway backed up and leaned against the white oak, blood leaping from the upraised wrist onto his shirt and denim breeches. The other sawyer stared at Galloway's wrist, then at the severed hand as if unable to reconcile that one had once been part of the other. The youth let the axe handle slip from his hands. The two workers appeared incapable of movement, even when Galloway's legs folded. His back was still against the tree, and the bark scraped audibly against Galloway's flannel shirt as he slid into a sitting position.

Serena dismounted and took off her coat, revealing the condition it had concealed for months. She lifted a pocketknife from her saddle pack and slashed free the Arabian's rein and tied it around the stricken man's forearm. She tightened the leather, and blood ceased pouring from Galloway's wrist. The men lifted their wounded foreman and held him upright on the horse until Serena mounted behind him. She rode back to camp, one arm around Galloway's waist, pressing the worker against her swollen belly.

Once at camp, Campbell and another man lifted Galloway off the gelding and carried him into Doctor Cheney's caboose. Pemberton came in a few moments later and believed he looked at a dead man. Galloway's face was pale as chalk, and his eyes rolled as if unmoored, his breathing sharp pants. Cheney emptied a bottle of iodine on the wound. He wiped blood off the forearm to check the tourniquet.

"Damn good job whoever tied this," Doctor Cheney said, and turned to Pemberton.

"You'll have to get him to the hospital if he's to have a chance," the doctor said. "Do you want the bother of that or not?"

"We need the train here," Pemberton said.

"I'll take him in my car," Campbell said.

Pemberton turned to Serena, who watched from the caboose door. She nodded. Campbell motioned to the worker who'd helped bring Galloway in. Together they lifted the injured man off the table. They placed his arms around their shoulders and dragged him to Campbell's Dodge, Galloway's boot toes plowing two small furrows in the soaked earth. Only when they got to the car did Galloway rouse himself enough to speak, turning his head toward the caboose door where Pemberton and Doctor Cheney watched.

"I'll live," Galloway gasped. "It's done been prophesied."

As Campbell's car sped off, Pemberton looked for Serena and saw her on the Arabian, already on her way back to Straight Creek. Serena's coat had been left in the woods, and Pemberton noticed several men stared at her stomach in amazement. He suspected the workers thought of Serena as beyond gender, the same as they might some phenomenon of nature such as rain or lightning. Doctor Cheney had been as oblivious to her pregnancy as the rest of the camp, reaffirming Pemberton's belief that the physician's medical knowledge was pedestrian at best.

Pemberton was about to return to his office when he glanced toward the stringhouses and saw Galloway's mother on the porch, her clouded eyes turned in the direction of all that had just transpired.

A week later Galloway walked back into camp. He'd witnessed enough men hurt to know Pemberton Lumber Company took no charity cases, especially when every day men arrived begging for work. Pemberton assumed Galloway had come to get his mother and take her back to their old home on Cove Creek. But when Galloway came to his stringhouse, he did not pause but kept walking, his body listing slightly rightward as if unwilling to acknowledge the lost hand. He left the valley and crossed the ridge to where the timber crews worked. For a few moments Pemberton contemplated the possibility that Galloway planned to avenge the loss of his left hand, not necessarily a bad thing since it might make other workers more careful in the future.

Pemberton was in the back room with Doctor Cheney when Galloway returned, walking beside Serena and the stallion. It was almost full dark, and Pemberton had been watching out the window for her arrival.

Serena and Galloway passed the office and went on to the stable, Galloway adjusting his gait so he stayed beside the Arabian's hindquarters. They came out a few minutes later, Galloway still lagging behind Serena in the manner of a dog taught to heel. She spoke to him briefly. Then Galloway walked toward the stringhouse where his mother was.

"We need to keep Galloway on the payroll," Serena said as she sat down and filled her plate.

"What good is he to us with just one hand?" Pemberton asked.

"Anything I bid him do. Anything."

"A right-hand man with only a right hand," Doctor Cheney said, looking up from his supper. "And for a left-handed woman, no less."

"You'll be surprised, Doctor, what a man such as Galloway can do with just one hand. He's very resourceful, and very willing."

"Because you saved his life?" Cheney asked. "As one who has saved numerous lives, dear lady, I can assure you such gratitude is fleeting."

"Not in this instance. His mother prophesied a time when he would lose much but be saved."

Doctor Cheney smiled. "No doubt a reference to some brush arbor meeting where his soul would be saved for the contents of his billfold."

"Saved by a woman," Serena added, "and thus honor bound to protect that woman and do her bidding the rest of his life."

"And you believe you are that woman," Doctor Cheney said, mock disappointment in his voice. "I would have assumed a woman as enlightened as you would deny belief in augury."

"What I believe doesn't matter," Serena said. "Galloway believes it."

Nineteen

TWO MORE ACCIDENTS OCCURRED THE FOLLOWING week on Shanty Mountain. A log slipped free of the main cable line and killed a worker, and two days later the skidder's boom swung a fifty-pound metal tong into a man's skull. Some workers began wearing hand-whittled wooden crosses around their necks while others carried rabbit's foots and loadstones, salt and buckeyes and arrowheads and even half-pound iron horseshoes. Still others carried talismans for specific dangers—madstones to stop bleeding, mistletoe to avoid lightning strikes, agates to prevent falls, all manner of lucky coins, playing cards from deuce to ace set rakishly in their hatbands. Several men were Cherokee and brought their own charms, fairy crosses and feathers, certain plants. A few believed the best response to the rash of accidents was a stashed whiskey bottle. Some adopted the bright and various coloration of Snipes and could be seen from great distances as they ascended the slopes, resembling not so much loggers as a tribe of deposed harlequins en route to a more hospitable court. Several men threatened to quit. Most grew more careful but still others grew less cautious, resigned to a violent end.

Snipes' crew worked a gap in Big Fork Ridge that looked as though a monolithic block wedge had parted the escarpment into two sections. A small creek ran through the gap and trees lined it, a few yellow poplars but mainly sycamore and birch and hemlock. Snipes and Campbell hadn't believed the trees worth the bother to harvest. To do so would be slow going, and particularly dangerous since they'd be working in close proximity to one another. But Pemberton insisted.

After another close call when a log slipped free of its tongs, Snipes gave his men a break. It wasn't time for one, but the foreman figured the fifteen minutes would cost Pemberton Lumber Company less than the time it'd take to haul an injured man back to camp. The workers gathered beside the creek.

Though it was early afternoon, little light fell into the gap. The sparse-leaved trees rose around them bleak and skeletal, particularly sycamores that the winter had bleached white. The men had been in the gap since noon yesterday, and Snipes believed the unrelenting gloaming put the workers in a darker more fatalistic state of mind, less careful than they otherwise might be. He felt it provident to make the crews aware of this.

"They's a philosophical reason the positive outlook is called a sunny disposition," Snipes said, his face tented by the newspaper he perused. "Anybody that's out in a place where the sun lays on you all day ain't got a care in the world."

Ross finished sifting tobacco onto his rolling papers and looked up.

"So if I was out in the middle of the desert and had no water and there wasn't any for miles I'd not have a care in the world," Ross said, then returned his attention to the construction of his cigarette.

"That ain't exactly what my notion is," Snipes replied, lowering his newspaper and looking at Henryson as well. "I'm saying the amount of sun you get can affect how you feel. You get down in a gloomy place like this and it's like what's outside gets inside you."

"Maybe that's what wrong with Preacher McIntyre," Stewart said. "He growed up in the most way-back holler in this county. He told me once it was so darksome in there they had to use a crowbar to get any light in."

"How's McIntyre doing?" Dunbar asked.

"Well," Stewart said. "They let him out of the nervous hospital over in Morganton last Friday. Now he's home under the bed covers most all the time, and he don't let ever a word come out of his mouth."

"Tell his missus to prop him up in the cornfield on a stick," Ross said. "He can get himself a sunny disposition whilst he's keeping crows out of the corn."

Henryson stood and stretched his back, looked over at his prone foreman.

"I see you found a patch to cover that space you had on your pants pocket, Snipes," Henryson said. "Is it purple or red? It appears to my eye somewheres betwixt them."

The men turned as one and contemplated the deranged rainbow that now covered every inch of their foreman's overalls.

"It's mauve," snipes said.

"I never heard of no such color," Dunbar said.

"Well," Snipes retorted. "You're looking right at it."

"No disrespect, Snipes, but I still can't see the wearing of such a outfit," Dunbar said. "You look like you been sewed up in a crazy quilt."

"I done explained the science behind it, same as I explained what darksomeness can do to a man," Snipes said, sighing deeply. "It's ever been the way of the man of science or philosophy. Most folks stay in the dark and then complain they can't see nothing."

Snipes folded his newspaper and rose, an unhinging brightness. He did not look at his crew but gazed eastward, as if communing with the spirits of his intellectual forbearers who, like him, had carried the lantern of enlightenment among those who wished only to snuff it. Ross struck a match on his boot heel and lit his cigarette. He held the match before him and watched it burn down to his finger and thumb, then extinguished it with a quick flick of his wrist, blew the wisp of smoke in Snipes' direction.

"Galloway's back," Dunbar said.

"There's some darkness for you, Snipes," Ross said. "It's like as if a black pall gets draped on everything he passes."

"That's the God's truth," Dunbar agreed.

"Or the devil's," Henryson said.

"I heard when that hand of his hit the ground it kept opening and closing like it was trying to strangle somebody," Dunbar said. "Kept on doing that for near five minutes."

"I'd not doubt it," Stewart said.

"Nobody'd touch that hand even after it quit moving," Dunbar added. "For all I know it's still out in them woods where it fell."

"I'd not have picked it up," Henryson said, "leastways without a pair of tongs and a glove."

"I'd sooner pet a mad dog than touch that hand," Dunbar said. "What Galloway's got is a sight worse than the rabies."

"I'd not argue that," Ross said, tapping ash off his cigarette. "I'm just glad he's working on the other front, and her that thought him worth saving being over there as well."

Several men murmured in assent.

"They's some claim it wasn't a tourniquet stopped that bleeding," Dunbar noted. "She just commanded it to stop and not a drip flowed out after that."

Stewart grimaced. "I'd just as lief not heard about Galloway's hand opening and closing, nor any of the rest of it. It'll be fretting me the rest of the day."

"Well, if we work hard we'll be out of this gap by tomorrow and we'll all be feeling better," Snipes said, checking his watch. "Time to get back to it."

Dunbar and Ross followed their foreman across the creek to a yellow poplar that was the biggest tree in the gap. Snipes notched the tree to fall opposite where the crew worked, aiming it so as not to snag on a cliff hang. Dunbar and Ross used the eight-foot cross-cut saw, and Snipes used the biggest wedge. As the poplar fell, its branches hit a neighboring sycamore and snapped free a piece of limb thick and long as a fence rail. Minutes passed as the limb dangled sixty feet up in the sycamore's higher junctions, one end quilled with smaller branches, the other sheared to a narrowing sharpness. Then it slipped free only to be caught again a few inches farther down, the sharp end tilting earthward as the limb hung in abeyance a few moments longer, as if deciding.

The limb fell toward Dunbar, whose back arched as his ax struck wood the same instant the sycamore limb entered between his collar bone and spine. Dunbar's face smashed against the ground as his knees hit, the rest of his body buckling inward. The white limb had not snapped or slipped free from the flesh. It remained embedded in Dunbar's back like a stalled lightning bolt, and as the limb's angled weight succumbed to gravity, Dunbar's body slowly, almost reverently, lifted to a kneeling position, as if to be given a last look at the world. Snipes knelt and laid his hand on the dying man's shoulder. Dunbar's eyes shifted in awareness of Snipes's presence, but as he left the world he offered no last words or even a final sigh, only one tear that welled in the corner of his right eye before slowly rolling down his cheek. Then he was dead.

"IT seems the men are getting killed at a rather prodigious rate these last few weeks," Doctor Cheney said that evening at dinner. "When Wilkie and Buchanan were here, there seemed to be fewer deaths."

"The men are working steeper inclines now," Serena said, "and the heavy rains make the footing tenuous."

"Much more rain than the previous years," Pemberton added.

Doctor Cheney raised his fork and knife and cut a rind of fat from his piece of ham.

"Ah, so that's the difference. Anyway, this continuing depression assures ready replacements. Men will ride a boxcar two hundred miles just on the rumor of work. I saw twenty or so at the train depot just yesterday. They were ragged as scarecrows and nearly as gaunt."

There was a knock on the door, and two young women came in with cups and a coffee pot. As the servers left, Doctor Cheney saw Galloway standing beside the office window. The light was not on, and Galloway stood so motionless as to appear a thicker shadow among other shadows.

"This latest addition to your menagerie, Mrs. Pemberton, he seems more dog than man the way he follows you about," Doctor Cheney said, lifting a piece of ham with his fingers and holding it as if he might fling it onto the office floor. "Do you allow Galloway to eat table scraps?"

Serena raised the coffee cup to her mouth and tipped it lightly. Pemberton watched as the gold flecks in Serena's irises sparked. She set the cup down, only then turned to acknowledge Cheney had spoken to her.

"First an eagle, now a two-legged dog," Doctor Cheney continued. "You acquire the strangest pets, Mrs. Pemberton, and yet you train them so well. Do you think you could teach one of those comely maidens who just retrieved our dishes to follow me to bed each night?"

"To what purpose, Doctor?"

"A remedy for their maidenhood."

Serena closed her eyes for a moment and then reopened them, as if to focus better on Cheney before she spoke. Her gaze became placid, the irises revealing only a gray muted disdain.

"But such a cure is beyond any nostrum you possess," Serena said.

"My lady, your jests are rather unjust." Cheney said, adopting a mockingly archaic tone. "And they lack humor."

"The lack of humour is yours, Doctor, not mine. Yours is choleric while mine's phlegmatic."

"A rather antiquated form of diagnosis," Cheney said.

"In some ways," Serena answered, "but I believe it still applies to the essence of our natures. Fire found fire when Pemberton and I met, and that will be the humour of our child."

"How can you be so sure?" Cheney asked. "Your own parents misconstrued your nature."

"How so?"

"Your Christian name."

"Another jape your lack of humor missed," Serena said. "My parents named me before I left the womb, because I kicked so fiercely to get out."

"But how did they know you'd be a female?"

"The midwife told them."

"A midwife told them," Doctor Cheney mused. "Colorado sounds even more medieval than western Carolina."

Cheney dabbed his mouth with a napkin and stood. He glanced out the window.

"There's light enough to search a creek for leeches," he commented dryly. "Perhaps after that I'll read up on my phrenology. Then early to bed. No doubt more casualties will come Monday."

Doctor Cheney stood and took a last swallow of coffee and left the room. Good dog, Cheney said to Galloway as he passed through the office. Pemberton looked at Serena's waxing belly. Fire finding fire, he thought, repeating Serena's words to himself.

"What news today, Pemberton?" Serena said.

"Nothing much, other than Harris calling," Pemberton replied. "It turns out that the Cecils weren't the ones backing Webb and Kephart on the Jackson County tract."

"How did Harris find that out?"

"He wheedled it out of the Cecils' banker in Asheville. But Harris still swears he'll find out who did back them."

"I don't think anyone was backing them," Serena said. "I think that it was all a ruse to get Harris interested in that tract instead of Townsend's. And it worked."

Twenty

REPAIRS ON THE CABIN WERE NEEDED, THINGS that should have been done during the first warm days of spring, but Rachel had been so worn down by her camp work and caring for Jacob that she'd put it off for months. When she'd flipped the Black Draught calendar in the kitchen to June, Rachel knew the repairs could wait no longer, so the following Sunday she and Jacob didn't walk down to Waynesville and take the train to the camp. Instead, she put Jacob in the smock Widow Jenkins had sewn from overalls Rachel had taken from her father's chest of drawers. Then she dressed herself in her raggiest gingham dress.

Rachel set Jacob on the grass with the toy train engine Joel had given him for a Christmas present. She leaned the Indian ladder against the cabin. Cowhide knotted the rungs to the two locust poles, and the dried leather lashing creaked with each upward step. Once on the roof, Rachel searched for what her father had taught her to look for. On the gable end, where last winter's afternoon sun had melted the nighttime freeze, the sill showed signs of early rot. She took up the broad axe and balanced its weight in her hands.

Rachel carefully lifted the axe to hew the wide new sill, setting her feet as solidly as she could. The axe was heavy and became heavier with each stroke. Her muscles would ache come morning. After ten minutes she knelt to rest and caught sight of the gable's half-dovetail notching, the precision of it. Her father had made this cabin with care, even where he'd placed it, searching until he'd found a lean slab of granite for a hearthstone and a pasture spring that wouldn't go dry, what older folks called lasting water. Building the cabin itself with white oak logs and cedar shingles. What she'd liked best was that her father chose the west slope, the sun late arriving but holding its light longer into the day and early evening.

Rachel picked up the axe again. Her arms were leaden and watery blisters ridged her palms. She thought of how nice it would be if she was at church, not only because of the fellowship and how Preacher Bolick's words were a comfort but just the easefulness of sitting there, not having to do anything but hold Jacob, sometimes not even that because Widow Jenkins would always set him on her lap part of the service. Seven more days before I get that again, she thought.

Rachel did not stop until the hewing was done, then climbed down the ladder and sat beside Jacob. She studied the cabin as the sun finally made its way above the eastern ridgeline, sipping up the morning's last shadows. The chinking was fractured in places, slivers of light passing through a few. Which was no surprise but just part of a cabin settling and a long winter of freezing and thawing. Rachel went to the woodshed and found the trowels and a feed bucket. She gathered old horse droppings and then mud from a boggy seep below the spring, mixed it to the consistency of cornbread batter, the same lumps and heaviness. She handed one of the trowels to Jacob.

"There may come a time you need to know how to do this," she told the child. "So watch me."

Rachel dipped the trowel in the bucket and plopped several scoops onto a plank of wood. Holding the plank in her left hand, Rachel smoothed a gob of the chinking between the logs as she might apply a salve.

"Let's let you do it now."

She molded her hand around Jacob's, helped him dip the trowel into the bucket and balance a clump on the blade's flat end.

"Daub it on good," Rachel said, and led his hand to a gap between two logs.

After a while it was noon-dinner time, so Rachel stopped and went inside. She made Jacob a mush out of milk and cornbread. She ate a piece of cornbread but drank water herself. Milk always made cornbread taste better, and Rachel hoped by next spring she'd have money enough to buy a calf and have all the milk she and Jacob could drink. It seemed possible, because the coffee can on the pantry's upper shelf was slowly filling, mainly with quarters and dimes and nickels but a few dollar bills. Eight Mason jars of honey now stocked the pantry shelves as well, half of which she'd sell to Mr. Scott.

When Jacob finished eating, they went back outside. Rachel placed Jacob in the thin shadow next to the cabin and mounted the ladder to chink the highest logs. She checked occasionally to the west for rain clouds, because changes in humidity would mottle the work. All the while Jacob below her, contentedly daubing logs more than gaps. A woodcock burbled in the woods behind the cabin, and a flock of goldfinches passed overhead soon after, confirmation that full summer had almost come.

An hour passed and Jacob's swaddlings were surely wet, but he wasn't fussing, so Rachel decided to go ahead and repair the chimney. Blustery winter winds had displaced four of the flat field stones. One lay shattered near the fence edge. Rachel fetched a cabbage sack from the woodshed and placed it beside the three good stones before walking down the creek to get a fourth. She found one that suited beside a shady pool, the stone's roughness softened by green lichens that peeled away like old paint. Beard-tongue brightened the bank, and Rachel smelled the wintergreen odor of the blooms, the best kind of smell on a warm day because breathing it in seemed to cool you off from the inside out. For a few moments Rachel lingered. She gazed into the pool, seeing first her own reflection, below it tadpoles flowing across the creek's sandy bottom like black tears. The kind of thing you could see as an omen, Rachel knew, but chose instead to see an omen in the blooming beard-tongue that had, like her, survived a hard winter. She picked up the rock and walked back.

Swinging the cabbage sack over her shoulder, Rachel climbed the ladder one handed, leaning her body as she crossed the pitched roof to the chimney. Placing the stones was like solving a wobbly puzzle, finding the one that fit most snug in each of the chimney's cavities. The last stone finally locked into place, and the chimney was again as it once had been.

Rachel did not leave the roof immediately, instead looked westward. She let her eyes cross the horizon toward the higher mountains that rose where North Carolina became Tennessee. She thought of the map in Miss Stephens' classroom, not the time in the fifth grade when Joel had been such a smart aleck but a morning in first grade, just months after her mother had left, when Miss Stephens had stood by the map whose different colors were like patches on a quilt. The first state they'd learned was North Carolina, long and narrow like an anvil, everything within its lines green. And that had made sense to Rachel at six, because come winter there were still holly bushes and firs and rhododendron, even in the gray trees bright-green clumps of mistletoe. But when Miss Stephens showed them Tennessee, the red hadn't seemed right. When her father pointed out mountains that were in Tennessee, they'd always been blue. Except at sunset, when the mountains were tinged with red. Maybe that was why, she'd thought as Miss Stephens began pointing out other states.

Rachel gave the chimney a last inspection, then eased down the ladder. Once back on the ground, she picked up Jacob and studied the cabin a few moments.

"That'll get us through another winter," she said, and was about to go inside when she saw Widow Jenkins coming up the road, still dressed in her Sunday finery, a peach basket covered with a dish towel in her gnarled hand.

Rachel went to meet her, Jacob already waving at the older woman.

"I figured hard as you had to work on your day off, I'd fix you a supper," Widow Jenkins said, nodding at the basket. "There's fried okra and bacon in there, some hominy too."

"That was awful kind of you," Rachel said. "It has been some work."

Widow Jenkins looked at the roof and chimney and studied it a few moments.

"You done a good job," she said. "Your own daddy couldn't have done better."

They walked over to the porch. Rachel sat on the steps, but when the older woman set the basket down she did not sit herself.

"That cloth ought to keep those victuals warm long enough for me to hold that rascal a minute," Widow Jenkins said, taking Jacob and jostling him until he laughed. "The way he's growing these old arms won't be able to do that much longer."

She gave Jacob a final nuzzling before handing the child back to Rachel.

"I better be on my way so you can eat and get some rest."

"Sit with us a few minutes," Rachel said. "I'd like the company."

"All right, but just a few minutes."

The sun had fallen enough now that the air was cooling, the day's first breeze combing the white oak's highest branches. The bullfrog that lived above the springhouse made its first tentative grunts. Rachel knew the katydids and field crickets would soon join in. All soothing dependable sounds that always helped her fall asleep, not that she'd need them tonight.

"Joel Vaughn asked about you at the service today," Widow Jenkins said. "He was worried you or the young one was feeling puny. I told him you had some chores needing done."

Widow Jenkins paused and looked straight ahead, as if observing something in the woods beyond the barn.

"He's turned into a right handsome young man, don't you think?"

"Yes ma'am," Rachel said. "I suppose so."

"I think he'd make you a good sweetheart," Widow Jenkins said.

It was the kind of comment that would normally make her blush bright, but Rachel didn't. She shifted Jacob on her lap, let her fingers smooth the down on the back of his neck.

"I'm beginning to think us Harmons don't do very well when it comes to love," Rachel said. "It didn't for Daddy and Mama, and it didn't for me."

"Young as you are you could yet be surprised," Widow Jenkins said, "and I expect someday you probably will be."

For a few moments neither of them spoke.

"Do you know where my mother went when she left? Daddy never told me, even when I asked."

"No," Widow Jenkins said. "Your daddy met her in Alabama when he was in the army. Maybe she went there, but I don't know for sure. The one time your daddy talked about it, he said your mama never said where she was going. All she told him was that life up here was too hard."

"Hard how?"

"The farm land being so rocky and hilly, the long winters and the loneliness. But she told him the hardest thing was the way the mountains shut out the sun. She said living in this cove was like living in a coal mine."

"Did she want to take me with her?"

"She tried. She told your daddy if he really loved you that he'd let you go, because you'd have a better life if you left here. A lot of folks argued against him for not letting you. They claimed what she said, that if he really loved you he'd have let you go. They thought he did it to spite your mother."

Widow Jenkins paused and took off her glasses, rubbed them on her black skirt. It was the first time Rachel had seen the old woman without them. Eyes that had appeared pop-eyed now receded into her face. Widow Jenkins had never looked younger than at this moment—the eyes usually fogged by the thick spectacles a bright blue, the lashes long, the high-boned cheeks smoother than when the gold rims creased them. *She was my age once,* Rachel thought with a kind of wonder.

"Why do you think he wanted me to stay with him?" Rachel asked.

"I don't like to speak any ill about the dead," the old woman said after a few moments. "All I'll say is that he had a temper and he could hold a grudge, like every Harmon I've ever known. Your granddaddy was the same way. But your father loved you. I never doubted that and you shouldn't either. I'll tell you something else I think. It would have been wrong to take you away from these mountains, because if you're born here they're a part of you. No other place will ever feel right."

Widow Jenkins put her glasses back on. She turned to Rachel and smiled.

"Maybe that's just an old woman's silly notion, about the mountains I mean. What do you think?"

"I don't know. How can I if I've never been away from them?"

"Well, I never have either, but you're young and young folks these days get restless," Widow Jenkins said, slowly lifting herself from the steps, "so if you ever do find out you'll have to let me know."

Widow Jenkins bent down and tousled Jacob's hair.

"I'll see you in the morning, buster."

After Widow Jenkins left, Rachel lingered a few more moments on the porch. The sun had fallen behind the mountains now, and the cove seemed to settle deeper into the earth, the way an animal might burrow into leaves to make a nest before it slept. All the while, the thickening shadows made the mountains appear to fold inward. Rachel tried to imagine what living here had been like for her mother, but it was impossible, because what had felt like being shut in to her mother felt like a sheltering to Rachel, as if the mountains were huge hands, hard but gentle hands that cupped around you, protecting and comforting, the way she imagined God's hands would be. She supposed Widow Jenkins was right, that you had to be born here.

Rachel lifted Jacob into her arms.

"Time for us to eat some supper," she told the child.

Twenty-one

MEN SEEKING WORK CAME TO THE CAMP IN A steady procession now. Some camped out in the stumps and slash, waiting days for a maimed or killed worker to be brought from the woods in hopes of being his replacement. These and others more transient gathered six mornings a week on the commissary porch, each in his way trying to distinguish himself from the others when Campbell walked among them. Some went shirtless to show off powerful physiques while others held axes brought from farms or other timber camps, ready at a moment's notice to begin chopping. Still others carried Bibles and read them with great attentiveness to show they were not blackguards or reds but Godly men. Some bore tattered pieces of paper testifying to their talent and reliability as loggers or discharge papers for military service, and all brought with them stories of hungry children and siblings, sick parents and sick wives that Campbell listened to with sympathy, though how much such stories influenced his choices none of the workers could discern.

Serena continued to go out with the lead crews each morning. Galloway trailed behind her, the nubbed arm dangling like rotten fruit clinging to a branch. As Serena moved from crew to crew, no man spoke to her of the coming child, and none let his gaze settle on her stomach. Yet all in their way acknowledged her waxing belly, some offering dipperfuls of spring water, hats holding raspberries and blackberries, ferns twined around chewy combs of sourwood honey. Others gave Galloway pint mason jars filled with spring tonics made of milkweed and sassafras, mandrake and valerian root. One logger offered a double-beveled broad axe to place under Serena's birth bed to cut the pain, still another a bloodstone to prevent hemorrhaging. Foremen came running when Serena appeared so she wouldn't have time or need to dismount. On warm days, the crew bosses led the Arabian into uncut trees so Serena would be shaded.

She often drank the spring water, occasionally ate some of the proffered berries and honey. Galloway placed the tonics in his tote sack. Whether Serena drank them none knew. As Galloway followed Serena from crew to crew, the jars clinked against each other softly, like wind chimes.

Snipes' crew worked alone, having ascended to the summit of Shanty Ridge. As they took a morning break, the men watched Serena moving among the crews to the south. Stewart shook his head in dismay.

"If Preacher McIntyre was here he'd say them carrying on like that is nothing short of idolatry."

"He surely would," Snipes agreed. "He any better, McIntyre I mean?"

"A tad," Stewart said. "Enough that his wife ain't let them doctors electrocute him."

"That's too bad," Ross said. "I was hoping we could fling him in the river and he'd shock us up a mess of catfish. Bring them up the same way you do cranking a telephone."

Snipes unfolded his newspaper and perused the front page.

"What's the scuttlebutt, Snipes?" Henryson asked.

"Well, them park folks seem to be honing in on Colonial Townsend's land over in Tennessee. Says here they've about reached an agreement."

"That tract's big as the one they got Champion to sell them, ain't it?" Henryson asked.

"Says here it is."

"I figured the Pembertons to have bought it," Henryson said. "They was hot after it for a while there till Harris steered them over to Jackson County."

"I heard Harris has got him some geologists over there in Jackson trying to root up a big copper vein," Stewart said.

"Copper?" Henryson said. "I heard it was coal he was looking for."

"I been hearing near everything from silver and gold to Noah's ark to the Big Rock Candy Mountain," Ross said.

"What do you think it is?" Stewart asked Snipes.

"Well," Snipes said reflectively. "It could be a quest for one of the world's immortal treasures, as many a rich man would wish to have his name recorded in the anus of history, but knowing Harris I'm not of a mind to think he'd care much about that."

Snipes paused and picked up a pebble, rubbed it between thumb and forefinger as he might a coin he was unsure he wanted to spend.

"What I'm thinking is that, at least as the crow flies, Franklin ain't but thirty miles away," Snipes concluded. "I'd say that ought to fill in enough of the puzzle pieces for you to figure the rest."

The men were silent for a few moments. Snipes returned to his newspaper as the others continued to look southward. They watched as Serena followed the new spur line into the woods.

"I heard she's just eating bloody beef for her breakfast and supper," Stewart said. "To make that young one of hers all the fiercer. And that ain't the half of it. Come the night she bares her belly to the moon, soaking in all its power."

"I'd say somebody's bull-ragging you, Stewart," Henryson said.

"Maybe so," Ross interjected, "but if somebody told you a year ago she'd train a eagle to go flitting around picking up timber rattlers long as your arm you'd have thought that a rusty too."

"That's true," Henryson said. "We've not seen the like of her in these hills before."

IT was in the eighth month of her pregnancy that Serena awoke with pain in her lower abdomen. Pemberton found Doctor Cheney in the caboose ministering to a worker who had a three-inch splinter embedded in the sclera of his eye. The doctor used a pair of tweezers to work the splinter free, washed the wound with disinfectant and sent the man back to his crew.

"Probably something has not lain well on her stomach," Doctor Cheney said as they walked to the house.

Galloway waited on the porch, Serena's horse tacked and tethered to the lower banister.

"Mrs. Pemberton will be staying in today," Pemberton told him.

Galloway made no reply but gazed intently at Cheney's heavy black physician's bag as Pemberton led the doctor into the house.

Serena sat on the bed edge. Her face was pale, gray eyes seemingly focused on something far away, her shallow breaths such as one might use while holding something fragile or dangerous. Serena's peignoir lay open, the dark-blue silk rippling back to reveal her rounded belly.

"Lie down on your side," Doctor Cheney said, and took a stethoscope from his bag. The doctor pressed the instrument to Serena's stomach, listening attentively a few moments. He nodded to himself and lifted the bright-steel bell from Serena's skin, freed the stethoscope's prongs so the instrument hung around his neck.

"All is well, madam," Doctor Cheney said. "It's normal for women to be susceptible to minor, sometimes even nonexistent pains, especially when with child. What you're feeling is probably a mild gastrointestinal upset, or to put it less delicately, excessive gas."

"Mrs. Pemberton is no malingerer," Pemberton said as Serena slowly raised herself to a sitting position.

Doctor Cheney placed the stethoscope back in his physician's bag, pinched its metal snap closed.

"I don't mean to imply such. The mind is its own place, as the poet tells us, and has its own peculiar reality. What one feels one feels."

Pemberton watched Cheney flatten his hand as if preparing to pat his patient on the shoulder, but the physican wisely reconsidered and let the hand remain by his side.

"I assure you that she will be better by tomorrow," Doctor Cheney said when they stepped back out on the porch.

"Is there anything that will help until then?" Pemberton asked, nodding at Galloway sitting on the steps. "Galloway can go to the commissary, to town if necessary."

"Yes," Doctor Cheney said, addressing Galloway. "Go to the commissary and fetch your mistress a bag of peppermints. I find they do wonders when my stomach is sour."

Serena stayed in bed all day. She insisted Pemberton go to the office, but he did so only when she agreed to have Galloway stay in the front room. When Pemberton returned to check on her at noon and then later in the evening, Serena told him she felt better. But she remained pale. They went to bed early, and as they settled into sleep Serena pressed her back and hips into Pemberton's chest and groin, took his right hand and placed it on the undercurve of her stomach as if to help hold the baby in place. Music filtered up from the dining hall porch. Pemberton drifted to sleep as a worker sang of a woman named Mary who walked the wild moors.

The next morning Pemberton was awakened by Serena sitting up in the bed, the covers pushed back to her feet, left hand pressed between her legs. When Pemberton asked what was wrong, Serena did not speak. Instead, she raised the hand to him as if making a vow, her fingers and palm slick with blood. Pemberton jerked on pants and boots, a shirt he didn't bother to button. He wrapped Serena in the peignoir and lifted her into his arms, snatching a towel from the rack as he passed the bathroom. The train was about to make an early run to the saw mill and men had collected around the tracks. Pemberton yelled at several loitering workers to uncouple all the cars from the Shay except for the coach. Mud holes pocked the ground, but Pemberton stumbled right through them as men scurried to separate the cars and the fireman frantically shoveled coal into the tender. Campbell rushed from the office and helped get Serena into the coach and lain lengthways on a seat. Pemberton told Campbell to call the hospital and have a doctor and ambulance waiting at the depot, then to drive Pemberton's Packard there. Campbell left the coach car and Pemberton and Serena were alone amidst the shouts of workers and the Shay engine's gathering racket.

Pemberton sat on the seat edge and pressed a towel against Serena's groin to try and stanch the bleeding. Serena's eyes were closed, her face fading to the pallor of marble as the engineer placed his hand on the reverser, knocked off the brakes and opened the throttle. Pemberton listened to the train make what seemed its endless gradations toward motion, steam entering the throttle valve into the admission pipes and into the cylinders before the push of the pistons against the rod, and the rod turning the crankshaft and then the line shaft turning through the universal joints and the pinion gears meshing with the bull gears. Only then the wheels ever so slowly coming alive.

Pemberton closed his eyes and imagined the engine's meshing metal akin to the inner workings of a clock, bringing back time that had been suspended since he'd seen the blood on Serena's hand. When the train gained a steady rhythm, Pemberton opened his eyes and looked out the window, and it was as if the train crossed the bottom of a deep clear lake. Everything behind appeared slowed by the density of water—Campbell entering the office to call the hospital, workers coming out of the dining hall to watch the engine and coach car pull away, Galloway emerging from the stable, his stubbed arm flopping uselessly as he ran after the train.

The Shay began its ascent up McClure Ridge, the valley falling away behind them. Once over the summit, the train gained speed, dense woods now surrounding the tracks. Pemberton remembered what Serena had once said about only the present being real. *Nothing is but what is now,* he told himself as he held Serena's wrist, felt her pulse fluttering weakly beneath the skin. As the train crossed the declining mountains toward Waynesville, Pemberton pressed his lips against the limp wrist. Stay alive, he whispered, as though speaking to what blood remained in her veins.

By the time the train pulled into the depot, the towel was saturated. Serena hadn't made a sound the whole way. Saving her strength to stay alive, Pemberton believed, but now she'd lapsed into unconsciousness. Two attendants in white carried Serena off the train and into the waiting ambulance. Pemberton and the hospital doctor got in as well. The doctor, a man in his early eighties, lifted the soggy towel and cursed.

"Why in God's name wasn't she brought sooner," the doctor said, and pressed the towel back between Serena's legs. "She's going to need blood, a lot of it and fast. What's her blood type?"

Pemberton did not know and Serena was past telling anyone.

"Same as mine," Pemberton said.

Once in the hospital emergency room, Pemberton and Serena lay side by side on metal gurneys, thin feather pillows cushioning their heads. The doctor rolled up Pemberton's sleeve and shunted his forearm with the needle, then did the same to Serena. They were connected by three feet of rubber hose, the olive-shaped pump blooming in the tubing's center. The doctor squeezed the pump. Satisfied, he motioned for the nurse to take it and stand in the narrow space between the gurneys.

"Every thirty seconds," the doctor told her, "any faster and the vein can collapse."

The doctor stepped around the gurney to minister to Serena as the nurse squeezed the rubber pump, checked the wall clock until half a minute passed, and squeezed again.

Pemberton raised his shunted arm and gripped the nurse's wrist with his hand.

"I'll pump the blood."

"I don't think . . ."

Pemberton tightened his grip, enough that the nurse gasped. She opened her hand and let him take the pump.

Pemberton watched the clock, and when fifteen seconds passed he squeezed the rubber. He did so again, listening for the hiss and suck of his blood passing through the tube. But there was no sound, just as there was no way to see his blood coursing through the dark-gray tubing. Each time he squeezed, Pemberton closed his eyes so he could imagine the blood pulsing from his arm into Serena's, from there up through the vein and into the right and left atria of her heart. Pemberton imagined the heart itself, a shriveled thing slowly expanding as it refilled with blood.

A grammar school was across the road, and through the emergency room's open window Pemberton heard the shouts of children at recess. An attendant entered the room and helped lift Serena's legs and hold them apart as the doctor performed his pelvic exam. Pemberton closed his eyes again and squeezed the pump. He no longer checked the clock but tightened his hand as soon as he felt the rubber fill with blood. A bell rang and the sounds of the children dimmed as they reentered the school. The doctor stepped away from Serena and nodded at the attendant to lower Serena's legs.

"Get the mayo stand and a lap pack," the doctor told the attendant.

The nurse fitted a mask over Serena's face and dripped chloroform onto the cloth and wire. The attendant rolled the stand beside Serena's bed, opened the white cotton sheeting to reveal the sterilized steel. Pemberton watched the doctor lift the scalpel and open Serena's body from pubis to navel. Pemberton squeezed the pump again as the doctor's right hand disappeared into the incision, lifted up the purplish blue umbilical cord for a moment before resettling it. Then the doctor dipped both hands into Serena's belly, raised something so gray and phlegmy it appeared to be made not of flesh but moist clay. Blood daubing the body was the only indication to Pemberton it could have ever held life. The umbilical cord lay coiled on the baby's chest. Pemberton did not know if it was still connected to Serena.

For a few moments the doctor stared at the infant intently. Then he turned and handed what filled his hands to the attendant.

"Put it over there," the doctor said, and motioned to a table in the corner.

The doctor turned back to Serena but not before asking the nurse how much blood Pemberton had given.

"Over 500 cc's. Should I try and stop him?"

The doctor looked at Pemberton, who shook his head.

"I guess not. He'll be too weak before long to squeeze it anyway, or he'll pass out."

As the doctor wove dark thread through Serena's skin, Pemberton turned his head toward her. Pemberton listened to her soft inhalations and matched his breathing precisely to hers. He became lightheaded, no longer able to focus enough to read the clock or follow the words passing between the doctor and nurse. Another group of children ran out onto the grammar school's playground, but their shouts soon evaporated into silence. Pemberton squeezed the pump, his hand unable to close completely around it. He listened to his and Serena's one breath, even as he felt the needle being pulled from his forearm, heard the wheels of Serena's gurney as it rolled away.

PEMBERTON still lay on the gurney when he awoke. The doctor loomed above, an orderly beside him.

"Let us help you up," the doctor said, and the two men raised Pemberton to a sitting position.

He felt the room darken briefly, then lighten.

"Where's Serena?"

The words came out halting and raspy, as if he'd not spoken in days. Pemberton looked at the clock, its hands gradually coming into focus.

Had one been on the wall, he would have checked a calendar to discern the day and month. Pemberton closed his eyes a few moments and raised his forefinger and thumb to the bridge of his nose. He opened his eyes and things seemed clearer.

"Where's Serena?" he asked again.

"In the other wing."

Pemberton gripped the gurney's edge and prepared to stand, but the orderly placed a firm hand on his knee.

"Is she alive?"

"Yes," the doctor said. "Your wife's constitution is quite remarkable, so unless something unforeseen occurs, she'll recover."

"But the child is dead," Pemberton said.

"Yes, and there's another matter I'll need to discuss with you and your wife later."

"Tell me now," Pemberton said.

"Your wife's uterus. It's lacerated through the cervix."

"And that means what?"

"That she can have no more children."

Pemberton did not speak for a few moments.

"What was the child's sex?"

"A boy."

"Had we gotten here earlier, would the child have survived?"

"That doesn't matter now," the doctor said.

"It matters," Pemberton said.

"Yes, the child probably would have survived."

The orderly and doctor helped Pemberton off the gurney. The room wavered a few moments, then steadied.

"You gave a lot of blood," the doctor said. "Too much. You'll pass out if you're not careful."

"Which room?"

"Forty-one," the doctor said. "The orderly can go with you."

"I can find it," Pemberton said, and walked slowly toward the door, past the corner table where nothing now lay.

He stepped out of the emergency room and into the corridor. The hospital's two wings were connected by the main lobby, and as Pemberton passed through he saw Campbell sitting by the doorway. Campbell rose from his chair as Pemberton approached.

"Leave the car here for me and take the train back to camp," Pemberton said. "Make sure the crews are working and then go by the saw mill to make sure there are no problems there."

Campbell took the Packard's keys from his pocket and gave them to Pemberton. As Pemberton turned to leave, Campbell spoke.

"If there's someone asks how Mrs. Pemberton and the young one are doing, what do you want me to say?"

"That Mrs. Pemberton is going to be fine."

Campbell nodded but did not move.

"What else?" Pemberton asked.

"Doctor Cheney, he rode into town with me."

"Where is he now?" Pemberton asked, trying to keep his voice level.

"I don't know. He said he was going to get Mrs. Pemberton some flowers, but he ain't come back."

"How long ago was that?"

"Almost two hours."

"I've got some business with him I'll settle later," Pemberton said.

"You're not the only one," Campbell said as he reached to open the door.

Pemberton stopped him with a firm hand on the shoulder.

"Who else?"

"Galloway. He come by an hour ago asking where Doctor Cheney was."

Pemberton took his hand off Campbell's shoulder, and the overseer went out the door. Pemberton walked across the lobby and up the opposite corridor, reading the black door numbers until he found Serena's room.

She was still unconscious when he came in, so Pemberton pulled a chair beside her bed and waited. As late morning and the afternoon passed, he listened to her breath, watched the gradual return of color to her face. The drugs kept Serena in a drifting stupor, her eyes occasionally opening but unfocused. A nurse brought Pemberton lunch and then supper. Only when the last sunlight had drained from the room's one window did Serena's eyes open and find Pemberton's. She appeared cognizant, which surprised the nurse because the morphine drip was still in Serena's arm. The nurse checked the drip to make sure it was operating and then left. Pemberton turned in his chair to face her. He slid his right hand under Serena's wrist and let his fingers clasp around it like a bracelet.

She turned her head to see him better, her words a whisper.

"The child is dead?"

"Yes."

Serena studied Pemberton's face a few moments.

"What else?"

"We won't be able to have another."

Serena remained silent for almost a minute, and Pemberton wondered if the drugs were taking hold again. Then Serena took a breath, her mouth kept open as though about to speak as well, but she did not speak, not at that moment. Instead, Serena closed her eyes and slowly exhaled, and as she did her body seemed to settle deeper into the mattress. Her eyes opened.

"It's like my body knew all along," she said.

Pemberton did not ask what she meant. Serena closed her eyes a few moments, opened them slowly.

"And yet . . ."

Pemberton nodded and squeezed Serena's wrist, felt again the pulse of their blood. Serena's eyes shifted to Pemberton's bruised inner elbow, the square of gauze taped to it.

"Your blood merged with mine," Serena said. "That's all we ever hoped for anyway."

PART III

Twenty-two

SHE LEFT THE HOSPITAL SOONER THAN THE doctors or Pemberton wished. I need to be back at the camp, she told them. Serena was carried out of the hospital the same way she'd been carried in. Campbell and Pemberton lifted her into the train's coach car, the gurney settled on a foot-thick pallet of blankets to cushion her against the train's jarring. When the train got to camp, they carried her to the house. It was supper time and the workers dropped their forks and knives and gathered on the porch. Most watched from a distance, but some, mainly crew bosses she'd worked with, ventured closer, their hats off as the gurney passed before them. Serena was pale but her gray eyes were open and staring at a sky she'd not seen in seven days. The workers watched in silence as Campbell and Pemberton carried her through the camp to the house. They watched in wonder as well, especially men whose mothers and sisters and wives had died from what Serena survived.

Vaughn opened the door to the house, and Galloway and Pemberton carried her into the bedroom. They eased Serena into the bed, and Pemberton shut the curtains in hopes it would help her sleep. Early evening was the time the workers played and sang their music, or, even tired as they were, sometimes arranged baseball games and wrestling matches, gathered around an outbreak of fisticuffs. But this evening the camp was hushed, oddly vigilant, like the afterward of a violent storm.

Pemberton checked the cotton gauze over her wound for any drainage of blood or jaundiced fluid, gave Serena water and the Feosol the doctor prescribed for her anemia. As the days passed, Pemberton fed her a soft diet of eggs and pureed meat until she could lift the fork and spoon herself. He emptied the bedpan and tried, vainly, to get Serena to take the codeine for her soreness. She grew stronger each day, soon leaving the bed to use the bathroom and to make short walks around the house while Pemberton held her arm. Serena insisted he continue working, especially in pursuing investors, but Pemberton did so only after moving his office into the front room. While Serena lay in the darkened bedroom, Campbell ran the day-to-day business from the office with his usual efficiency, Vaughn taking over lesser duties.

All the while Galloway remained on the porch, allowing no trespass, taking inside himself what food or medicine or well wishes were brought. Come evening, he made a pallet in front of the door. One night Pemberton looked out the window and saw Galloway asleep on the pallet, wearing the same clothes he'd worn since the day Serena had come home. Galloway's knees were tucked tight to his stomach, head bowed inward, the nubbed wrist pressed childlike to his mouth while his hand gripped the handle of a sprung switchblade knife.

As she strengthened, Serena talked about Brazil, about going there as soon as they finished in Jackson County. Obsessed with it, Pemberton believed, especially after Pemberton had found potential investors in Asheville. Men who would be interested only in local investments, Pemberton told her, but Serena believed otherwise. I can convince them, she said. As Pemberton sat in the darkened bedroom, his chair pulled close to the bed, Serena spoke of Brazil's untapped resources, its laissez-faire attitude toward businesses, how she and Pemberton should go there and scout tracts as soon as the Jackson County camp was up and running. Not even an empire, Pemberton, a world, she told him, and spoke with such fervor Pemberton at first feared an infection might have set in and raised her temperature. What reservations Pemberton had, he kept to himself. They did not speak of the dead child.

By the second week Serena was out of bed and sitting in a chair, sending Vaughn out on horseback to monitor the work crews' progress and relay messages back and forth from the foremen. Documents and statistics and reports about Brazil, which Pemberton had not even known existed, were exhumed from Serena's Saratoga trunk. Also, a wax-engraved map of South America, which, once unfolded, consumed half the front room. The map covered the floor for days, a cane back chair set upon it so Serena could peruse its expanse more diligently, the chair occasionally lifted like a chess piece and set back down on a different square of the map.

Something planned for years, Pemberton now realized. Serena sent telegrams and letters to sources and contacts in Washington and South America. Possible investors as far away as Chicago and Quebec were contacted as well. Serena did all this with a frenetic alacrity, as if her mind had to make up for her body's inactivity. Minutes and hours seemed to move quicker, as if Serena had wrenched time itself into a higher gear. At the end of the second week, Serena insisted Pemberton return to the office where, as efficient as Campbell was, invoices and work orders and payrolls piled up.

With the help of the mild spring, they were on schedule to finish in Cove Creek Valley by October, so an increasing number of workers were being sent east to Jackson County to set down rail lines and raise buildings for the new camp. Harris had his men in Jackson County as well, teams led by geologists making exploratory sorties into cliffs and creek banks. Harris was tight-lipped about what these men searched for, but he'd also bought an adjacent hundred acres that enclosed the upper watershed. These mountains are like the finest ladies, Harris told Pemberton. They won't give you want you want until you spend a lot of time and money on them.

On Pemberton's first Saturday back in the office, a foreman drove over from the saw mill with his payroll ledger. Pemberton set a fountain pen and box of envelopes on his desk, opened the safe and pulled out a tray of one-and five-dollar bills, a cloth bag holding rolls of quarters and dimes and nickels. When Pemberton opened the ledger, he saw a new name printed on the last line. *Jacob Ballard Age fifteen.* After a few moments, Pemberton raised his eyes to the top of the ledger. He wrote a name on an envelope, placed two fives and two ones inside. But even as he sealed the envelope, Pemberton's eyes drifted to the bottom of the page, unable to shake the sensation of seeing the child's first name in print. He studied the five letters, the way the raised *J* and *b* shaped the word to look like a bowl waiting to be filled. Minutes passed until, for the first time since Serena's miscarriage, Pemberton took the photograph album from the bottom drawer. He set it beside the ledger and opened it to the last two pages. The photograph of himself as a two-year-old was on the left, but it was the photograph on the opposite page that held his attention. Pemberton eased the ledger closer so Jacob and the child's photograph lay side by side.

THAT afternoon Snipes' crew was cutting on Big Fork Ridge when the main cable's tail block broke free from a stump. Snipes believed that if the skidder crew got a break his men should as well, so they sat on the logs they'd just cut. A large woodpecker glided low overhead, a white lining on the black underwings, its round head tufted a brilliant red. The bird flapped its wide wings once and vanished into the uncut trees.

Henryson looked wistfully toward the woods where the bird had disappeared.

"Wish he'd have dropped off one of them head feathers," he said.

Snipes' crew was a bright-spangled assemblage now, for after Dunbar's death all to varying degrees had adopted the heraldry of their foreman. Henryson stuffed his hatband with goldfinch and jay and cardinal feathers to create a variegated winged halo around his head while Stewart wore green patches on his shoulders like chevrons and a white handkerchief sewn onto his bib, crayoned in its center a smudgy red cross. Ross bore a single patch of orange across his crotch, though an act of derision or belief no one but he knew. Snipes himself had further brightened his wardrobe by replacing his leather bootlaces with orange dynamite wire.

Most of the men rolled cigarettes and smoked while they waited. Snipes took his pipe and glasses from his bib before pulling a section of the *Asheville Citizen* from his overalls' back pocket. Snipes set the newspaper on his lap and took off his glasses, wiped the inner rims carefully with his handkerchief before perusing the page.

"Says here they still ain't got no suspects in the recent demise of Doctor Cheney," Snipes said. "The high sheriff in Asheville argues that some hobo hanging around the train station done it and then hopped the next freight out of town. He figures they'll likely never catch the perpetrator."

"Didn't the high sheriff find it kindly curious that hobo didn't take the train ticket to Kansas City they found in Doctor Cheney's pocket, nor his billfold for that matter?" Henryson asked. "Or why a hobo would sit the good doctor in a bathroom stall with his tongue cut out and a peppermint in each hand."

"Or figure the fellow who's driving the very car the late doctor used to drive might be the least bit involved?" Ross added.

"No sir," Snipes said. "That's what the law calls immaterial evidence."

Ross raised his head and looked upward at the blue sky, let a slow drift of smoke rise from his pursed mouth before speaking.

"I doubt they'll be looking for any other kind of evidence since the sheriff's on the Pemberton Lumber Company payroll."

"You mean the high sheriff in Asheville, not Sheriff McDowell?" Stewart asked.

"That's right," Ross said.

"I don't think Sheriff McDowell can be bought," Stewart said.

"We'll find out soon enough," Ross replied. "These folks seem to be picking up steam far as their killings. Didn't bother to make this one look like no accident neither, the way they done with Buchanan. They'll be needing every lawman in this state on their payroll at the rate they're going."

"They ain't never got to McDowell before, and we all know they've tried. I don't think they will now," Henryson said with uncharacteristic optimism.

The men paused to listen to a staccato tapping coming from the deeper woods. Henryson cocked his head slightly to better gauge the bird's location, but the tapping ceased and the woods grew silent.

"Got anything new about that park in your paper?" Ross asked Snipes.

"Just that Colonial Townsend did sell his land to the guvment," Snipes said. "The paper gives Townsend and the park folks both a big huzzah for that."

"That's bad news for my brother-in-law," Henryson said, shaking his head and looking west toward Tennessee. "He's been a sawyer for Townsend for nigh on ten years. Him and my sister got four young ones to feed."

"Is he a good worker?" Snipes asked.

"He can handle a axe good as any man I know."

"I'll put in a word for him with Campbell," Snipes said, "but so many folks is perched on them commissary steps now you about have to draw lots for a seat. They's workers already herding at the new camp and it not even open yet."

"Who told you that?" Henryson asked.

"Nobody told me," Snipes said. "I seen it my ownself last Sunday. One of them on the porch steps picked up his axe and said he was headed to Jackson County, and a good dozen men up and followed like he was Moses leading them to the promised land."

"Your brother-in-law don't do no doctoring, does he?" Ross asked Henryson. "Got an opening there."

"No," Henryson replied, "but even if he was I'd as lief have him stick to the logging. At least you've got a chance to dodge a tree or axe blade. I ain't of a mind to say the same of Galloway."

Twenty-three

SHE'D BEEN TOLD TO STAY IN BED FOR SIX weeks, but when a month had passed Serena resumed supervising the cutting crews. When she stepped off the front porch, Galloway waited. They went to the stable together and Serena came out on the Arabian, the eagle on its perch. She rode slowly out of camp, Galloway following in his shambling gait, a constant and resolute shadow. The land had been cleared up Rough Fork to Wash Ridge. From a distance, the valley's forests appeared not so much cut down as leveled by some vast glacier. Though the rains had lessened, silt-stalled creeks continued to make traversing the bottomland a precarious business. Men stumbled and slipped, came up cursing and wiping mud from their faces and clothes. Two workers broke bones in the miasma and several more lost tools. A sawyer who'd once logged on the coast said the only difference between the valley and a Charleston County swamp was the absence of cottonmouth moccasins.

Pemberton watched from the office porch as Serena and Galloway slogged on through the wasteland and disappeared up Cove Creek. As the morning passed, he worked on invoices and talked with Harris about meeting two potential investors. Every half hour, Pemberton got up from his desk and looked west to where Serena was. At eleven, it was time to check in with Scruggs, the man who'd overseen the saw mill operation since Buchanan's death. But Pemberton was reluctant to leave the camp, and not just because he was worried about Serena. For the first time he could remember, Campbell hadn't shown up for work. Pemberton found Vaughn and told him to stay in the office and answer the telephone. As Pemberton drove out of camp, he saw Serena and the horse ascending Half Acre Ridge. He remembered the workers' surprise at how the thin mountain air never affected her, even in her first days when she'd ridden into the tract's highest elevations. They forget where I'm from, Serena had told him.

When Pemberton arrived at the saw mill, he found Scruggs at the splash pond supervising two workers guiding timber toward the log buggy. Using their eight-foot-long jam pikes like acrobats, the men moved quickly across the splash pond's surface, stepping log to log with a confidence that belied the job's dangers. Pemberton saw that the older man was Ingledew, a foreman who'd worked at the saw mill since it had begun operation. Ingledew wore cutter boots, their steel points grabbing the wood like claws, but the youth with him still worked barefoot, despite being at the saw mill a month.

"Is that Jacob Ballard?"

"Yes sir," Scruggs said, a slight surprise in his voice. "I didn't know you knew him."

"I remember his name on the payroll," Pemberton said. "Why hasn't he bought his cutter boots yet?"

"I been telling him to," Scruggs said, "but he's sparking some girl over in Sevierville every Sunday. Young Ballard there would rather waste his money buying gewgaws for her."

Pemberton and Scruggs watched as the youth stepped barefoot across the pond's all but hidden surface, now wielding the jam pike like a harpoon as he jabbed and herded the timber into position for the log buggy, Ingledew behind him untangling timber as well. Most of the logjams gave readily, but some had knit together like stitches, the whole jam moving instead of a single log, forcing the two men to crouch and untangle the timber by hand.

"Good at it though, ain't he, especially to be so green," Scruggs said. "He glides over that pond like a water spider."

Pemberton nodded as they watched Ballard scamper to another log, prod more timber toward the buggy where a third worker waited to transport it onto the log carrier. Ballard was skinny but Pemberton could tell from the way he shoved the logs around that, like so many of the highlanders, he possessed a wiry strength.

Pemberton was about to leave when he saw Ingledew unlock another logjam and free the lower trunk of a large poplar, push it toward the single slab of timber Ballard rode. The poplar log bumped against a smaller one only a yard behind the younger worker, it in turn bumping the timber the youth rode. It was hardly more than a tap, but enough. The log rolled and Ballard slipped. He plunged feet first through a small breech in the timber as through a trap door. Legs, trunk, and then head fell in a blur, all vanished except for a hand and a few inches of wrist. Somehow Ballard managed to hold onto the jam pike with his right hand. For a few moments, Pemberton thought it might save him, because each end of the pike had snagged timber. Pemberton watched the hand gripping the pike, willing the boy to hold on while Ingledew hurdled logs to come help. As Ingledew came closer, his wake caused the timber near where the youth fell to shift, and the breech Ballard had fallen through became no wider than the fist poking through to clutch the jam pike.

Another five seconds and Ingledew might have been able to pull him out, but Ballard's hand let go of the jam pike to make a last clawing grab at a log, his fingertips breaking off a piece of oak bark. The last breech in the gap disappeared along with the hand. Ingledew frantically opened a hole in the timber, but Pemberton knew as well as the workers that under the splash pond's calm surface the creek's old currents yet swirled. Ingledew kept moving, prying open more holes nearby as Pemberton and Scruggs scoured the pond for a logjam rocked or swayed by Ballard pushing from underneath. The man operating the log buggy was on the water as well now, but Ballard was lost. After twenty minutes Ingledew and the other man gave up and came to shore.

Scruggs, the sole Catholic in the camp and perhaps the whole county, bowed his head and crossed himself.

"Them logs sealed that boy up like a coffin lid," Scruggs said softly.

Pemberton stared out at the pond's timbered surface, so calm now that the logs could have been perceived as resting on land, not water. The world suddenly appeared to Pemberton to widen in distance between the earth and sky, followed by a lightheadedness like what had caused him to pass out on the hospital gurney. For a moment, Pemberton feared his legs would give way. He bent his knees slightly and lowered his head, hands against thighs as he waited for the feeling to pass.

"You all right?" Scruggs asked.

"Just give me a second," Pemberton said and slowly raised his head.

Pemberton saw that not just Scruggs but also Ingledew and the other worker watched him. Scruggs reached out to steady him, but Pemberton waved the proffered arm away. He took slow breaths, let the space between the sky and world contract, steady itself.

"You want to sit in the office for a while, Mr. Pemberton?" Scruggs asked.

Pemberton shook his head. The lightheadedness had been replaced by nausea, and he wanted to be gone from this place before it got worse.

"Come into camp tomorrow and we'll get you a new man," Pemberton said, already walking back to his car, "and this time make it clear he buys cutter boots with his first week's pay."

"Yes sir," Scruggs said.

Pemberton got in the Packard and drove until he was out of sight of the saw mill. He pulled off the road and opened the door, waiting to see if his stomach was strong enough to hold its moiling contents.

Once back at camp, Pemberton found that Campbell still hadn't shown up, so he sent Vaughn instead to check on a problem with the second skidder. Pemberton went back to the invoices on his desk, but after getting up and standing by the window a third time, he placed the checkbook back in the Mosler safe and went to the stable after telling Vaughn that he'd return in the late afternoon. Pemberton mounted his horse and rode through slash and mud to Wash Ridge where he found Serena talking to a crew boss. The eagle's hooded head swung in Pemberton's direction as he approached.

"Come to check up on me, Pemberton?" Serena said as he rode up beside her.

"You'd do the same."

"True enough," Serena said, and reached out and touched his cheek. "But you're the one who looks a little peaked. Are you all right?"

"I'm fine," Pemberton said.

As the foreman asked Serena a final question, Pemberton thought of Ballard's hand grasping the jam pike. He imagined the youth hanging in the murky water, debating whether or not to let go, to try and save himself or wait to be saved. Those seconds would have felt like minutes, Pemberton knew, the same way it had been when the bear enveloped him. Closing over the youth like a coffin lid, Scruggs had said. It would have felt that way, Pemberton knew, just as black and hopeless.

The foreman nodded to Serena that he understood. He doffed his battered felt hat and went back to his men as Pemberton moved his horse alongside the Arabian.

"Harris called," Pemberton said. "We meet our potential investors at the Cecils this weekend."

"So I see the castle at last," Serena said. "What else did Harris say about them?"

"The Calhouns are old-money Charleston. They summer in Asheville and stay part of the time with the Cecils, which is why we're meeting there. Lowenstein's a businessman in New York City, a very successful one."

"Why is he here?"

"His wife has tuberculosis."

Pemberton paused and watched the workers as they walked into the deeper woods, still watching them as he spoke again.

"As far as Brazil, Harris told me they're only considering investments in this region."

"Then we'll have to change their minds," Serena said.

For a few moments neither of them spoke. The eagle's jesses and swivels rustled as the bird raised its wings. Serena stroked the eagle's keel with the back of her index finger and the bird calmed.

"We lost a man at the saw mill today," Pemberton said. "One of the new hires Scruggs was high on."

"If Scruggs liked him, then it is a loss. He's a good judge of workers," Serena said, pausing as she glanced east towards camp. "Has Campbell shown up?"

"No," Pemberton said. "I sent Vaughn to look for him, but he didn't have any luck."

"Then it's true."

"What's true?"

"A sawyer claimed that he's deserted us," Serena said. "We'll give him until morning before we send Galloway after him."

"Why bring him back? If he doesn't want to work for us, the hell with him."

"He knows who we've paid off and what for," Serena said, "which might become a problem. Besides, the workers need to understand the necessity of loyalty."

"Campbell will keep his mouth shut. If Galloway does bring him back, it'll look to the men like we can't run this place ourselves."

"He won't be bringing him back," Serena said, addressing both Pemberton and the man behind him.

Galloway leaned against a chestnut tree whose trunk outspanned his narrow shoulders. Despite wearing a blue denim shirt, Galloway had been so still Pemberton hadn't seen him. He didn't acknowledge Pemberton, but Pemberton knew Galloway had been listening all the while. Still listening. Pemberton looked down for a moment. His left hand folded inward slightly, and he saw that his thumb rubbed the index finger's gold. An image came to him from his childhood of a turbaned genie rubbing a lamp. He closed the hand completely and looked up.

"All right," Pemberton said.

"MCINTYRE'S doing some better," Stewart said that evening as the men set their tools down for the day, rested a minute before walking the half-mile back to camp. "Me and his missus done what you all suggested."

"Hung him up on a stick?" Ross asked.

"No, got him in the sunlight. He wouldn't leave his bed so me and his missus had to tote him out on it. We set him and that bed in the cow pasture where there ain't no shadows."

"Help any?" Henryson asked.

"Seemed to for a while," Stewart said. "He wasn't talking none but did get to where he'd pick up his axe and cut some firewood, but then a big hoot owl flapped over the pasture and give him the fantods again. He figured it for a portent of something bad a-coming."

Ross cleared his throat and spit, nodded across the quarter-mile of stumps and slash to the south where the Pembertons and Galloway had appeared. Galloway was on foot but the Pembertons rode on horseback, the eagle rigid as a sentinel as it perched on Serena's arm.

"You want a portent of something bad a-coming there it is," Ross said.

Henryson nodded. "They say death always comes in threes, and if that ain't the thing itself then I'm the king of England."

The men paused and stared out at the wasteland and watched the

Pembertons and Galloway pass below them, Serena's white gelding gleaming against the stark backdrop, Galloway trailing the procession, his hat brim low against the evening sun.

"Look at them rattles on Stub's hat," Ross said. "They's tilted up like a satinback ready to pour its teeth into you."

Henryson leaned over and raised his pant leg, examined a fist-sized bruise left by a limb whipping against it.

"I'm of a mind it's a good thing for Stub to have them rattles," he said, "especially if they give a little shake once in a while. Leastways you'd know he was around. That fellow could hide from his own shadow."

The men were silent a few moments.

"Campbell didn't come to work today," Henryson said.

"And that ain't like him," Stewart added.

"It ain't like him to haul a grip full of clothes and leave his front door open either," Henryson said, rolling down his pants leg. "Vaughn got up late last night to piss and seen him packing his car and heading out. I reckon Campbell read the writing on the wall. He was ever always a clever man."

"Like I told you," Ross noted, "Campbell's going to look after number one when things get too hot, like any other man."

"I think he was sick of being part of all their meanness," Stewart said. "You could tell he never cottoned to them, even if he never said so."

"They'll not abide his taking off like that," Henryson said, his eyes on the Pembertons and Galloway as he spoke.

"No," Ross agreed. "If you book keep, you know where the checks go, including the ones them senators in Raleigh stuff in their pockets."

"How long you figure her to give Campbell before she sics Stub there after him?" Henryson asked.

"I'd guess a day," Ross said, "just to give some sport to it."

"Some claims Galloway's mama helps him with his murderings," Stewart said. "All she's got to do is get a good look at you. Then she tells Galloway what he needs to do. That's what some say."

"There's some likely in that conclusion," Snipes said, finding a segue into the discussion. "Even your scientists and such argue some folks got uncertain ways of knowing things."

"Which is why you'll not hear me calling him Stub," Ross said to Henryson, "and I'd advise you not to call him that unless you're wanting to join the others he's taken a disliking to."

They watched the party enter the fold of land where Rough Fork Creek flowed into the valley. Their vanishing forms appeared to wobble and haze, miragelike. Then they were gone as if consumed by the air it-self.

Twenty-four

On Saturday evening Pemberton followed the blacktop through the declining hills and into the Pigeon River valley. A month earlier the last dogwood blossoms had wilted and fallen in the passing forests, the understory now the bright green of dogwood leaves and scrub oak, the denser green of mountain laurel and rhododendron. Pemberton suspected someday soon there'd be a poison to eradicate such valueless trees and shrubs and make it easier to cut and haul out hardwoods.

Pemberton raised his index finger and loosened the silk tie around his collar. He'd dressed up for the first time since his wedding. The white Indian cotton suit lay light over his body, but it still felt constrictive. Yet worth it to see Serena in the same dress she'd worn the first evening they'd met. Now as then the dress seemed in motion as it revealed her body's clefts and curves, its thin green current of silk coursing from neck to ankle. Pemberton placed his right hand on Serena's knee. As he felt the smooth skin beneath the smoothness of the silk, Pemberton tried to make its promise of later pleasure eclipse other concerns. But it didn't. As the road began its ascent from the valley, Pemberton lifted his hand and shifted the Packard into a lower gear.

"I heard McDowell came into the commissary last evening," Pemberton said, keeping his hand on the knob. "He was asking the men about Campbell."

"If he's asking questions, he must not have the answers," Serena replied, turning so her body angled toward Pemberton. "How is Meeks working out?"

"Considering it was his first week, pretty well. He has trouble with the local brogue, but he got the payroll numbers right."

The land leveled and then fell as they crossed the French Broad, the river brown and swollen from an afternoon rain. It was eventide and streetlights were flickering on as the Packard skirted Asheville. They crossed the Swannanoa River, then passed through the Biltmore Estate's main gate and began the winding three-mile drive to the mansion. The forest pressed close to the road, blotting out any light other than the Packard's beams.

The road curved and then straightened, revealing a grassy esplanade. Pemberton made the last turn, and the mansion appeared before them like a cliff of lights. Towers and spires surged upward in silhouette. Gargoyles leaned from the parapets, their scowling features backlit by the glow of windows. The limestone veneer bespoke solidity, a confidence that the Vanderbilt family's place in the world was beyond the vagaries of stock markets and industry.

"Chambord transported to the hinterlands," Serena said derisively as Pemberton braked, the Packard taking its place in line behind other cars.

At the mansion's main entrance, an attendant in black tails and top hat opened Serena's door and took the car keys. The Pembertons joined other guests walking up the wide steps. As they passed the marble lions, Serena placed her hand on Pemberton's forearm, held it firmly as she leaned closer and kissed him softly on the cheek. As she did, Pemberton felt some of his disquiet begin to lift.

They waited for three couples ahead of them to enter. Pemberton placed his hand on the small of Serena's back and moved his hand downward. Pemberton felt the silk cool against his fingers and palm as he caressed the flank of her upper hip. An image came back to him with such vividness that it might have been framed before him in glass—Serena in the dawn light of her Revere Street apartment, laying her Ram's Head overcoat on a chaise lounge as Pemberton entered the room behind her. She hadn't offered him something to drink or a place to sit, or even offered to take his coat. She'd only offered him herself, turning with her left hand already on the dress's green strap, pulling it off her shoulder and letting it fall, exposing the pale globe of her breast, the ruddy nipple beaded by the cold. The line shifted forward, bringing Pemberton out of his reverie.

In the entrance hall, a tuxedoed butler stepped forth and offered champagne flutes from a silver tray. Pemberton handed Serena one and took one for himself before they stepped forward to greet their hosts.

"Welcome to our domicile," John Cecil said, bowing after an exchange of names.

The host's left arm opened outward to the expansiveness behind him. Cecil's hand clasped Pemberton's as he kissed Serena demurely on the cheek. Cornelia Cecil stepped closer, let her lips brush Pemberton's cheek, then turned to Serena and embraced her.

"I'm so sorry, dear. Lydia Calhoun told me of your recent misfortune. To carry a child that long and lose it, such a terrible thing."

Mrs. Cecil broke the embrace but rested her hand on Serena's wrist.

"But you are here, and looking so well. That's something to be thankful for."

Serena's shoulders tensed as several other women came forth to offer condolences. Pemberton quickly took Serena's arm and told the women he needed his wife's presence for a few minutes. They walked to the far end of the room. As soon as they were alone, Serena took a long swallow from the crystal flute.

"I'll need another of these," she said as they made their way toward the music room.

In the music room a jazz band played "Saint Louis Blues." Several couples danced but most stood on the periphery with drinks in hand. Serena and Pemberton lingered by the doorway.

"My partners," Harris said loudly as he came up behind them.

Accompanying Harris was a man in a tuxedo who looked to be in his fifties. Both men moved in unsteadily gaits, whiskey in hand. Harris clasped Pemberton's shoulder with his free hand.

"Bradley Calhoun," Harris said, nodding at the man beside him. "I'll go get Lowenstein."

As Harris walked off, Pemberton offered his hand. Calhoun's handshake was firm and confident, but it could not hide the palm's plump softness. Calhoun took Serena's hand and bestowed a kiss upon it, his drink sloshing as he did so. After he let go her hand, Calhoun brushed back a lock of long yellow-gray hair with a flourish.

"The woman who tames eagles," Calhoun said in a cultivated Southern accent. "Your reputation precedes you, Mrs. Pemberton."

"I hope as a business partner as well," Serena replied.

Harris returned with Lowenstein, a man younger than Pemberton had expected. The New Yorker wore a dark-blue gabardine suit, which Pemberton assumed had been made in one of Lowenstein's own garment shops. Unlike the boisterous Calhoun, Lowenstein possessed the watchful reticence of a self-made man. Harris, his face already flushed by alcohol, raised his glass and the others did as well.

"To fortunes made in these mountains," Harris said, and they all drank.

"But why limit ourselves to just what's here," Serena added, still holding her champagne flute aloft. "Especially when there's so much more to be gained elsewhere."

"And where would that be, Mrs. Pemberton?" Lowenstein asked, his words precisely enunciated, perhaps to counter the vestiges of a European inflection.

"Brazil."

"Brazil?" Lowenstein said, giving Harris a puzzled look. "I'd assumed your plans were for local land investments."

"My husband and I are more ambitious than that," Serena said. "I think you will be also, once you learn of the possibilities."

Lowenstein shook his head.

"My hopes were something here, not Brazil."

"As was I," Calhoun said.

"Gentlemen, local purchases are certainly a possibility as well," Pemberton said, and was about to say more but Serena interrupted.

"Eight dollars on each dollar invested in Brazil, as opposed to two to one on your investment here."

"Eight dollars to one," Lowenstein said. "I find that hard to believe, Mrs. Pemberton."

"What if I can convince you otherwise by showing you land prices and costs of machinery and workers' pay," Serena replied. "I have the documents to prove everything. I'll bring them to Asheville tomorrow and let you peruse them for yourselves."

"Good Lord, Mrs. Pemberton," Harris sputtered, his tone balanced between amusement and annoyance. "You've barely allowed these gentlemen to sip their drinks before trying to hector them into some South America venture."

Calhoun raised his hand to halt Harris' protestations.

"I'd listen to such a proposal, tomorrow or any day for that matter, just for the pleasure of Mrs. Pemberton's presence."

"What about you, Mr. Lowenstein?" Serena said.

"I can't see myself investing in Brazil," he replied, "under any circumstances."

"Let's hear Mrs. Pemberton out, Lowenstein," Calhoun said. "Harris here claims she knows more about timber than any man he's ever met. Right, Harris?"

"No doubt about that," Harris said.

"But what about the new camp in Jackson County?" Lowenstein asked. "Won't that keep you in North Carolina for quite a while?"

"We're ready to begin cutting timber," Serena replied. "We'll be through there in a year at most."

"Brazil," Lowenstein mused. "What about you, Harris? Are you interested in Brazil, Inca gold perhaps?"

"No," Harris said. "As persuasive as Mrs. Pemberton can be, I think I'll stay in North Carolina."

"Too bad," Calhoun said. "How you and the Pembertons have profited by mining and logging the same land strikes me as rather brilliant."

"Yes," Harris said, signaling a waiter for another drink. "The Pembertons take what's above the ground and I take what's below."

"And what have you found below?" Lowenstein asked. "I'm not familiar with what is mined in this region."

"Mr. Harris has been rather reticent on that matter," Serena said.

"True," Harris admitted, "but since I've now bought the adjacent hundred acres and own the creek all the way to its source, I can be more forthcoming."

"Surely you don't mean gold?" Calhoun said.

Harris drained his glass and smiled widely.

"Better than gold. Near Franklin they've found rubies you measure by the ounce. I've seen one myself big as an apple. Sapphires and amethysts as well. All found within forty miles of our Jackson County site."

"So your tract looks promising for similar finds?" Lowenstein asked.

"Actually," Harris said, reaching into his pocket, "more than promising."

Harris opened his hand in the manner of a magician showing a vanished coin, revealing instead a small silver snuff tin. Harris unscrewed the lid and poured the contents into his palm.

"What are they?" Lowenstein asked, peering at a dozen stones shaped and sized like teardrops, all the color of dried blood.

"Rubies," Harris said. "These are too small to be worth more than a few dollars, but you can bet there are more, especially since I found these in and around the creek."

"Washed downstream from a whole cache of them, you mean?" Calhoun asked.

"Exactly, and it's often only the smaller ones that do get washed down."

Harris poured the stones back into the snuff tin, then reached into his pocket again and took out another stone the same size as the others, though this one was violet.

"Amethyst," Harris said. "The damn thing was right by the farmhouse, if you can believe that. Rhodolite garnets all over the yard as well, a sure sign you're in the right place to find more of what I just showed you."

"Sapphires and rubies," Calhoun exclaimed. "It sounds like a veritable El Dorado."

"I would never have believed such riches could be in these hinterlands," Lowenstein said.

"It was evidently so hard to believe there was no use mentioning it before we signed the papers," Serena said. "Right, Harris?"

Harris laughed. "You've found me out, Mrs. Pemberton."

Serena turned to Pemberton.

"I'm sure Mr. Harris realizes that our contract does not allow him to begin his mining operations until the timber is cut."

"Indeed," Pemberton said. "We may decide certain sites should remain uncut a whole decade."

Harris' face sagged a moment, then reset into a craggy grimace.

"Damn if I shouldn't put a clamp on my tongue whenever I drink," Harris muttered. "I won't go more than ten percent."

Calhoun shook his head admiringly.

"Not many could outfox this old fox. I'd hold out for twenty percent, Mrs. Pemberton, really make him pay for his skullduggery."

"I doubt it matters," Serena replied. "These rubies, Harris, how far upstream did you find them?"

"Not far at all," Harris replied. "I'd barely got to the creek when I saw the first one."

"How far did you go that first day?" Serena said. "Up the creek I mean."

"A third of a mile, but I've been all the way to the springhead since. That's nearly a whole mile."

"But how far upstream did you find the rubies?"

"What are you getting at, Mrs. Pemberton?" Lowenstein asked.

"Not far," Harris said, and raised his nose slightly as if detecting the first whiff of an unpleasant odor.

"I would suspect within fifty yards of the farmhouse," Serena said.

You don't think," Harris stammered. "But the stones weren't cut or cleaned off. Most people wouldn't even have known they were rubies. There weren't any footprints, not even around the waterfall."

Harris didn't speak for a few moments. His blue eyes widened in understanding even as his head swayed back and forth, as if part of his body hoped yet to dissuade him of the truth.

"That son-of-a-bitch Kephart waded up that creek," Harris said, and raised the crystal tumbler in his hand, seemingly ready to fling it against the wall. "God damn them."

Harris swore his oath again, this time loud enough that several nearby couples looked his way. Serena's face remained placid, except for her eyes. Pemberton thought of Buchanan and Cheney, who'd received similar looks. Then, as if a shutter had fallen, Serena's self-control reasserted itself.

"I saw Webb in the billiard room," Harris said, his face coloring. "I'll have a few words with him this evening. I'll catch up with Kephart later."

Pemberton looked over at Calhoun, who appeared amused, and Lowenstein, who seemed unsure if he should be listening or easing away.

"Let's not dwell on old matters," Serena said, "especially when we have such promising new ventures before us."

Harris finished his drink, wiped a drop of the amber-colored whiskey from his moustache. He looked at Serena with unconcealed admiration.

"Would I have married a woman like you, Mrs. Pemberton, I'd be richer than J.P. Morgan now," Harris said, and turned to Lowenstein and Calhoun. "I haven't heard a word about this Brazil business, but if Mrs. Pemberton thinks it can be successful I'll buy in, and you'll do well to do likewise."

"We'll all talk tomorrow in Asheville," Calhoun said.

Lowenstein nodded in agreement.

"Good," Serena said.

The band began playing "The Love Nest," and several couples strolled hand in hand onto the dance floor. Harris' face suddenly soured when he saw Webb standing in the lobby.

"Excuse me," he said. "I'll have a word with that man."

"No fisticuffs, Harris," Calhoun said.

Harris nodded, not entirely convincingly, then left the room.

As the song ended, Cecil stepped onto the jazz band's podium and announced it was almost time for dinner.

"But first to the Chippendale Room to show you the Renoir," the host said, "newly reframed to better show its colours."

Mr. and Mrs. Cecil led the guests up the marble stairs and into the second floor's living hall. They passed a life-sized portrait of Cornelia, and Serena paused to examine the painting more closely. She shook her head slightly and turned to Pemberton, who lingered beside her as the others walked on.

"I cannot understand how she endured it."

"What?" Pemberton asked.

"So many hours of stillness."

The Pembertons moved down the wide hallway, passing a portrait of Frederick Olmsted and then a Currier & Ives print. Beneath them a burgundy carpet softened their footsteps as the passageway veered left into another row of rooms. In the third, they rejoined the Cecils and the other guests, who huddled around the Renoir.

"It is magnificent," a woman in a blue evening dress and pearls declared. "The darker frame does free the colors more, especially the blue and yellow on the scarf."

Several guests respectfully stepped back to allow an elderly white-haired man to approach. His feet moved with short rigid steps, in the manner of some mechanical toy, a likeness enhanced by the metal band around his head, its dangle of wires connecting the metal to a rubber earpiece. He took a pince-nez from his coat pocket and examined the painting carefully. Someone behind the Pembertons whispered he was a former curator at the National Gallery of Art.

"As pure an example of the French modernist style as we have in this country," the man proclaimed loudly, then stepped back.

Serena leaned close to Pemberton and spoke. Harris, who was close by, chuckled.

"And you, Mrs. Pemberton," Cecil said. "Do you also have an opinion on Renoir?"

Serena gazed at the painting as she spoke.

"He strikes me as a painter for those who know little about painting. I find him timid and sentimental, not unlike the Currier & Ives print in the other room."

Cecil's face colored. He turned to the former curator as if soliciting a rebuttal, but the old man's hearing device had evidently been unable to transmit the exchange.

"I see," Cecil said and clasped his hands before him. "Well, it's time for dinner, so let's make our way downstairs."

They proceeded to the banquet hall. Serena scanned the huge mahogany table and found Webb at the far end near the fireplace. She took Pemberton's hand and led him to seats directly across from the newspaperman, who turned to his wife as the Pembertons sat down.

"Mr. and Mrs. Pemberton," Webb said. "The timber barons I've told you so much about."

Mrs. Webb smiled thinly but did not speak.

The waiters brought lentil and celery soup for the meal's first course, and the room quieted as guests lifted their spoons. When Pemberton finished his soup, he contemplated the Flemish tapestries, the three stone fireplaces and two massive chandeliers, the organ loft in the balcony.

"Envious, Pemberton?" Webb asked.

Pemberton scanned the room a few more moments and shook his head.

"Why would anyone be envious," Serena said. "It's merely a bunch of baubles. Expensive baubles, but of what use?"

"I see it as a rather impressive way to leave one's mark on the world," Webb said, "not so different from the great pharaohs' pyramids."

"There are better ways," Serena said, lifting Pemberton's hand in hers to rub the varnished mahogany. "Right, Pemberton."

Mrs. Webb spoke for the first time.

"Yes, like helping make a national park possible."

"Yet you contradict your husband," Serena said, "leaving something as it is makes no mark at all."

Waiters replaced the soup bowls and saucers with lemon sorbet garnished with mint. Next were filets of fresh-caught bass, the entrée served on bone china with burgundy circles, at the center GWV engraved in gold. Serena lifted a piece of the Bacarrat crystal, held it to the light to better display the initials cut in the glassware.

"Another great mark left upon the world," she said.

An intensifying reverberation came up the hall, and a few moments later a grand piano rolled into view, two workers positioning it just outside the main door. The jazz orchestra's pianist sat down on the bench as the singer stood attentively, waiting for a signal from Mrs. Cecil. The pianist began playing and the singer soon joined in.

One thing's sure and nothing's surer
The rich get richer and the poor get—children.
In the meantime,
In between time

"This song," Mrs. Webb said, "is it a favorite of yours, Mrs. Pemberton?"

"Not really."

"I thought perhaps Mrs. Cecil had it played in your honor. A way of cheering you up after your recent misfortune."

"You show more wit than I'd have thought, Mrs. Webb," Serena said. "I'd assumed you a dullard, like your husband."

"A dullard," Webb said, musing over the word. "I wonder what that makes Harris? He accosted me in the lobby. It seems he bought a salted claim."

"If he'd been forthright with us, we'd have figured it out," Serena said tersely.

"You may be right, Mrs. Pemberton," Webb said, "yet someone obviously counted on the fact that Harris would betray a partnership for his own self-interest."

"I think betrayal is a bit strong for what he did," Pemberton said.

"I don't," Serena said.

Webb waved his hand dismissively.

"Regardless, Colonel Townsend has accepted Albright's offer, and all the documents have been signed. That land was the lynchpin, you know. The whole project could have easily fallen through without it, but now all the parkland on the Tennessee side has been bought."

"Then that should be enough," Pemberton said. "You and your fellows can have the park in Tennessee and leave North Carolina alone."

"I'm afraid it doesn't work that way, Mr. Pemberton," Webb said. "This frees us to turn all our attention to North Carolina. With two-thirds of the proposed park land secured, eminent domain will be even easier to enact, maybe as soon as next fall from what Secretary Albright's told me."

"We'll have every tree in the tract cut down by then," Serena said.

"Perhaps," Webb admitted, "and it may take forty or fifty years before that forest will grow back. But when it does, it will be part of the Great Smoky Mountains National Park."

"Pemberton and I will have logged a whole country by then," Serena said.

For a few moments no one spoke. Pemberton looked for Harris and found him five seats away, laughing at some remark a young lady had made.

"But not this land," Webb replied. "As Cicero noted, *ut sementem feceris ita metes.*"

"Do you know how Cicero died?" Serena said. "It's certainly something a scribbler such as yourself should be familiar with."

"I've heard the story," Webb said. "I'm not easily intimidated, Mrs. Pemberton, if that's your intent."

"I don't know the story," Mrs. Webb said to Serena. "I'd prefer your threats be explained."

"Cicero made himself an enemy of Antony and Fulvia," Serena replied. "He could have left Rome before they came to power, but he believed his golden words could protect him. As your husband is aware, they didn't. Cicero's head was displayed on the Rostra in the Roman Forum, where Fulvia took golden pins from her hair and pierced his tongue. She left them there until the head was tossed out to the dogs."

"A history lesson worth heeding," Pemberton said to Webb.

"No more so than how Antony himself died, Mr. Pemberton," Webb replied.

THE Pembertons did not get back to camp until one A.M., but Galloway was waiting on the front steps.

"We won't need to wake him after all," Serena said when she saw Galloway.

Pemberton turned off the engine. The light from the office porch was not enough to see Serena's face as he spoke.

"What Harris did, I'm not so sure we wouldn't have done the same under those circumstances. And the money, we didn't lose that much."

"He made us vulnerable," Serena said. "It's like an infection, Pemberton. If you don't cauterize it, then it spreads. It won't be that way in Brazil. Our investors will be a continent away." Serena paused. "We should never have allowed it to be otherwise. Just us."

For a few moments neither spoke.

"Isn't that what we want?" Serena asked.

"Yes," Pemberton said after another pause. "You're right."

"Whether it's right wasn't my question," Serena said, her voice soft, something in it almost like sadness. "Is it what we want?"

"Yes," Pemberton said, glad the darkness concealed his face.

Pemberton opened the car door and went on inside the house while Serena talked on the porch with Galloway. He poured himself a stout dram of bourbon and sat down in the Coxwell chair that faced the hearth. Though cool weather was still months away, a thick white oak log had been placed on the andirons, newspaper and kindling set around it. Serena's voice filtered through the wall, the words muffled but the tone calm and measured as she told Galloway what she wanted done. Pemberton knew if he could see Serena's face it would be just as placid, no different than if she were sending Galloway to Waynesville to mail a letter. He also realized something else, that Serena would be able to convince Lowenstein and Calhoun to invest in her Brazil venture. Like her husband, they would believe her capable of anything.

Twenty-five

BEFORE THE FIRST STRINGHOUSE HAD BEEN set on Bent Knob Ridge, the dining hall or train track or commissary built, an acre between Cove Creek and Noland Mountain had been set off for a graveyard. As if to acknowledge the easy transition between the quick and the dead in the timber camp, no gate led into the graveyard and no fence surrounded it. The only markers were four wooden stobs. By the time they'd rotted, enough mounds swelled the acre to make further delineation of boundaries unnecessary. Occasionally, a deceased worker would have his body taken from the valley to a family graveyard, but the majority were buried in camp. The timber that had brought them here and killed them, and now enclosed them, also marked most of the graves. These wooden crosses ranged in elaborateness from little more than two sticks tied together to finely sawn pieces of cherry and cedar with names and dates burned into the wood. On these graves, sometimes on the crosses themselves, the bereaved always placed some memento. A few evoked a fatalistic irony, the engraved axe handle that felled the tree that in turn felled the owner, an iron-spiked Kaiser's helmet worn by a man struck by lightning. But most of what adorned the graves attempted to brighten the bleak landscape, not just wildflowers and holly wreaths but something more enduring—yellow-feathered hadicaws, Christmas ornaments, military medals trailing hued ribbons, on the grave itself bits of indigo glass and gum foil and rose quartz, which sometimes were cast over the loose soil like seeds for planting, other times set in elaborate patterns to spell what might be as discernable as a name or obscure as a petrograph.

It was upon this graveyard that Ross and his fellows gazed as the crew took its afternoon break. Rain had fallen off and on all day, and the men were wet and muddy and cold, the low gray sky adding to their somberness.

"The boy killed yesterday by that skidder boom," Ross said. "There was a hell of a thing. In the ground with dirt over him before he'd worked a week. A fellow used to could count on at least a pay stub before getting killed."

"Or live long enough to shave something besides peach fuzz off his chin," Henryson added. "That boy couldn't have been no more than sixteen."

"I expect before long they'll be fittin us for coffins ahead of time," Ross said. "You'll be planted in the ground before you've got a chance to stiffen up good."

"They ever find out who his people was?" Stewart asked. "That boy, I mean."

"No," Henryson said. "Jumped off one of them boxcars coming through so there ain't no telling. Wasn't nothing in his billfold but a picture. An older woman, probably his mama."

"Nothing writ on the back of it?" Stewart asked.

Henryson shook his head.

"Nary a word."

"Your people not knowing where you're buried," Stewart said sombery. "That's a terriblesome thing. There'll be never a flower nor teardrop touch his grave."

"I heard back in the Confederate War them soldiers pinned their names and where they was from on their uniforms," Henryson said. "Leastways their folks would know what happened to them."

Snipes, who'd been trying to unfold his sodden newspaper without tearing it, nodded in affirmation.

"It's the truth," he said. "That's how they knew where my grandpappy was buried. He got killed over in Tennessee fighting for the Lincolnites. They buried him right where he fell, but leastways his mama known where he was laid."

"Anything more on Harris in your newspaper?" Ross asked.

Snipes delicately set the wide wings of the paper onto his lap.

"There is. Says here the county coroner still has the brass to claim Harris' death was an accident, and that's after Editor Webb's article about the coroner being in the Pembertons' pocket."

"Makes you wonder who's next, don't it?" Henryson said.

"I'd not be surprised if Webb's moved up a spot or two with that editorial," Ross said. "I hope his house don't have a second floor. He might take the same tumble Harris did."

The men grew silent. Stewart unfolded the oilcloth that kept his Bible dry and began reading. Ross reached into his pocket and brought out his tobacco pouch. He removed his rolling papers and found them sodden as Snipes' newspaper. Henryson, who also was anticipating a cigarette, found his papers in the same condition.

"I was at least hoping my lungs might be warm and dry a minute," Ross complained.

"You'd think there'd be one little pleasure you could have, even on a day scawmy as this one," Henryson said. "You ain't got no rolling papers, do you Stewart?"

Stewart shook his head, not raising it from his Bible.

"How about a few pages of your Bible there?" Ross asked. "That'd make a right fine rolling paper."

Stewart looked up incredulously.

"It'd be sacrilegious do such a thing as that."

"I ain't asking for pages where something important's being said," Ross entreated. "I'm just asking for two pages where there's nothing but a bunch of so and so begot so and so. There ain't nothing to be missed there."

"It still don't seem right to me," Stewart said.

"I'd say it's exactly the Christian thing to do," Henryson countered, "helping out two miserable fellows who just want a smoke."

Stewart turned to Snipes.

"What do you think?"

"Well," Snipes said. "Your leading scholars has argued for years you'll find cause to do or not do most anything in that book, so I'm of a mind you got to pluck out the verse what trumps the rest of them."

"But which one's that?" Stewart asked.

"How about love thy neighbor," Henryson quickly volunteered.

Stewart bit his lower lip, deep in thought. Almost a minute passed before he opened the Bible and turned to Genesis. Stewart perused some pages before carefully tearing out two.

ON the following Sunday afternoon, the Pembertons mounted their horses for a ride to Shanty Mountain. Pemberton hadn't especially wanted to go, but as it was something Serena expected of him, he followed her to the barn. A sawyer had been killed by a snapped cable on Saturday morning, and as Pemberton and Serena made their way out of the camp, they encountered a funeral party proceeding toward the cemetery where an unfilled grave waited amid the stumps and slash. Leading the mourners was a youth wearing a black armband on his sleeve, in his hands a three-foot-tall oak cross. Two workers carrying the coffin came next, then a woman dressed in widow's weeds. Reverend Bolick and a dozen men and women followed. Two of the men walked with shovels leaned on their right shoulders, like military men at arms. Reverend Bolick carried his Bible, its black weight held skyward as if to deflect the sun's glare. Last came the women, bright-hued wildflowers in their hands. They moved through the blighted landscape slowly, looking as much like refugees as mourners.

Pemberton and Serena traveled west, the land rising quickly, the air stingier. An hour later the Pembertons made the last switchback in the trail and stood atop Shanty Mountain. They had not spoken the whole way. Serena and Pemberton looked over the valley and ridges and surveyed what timber remained.

"What Harris did, it was a needed reminder," Serena said, breaking their silence.

"A reminder of what?" Pemberton asked, still staring out at the valley.

"That others can make us vulnerable and the sooner such vulnerabilities are dealt with the better."

Pemberton met her eyes, and saw within Serena's gaze a stark unflinching certainty, as though to think otherwise was not just erroneous but unimaginable. She patted the Arabian's flank and moved off a few paces to check the depth a steel cable had bitten into a hickory stump. Pemberton looked down at the camp. The sun shone full on the train tracks, and the linked metal gleamed. Soon it would be time to pull up the rails, starting with the spurs and moving backward to undo what they'd bolted to the land.

Just remember you were warned, Mrs. Lowell had said that first night in Boston. Serena told him later she'd come only because she'd heard a timber man named Pemberton would be present at the party. She'd made a few inquiries to people in the business and decided it worth her time to meet him. After Mrs. Lowell had introduced them, Pemberton and Serena quickly left the others and talked on the verandah until midnight. Then she'd taken him to her apartment on Revere Street and he'd stayed until morning. Weren't you afraid that first evening I'd think you a strumpet with such boldness, he'd teased her later. No, she'd replied. I had more faith in us than that. Pemberton remembered how Serena had not spoken as she unlocked the apartment's door. She'd just stepped inside, leaving the door open. Serena had turned and fixed her eyes on him. Then, as now, they'd contained the utter certainty that Pemberton would follow her.

As they rode back, the sun's last light embered on the western ridge tops. A breeze had cooled the air on Shanty, but as Pemberton and Serena made their descent the air became stagnant, humid. In the graveyard only one worker remained, methodically shoveling the last clods of dirt over the coffin.

Serena and Pemberton ate their supper in the back room and alone, as they always did now, then returned to the house. At eleven Pemberton went into the back room to prepare for bed. Serena followed him but did not begin to undress. Instead, she sat in a chair across the room, watching him intently.

"Why aren't you undressing?" Pemberton asked.

"I have one more thing to do tonight."

"It can't wait till morning?"

"No, I'd rather get it done tonight."

Serena rose from the ladderback chair, came over and kissed Pemberton full on the mouth.

"Just us," she whispered, her lips still touching his.

Pemberton followed her to the door. As Serena stepped onto the porch, Galloway, seemingly unbidden, emerged from the shadows.

Pemberton watched as they walked to the office. Vaughn came out a few moments later and brought Galloway's car from behind the stable. When Galloway and Serena stepped onto the office porch, Pemberton saw something was in Serena's hand. As she passed directly under the porch's yellow light bulb, it gave off a silvery wink.

Galloway handed Vaughn a pen and notepad, and the youth wrote on it, pausing a moment to make movements with his index finger when

Galloway asked something further. Pemberton watched Serena and Galloway drive off, his gaze following the headlights as the automobile moved across the valley floor, then disappeared. Vaughn, who'd watched the car beams diminish as well, went inside the office and closed the door. In a few minutes, Vaughn came out. He turned off the porch light and walked rapidly toward his stringhouse.

Pemberton went back into the house but did not go to bed. He set invoices before him on the kitchen table, attempting to lose himself in calculations of board feet and freight costs. Since the moment Serena and Galloway had driven off, he'd tried to block his mind from imagining where they were going. If he didn't know, he couldn't do anything about it.

But his mind worked in that direction anyway, wondering if what Serena had whispered was not "just us" but instead a single word. He figured the only way to stop the flow of thoughts was with the half-filled bottle of Canadian bourbon in the cabinet. Pemberton didn't bother with a glass. Instead, he tipped the bottle and drank until he gasped for breath, the bourbon scalding his throat. He drank again and finished off the bottle. He sat in one of the Coxwell chairs and closed his eyes, waited for the whiskey to take hold. Pemberton hoped the half-quart was enough and tried to help it along. He imagined the thoughts seeking connection in his head were like dozens of wires plugged into a switchboard, wires the whiskey would begin pulling free until not a single connection was possible.

In a few minutes, Pemberton felt the alcohol expanding in his skull, the wires pulling free, one at a time, the chatter lessening until there was no chatter at all, just a glowing hum. He closed his eyes and let himself sink deeper into the chair.

When the clock on the fireboard chimed midnight, Pemberton stepped back out on the porch. The whiskey made his gait unsteady, and he held onto the porch railing as he looked down at the camp. No light glowed through the office window, and Galloway's car was still gone. A dog barked near the commissary, then quit. Someone in a stringhouse played a guitar, not strumming but plucking each string slowly, letting the note fade completely before offering another. In a few minutes the guitar stopped, and the camp was completely silent. Pemberton raised his head, felt a moment of vertigo as he did so. Soon the last coal-oil lamp in the stringhouses was snuffed. To the west, a few mute spasms of heat lightning. Dark thickened but offered no stars, only a moon pale as bone.

Twenty-six

SHERIFF MCDOWELL DROVE INTO CAMP AT MID-morning. He didn't knock before entering the office. Pemberton found the sheriff's manner typically insolent and remembered it was Wilkie who'd advocated McDowell remain in office when the timber camp first opened. It will mollify the locals to have one of their own in the position, Wilkie had argued. Pemberton did not offer McDowell a seat, nor did the sheriff ask for one. Pemberton still felt the effects of the whiskey, not just the hangover but a residue of drunkenness as well.

"What brings you here that a telephone call couldn't convey?" Pemberton asked, looking at the invoices on his desk. "I've got too much work to deal with uninvited guests."

McDowell did not speak until Pemberton's gaze again focused on him.

"There was a murder up on Colt Ridge last night."

The sheriff's eyes absorbed Pemberton's surprise. The only sound in the room was the Franklin clock on the credenza. As Pemberton listened, the clock's ticking seemed to gain volume. Wires the alcohol had severed reconnected. Pemberton felt something shift inside him, something small but definite, the way a knob's slight twist allowed a door to swing wide open.

"A murder," Pemberton said.

"A murder," the sheriff repeated, emphasizing the first syllable. "Just one, Adeline Jenkins, an old widow-woman who never harmed anyone. Her throat was slashed. Cut left to right, which means whoever did it was left-handed."

"Why are you telling me this, Sheriff?"

"Because whoever did it didn't bother to step around the blood on the floor. I found two sets of boot prints. One's just a brogan, nothing special about it except small-sized for a man, but the other is something fancy. Narrow toed, nothing you'd buy around here. From the size and shape I'm betting it's a woman's. All I've got to do is find a match, and the fact that I'm here should tell you I know where to look."

"I'd be careful about any accusations," Pemberton said. "I have no idea who this Jenkins woman is. She doesn't work for me."

"Your wife and that henchman of hers thought she'd tell them where the Harmon girl and her child were. That's what I think. They went to the girl's cabin first. The door was wide open this morning, and I know for a fact it was fastened last night. Cigarette butts by the barn as well. Only I don't know which one they were after." McDowell paused. "Which one was it, the child or the mother? Or was it both?"

"The Harmon girl and the child," Pemberton said. "You're saying they weren't harmed?"

"Ask your wife."

"I don't need to," Pemberton said, his voice not as assertive as he wished. "Whatever happened, she wasn't involved. Any tramp off a train could have killed that old woman. If you're looking for a suspect, you should go down to the depot."

McDowell looked at the floor a few moments as if studying the grain of the wood. He slowly raised his eyes and stared directly at Pemberton.

"Do you people think you can do anything?" McDowell asked. "I went over to Asheville last week and found out more about Doctor Cheney's killing. There were at least five possible causes of death and all of them slow. Campbell at least got killed quick, the Nashville sheriff says. Harris did too."

"Harris fell and broke his neck," Pemberton said. "Your own coroner said it was an accident."

"Your coroner, not mine," McDowell replied. "I'm not the one paying him off every month."

The sheriff's uniform was rumpled, as if he'd slept in it the night before. McDowell suddenly seemed conscious of this, and tucked his shirt tail tighter into his pants. As he raised his eyes, his features pinched into a rictus of loathing.

"I can't do anything about Buchanan or Cheney or Harris, maybe not Campbell either, but I vow I'll do something about the murder of an old woman, and I'll not let a mother and her child be killed," McDowell said, then more softly. "Even if it is your child."

For a few moments neither man spoke. The sheriff splayed his fingers and ran them through hair he'd obviously not combed that morning, revealing a few streaks of gray Pemberton had never noticed before. The sheriff let the raised hand settle over the right side of his face. He rubbed his forehead as if he'd banged it against a door jamb or window sill. The hand was withdrawn, resettled on the side of McDowell's leg.

"When's the last time you saw that boy?"

"January," Pemberton answered.

"Amazing how much he favors you. Same eyes, same hair color."

Pemberton nodded at an invoice on the desk.

"I've got work to do, Sheriff."

"Where's your wife?"

"Out with the cutting crews."

"How far from here?"

"I don't know," Pemberton said. "She could be anywhere between here and the Tennessee line."

"That's convenient."

McDowell looked at the clock, kept his eyes on it a few moments.

"I'll be back," he said, and turned and walked toward the door, "and I'll have an arrest warrant next time."

Pemberton watched from his window as the sheriff got in his car and drove across the valley toward Waynesville. He went to the gun rack and opened the drawer beneath the mounted rifles. The hunting knife was in the same place as before, but when Pemberton pulled its elk-bone handle from the sheath, he saw that blood stained the blade. The blood was black, clotted. Pemberton scratched a fleck free and rubbed it between his thumb and forefinger. He felt a residue of moisture.

The phone rang and Pemberton almost didn't answer it, picking up the receiver only after the eighth ring. Calhoun was on the line, asking a question about the contract Serena had shown him and Lowenstein. Pemberton's voice felt hardly a part of himself as he told Calhoun that the paperwork was nearly done.

Pemberton did not set the receiver back on the hanger. Instead, he made a call to Saul Parton in Waynesville and left a message with the coroner's wife. The knife still lay on the desk, and Pemberton picked it up, briefly considered taking the weapon to the saw mill and throwing it in the splash pond. But it was, Pemberton reminded himself, his wedding present. For a few moments, he allowed that scalding thought to resonate through him. Then he wet a handkerchief with his spit and wiped off the blood. Pemberton slipped the knife in the sheath and placed it back in the gun rack's drawer. He picked up the receiver again and told the operator he wished to make a call to Raleigh.

Afterwards, Pemberton left the office and searched for Vaughn but had no luck. He did find Meeks in the dining hall, discussing next month's payroll with the head cook. The conversation was a halting exchange, the North Carolina highlander and New England yankee struggling with each other's dialects like two ill-trained interpreters.

"I've got to go to Waynesville," Pemberton told Meeks. "Stay in the office and answer the phone. If Saul Parton calls, tell him not to send his report to Raleigh until I see him."

"Very well," Meeks said with exasperation, "though I'm a bookkeeper, not a linguist. If your callers speak the same barbarous parlance as this fellow I'll have no idea what they are saying."

"If you see Vaughn, he can spell you. I'll be back as soon as I can."

As he drove out of the valley, Pemberton saw Galloway sitting on the commissary steps, a half-eaten apple in his hand, enjoying a day off for working late last night. Pemberton wondered if Galloway had seen the sheriff's car. As the Packard passed, Galloway's gray eyes looked up, but they were as blank and fathomless as his mother's.

McDowell's patrol car was parked outside the courthouse, a relief since Pemberton wouldn't have to search around town for him. Pemberton found a parking place and walked up the sidewalk, crossed the courthouse lawn. Only the desk's lamp was on when he entered the office, and Pemberton's eyes took a moment to adjust to the gloaming. McDowell was in the room's one cell pulling a dingy mattress off its spring base. As the sheriff did so, dust motes floated upward, suspended in the cell window's barred light as if in a web.

"Checking for hacksaws and files, Sheriff?"

"Bedbugs," McDowell replied, not looking up. "I suspect you and Mrs. Pemberton have them as well. They aren't particular about who they lay down with."

Pemberton seated himself in a rickety shuck bottom chair set in front of the sheriff's desk. Above, a ceiling fan stirred the air with no noticeable effect. McDowell took the mattress from the cell and down the narrow hall to the open back door and set it outside. He came back in and repositioned the regulator clock's calendar hand. Only then did he sit down behind his desk.

"Come to turn in your wife?" McDowell asked.

"I've come to make an offer for your cooperation," Pemberton said, "a final one."

"You know my answer. You've known it for three years."

Pemberton eased back into the chair he suspected the sheriff deliberately wanted uncomfortable, spreading his legs to better balance his two-hundred pounds.

"It's not just money this time. It's whether you want to continue being sheriff."

"Oh, I'm going to continue," McDowell replied. "I found me a fisherman who saw Galloway's Ford crossing the bridge near Colt Ridge last night. Since Galloway doesn't have a left hand, I'd say that kind of narrows who did the actual killing."

"I just got off the phone to a state senator who can have you fired within a week," Pemberton said. "You want to keep your job or not?"

McDowell looked intently at Pemberton.

"What's interesting to me is how you were surprised this morning. I guess I can take that a couple of ways, can't I?"

"I don't know what you're talking about," Pemberton answered.

"No, maybe you don't," McDowell said after a few moments. "Maybe you're such a worthless son-of-a-bitch that you wanted it done same as she did, but you were too gutless to go with her."

McDowell stood up, his chair scraping against the wood floor as he shoved it backward. He was not nearly as big a man as Pemberton, no more than five-ten. Yet there was a visible strength in McDowell's body, wiry but muscled in the biceps and forearms, wrists thicker than expected for his frame. No gun and holster clinched around the sheriff's waist. Pemberton stood up as well. It would be a good fight, Pemberton told himself, because the highlanders considered it a matter of honor never to cut and run, or quit once a brawl had begun. He'd be able to pummel McDowell for ten or fifteen minutes. Adrenaline surged through his veins, and with it Pemberton felt a revived sense of his own strength that had been dormant too long. The world suddenly became simpler than it had been in a long while.

But before they could start, there was a knock on the door, another soon after, still light but more insistent. McDowell looked toward the door. Pemberton thought the lawman would walk over and lock it, and perhaps he would have, but at that moment the brass doorknob turned and the door opened. An older woman, her gray hair tied in a taut bun, entered the office, behind her Rachel Harmon, the child in her arms.

Pemberton looked at Jacob and saw the sheriff was right about his features, even more obvious now than in January. He thought about the photograph of himself and wondered if Serena had found it last night as she searched for the hunting knife. She might have opened the desk drawer and found the album, turned the pages until she came to the last two. It suddenly occurred to Pemberton then that Serena might have taken not only the knife but also a photograph with her.

Sheer lunacy to imagine such a thing, Pemberton told himself, but his mind continued to assemble its own fevered logic. Pemberton remembered the glint of the knife blade when Serena stepped onto the porch last night. He tried to recall if something had been in her right hand as well. It could have easily been there, a photograph taken to confirm a child that, as far as Pemberton knew, Serena had never seen. Taken to make sure—except it wouldn't be the photograph of Jacob as an infant, Pemberton suddenly realized. Because even if Serena knew it was a picture of Jacob, she'd need a picture of the child the way he looked *now*, at two years of age. Serena would have taken the photograph of Pemberton.

Pemberton continued to stare at Jacob. It was impossible not to. The dark-brown eyes solemnly stared back at him. The Harmon girl noticed and turned the boy away. For a few moments no one moved, as if all awaited someone else to enter the office and set something yet unknown into motion. The only sound was the tick of the brass chain against the ceiling fan's motor.

McDowell opened the desk drawer and pulled out his revolver. The sheriff clicked off the safety and pointed it at Pemberton.

"Get out of here."

Pemberton was about to speak, but McDowell thumbed back the hammer and aimed directly at Pemberton's forehead. The sheriff's raised arm and hand did not tremble as the index finger settled against the trigger.

"If you say a word, one single word, I swear to God I'll kill you," McDowell said.

Pemberton believed him. He stepped away from the desk and walked across the room, the Harmon girl clutching the child tighter in her arms as if Pemberton might try to snatch away the boy. Pemberton opened the door and stepped blinking into the midday light.

The town was still there, the streetlamps and shops and the not quite obsolete hitching post, the clock face on the courthouse steeple. Pemberton watched as the ponderous minute hand lurched forward and nudged away another bit of time. He recalled one of the few occasions he'd attended his physics class at Harvard, the professor lecturing on an idea espoused by an Austrian scientist about the relativity of time. It seemed that way to him now, as if time was no longer brisk measured increments but something more fluid, with its own currents and eddies. Something that could easily sweep him away.

A Model T blared its horn and pulled around him. Only then did Pemberton realize he stood in the middle of the street. Pemberton walked to his car and got in, but he did not turn the key and press the starter button.

In a few minutes the office door opened. The older woman went up the street, but the girl and child got in the sheriff's car. Pemberton let them get far enough away and then pulled out and followed the sheriff's car west. After a while the blacktop became dirt, and gray roostertails of dust rose in the police car's wake. Pemberton dropped farther behind, no longer following the car but the haze of dust. The dust trail soon left the main road, turned down the washout that led to Deep Creek. Pemberton knew where they were headed.

Pemberton did not follow but drove fifty yards past. He turned the Packard around and parked it on the road's weedy shoulder. The day was warm, but he didn't roll down the passenger window. He wanted to blame the heat for the sweat matting his shirt. Twenty minutes later the sheriff's car came back up the secondary road and turned toward Waynesville.

There was a two-foot-long Stillson wrench in the trunk, and for a few minutes he imagined the ten pounds of iron in his grasp. It would be enough. Or he could simply make a phone call to Meeks, a few words passed on to Galloway. He turned the key and his foot pressed the starter button. Pemberton let his hand settle over the black gear shift knob. He squeezed and felt the ball of hard rubber in his grip. He pressed the clutch and paused a moment longer, then shifted the Packard into gear. When he came to the Deep Creek turnoff, Pemberton did not slow but kept on going. He drove into Waynesville, on past the hospital and elementary school and the train depot, then on toward Cove Creek Valley.

As Pemberton passed the saw mill, he remembered his father's funeral, though "remembered" didn't seem as apt a word to him as "recovered." He could not recall the last time he'd thought of the funeral since his return from Boston. Or when he'd last thought of his mother or two sisters. The letters they'd written him those first months had been thrown away unopened. Partly it had been his freeing himself of the past, as Serena advocated, but it had also been a self-willed amnesia, a spell willingly succumbed to.

Pemberton was halfway to the camp when he pulled off at the summit where he'd first shown Serena the lumber company's holdings. He stepped to the precipice and looked down at the vast dark gash they'd made on the land. Pemberton stared at the razed landscape a long time, wanting it to be enough. He looked beyond the valley and ridges and found Mount Mitchell. The highest point in the eastern United States, Buchanan had claimed, and so it appeared to be, its tip closer to the clouds than any other in sight. Pemberton gazed at the peak a long time, then let his eyes fall slowly downward, and it was as if he was falling as well, falling slow and deliberate and with his eyes open.

Twenty-seven

BEFORE SHE SAW THE LATE MORNING LIGHT, Rachel had felt it, the sun's heat and brightness lying full on her closed eyelids. She heard Jacob's steady breaths and something, something not remembered in those first moments of waking, caused her to know the importance of his breaths, that he *was* breathing. She reached her arms around the child, pressed him closer. He made a soft complaint, but his breath soon soothed into the calmness of sleep. It all came back to her then—the sheriff at the cabin door, a dress and shoes quickly pulled on and a carpetbag stuffed with what Jacob would need. Maybe nothing, just a rusty, the sheriff had told her, but he didn't want to take a chance. He'd brought her to the boarding house, given her and Jacob his own room for the night. Rachel had listened to the grandfather clock in the hallway chime the hours toward dawn, unable to sleep until first light filtered through the window and

Jacob had whimpered and she'd suckled him. Only then did she fall asleep.

Now, in the early afternoon, she and Jacob were in the back seat of Sheriff McDowell's police car, heading down what was little more than a skid trail along Deep Creek. They made another turn, the road now nothing more than a winding gap between trees. Sapling branches raked the car's sides, the seat springs creaking and bobbing beneath her and Jacob. The road made a sharp final bend and then was simply gone. Nothing but a stand of maple trees, a foot-wide path leading into them. The sheriff backed up and turned the car around to face the way they'd come. He cut off the engine but did not make a move to get out. Rachel had no idea where they were. When she'd asked the sheriff where they were going, the only words she'd spoken since his landlady had brought her and Jacob to the courthouse, he'd just answered somewhere safe. The sheriff looked in the rearview mirror, met her eyes.

"You'll be staying down here a few hours with a man named Kephart. You can trust him."

"It could have been just a rusty somebody was playing, couldn't it, like you said?"

The sheriff turned and placed his arm on the seat.

"Adeline Jenkins was murdered last night. I think the folks who killed her thought she could tell them where you and that child were."

The car's metal and cloth upholstery seemed to thin and lighten, the seat beneath her and Jacob seeping away, a sense of weightlessness like the moment between the rise and fall on a rope swing. She pressed Jacob tighter, closed her eyes for a few moments, opened them.

"You mean the Widow?" Rachel said, saying it that way because if it was a question it could still, for a few moments longer, be a question and not a confirmation.

"Yes," McDowell said.

"Who would do such a thing?"

"Serena Pemberton and a man who works for her named Galloway. You know who he is, don't you?"

"Yes sir."

Jacob squirmed in her lap. Rachel looked down and saw his eyes were open.

"Mr. Pemberton . . . ," Rachel said, and could think of no more words to follow.

"He wasn't up there, I know that," the sheriff said. "I'm not even sure he knew what they were going to do."

McDowell let his gaze settle on Jacob.

"I've got my own ideas about why she'd do this, but I'd be interested in yours."

"I think it's because I could give him the one thing that she couldn't," Rachel said.

The sheriff gave a nod so slight it seemed to Rachel more an acknowledgment that he'd heard her than a sign of agreement. He turned back around, seemingly lost in his own musings. Somewhere in the trees Rachel heard a yellowhammer tapping at a tree. It started up, then paused, then started again, like someone knocking on a door and waiting for a response.

"You're sure she's dead?" Rachel said, "not just hurt bad?"

"She's dead."

They did not speak for a few moments. Jacob fussed again but when Rachel checked his swaddling it was dry.

"If he's hungry I can get out and give you some privacy," Sheriff McDowell said.

"It's too soon for him to be hungry. He's just put out because I forgot to bring him some play-pretties."

"We'll stay here a couple more minutes," McDowell said, checking his watch, "just to be sure we weren't followed. Then we can walk down to Kephart's place. It's not far."

Jacob fussed some more, and she took the sugar teat from the carpetbag, put it in his mouth. The child calmed, a soft kissing sound as he worked the cheesecloth and sugar between his gums.

"What it was that happened," Rachel asked. "They done it to her in her house?"

"Yes."

Rachel thought about Widow Jenkins, how the old woman had loved this child in her arms. As far as Rachel knew, the one other person in the world who loved him. She thought of the old woman in her chair by the hearth, knitting or just watching the fire and hearing a knock on the door and probably thinking it could only be Rachel, thinking that maybe Jacob had the flux or a fever and Rachel needed her help.

"They had no cause to kill her," Rachel said, as much to herself as to Sheriff McDowell.

"No, they didn't," the sheriff replied, and reached for his door handle. "We can go now."

McDowell carried the carpetbag and Rachel carried the child. The trail was steep and narrow, and she watched for roots that could send her and Jacob sprawling. Purple-tinged pokeberry clustered beside the path, the berries shiny-dark as water beetles. Come the first frost, Rachel knew the stems would sag and the berries wither. Where will me and this young one be then, she wondered. They crossed a weathered plank that wobbled over a tight rush of whitewater, and the land leveled out.

The cabin was small but well built, the wattle and clay daubing packed with care between the hand-hewn logs, not so different from her and Jacob's cabin. A drift of smoke rose from the corbelled chimney, the door partway open.

"Kephart," the sheriff said, addressing not just the cabin but the nearby woods.

A man Rachel guessed to be in his late sixties appeared in the doorway. He wore denim breeches and a wrinkled chambray work shirt. His gallouses were unstrapped from his shoulders, and a gray stubble showed he hadn't shaved in several days. The skin below his eyes was puffy and jaundiced looking, the eyes themselves bloodshot. Rachel knew from being around her father what that meant.

"I need a favor," Sheriff McDowell said, and nodded toward Rachel and Jacob. "They need to stay here, maybe just till this evening, maybe till morning."

Kephart looked not at Rachel but at the child, who'd fallen back asleep. His tan weathered face revealed neither pleasure nor irritation as he nodded and said all right. Sheriff McDowell stepped onto the porch and set the carpetbag down, turned and looked at Rachel.

"I'll get back soon as I can," he said, and walked down the trail and soon disappeared.

"I have a bed you can lay him on if you like," Kephart said after an awkward minute had passed.

Kephart's voice sounded different from any she'd heard before. Flatter, leveled out as if every word had been sanded to a smooth sameness. Rachel wondered where he was from.

"Thank you," Rachel said and followed him into the cabin. It took a few moments for her eyes to adjust to the darkness, but then she saw the bed in the back corner. Rachel laid the child on the bed and opened the carpetbag, removed first Jacob's bottle and then the pins and clean swaddlings. Shadows cloaked the cabin's corners, and Rachel knew that even had the two oil lamps been lit shadows would remain, like a root cellar where so much dark had gathered for so long it could never be gotten completely rid of.

"When's the last time you two ate?' Kephart asked.

"I fed him near noon."

"And you?"

It took Rachel a few moments to remember.

"Supper last night."

"I've got beans simmering in that kettle," Kephart said. "That's about all I have but you're welcome to it."

"Beans is fine."

He filled a bowl and placed it on the table with a tin of cornbread.

"You partial to sweet milk or buttermilk?"

"Buttermilk would be my rathering," Rachel said.

Kephart took two pint jelly glasses outside. He came back with one brimmed with buttermilk, the other sweet milk.

"I figure that chap will be hungry again before too long," he said. "I got another pot to put on the fire if you want to warm him a bottle."

"That's alright. He's learned to drink it cold."

"Get your bottle then. I'll pour this in and set it in the springhouse so it'll be ready when he wakes up. Got some graham crackers too if he wants something to nibble."

Rachel did what he suggested, knowing he'd done these things before, maybe a long time ago, but sometime. She wondered where his wife and children were and almost asked.

"Have a seat," Kephart said, and nodded at the table's one chair.

Rachel looked around the room. Another chair and table were in the corner opposite the hearth. On the table was one of the room's oil lamps, beside it paper and a typewriter, the words REMINGTON STANDARD stamped in white beneath the keys. A mason jar filled with a clear liquid was also on the table. The lid lay beside the jar.

While she ate, Kephart took Jacob's bottle to the springhouse. Rachel was ravenous and ate every bean in the bowl. Kephart refilled her jelly jar and she drank half, then crumbled a square of cornbread in it. It struck her how eating was a comfort during a hard time because it reminded you that there had been other days, good days, when you'd eaten the same thing. Reminded you there *were* good days in life, when precious little else did.

When Rachel finished, she went out to the creek with the bowl and spoon. She laid them on the mossy bank and went into the woods to squat. She came back to the creek and cleaned the bowl and spoon with water and sand and brought them inside. Jacob was awake, clutching the bottle to his mouth. Kephart sat on the bed beside the child.

"He wasn't of a mind to wait for you, so I figured I'd oblige him."

Kephart lingered a few moments longer and then went outside. When Jacob finished the bottle, Rachel burped him and changed his swaddlings. The room felt cozy, but it didn't seem right to be in the cabin without Kephart there, so she took Jacob outside. Rachel sat on the lowest porch step and placed the child on the grass. Kephart came and perched on the top step. Rachel tried to think of something to make conversation, hoping it'd take at least some of her thinking off Widow Jenkins, them that would do the same to her and Jacob.

"You live here all the time?" Rachel asked.

"No, I got a place in Bryson City," Kephart answered. "I come out here when I'm tired of being around people."

He hadn't said the words in a mean sort of way, the way he would have if he meant to make her feel bad, but they made Rachel feel even more like a bother. Half an hour passed and they didn't speak again. Then Jacob began to fuss. Rachel checked his swaddlings and set him on her lap, but he continued to whine.

"I got something in the shed I bet he'll like," Kephart said.

Rachel followed him behind the cabin. He opened the shed door. Inside two fox kits nestled against each other on a bed of straw.

"Something got their mama. There was another one, but it was too weak to live."

The kits rose, mewing as they came to Kephart, who scratched them behind their ears as he might pups.

"How do you feed them?" Rachel asked.

"Table scraps now. The first few days cow milk in a medicine dropper."

Jacob reached out his hand toward the kits, and Rachel stepped inside, kneeled as she held Jacob by the waist.

"Pet them soft, Jacob," Rachel said, and took the child's hand and brushed it over one of the kit's fur.

The other kit nudged closer, pressed its black nose against Jacob's hand as well.

"It's about time for them to go out and fend for themselves," Kephart said.

"They look fat and sassy enough," Rachel said. "You look to have been a good parent."

"It'd be the first time," Kephart said.

After a while, Rachel and Jacob went back to the front steps and watched as the afternoon settled into the gorge. It was the kind of early fall day Rachel had always loved, not warm or cold, the sky all deep-blue and cloudless and no breeze, the crops proud and ripe and the leaves so pretty but hardly a one yet fallen—a day so perfect that the earth itself seemed sorry to let it pass, so slowed down its roll into evening and let it linger. Rachel tried to lose herself in that, let it clear her mind, and for a few minutes she could. But then she'd think of Widow Jenkins, and she could just as well have been sitting in a hailstorm for the comfort the day gave her.

Soon shadows splotched the yard and began to spread. The air cooled and a breeze stirred the higher branches. In that breeze Rachel felt a tinge of the cold weather coming. Kephart went back into the cabin, and the typewriter's rat-tat-tat began. A few minutes later, as if in reply, the yellowhammer found a closer tree to peck. The typewriter's sound seemed to soothe Jacob, because he soon crawled into Rachel's lap and napped.

IT was early evening when Rachel heard footsteps coming up the path. The sheriff stepped into the clearing, a cardboard container slightly smaller and shallower than a cigar box in his right hand.

"Something for him when he gets fussy," the sheriff said, handing the container to Rachel. "Got them from Scott at the general store."

She set the container between her and Jacob, the contents shifting and rattling inside. Rachel lifted the lid and found it held marbles.

"Scott said there's cat eyes and solids and swirls. Some steel shooters in there too."

Kephart, who'd come out on the porch, shook his head and smiled.

"What?" McDowell asked.

"They're usually not shooting marbles till they're a tad older."

The sheriff's face reddened.

"Well, I guess he can grow into them."

"Look here, Jacob," Rachel said, and lifted the box slightly so marbles rolled and clacked. The child placed his hand inside, lifted as many as he could hold and let them drop back in. He picked up more, dropped them as well. Rachel watched to make sure he didn't put one in his mouth.

"We'd better go," Sheriff McDowell said, and stepped onto Kephart's porch to get the carpetbag.

"Just a moment," Kephart said, and disappeared into the cabin, came back with a gray wool sock. "There's only one thing for a boy to keep his marbles in, and that's a sock."

Kephart kneeled beside Jacob, the sock soon bulging with marbles. He knotted the sock above the heel.

"There. Now they'll not be spilling out like they would in that cardboard."

Rachel took the sock, its heft more than she'd imagined, at least a pound. She lifted Jacob with one arm and handed the sock to the child, who clutched it like a poppit-doll.

"Thank you for letting them stay here," Sheriff McDowell said.

"Yes, thank you," Rachel said. "It was a considerable kindness."

Kephart nodded.

They walked out of the yard and down the path. Rachel glanced back and saw Kephart watched from the porch, the mason jar now in his hand. He raised it slowly to his lips.

"Where's Mr. Kephart from?" Rachel asked once they had entered the woods.

"The midwest," Sheriff McDowell said. "Saint Louis."

When they got to the trail end, the police car had been replaced by a Model T Ford.

"This car will be less conspicuous," the sheriff said.

"I ain't got clothes and swaddlings but for two days," Rachel said as they drove out of the gorge. "Can we go by my cabin?"

The sheriff didn't say anything, but when the road forked a few miles later he turned toward Colt Ridge. The sheriff drove faster now, and the automobile's rapid motion seemed to make her mind move faster as well. So much had happened so quickly she hadn't even begun to take it all in. While she'd been at Kephart's cabin, it all hadn't felt quite real, but now what had happened to Widow Jenkins and what could have happened to her and Jacob came full at her, and it was like running ahead of a barn-high wave of water. Running hard to stay ahead of it, Rachel thought despairingly, because when it all did take hold of her she didn't know if she could bear the burden of it.

They parked next to the cabin. Rachel set Jacob on the ground beside the porch steps as the sheriff opened the trunk.

"We'll put the things you need in here," Sheriff McDowell said, following Rachel onto the porch. "I can help you carry out what you need."

"You think it could be a long while before we come back here?"

"Probably. Leastways if you want that child to be safe."

"There's a box trunk in the front room," Rachel said. "If you can fetch it I'll get the rest."

Rachel stepped inside, the cabin somehow different than when she'd left it last night. It appeared smaller, and darker, the windows letting in less light. Nothing had been disturbed that she could tell except that the loft ladder had been set upright. Thinking me and Jacob might have hid up there, Rachel knew. She gathered what she needed as quickly as she could, including Jacob's toy train engine. As she moved through the cabin filling the carpetbag, Rachel tried not to think about what could have been.

"I'll put that in the trunk for you," the sheriff said when she came outside. "You get the boy."

Rachel kneeled beside Jacob. She took the child's hand and pressed it to the dirt. Her father had told Rachel that Harmons had been on this land since before the Revolutionary War.

"Don't ever forget what it feels like, Jacob," she whispered, and let her hand touch the ground as well.

The woodshed's door was open, and a barn swallow swung out of the sky and disappeared into its darkness. A hoe leaned against the shed wall, its blade freckled with rust, beside it a pile of rotting cabbage sacks. Rachel let her gaze cross the pasture, the spring clotted with leaves, the field where only horseweed and dog fennel grew over winter-shucked corn stalks, no more alive than the man who'd planted them.

They got back in the car. As they approached the Widow's house, Rachel remembered the cradle her father had made.

"There's something I got to get from Widow Jenkins' house," she said. "It'll just take a second."

The sheriff pulled up beside the farmhouse.

"What is it?"

"A cradle."

"I'll go in and get it," the sheriff said.

"I don't mind. It ain't heavy."

"No," Sheriff McDowell said. "It's best I get it."

Rachel understood then. You'd have walked right in and not realized until you seen the blood or whatever else it is he don't want you to see, she told herself. But as Rachel watched the sheriff enter the front door, it was hard to believe the farmhouse itself was still there, because a place where something so terrible had happened shouldn't continue to exist in the world. The earth itself shouldn't be able to abide it.

Sheriff McDowell placed the cradle in the trunk. When he got back in the car, he passed back a brown paper bag.

"It'll be a while before we get where we're going, so I got you a hamburger and co-cola. I loosened the cap, so you won't need an opener."

"Thank you," Rachel said, setting the bag beside her, "but what about you?"

"I'm fine," the sheriff said.

Rachel smelled the grilled meat and realized she was hungry again despite the bowl of beans, the cornbread and buttermilk. She settled Jacob deeper into her lap, then unwrapped the wax paper moist with grease. The meat was still warm and juicy, and she pinched off a few bits for Jacob. She took out the drink and pressed her thumb against the metal cap, felt it give. A kindly thing for him to have done that, Rachel thought, just his thinking to do it, same as buying the marbles. When she'd finished, Rachel put the bottle and wrapper in the bag and set it beside her.

They skirted Asheville and passed over the French Broad. As Rachel stared at the river, she told herself to think of something that wasn't fretful, so she thought of the sheriff's room, how you'd have known it was a man's room as much from what wasn't in it as what was—no pictures on the wall or lacy curtains over the window, no flowers in a vase. But there had been a neatness she'd have not have reckoned on. On the bedside table, a shellcraft pipe and stringed cloth tobacco pouch, a pair of wire-rimmed glasses and a pearl pen knife he'd pare his nails with. Across the room on the bureau, a looking glass, in front of it a black metal comb, a straight razor and its lather bowl and brush. On the chest of drawers, a Bible and a *Farmers' Almanac,* a tall book titled *Wildlife of North America* and another called *Camping and Woodcraft,* all stacked in a tidy row like in a library. Everything looked to have its place, and that place seemed to have been set and determined for a long time. A lonely sort of room.

In a while they passed a sign that said Madison County. The mountains around them rose higher, blotted out more of the sky.

"Where are we going?" Rachel asked.

"I called a relation of mine," the sheriff said. "She's an older woman who lives by herself. She's got an extra room you can stay in."

"She your aunt?"

"No, that would be too close of kin. A second cousin."

"Where does she live?"

"Tennessee."

"Her name McDowell too?"

"No, Sloan. Lena Sloan."

They drove west now, the road rising steadily toward mountains where the day's last light limned the ridge tops red. Jacob waked for a few minutes, then nuzzled against Rachel's breast and fell back asleep. It was full dark when she and Sheriff McDowell spoke again.

"You ain't tried to arrest them?"

"No," Sheriff McDowell said, "but I think soon I'll get enough on them that I can. I'm going to have the state coroner in Raleigh help me. But until then you've got to stay as far from them as possible."

"How'd you know they was coming after us?"

"A telephone call."

"A call last night?"

"Yes."

"And they said Jacob was in danger, not just me?"

"Yes, both of you."

"Do you know who it was, the one that called?"

"Joel Vaughn."

"Joel," Rachel said.

For a few moments she didn't speak.

"They'll kill him for that, won't they?"

"They'll try."

"Do you know where he is?"

"I drove him to Sylva this afternoon so he could hop a freight car," Sheriff McDowell answered, "one that wouldn't be going near Waynesville or Asheville."

"Where's he going?"

"If he did what I told him, as far from these mountains as possible."

The road leveled out a few yards before unfurling downward. Below in the distance were a few muted clusters of light. Rachel remembered how a month ago she'd sat before a hearth of glowing coals and listened to Jacob's breathing, thinking how after her mother had left when Rachel was five there'd been so much emptiness in the cabin she could hardly bear to be inside it, because everywhere you looked there was something that had reminded her that her mother was gone. Even the littlest thing like a sewing needle left on the fireboard or a page turned down in the Sears, Roebuck catalog. The same after her father died. But that night a month ago, as she'd listened to Jacob breathing, the cabin had felt fuller than it had in a long time. More alive too, a place where the living held sway more than those dead or gone.

Now everywhere was emptiness, the only thing left the child sleeping in her lap. She thought about Widow Jenkins and Joel, gone now as well. A part of her could almost wish Jacob too were gone, because it would all be so much easier. If it was just her left, she wouldn't even have to be afraid because all they could take from her was her life, and that seemed a piddling thing after all that had happened. Rachel thought about the bowie knife in the box trunk, how easy it would be to hide in her dress pocket, then wait until the last light in the camp went out and walk up to the Pemberton's house.

But Jacob was alive, and she'd have to protect him because there was nobody else to. She'd have to be afraid, for the both of them.

"We just crossed into Tennessee," Sheriff McDowell said. "They won't find you here. Just don't use your real name and don't take the young one with you when you go into town."

"Besides them two you told me about, is there anyone else you figure might come after us?"

"Maybe Pemberton, but I doubt it. Probably not her either. Most likely it'll be Galloway."

Rachel looked out the window.

"I've never been to no other state before."

"Well, you have now," Sheriff McDowell said. "Not much difference though, is it?"

"Not from what I can see."

The blacktop curved and the sheriff shifted gears. The road made a last brief rise and then plunged downward. They drove another thirty minutes before coming into a town. The Model T turned and bumped over railroad tracks, then passed a depot before stopping in front of a small white house.

"Where are we?" Rachel asked.

"Kingsport."

Twenty-eight

"A RATHER DAINTY APPETITE TONIGHT," SERENA said. "Are you feeling ill?"

They sat across from each other in the back room, the table's width between them, the empty chairs set against the walls. Pemberton noted the sound of Serena's silver cutlery ringing against the bone china, how it further accentuated the room's emptiness. Serena set her knife down.

"No," Pemberton said, and poured himself a fifth glass of red wine, staring at the crystal and its contents for a few moments before lifting the glass to his lips and drinking deeply. He set it back down, half emptied.

"You didn't used to drink this much."

The words were not spoken in a harsh or chiding way or even in a tone of disappointment. Pemberton looked up, and saw only concern on Serena's face.

"You haven't asked about the other night," Serena said, "when I went to Colt Ridge."

Pemberton reached for the glass but Serena lunged across the table, grabbing Pemberton's wrist so violently that the wine splashed onto his shirt sleeve. She leaned her face near as she could, not letting go her hold.

"We've both killed now," Serena said urgently. "What you felt at the depot, I've felt too. We're closer, Pemberton, closer than we've ever been before."

Madness, Pemberton thought, and remembered the first evening back in Boston, the walk down the cobbled streets to Serena's lodging, the hollow sound of their footsteps. He remembered the moment he'd stood on the icy top step as Serena unlocked the door and went inside, pressed the front room light on. Even when Serena had turned and smiled, Pemberton had lingered. Some dim troubling, almost visceral, keeping him there on the step, in the cold, outside the door. He remembered how he'd pulled off his gloves and stuffed them in his overcoat pocket, brushed some snow flurries off his shoulders as he delayed his entrance a few more moments. Then he'd stepped inside, stepping toward this room as well, into this moment.

Serena withdrew her hand and sat back. She said nothing more as Pemberton poured himself more wine.

The day had been warm so the window was open. Someone on the commissary steps strummed a guitar and sang about a big rock candy mountain. Pemberton listened to the words intently. It was the same tune he'd heard the porter whistling on the train the day Pemberton had brought Serena from Boston. Just twenty-six months ago, but it felt so much longer than that. The servers came and brought dessert and coffee. Pemberton finally felt the alcohol spread its calming glow inside his head. He let the wine have its way with him, glide him past where he didn't want to dwell.

Pemberton and Serena were finishing their coffee when Galloway came in. He acknowledged only Serena.

"I got something to tell you."

"About what?" Serena said.

"Vaughn," Galloway said. "Had me a little chat with the switchboard operator. I figured that old biddy would of been listening in. It was Vaughn tipped off McDowell, which explains why the little piss ant's skedaddled." Galloway paused. "And that ain't the only thing. A sawyer seen McDowell driving toward Asheville Monday evening with that Harmon girl and her young one. The dumb son-of-a-bitch didn't think it worth telling anybody till today."

"That explains a lot," Serena said.

After Galloway left, Serena and Pemberton finished their meal in silence, then walked to the house. The porch light had not been turned on, and Pemberton stumbled on the steps, would have fallen if Serena had not caught his arm.

"Careful, Pemberton," she said, then ever so softly. "I don't want to lose you."

EDMUND Wagner Bowden the Third arrived at the camp office the following morning. He was a recent Duke graduate and, according to the senator who'd sent him, fancied the job might do for him what being police commissioner in New York had done for Teddy Roosevelt. Though, the senator had hastened to add, Bowden was no follower of Roosevelt in other ways. Bowden was exactly what Pemberton expected—soft and florid, a reflexive smirk behind a few tentative hairs attempting to pass as a moustache. The smirk disappeared when Serena quickly exhausted the young man's conversational Latin.

Bowden departed mid-morning for his first full day as the new Haywood County sheriff. He'd been gone less than an hour when he called Pemberton's office.

"Mr. Luckadoo from the savings and loan just came by to tell me that McDowell and a police detective from Nashville are at Higgabothom's Café. They've been there all morning with Ezra Campbell's brother. Mr. Luckadoo said you'd want to know."

"Did the detective come and see you first?"

"No."

"Go tell him he's collaborating with a man indicted for malfeasance," Pemberton said. "Tell him that if he's got questions you are the law in town, not McDowell."

Seconds passed and all Pemberton heard was static.

"Speak, damn it."

"This Campbell fellow is telling the detective and anyone else who'll listen not to trust me. He's claiming his brother said you and Mrs. Pemberton would try to kill him."

"What's the detective's name?"

"Coldfield."

"Let me make a few phone calls. Then I'll come over there. If they look like they're going to leave, tell Coldfield I'm on my way to talk to him."

Pemberton hesitated a moment.

"Tell McDowell I want to talk to him as well."

Pemberton hung up the receiver and went to the Mosler safe behind the desk. He stood before it and turned the black dial slowly left and right and then left, listening as if he might hear the tick of the tumblers as they found their grooves. He pulled the handle, and the immense metal door yawned open. For almost a minute, he simply stared at the stacks of bills, then gathered up enough twenties to fill an envelope. He closed the metal door slowly, the safe's contents sinking back into darkness, a crisp snap as the door locked into place.

Pemberton took the photograph album from the desk drawer. He'd tried to dismiss the idea of Serena using his photograph to identify the child, but the thought had seized his mind like a snare he couldn't pull free from. Pemberton hadn't opened the bottom drawer, although several times in the last few days he'd allowed his hand to settle on its handle. Now he did. He opened the album and found the photograph of himself still there, as was the one of Jacob. But what did that prove or disprove, Pemberton thought. Like the hunting knife, it could have been taken and returned. He carried the photograph album to the house, shuffling papers and ledgers aside to place it at the bottom of the steamer trunk.

As Pemberton drove out of the camp, he saw Serena on Half Acre Ridge, Galloway close behind. The eagle was aloft, making a slow widening circle over the valley. Their prey believes if it stays still long enough, it won't be noticed, Serena had told him, but the prey eventually flinches, and when it does the eagle always sees it.

When Pemberton arrived at the sheriff's office, Bowden told him that Campbell's brother had left but that the Nashville detective and McDowell remained at the café.

"Do you want me to go with you?"

"No," Pemberton said. "This won't take long."

Pemberton walked across the street to the café. He'd thought McDowell might go quietly, in part because the day he'd been forced to resign McDowell simply left his keys and badge and state-issue pistol on the office desk, his uniform hung neatly on the coat rack. There'd been no curses or threats, no calls to a congressman or senator. The man had simply walked out, leaving the door wide open.

Coldfield and McDowell were in the back booth, green coffee cups in front of them. Pemberton pulled a chair from the closest table and sat down. He turned to the man sitting opposite McDowell.

"Detective Coldfield, my name is Pemberton."

Pemberton held out his hand, and the detective looked at it as if he'd been offered a piece of rancid meat.

"I talked to Lieutenant Jacoby half an hour ago," Pemberton said, lowering his hand. "He and I have some mutual friends."

A waitress approached with her pencil and pad but Pemberton waved her away.

"Lieutenant Jacoby said you should call him immediately. Do you need me to write down his telephone number for you?"

"I know his number," Coldfield said tersely.

"There's a telephone in the sheriff's office across the street, detective,"

Pemberton said. "Just tell Sheriff Bowden you have my permission to make the call."

Coldfield got up without comment. Pemberton watched through the window as the detective walked across the street and into the sheriff's office. Pemberton pulled his chair back a few inches and studied McDowell, who stared where Coldfield had sat. McDowell seemed to be studying a small tear in the booth's padding. Pemberton placed his hands on the table and clasped them, spoke quietly.

"You know where that Harmon girl and the child are, don't you?"

McDowell turned and stared at Pemberton. The ex-lawman's amber eyes registered incredulity.

"Do you think I'd tell you if I did?"

Pemberton took the envelope from his back pocket and laid it on the table.

"That's three hundred dollars. It's for her and the child."

McDowell stared at the envelope but didn't pick it up.

"I don't want to know where they are," Pemberton said, sliding the envelope toward McDowell as he might a playing card. "Take it. You know they'll need it."

"Why should I believe this isn't a trick to find out where they are?" McDowell asked.

"You know I had nothing to do with what happened on Colt Ridge," Pemberton said.

McDowell hesitated a few moments longer, then took the envelope and placed it in his pocket.

"This doesn't change anything between us."

"No, nothing changes between you and me," Pemberton said, looking toward the entrance. "You'll soon enough see the truth of that."

The bell on the café door rang and Coldfield walked toward them, but the detective didn't sit down or look at either man.

"Lieutenant Jacoby's decided I should let Sheriff Bowden take care of the investigation on this end."

Coldfield raised his eyes, met Pemberton's gaze.

"I will tell you one thing, Mr. Pemberton. Campbell's brother has been at the station every day since his brother got killed, which is why I'm here in the first place. He won't give up."

"I'll keep that in mind," Pemberton said.

The detective tossed a quarter beside his coffee cup. The silver rang hollowly against the formica surface.

"I'll be on my way now," Coldfield said.

Pemberton nodded, and stood up to leave as well.

"YOU'D a thought at least the women and children was safe," Henryson said on Sunday afternoon as Snipes' crews sat on the commissary steps.

"It ain't enough that they killed an old woman," Snipes said. "Now they're after that girl and her child."

Henryson nodded.

"The wonder of it is they don't kill us, just for practice."

"They's content to let the saws and axes and falling limbs kill us off," Ross said. "Frees up Galloway to do his traveling."

The men sat in silence a few moments, listening to a guitar strum the last notes of "Barbara Allen." The song's plaintive refrain put the men in a pensive mood.

"Campbell's brother is in town," Ross said. "I seen him my ownself the other day."

"The one Campbell was staying with in Nashville?" Henryson asked.

"That one, the guitar picker. He was out on the courthouse steps telling how he come home from his show and found Campbell laying in bed with a hatchet back of his head. To hear tell how deep that blade was in him, you'd think Campbell's head was no more than a pumpkin."

"That's a terrible way to die," Henryson said.

"Better than what Doctor Cheney got," Snipes said.

"Campbell at least got the record for getting farthest before Galloway caught up with him," Ross said. "Hell, Campbell even made it out of the state. I reckon that's a sort of victory."

"For sure," Henryson said. "Harris didn't even make it out of his house."

"Proves one thing, though," Ross said. "One day's head start ain't enough."

"No, it ain't," Henryson agreed. "I'd say you'd likely need at least a week to even get betting odds."

"The Harmon girl and her young one likely won't get that," Ross said. "Vaughn might though. Even Galloway can't be in two places at once."

"That boy always had a good head on his shoulders," Snipes said. "He figured the right time to take off."

"Just like quail," Ross said. "They figure if they all flush in different directions there's a chance one of them will make it."

"Has Galloway started after anybody yet?" Stewart asked.

"No, but he's liable to any time now," Snipes said. "He was at the commissary last night, trying to get fellers to help figure out what town his mama was visioning. Said he'd pay a dollar to the one named it."

"What sort of visioning did that old witch have?" Henryson asked.

"Claimed the Harmon girl and her young one was in Tennessee, a town where there was a train track. Which don't tell you much of nothing, of course, but she also told Galloway the place was a crown set amongst the mountains."

"A crown?" Ross asked, reentering the conversation.

"Yes, a crown. A crown set amongst the mountains. Them's the exact words."

"It might could be the top of a mountain," Henryson said. "I've heard peaks called crowns before."

"But it was *set* amongst the mountains," Ross noted, "not part of the mountain."

"Which would argue for it being a crown like them that royalty wears," Snipes added.

"Anybody figure it out?" Henryson asked Snipes. "Last night, I mean?"

"One of the cooks claimed there was a Crown Ridge over near Knoxville. That was all they come up with, and Galloway had already gone over there the day before and caught nary a scent of them."

Ross stared west toward the Tennessee line and slowly nodded to himself.

"I know where they are," he said. "Or leastways I can narrow it to two places."

"You ain't going to tell Galloway, are you?" Stewart asked.

"No," Ross said. "Maybe there's nothing I can do to stop them, but I damn well won't help them. I can give that girl a few more hours head start."

Henryson shook his head.

"I'd still not give you a dime to a dollar they'll survive another week."

Ross was about to speak in agreement when he saw a curious assemblage making its way into the camp.

"What in the name of heaven is that?" he said.

Three horse-drawn prairie schooners led the procession. Grimy muslin stretched over the iron hoop frames, and each tarp bore a different proclamation. HAMBYS CARNIVAL DIRECT FROM PARIS said the first, the second SEEN BY EUROPES ROYALTY, the third ADULTS A DIME. CHILDREN A NICKEL. Behind the wagons came a tethered menagerie, around each animal's neck a wooden placard naming the species. The animals traveled two abreast, led by a pair of slump-backed Shetland ponies. Next came two ostriches, their serpentine necks bowed as if embarrassed to be part of such an entourage, then two white horses striped with what appeared to be black shoe polish. ZEBRA, their placards proclaimed. A flatbed wagon ended the parade, a steel cage filling its wood-plank bottom. WORLDS DEADLIEST CREATURE was written on a tarp concealing the cage's bottom half.

The first wagon halted in front of the commissary steps. A portly man adorned in a rumpled beige cotton suit doffed his black top hat with a flourish and bid Snipes and his fellows a good afternoon. The stranger spoke with a nasal accent none of the men had ever heard before but Snipes immediately suspected had been cultivated at a European university.

"Appears you've took a wrong turn," Ross said, nodding at the paired animals. "That ark I notion you're searching for ain't around here. Even if it was, you're a tad late to get a seat on it."

"Our destination is the Pemberton Lumber camp," the man said, puzzled. "Is this not it?"

Snipes stood up. "Yes sir, it is, and unlike Mr. Ross here I'm a man of some culture and respectful of others that has it as well. How may I assist you?"

"I need to speak with the camp's owners, for permission to perform this evening."

"That would be Mr. and Mrs. Pemberton," Snipes said. "They like to ride their horses on Sundays, but they ought to be heading back in soon enough. They'll come right by here, so's the best thing to do is just sit and wait."

"Your suggestion appears a sound choice," the man said, and despite his considerable bulk leaped off the buckboard and landed with surprising light-footedness, the top hat wobbling but remaining on his head. "My name is Hamby, and I am the owner of this carnival."

Hamby knotted the horse's reins to a porch rail and clapped his hand twice. The other three men, who up until this moment had been inanimate as statues, now tethered their wagons as well. They immediately went about various tasks, one watering the menagerie while another searched possible sites to raise the tent. The third, a small swarthy man, disappeared into his wagon.

"Say you been doing your show across the ocean," Henryson said, nodding at the second wagon.

"Yes sir," the carnival owner said. "We're only back in this country for a limited engagement. We're headed to New York, then back to Europe."

"Kind of a roundabout way to get to New York, coming through these mountains," Ross said.

"Indeed it is," Hamby said, weariness tinting his voice, "but as professional entertainers, we feel a need, dare I say a moral obligation, to bring culture to those such as yourself exiled to the hinterlands."

"Awful kind of you to do that for us," Ross said.

At that moment, the man who'd entered the wagon reemerged in black tights and a black-and-white checked shirt made of the same pliable material, four bowling pins dangling from his hands. But it was what adorned his head that most intrigued Snipes and his crew, a piece of haberdashery concocted from red and green felt and silver bells, splayed atop the man's skull like an exhausted octopus.

"What do you call that thing on your noggin?" Snipes asked.

"A cap and bells," the man said in a thick accent, then began juggling the bowling pins.

"A cap and bells," Snipes repeated. "I've read of them but yours is the first I ever seen. I'd of not notioned it to have so much color."

Snipes joined the other crew members who'd gathered around the last wagon. The worker who'd been tending to the animals walked toward it as well, a bantam chicken squawking and flapping in his grip. The worker lifted the tarp and with obvious trepidation shoved the chicken and as little of his flesh as possible between the steel bars. He jerked his hand back and looked at it dubiously, as if surprised it was still there. Something very large and very powerful lunged against the cage with such force the whole wagon shook, the wheels rocking a few inches forward. A flurry of feathers rose into the cage's upper realm, seemed to hang a few moments before slowly floating down. One slipped through the bars, and Henryson reached out so it might settle in his hand. He peered at the feather and spoke.

"Favors chicken, does it?"

The carnival worker gave an enigmatic smile that did not balance the flinty look in his eyes.

"It favors anything that's got meat on it."

Hamby joined Snipes and the others. For a few moments the only sound came from within the cage, a brisk crunching of bones.

"I reckon you got to pay to know what sort of critter you got in there?" Henryson asked.

"Not at all, sir," Hamby said, opening his hands and arms in an expansive gesture. "It's a dragon."

Ross nodded at the zebras, one of which was licking a stripe off its shoulder, the long tongue black as licorice.

"I hope it's a sight more convincing than them."

"Convincing," Hamby spoke the word as if it had a pleasant taste. "That's the main purpose of our show, to convince our audience it has seen, in the flesh, the world's most dangerous creature. My dragon has fought a jaguar in Texas, an alligator in Louisiana, an orangutan in London, innumerable breeds of canine and several men now deceased."

"And never lost?" Stewart asked.

"Never," Hamby said. "So whatever manner of ferocious beast these mountains offer, bring it tonight, gentlemen. I welcome wagers on the side as well, to make it more sporting."

Henryson stared intently at the cage.

"How much you charge to look at it? Right now, I mean?"

"Free of charge for you men, just so you'll tell your friends of the terrifying wonder you have witnessed with your very own eyes."

Hamby nodded to the worker who'd fed the creature, and he pulled a frayed hemp cord. The muslin tarp fell away from the cage, revealing a creature shaped much like an alligator, though its skin was dusty and gray. A forked purple tongue stabbed the air as its head swayed slowly back and forth.

"Seven feet in length and two hundred pounds of reptilian muscle and meanness," Hamby said. "Trapped on the isle of Komodo, its native habitat."

As the men stepped closer to the cage, Hamby motioned behind them.

"You sir, you can see the world's deadliest creature for free as well."

Galloway came forward, stared at the reptile impassively.

"Say you'll fight it against anything," Galloway said after a few moments.

"Anything," Hamby replied, signaling his cohort to raise the tarp. "Bring your champion tonight, and your billfolds, for the ultimate test against the ultimate foe."

BY nightfall the canvas tent had been raised, lamps and torches lit, at the center a waist-high steel-mesh fence linked to make a ring, inside of which the man in black tights juggled before swallowing fire and pieces of colored glass and, finally and most dramatically, a sword. The menagerie then paced around the ring while Hamby, dressed now in a red swallow-tailed coat, top hat set on the crook of his arm, held forth with great originality on the animals' various attributes and origins. Only after all this was the dragon brought forth, one section of the fence unlocked so the cage door filled the gap. A carnival worker climbed atop the steel bars and lifted the door, the dragon swaggering forth into the pit. As its purple tongue probed the new surroundings, several men tested the interlocked metal holding the creature in and decided to watch from a farther vantage point. Hamby had set up a table beside the cage. Money and paper scraps with names and initials and in a few cases distinctive X's quickly covered its surface, though the largest wager had already been made with Serena. Side bets with the carnival's other workers were more informal, including one between Snipes and the juggler.

Several men cheered when Serena entered the tent, the eagle on her arm. She raised her free hand and the men grew silent. Serena told all the workers to be as quiet and still as possible, then motioned for those closest to the fence to back up at few feet. Serena placed the eagle, still hooded, on her fist. She spoke to the Berkute in a calm voice, then softly stroked the bird's keel with the backs of two fingers. The dragon still paced but it had moved into the far corner, like a boxer awaiting the bell.

Serena nodded to Galloway, who stood where the cage closed the ring's one entry point. Galloway shoved hard against the cage bars and created an opening, small but enough. By the time Hamby and the other onlookers realized what was happening, Serena had stepped into the ring.

"Get her out of there," Hamby shouted at one of his workers, but Galloway flashed a knife.

"She comes out when she decides, not you," he said.

After speaking to the bird a last time, Serena removed its hood. The dragon and the eagle acknowledged each other at the same moment. The dragon had moved into the ring's center, but now it paused in its pacing. The eagle's head swiveled downward. As the two creatures stared at each other, something summoned forth from an older world passed between them.

Serena lifted her hand and the Berkute flapped awkwardly over the ring and landed on the fence's back portion where no lamp or torch burned and the shadows deepened. As the bird passed overhead, the dragon lunged upward with a speed and dexterity that belied its bulk.

"Another six inches and we'd have had it ended before it even started," Snipes told Stewart in a hushed tone.

The eagle did not move again for almost a minute, though its gaze remained on the dragon, which resumed pacing around the ring's center. Though she was still in the ring, the reptile appeared oblivious to Serena, who now blocked its one exit point from the pit.

"I thought dragons could breathe fire," Stewart whispered to Snipes.

"They used to a far back ago," Snipes replied softly, "but they evolutioned out of it to survive."

Stewart leaned toward Snipes' ear.

"How come? It's a mighty powerful weapon to have, breathing fire."

"Too powerful," Snipes said. "They was scorching all the meat off their prey. Wasn't none left to eat."

The third time the dragon passed below the eagle, the bird pounced, wings outspread as its talons grasped the reptile's face. The dragon whipped its head back and forth, shaking free not just the eagle but a few of its feathers, but not before the eagle's talons had pierced the reptile's eyes. The bird half-leaped, half-flew back onto Serena's arm as its adversary plunged blindly into the metal, making the whole fence shudder. The dragon turned and lunged in the other direction, its slashing tail raising spumes of strawy dust off the earthen floor. It slammed against the fence's other side, only a few feet from where Serena stood, both she and the bird placid amid the dragon's frantic rushes. The mesh shuddered again.

"That fence ain't gonna hold it in," a worker shouted, eliciting a frantic rush that almost collapsed the tent as a number of onlookers shoved their way out the entrance and into the night.

Hamby now pressed his considerable bulk against the ring, causing the metal to give enough that the fence was further destabilized. The carnival owner leaned over the railing and raised both arms out, imploring his champion to rally.

The dragon's lunges were weakening, a white froth coating the rim of its mouth. The dragon turned back toward the ring's center, making a slower and slower circle, its belly dragging against the earth. Serena waited a few moments more, then lifted her arm and the eagle swooped down and landed on the dragon's neck. The bird stabbed the base of the reptile's head with its hallux talon, piercing the skull with the same force and result as a well-struck sixteen penny nail. The eagle arose and this time flew onto one of the tent's rafters as the dragon rolled over on its back, feebly righted itself. Hamby tumbled into the ring, his top hat falling off his head. He got up and watched his champion use what life it yet had to drag itself to the ring's far corner.

Hamby called for more light, and the juggler tossed him a torch. The carnival owner kneeled beside his reptile, the torch lowered so all could see that the dragon was indeed dead, its split purple tongue laid on the ground like a flag in defeat. Hamby remained hunched over the creature almost a minute, then looked up. He reached into the front pocket of his swallow-tailed coat and brought forth an elegant white handkerchief with the initials D. H. embossed on the center. The carnival owner opened his handkerchief with great formality and gently placed it over the dragon's head.

Henryson walked toward the tent's exit, Snipes joining him, now wearing the cap and bells.

"I don't see Ross picking up his winnings," Henryson noted as they passed the table where bets were being settled. "That's the first wager I've seen him lose in a coon's age."

Snipes nodded at Mrs. Pemberton, who was taking the eagle back to the stable, Galloway walking behind her with a thick stack of bills in his hand.

"Looks like she done pretty good for herself, though."

"Yes, sir," Henryson agreed. "I'd say she just bankrupted a whole carnival. I wouldn't be surprised to see the lot of them on the commissary steps tomorrow."

They stepped out of the tent and followed other workers up the ridge. Above them, the locust pole foundations made the stringhouses look like shaky dry-docked piers.

"I bet if you tugged good on just one pole every one of them stringhouses would tumble off this ridge," Henryson said. "That would be a wager near certain as betting on that eagle tonight."

Henryson paused and glanced back at the tent.

"I wonder what notion got into Ross's head to make him think her and that eagle could be beat."

"It wasn't in his head," Snipes said.

Twenty-nine

RACHEL DIDN'T SLEEP WELL THE FIRST NIGHTS in Kingsport. Every passing train waked her, and once awake she could think only of Serena and her henchman. She'd removed the pearl-handled bowie knife from the trunk and placed it under her pillow. Each time the house creaked and settled, Rachel grasped the knife's smooth handle. The child slept beside her, closest to the wall.

It wasn't until the fifth day that Rachel took Jacob outside. On an earlier trip to the grocery store, she'd found a rhubarb patch across the tracks from Mrs. Sloan's house. I can at least make her a pie, Rachel figured, a little something to thank the older woman for her kindness. She and Jacob crossed the tracks, the bowie knife and an empty tote sack in her free hand. The rhubarb was near a rusty boxcar so long motionless its wheels had sunk deep in the ground. She moved through a blackberry patch, the briars clutching at her dress. The boxcar cast a square of shade, and Rachel set the child in it. She took the sock from her dress pocket and spilled its contents before him. Now don't be putting them near your mouth, Rachel told him. Jacob placed the marbles in small groups, then pushed them farther apart.

Rachel began cutting the rhubarb, topping the plants the same way she would early-summer tobacco. It wasn't the sort of work she'd ever have thought you could miss, the purplish stalks so twiny it was like cutting rope, but it felt good to be doing something outdoors, something that had a rhythm you could fall into because you'd done it all your life. Next year I'll plant me a garden, she told herself, no matter where we are.

Soon small bouquets of crinkled leaves lay scattered around her. Rachel gathered up a handful of stalks, placed them in a stack like kindling. Jacob played contentedly, appearing glad as Rachel to be outside. A train came up the track, moving slow out of the depot. As it passed, a flagman waved from the caboose's railing. A pair of bright-red cardinals flew low across the tracks, and Jacob pointed at them before turning his gaze back to the marbles.

The sun had narrowed the boxcar's shadow by the time she'd cut the last stalk, stuffed the pile into her tote sack. More than enough rhubarb for five pies, but Rachel figured she and Mrs. Sloan could find a use for the extra. When she and Jacob recrossed the tracks, the sheriff's Model T was parked in front of the house.

"Looks like we got company," she told Jacob.

McDowell sat at the kitchen table with Mrs. Sloan, his right hand gripping a sweating glass of iced tea. An envelope lay on the table before him. Rachel set the rhubarb on the kitchen counter and sat down as well, but Jacob squirmed, began to whine.

"Probably needs changing," Rachel said, but Mrs. Sloan got up before she could and took the child into her arms.

"I'll do it." Mrs. Sloan said. "Then I'll take him out on the porch. You and the sheriff need to talk."

"Here," Rachel said, and gave the older woman the sock filled with marbles. "For if he gets fussy."

Mrs. Sloan jiggled the child in her arms, and Jacob laughed.

"Let's get you changed," she said, and disappeared with the child into the back bedroom.

McDowell took a sip of tea, set the glass before him.

"Likes the marbles, does he?"

"He plays with them every day."

"And doesn't try to eat them?"

"No, leastways not yet."

Mrs. Sloan and Jacob came out of the back bedroom and went out on the porch.

"What is it?" Rachel asked when McDowell didn't speak.

He looked out the front window where Mrs. Sloan held Jacob in her arms, the child reaching for a wind chime that dangled from the porch ceiling.

"I'm not sheriff anymore. They fired me and got them a lawman they can control."

"So there ain't nothing left to do but run and hide from them," Rachel said.

"I'm not running," McDowell said. "There's ways to beat them that don't need a sheriff's badge."

"If you do, we can go back home?"

"Yes."

"How long before you try to do something about them?"

"I have been trying," McDowell said bitterly. "My mistake was believing the law might help me. But I've come to the end of that row. If it's to be done I'll be doing it myself."

The ex-sheriff paused. He still looked out the window, but his gaze seemed upon something farther away than Mrs. Sloan and the child.

"You're going to try and kill them, ain't you?" Rachel asked.

"I'm hoping there'll be another way."

"I'd kill them if I didn't have Jacob to look after," Rachel said. "I would."

"I believe you," McDowell said, meeting Rachel's eyes.

A train hooted as it left the depot, the tea glass trembling as the train passed behind the house. McDowell reached out and held the glass still as the train clattered on south towards Knoxville. He stared at the glass as he spoke.

"If things don't work out the way I hope, you'll need to get you and the boy farther away than here."

"How far?"

"Far as this can get you," McDowell said, pushing the envelope toward her. "There's three hundred dollars in there."

"I wouldn't feel right taking your money," Rachel said.

"It's not my money."

"Where'd it come from then?"

"That doesn't matter. It's yours and the boy's now, and it may be all that keeps them from catching the both of you."

Rachel took the envelope and placed it in her dress pocket.

"You think they're still looking for us, right now I mean?"

"I know they are. If it's safe to come back, I'll come get you." McDowell said, pushing back his chair and standing up. "But until then don't take that child outside any more. I don't think they can track you here, but these folks ain't the kind you want to underestimate."

Rachel walked out on the porch with him and watched as he got back in the Model T and drove away. Then Rachel went back inside, fixed some oatmeal for Jacob. She set him on the floor and began cutting the stalks into inch-long pieces. Rachel raised a piece to her mouth, tasted its sourness and knew she'd need plenty of sugar. A freight train rattled the house, and she felt the boards beneath her shudder. Crockery shook in the cabinet.

Rachel wondered where the train was headed and remembered something from her last year of school. Where would you most want to go, Miss Stephens had asked, if you could choose anywhere on this map?

One student raised a hand and said Washington, D.C., and another New York and another said Raleigh. Bobby Orr said Louisiana because he'd heard folks there ate crawdads and he'd like to see such a thing as that. Joel Vaughn, taking a notion to be a smart-aleck, said as far away from the school as possible. Now where would that be, Joel, Miss Stephens had asked, and made him come up to the front of the room. She'd taken a ruler from her drawer and made Joel go to the map and measure until he found the farthest dot, which was Seattle, Washington. I went there once, Miss Stephens had said. It's a pretty place. There's a river and a pretty blue harbor and mountains so high they have snow on them all year long.

Thirty

By early October, the railroad track to the new camp in Jackson County had been laid down and connected to the Waynesville line. Spurs sprouted into the surrounding forests, and the site itself had been cleared by workers who'd been in the Cove Creek camp just weeks before, their stringhouses set on flat cars and sent east with them. The farmhouse had been converted into a dining hall, and work had begun on houses for Meeks and the Pembertons. Little would change other than the locale.

Snipes' crew was among the ones left in the Cove Creek camp. On those last mornings they ascended the far western slopes of Shanty Mountain and Big Fork Ridge, the few acres yet unlogged. They were still one worker short due to Dunbar's death in the gap. A replacement had been brought in, but on the second morning a sapling under a felled hickory sprang free and fractured his skull, making Snipes both lead cutter and sawyer. By the time the men stopped midday to eat, Snipes was so exhausted he lay on the ground, his eyes closed.

Henryson took a bite from his sandwich. His nose wrinkled as he chewed the soggy bread and fatback, swallowed it with the relish he might a mouthful of tacks. He set the sandwich aside.

"I heard your preacher was out in his cabbage patch the other evening," Henryson said to Stewart. "He must be doing some better."

"He is, but he still ain't of a mind to say much. My sister got him a funeral to preach over there at Cullowhee, figured it would cheer him up a considerable bit, but he just shook his head at her."

"Well, there ain't nothing like seeing somebody laid in the ground to cheer a fellow up," Ross said.

"It used to done him that way," Stewart said. "He told me once the only thing he hated about dying was he wouldn't be around to do his own funeral."

Snipes eyes were still closed as he spoke.

"That's another example of the duality of man you're speaking of, Stewart. We want what's in this world but we also want what ain't."

"I don't quite get your meaning," Henryson said to Snipes.

Snipes turned his head a few inches to address Henryson, the foreman's eyelashes fluttering a few moments like insect wings vainly attempting to take flight.

"Well, I'm too tuckered to explain it right now."

The crew foreman resettled the back of his head on the ground. He placed a piece of the cap and bells' pennant-shaped cloth over each eye to blunt the sun and was soon snoring.

"If we don't get another worker soon, Snipes is going to be worn to a frazzle," Henryson said.

"Maybe they'll hire McIntyre back," Ross said. "It ain't like a man's got to wag his tongue to be a good sawyer."

"What do you think, Stewart?" Henryson asked. "Think McIntyre might come back?"

"Maybe."

"If funerals perk him up, he couldn't do better than here," Ross noted. "There's men falling dead near about fast as the trees."

A breeze stirred a white oak's high limbs. It was the last hardwood on the ridge, and a few scarlet leaves fell like an early surrendering. One drifted toward Ross, who picked it up and examined it carefully, turning the leaf to and fro as though something never seen before.

"I reckon there'll be a couple of new graves over in Tennessee in a day or two," Henryson said. "Galloway or his mama finally figured out that it wasn't so much the crown as what it stood for."

"Meaning?" Stewart asked.

"Meaning what wears one. There's a Kingston and a Kingsport, and they're both in the mountains."

"And they both got rail lines," Ross said, still studying the leaf as he spoke.

"Was that the places you figured?" Stewart asked, "when you said you knowed where they was the other day?"

Ross nodded.

"Yes it was. I knew it'd come to them sooner or later."

"Which one is Galloway going to first?" Stewart asked Henryson.

"He didn't say," Henryson replied. "All I know is he's headed out tonight."

"I reckon we'll know soon enough if Galloway picked right," Ross said.

"You figure?" Henryson asked. "He could leave them in the woods for the varmints to eat or stuff them down a dry well and none would be the wiser."

"He could but he won't. These folks ain't about you having any doubts concerning their meanness. They want it right out there in the open."

"I reckon you're right," Henryson agreed. "You heard about them finding young Vaughn's cap on the bridge with that note pinned to it. His mama claimed it for his handwriting."

"What'd it say?" Stewart asked.

"Just that he was sorry."

"I reckon he figured to save Galloway the bother of tracking him down," Ross said.

"I can understand him getting it over with," Henryson said. "That'd be a terriblesome thing to take nary a breath for the rest of your life without worrying Galloway was sneaking up behind you. I'd be tempted to get it over with too."

"But they ain't found his body yet," Stewart noted. "There's some hope in that."

"He was always a clever lad," Henryson said. "He might have been trying to throw them off his trail."

"No," Ross said, a discernable weariness in his voice. "What's left after the crawdadders and mudcats have their way with that boy will bob up somewheres downriver. Just give it a few days."

"MEEKS told me Albright called," Serena said that night as she and Pemberton prepared for bed.

"He's starting eminent domain proceedings next week," Pemberton said, "unless we take his offer."

"Is his offer what it was before?"

Pemberton nodded as he leaned to take off his boots, but did not raise his eyes..

"We'll take it then," Serena said. "Thirty-four thousand acres of stumps and slash will buy a hundred thousand acres of mahogany in Brazil."

Serena removed the last of her clothing. Pemberton noted that the scar across her stomach had not changed Serena's lack of self-consciousness. She stepped toward the chifforobe with the same feline grace and suppleness as she'd done that first night in Boston. Pemberton remembered the evening she'd returned from the hospital, how she'd stood naked in front of the mirror, studying the scar carefully, letting her finger glide across it as she stared into the mirror. My Fechtwunde, she'd told Pemberton. She'd taken his hand and had him trace the scar's length as well.

"So the Chicagoans are ready to sign?" Serena said as she placed her shirt and pants inside the chifforobe.

"Yes," Pemberton said.

"I'm assuming Garvey won't venture this far south."

"No, he's sending his lawyer to sign the contract."

"Even in the North I'm sure it's hard for him to find investments," Serena said. "He may become our best long-term partner. What about our investors from Quebec?"

"They have more questions before they sign."

"They'll sign," Serena said. "You told them of your birthday party?"

"Yes," he said tersely.

"Don't be so grim about it, Pemberton. This may well be the last time that we see any of them. Once we're in Brazil, they'll be nothing more than names on checks."

Serena stepped to the window and opened the curtains, looked toward the ridge.

"I talked with Mrs. Galloway today. I never had before but she was at the commissary. I must say I find her augury deficient," Serena said, her voice becoming more reflective. "Which may explain why the lamp in her stringhouse is still off."

Serena opened the curtains wider. She angled her head close to one of the higher panes, as if to frame it inside the mullion.

"The lunar eclipse is tonight," she said. "I've always found it stunning, not just the brightness but how the hues change. Galloway calls it a hunter's moon. He says there's not a better night to hunt."

Serena didn't turn around as she spoke. Her eyes peered beyond the stringhouses and the ridge, into a sky that had yet to usher forth its moon and stars. Pemberton's fingers paused on a shirt button as he let his gaze settle on the crescent line where the paleness of Serena's upper back and shoulders darkened at the neck. His fingers and lips had often traced that demarcation between the part of herself Serena allowed others to see and what was seen only by Pemberton. He allowed his gaze to follow the curved flex of Serena's back as she twisted to look out the windowpane, then down the tapering waist and on to the hips and the muscled calves and the ankles and finally the feet themselves, heels uplifted as Serena's weight balanced on the balls of her feet. She did not move from the window, as if holding a pose for him. A pose that that even in its stasis embodied motion as well, like a stream current beneath a calm surface.

Pemberton knew Serena was waiting for him to come and press his chest against her back, cup her breasts in his hands, feel her nipples harden against his palms as her hips pushed into his groin, her mouth turning to meet his. He did not go to her. After a while Serena turned from the window, leaving the curtains open. She got into bed and lifted the covers as Pemberton finished unbuttoning his shirt.

"Come on to bed," Serena said softly. "Let me finish undressing you."

Pemberton lay down and felt the bed's feather mattress and springs give under his back. Serena placed her knees athwart his hips and leaned over him, her hands pulling the shirt off his shoulders, freeing his arms one at a time from the cloth. Serena's hands traced a path up his ribcage as she leaned closer, pressed her lips to his as her body settled over him. He did not respond.

Serena finally eased herself off Pemberton and lay beside him, her hand resting lightly on his chest.

"What's wrong, Pemberton?" Serena said. "Is your mind elsewhere?"

Thirty-one

RACHEL CROSSED THE TRACKS AND SOON WAS on the sidewalk, in her pocket one of the twenty-dollar bills to buy groceries. At the curb a wagon creaked by, a Holstein's black-and-white head poking through the board slats. Rachel smelled the manure and straw, so much more clear and familiar than the stew of odors in Kingsport. Probably going to be someone's milk cow, she thought, and took one step off the curb. She did not take another.

What she saw first was absence, a gap in the human form where wrist and hand should be. He lounged outside the post office, a matchstick in the corner of his mouth. Even at a distance, there was no doubt in her mind. The slick black hair and small wiry frame, the way his head cocked slightly to the side. The day's waning sunlight suddenly felt thicker, more contained, almost as if she could wave a finger through it and find her skin tinged yellow.

Rachel stepped back slowly, afraid a quick movement would divert his gaze from those who passed nearer.

When she was out of sight she ran, at first toward Mrs. Sloan's house. Then her body and mind swerved as one, and she ran instead toward the depot. When she made it to the entrance, Rachel paused to calm herself before stepping inside. He didn't see you, and he don't know where we're staying, she told herself. We got time.

Behind the ticket booth, a stout moon-faced man studied numbers in a wire-bound notebook. When he looked up, Rachel searched for something in his features to reassure herself and found it in his bow tie and spectacles. Like what a doctor would wear, she thought.

"Yes, ma'am," he said, his tone neither friendly nor unfriendly.

"A man who's got only one hand, not much taller than me. Has he been in here?"

"You mean today?"

"Today or yesterday."

The man shook his head.

"Not to my recollection."

"Are you sure? It's important."

"I see a lot of folks," the man said, "but I think I'd remember someone like that."

Rachel turned and glanced out the window, then placed the twenty-dollar bill on the counter.

"How far will this get me and a young one."

"Which direction you headed?"

For a few moments, Rachel did not answer. On the wall behind the ticket master was a map of the United States, black lines woven across it like a spider's web. She found Tennessee, then let her eyes follow the knitwork of lines northwest.

"We want to go to Seattle, Washington."

"Twenty dollars would get you far as Saint Louis," the man said.

For a few moments Rachel contemplated going to the house to get more money.

"Once on the train we can get tickets for the rest of the way?"

The ticket master nodded.

"Part way will have to do," Rachel said. "When does it leave?"

"An hour and a half."

"Is there one leaves sooner?"

"Nothing but freight trains."

Rachel paused a few moments, then handed over the bill.

"These will get you to Saint Louis," the man said, placing two tickets before her and the two quarters in change.

Rachel picked up the tickets but left the quarters.

"That fellow I told you about. If he comes around asking . . ."

The man lifted the silver from the counter and placed it in his vest pocket.

"I've not sold any tickets to a woman and a child," he said.

She paused at the depot's doorway, looking back toward town before crossing the tracks and entering the house. Mrs. Sloan sat at the kitchen table peeling apples, Jacob in the back room napping.

"That man the sheriff told me to watch for," Rachel said. "I seen him uptown."

Rachel hurried on to the back room. She took the money and bowie knife from under the pillow and stuffed them in the carpetbag with what items she thought most needed. Mrs. Sloan came into the room.

"What can I do to help you?"

"Get yourself over to your sister-in-law's and stay there," Rachel said, and lifted Jacob from the bed. "Call the sheriff and tell him Galloway's here."

The older woman came to her, the toy train engine and sock of marbles in her veiny hands.

"Don't forget these," Mrs. Sloan said, stuffing the toy train engine in the sock as well and knotting it. "He'd be put out something awful if you left them."

Rachel placed the sock in her dress pocket, and she and Jacob were quickly out of the house and crossing the tracks to the boxcar, the best place to wait because she could see both the house and the depot. See but not be seen, Rachel told herself. She crossed the last rail and looked over her shoulder toward town and saw no one. Jacob whimpered.

"Hush now," she said.

Rachel stepped quickly through the blackberry bushes, not pausing when briars clutched her dress. She lifted Jacob and the carpetbag into the boxcar before getting in herself.

At first there was only gloaming. As her eyes slowly adjusted, Rachel saw a mattress made from corn shucks stuffed between two rotting quilts, beside it yellowing newspapers and an empty sardine can. Whoever he is, he'll not come back till it cools off some, Rachel thought. She set Jacob and the carpetbag down, then stepped to the back of the boxcar and pinched the quilts between her thumbs and forefingers to slide the makeshift mattress closer to the doorway. A gray blur shot out of the pallet, its body and long tail brushing an ankle as it passed between her legs and then on through the doorway. A rustling in the briars and then nothing.

Rachel prodded the pallet with her shoe. Nothing else emerged and she slid the pallet the rest of the way. She sat down, the shucks rasping as she leaned and lifted Jacob onto her lap. The boxcar rattled as a freight train passed, moving so slow Rachel could read the words and numbers on each car as it passed wide and high before her. Several of the freight cars' sliding metal doors were open. From one of them a hobo peered out.

After the caboose glided by, Rachel fixed her gaze on the house. Soon Mrs. Sloan came out, a suitcase in her hand. The old woman walked with a steadfast stride toward town. A few minutes later a man went inside the depot, came out and walked toward town as well. The day had been warm for early fall, and the boxcar had stored the day's heat like a kiln. Beads of sweat formed on Rachel's brow, the dress cloth beginning to stick between her shoulder blades.

Jacob leaned forward and pointed at a lizard clinging to the doorway. The lizard's back and legs were as bright green as a cinnamon fern. On its throat a red bubble of flesh expanded and contracted, but otherwise the creature lay completely still.

"Pretty ain't it," Rachel told Jacob.

After a few moments, the lizard crawled farther up the rusty metal and paused again. The lizard's green dulled to a light brown, and it soon blended so perfectly with the rusty metal as to be invisible. There's a trick we could sure use, Rachel thought.

Jacob settled deeper into her lap, sleepy enough not to fret about the boxcar's heat. His breath took on the cadence of sleep, and not long after that twilight settled in. A pale swollen moon appeared in the sky, crowding out the lesser stars as it pressed closer to earth. A thin whiteness spread over the ground like hoarfrost. Another freight train passed. Less than an hour, Rachel told herself, eyes shifting from the house to the depot.

The boxcar finally began to cool, the day's heat leaking away with the light. A man and woman stepped into the depot, came out and sat on the wooden bench to await the train. Soon several other travelers joined the couple. Lights flickered on and cast the depot in a yellow light. No one approached Mrs. Sloan's house. Something rustled near the boxcar door, and Rachel saw a rat's snout tentatively emerge.

"Shoo," she said and pulled a shuck from the pallet to throw if the rodent ventured closer, but at the sound of her voice it disappeared back into the undergrowth.

Jacob woke and began to fuss. Rachel checked his swaddlings but they were dry. Hungry then, she told herself, and set the child on the pallet. She took one of the graham crackers from the carpetbag and gave it to him. The moonlight continued to thicken, the train tracks gleaming as if gilded in silver. Not a wisp of cloud passed overhead. Rachel looked up at the sky and saw the moon was no longer white but deepening into an orange hue.

A smudge of light came on in the back room of Mrs. Sloan's house. The light disappeared and Rachel hoped it might be her imagining, but then it was in the kitchen, moving around like foxfire before briefly reappearing in the back room. Rachel squinted her eyes and watched for the glow of a flashlight crossing Mrs. Sloan's yard, if not that for some denser shadow.

But she saw nothing. Galloway had vanished as completely as the light held in his hand. Could be walking straight toward town or the depot or straight toward us, Rachel thought, and moved Jacob and herself deeper into the boxcar. Minutes passed though she'd not have believed so except she heard the passenger train coming. Rachel gathered up the carpetbag and Jacob. Briars grabbed her legs, and each time there was an instant she thought Galloway had her.

Rachel finally felt cinders beneath her feet. She did not step onto the glimmering tracks but walked the edge. The train whistle blew and she took a few more steps. A big oak rose near the depot, and its limbs snared some of the moonlight. Rachel stood beneath where the dark pooled, a few yards outside the depot light's glow. She studied the travelers gathered on the platform, looked through one of the depot's wide windows but saw no one. The train pulled into the station and shuddered to a stop.

Two men got off but that was all, and soon the train began to load its new passengers. Rachel took the tickets from her pocket and moved closer, almost ready to step onto the depot's porch when something stopped her. It was not something seen but something sensed, like the time as a child when she'd started to lift the spring guard and stopped, a black widow spider big as a quarter where her fingers would have gone. The last passengers boarded, but still Rachel did not move. Then she saw him, in the shadows on the depot's far side. The last ticket holder boarded and the train pulled away, the flagman's brass lantern sweeping back and forth in farewell.

Rachel turned from the depot's glow and could not see her feet in the oak's thick shade. If I trip and fall and this young one starts squalling, we'll be goners for sure, Rachel thought. Imaginings began to get the best of her, thinking how one wrong step to the left or right and there could be a ditch or a rusty stob that would trip her. You've got to follow the same path you come here on, she told herself. She took a step into the darkness because there was no choice. Rachel took another step, the foot set tentatively before her. Like crossing a pond on thin ice, she thought, and it seemed a part of her listened for that first crackle. Seven steps and she was out of the tree's shade.

Rachel walked on toward the boxcar, quicker now, hunched low so that she was little taller than the briars and weeds. The only thing she could think to do was try to get to town and find the town's lawman, but Sheriff McDowell had warned her to trust no one but his cousin, even if that someone wore a badge. The moonlight was so stark and intense now she could see Mrs. Sloan's house clearly. She remembered then that it was October, remembered how her father called this a hunter's moon and claimed blood on the moon meant blood on the land. Rachel walked faster and got herself and Jacob into the boxcar as quickly as she could, unable to shake the feeling that Mrs. Pemberton and Galloway held sway over even the moon and stars and clouds. That they'd waited for this night and this night alone to find her and Jacob. Don't look up and see it, she told herself. Rachel pushed farther into the boxcar, clutched Jacob more tightly in her arms.

She heard a train, not the one that had departed but one coming out of the mountains into the valley, a freight train. The engine stopped beside the coal chute on the station's opposite end. Rachel lifted Jacob and the carpetbag and made her way down the track to where she'd stood before. She studied the depot, the shadowy far corner where Galloway had been fifteen minutes earlier. He wasn't there. The last of the coal clattered from the chute, and the train began moving. The engine passed in front of the depot, and when several cars had done the same Rachel gathered up the carpetbag and Jacob and walked rapidly toward the train, exposed now not just by the moon but the depot's yellow glow. She stepped onto the closer track, the train passing slowly in front of her. The fifth car gaped open, but Rachel didn't reach it in time. Six more cars creaked by before another was open. She set Jacob and the carpetbag inside, then jumped in herself. The train moved past the old boxcar and soon the darkened backs of buildings.

He was coming, beside the caboose but closing the distance between them one boxcar at a time, not even running but still gaining steadily. He stumbled, got up, and came on. He was smiling and his index finger waved in admonishment. She'd never known fear had a taste, but it did. It tasted like chalk and metal. Rachel pushed Jacob deeper into the car, so deep the child's back pressed against the rattling steel. Rachel's ribs tightened around her heart like a vise-grip.

The train sped up but not enough. Galloway's face appeared beside the car. He trotted now, his hand outstretched. A lanyard made from a dingy piece of twine was around Galloway's neck, dangling from it a dagger. Rachel thought of the bowie knife, but there wasn't time to get it from the carpetbag. She pulled the sock from her dress pocket as Galloway reached out his hand and gripped the door, the dagger glinting as it swayed back and forth across his chest. He continued to trot beside them, gathering himself to leap inside. The train whistle screamed like a final warning.

Galloway shoved himself halfway into the car, his head and belly on the metal floor, legs yet dangling. Rachel raised the sock to ear level. She paused, willing the pound of glass and steel to be enough, then brought it down as hard as she could on Galloway's leering face. His eyes went white. For a moment his body balanced half in and half out of the car. Then Rachel pressed her shoe heel against his forehead and shoved him earthward. Galloway tumbled into a gulley. Rachel leaned out and watched as the caboose passed where he'd fallen. She kept watching the tracks, but he did not rise. Jacob was squalling now and she gathered him into her arms.

"We're all right now," she told him. "We're all right."

There was hay on the boxcar's floor, and Rachel heaped some of it into a corner. She and Jacob lay on it, her arms around him. They were out of Kingsport now, headed south through the Smokies. They passed an occasional farmhouse, what wan light its windows shed skiffing the metal floor a moment, then gone. The rocking heartbeat of the train soon lulled the child asleep, herself as well. Rachel dreamed that she and Jacob stood in a cornfield where only a single green stalk grew. She and Jacob pulled shucks off the stalk's one ear and found not corn but a knife blade.

She woke in darkness, for a moment unsure where she was. Rachel spooned her body tighter around Jacob's and tried to fall back asleep but sleep did not come. She listened to the train passing over the rails, listened to Jacob's measured breaths. Rachel waited for the wheels to slow beneath her, and when they finally did she and Jacob got out and crossed rows of tracks, moving around stalled boxcars toward the depot. The sign above the front door said Knoxville. She went inside and checked the train schedule before asking to borrow the telephone mounted on the wall behind the counter. A collect call, she assured the depot master. She lifted the receiver to her ear and leaned toward the mouthpiece, Jacob clutching the black clothbound cord as Rachel spoke to the operator.

McDowell answered on the first ring.

"Where are you?" he asked, and as soon as she told him he asked when the next train left.

"The one we need don't leave for four hours."

"The next train," he said again, "to anywhere."

"There's one headed to Chattanooga in thirty minutes."

"Take it. Then when you get to Chattanooga buy the ticket to Seattle."

"You think he's already headed here, don't you?" Rachel said.

"I'd say it's likely."

For a few moments only static crossed the miles of lines between them.

"Just get to Chattanooga," McDowell said. "I'm going to end this tonight, end it for good."

"How?"

"That's not your concern. Go buy your tickets."

She did what he said. Thinking she hadn't offered enough money to the other depot master, Rachel handed this one a five-dollar bill. Then she described Galloway.

The depot master stared at the bill, a smile rising on his face that offered no comfort or sympathy.

"You must be in some serious trouble," the depot master said, "and one thing I've learned is folks with trouble ain't no different than folks with head lice or the shits. You get close enough to them and soon enough you'll get it your ownself."

The depot master looked past Rachel as he spoke, as if so pleased with his words he hoped a larger audience had heard them.

Rachel met the man's eyes, held his gaze until the smirk left his face. She no longer felt anger or fear or even weariness. What remained was just a numb acceptance that she and Jacob would or wouldn't survive. Something would happen or it wouldn't happen, and that was the way of it. Almost as if she was outside of herself, watching her and the child from some distant vantage point. As Rachel spoke, the coldness of her inflection felt outside herself as well.

"You'll help us or you won't, mister. You can make light of our troubles and smile at your own smartass sayings. You can refuse to take my money or take it and tell where we went anyway. You'll do what you want to do. But know one thing. If that man finds us he'll rake a knife blade across this young one's throat and bleed him dry like he was no more than a shoat in a hog pen. That blood will be on your hands, every bit as much as on him that does the killing. If you can handle knowing you done that, then go ahead and tell him."

The depot master placed a hand on the five-dollar bill but did not slide it toward himself. He no longer looked at Rachel but at Jacob.

"I won't tell him nor nobody else," he said, then handed the bill back to Rachel.

Thirty-two

THAT NIGHT IT WAS NOT THE GLARE OF FLAMES or the smell of smoke that roused Pemberton but a sound, something heard but not registered until other senses lifted him from a restless sleep. When he opened his eyes, the bed was a raft adrift on a rising tide of smoke and fire. Serena had awakened as well, and for a few moments they only watched.

The front of the house disappeared in a wide rush of flame, as did the foyer leading to the back door. The bedroom's window was five feet away but hidden by smoke. Each breath Pemberton took felt like a mouthful of ash singeing his throat and lungs. Waves of heat rolled over his bare skin. Smoke seemed to have clouded inside his mind as well as the room, and for a second he forgot why the window mattered. Serena held to his arm, coughing violently as well. They helped each other off the bed and

Pemberton wrapped a blanket around them, its fringe catching aflame when it touched the floor.

Pemberton used his last clear thought to gauge where the window would be. With his arm around Serena and hers around his waist, he led them stumbling and breathless toward the window. When Pemberton found it, he lowered his head and turned his shoulder and used what momentum they had to break the glass and wooden mullion. He and Serena plunged through the window clutching each other, the glass raining around them, twirling and refractive like a kaleidoscope. Their legs caught the sill a moment, slipped through. Then they were falling, so slowly it did not feel like falling but a suspension. Pemberton felt a moment of weightlessness as if they were submerged in water. Then the ground came rushing upward.

They hit and rolled free of the flaming blanket and pressed their naked flesh against each other's. He and Serena stayed on the ground, holding each other though coughs racked their bodies like seizures. Fire had burned Pemberton's forearm and a six-inch glass shard jagged deep into his thigh, but he did not break his and Serena's embrace. As the roof collapsed, orange sparks spewed upward, hovered a moment and dimmed. Pemberton shifted to cover Serena, ash and cinders stinging his back before expiring.

A tumult of shouting came toward them as what workers remained in the camp gathered to contain the fire. Meeks appeared out of the smoke and leaned over them, asking if Pemberton and Serena were all right. Serena said *yes*, but neither she nor Pemberton unclenched. As the heat washed over him, Pemberton thought of their stumbling rush toward the window and how, at that one moment, the world had finally revealed itself to him, and in it there was nothing but himself and Serena, everything else burning away around them. *A kind of annihilation.* Yes, he thought, I understand now.

Pemberton finally let go of Serena to pull free the glass shard. Meeks helped Serena and Pemberton to their feet, placing a bedsheet around them as he did so.

"I'll call a doctor," Meeks said, and walked briskly back to the office.

Serena and Pemberton began slowly walking in the same direction, arm in arm. The flames cast the whole camp into a pulsing translucence, light gathering and dispersing like brightened shadows. Pemberton made a quick inventory of what had burned inside the house that could not be replaced. Nothing. A foreman came up to Serena, his face damasked with a sooty sweat.

"I've got men checking to make sure it don't spread," he said. "When we get it put out, you want me to send the crews out?"

"Keep them around camp, just in case," Serena answered. "We'll let them rest up and get a full day from them tomorrow."

"You was lucky to have got out of there," the foreman said, looking toward the house.

Serena and Pemberton turned and saw the truth of his statement. The back portion was still aflame, but the front was a tumble of black smoking wood but for the brick steps that now rose toward nothing but singed air. A man in silhouette sat in a ladderback chair directly in front of the steps. The man watched the flames, seemingly oblivious to the workers who rushed and shouted around him. On the ground beside the chair was an empty ten-gallon canister of kerosene. Pemberton did not have to see the man's face to know it was McDowell.

PART IV

Thirty-three

IT WAS MID-MORNING BEFORE ENOUGH LIGHT filtered through the pall of smoke to see more than a few yards. Even then the ashy air brought tears to any lingering gaze. Much of the slash and stumps in the valley had burned along with the lean-tos of wood and tin assembled by squatters. Men begrimed by smoke and soot moved to and fro across the valley's smoldering floor, gathering sludgy buckets of water from the creek to smother what gasps of fire lingered. From a distance, they appeared not so much like men as dark creatures spawned by the ash and cinder they trod upon. Had there not been rain the day before, every building in the camp would have burned.

Snipes' crew sat on the commissary steps. With them was McIntyre, whose proven talent as a sawyer had gotten him rehired. The lay preacher had not spoken a single word since his return, nor did he now as the crew observed the black square that was once the Pemberton's house. Snipes lit his pipe and took a reflective draw, let the smoke purl from his rounded lips as if some necessary precursor to what wisdom the lips were about to impart.

"An educated man such as myself would of knowed better than try to kill them in their natural element," Snipes mused.

"Fire, you mean?" Henryson asked.

"Exactly. That's like throwing water on a fish."

"What would you have done?"

"I'd of planted a wooden stake in their hearts," Snipes said as he tamped more tobacco into his pipe. "Most all your best authorities argue for it in such situations."

"I seen Sheriff Bowden cuffing up McDowell earlier," Henryson said. "He was hitting at him, but it looked like he was doing no more than swatting flies off of him. Much as he's wanting to be, the new high sheriff ain't in them other three's league."

"I doubt there's not a one north of hell itself that is," Ross exclaimed.

For a few moments the men grew silent, their eyes turning one pair at a time to look at McIntyre, who in previous times would have gleaned half a dozen impromptu sermons after hearing the other men's comments. But McIntyre stared fixedly across the wasteland at the bleary western horizon. Since his return, McIntyre's silence had been a matter of much speculation among the men. Snipes suggested the lay preacher's experience had caused McIntyre to adopt a vow of silence in the manner of monks of long-ago times. Stewart retorted that in the past McIntyre had been vehemently opposed to all manner of things popish, but conceded that perhaps the flying snake had changed his view on this matter. Henryson surmised that McIntyre was waiting for some particular revelation before speaking.

Ross said maybe McIntyre just had a sore throat.

Yet none of the men laughed or snickered when Ross made his quip, and Ross himself seemed to regret the remark as soon as it left his mouth, for they all believed, even Ross, the most cynical of men, that the lay preacher had been truly and irrevocably transformed.

LATE that morning after being treated by the doctor summoned from Waynesville, Serena and Pemberton dressed in denim breeches and cotton shirts gleaned from what sundries remained in the commissary. They sent a worker to town to buy clothing and toiletries the commissary could not furnish. Serena gathered some of the kitchen staff to prepare Campbell's old house for them while Pemberton went to make sure any stray fires had been put out. As he followed the fire's leaps and sidles, Pemberton found that though acres of slash and stumps had burned, not a single building aside from the house had been lost. After these tasks had been done, he and Serena lingered in the office.

"I probably should go and ride the ridge," Serena said, "just to make sure the cables are undamaged."

Pemberton looked at the bills and invoices on the desk, then got up.

"I'll go with you. The paperwork can wait."

Serena came around the desk and placed her bandaged hand on the back of Pemberton's neck. She leaned and kissed him deeply.

"I want you with me," Serena said, "not just this morning but all day."

They went to the stable and saddled their horses. Serena freed the eagle from its roost and they rode out of the stable. The noon sun shone on the train tracks, and even in the dingy light the linked metal gave off a muted gleam. Soon it would be time to pull up the rails, Pemberton knew, starting with the spurs and moving backward. He looked forward to taking off his shirt and working with the men again, asserting his strength. It seemed so long since he'd done that, spending all his days in the office, poring over numbers like some drudge in a bank. With Meeks settled in, he'd be able to get out more, especially at the new camp.

Warm ash blackened the horses' hooves and forelegs as Pemberton and Serena rode across the valley floor. They passed exhausted workers washing soot off their faces and arms, the men looking not so much like loggers as minstrels unmasking after a performance. The men did not speak, the only sound their hacking coughs. The last flames doused were where the cemetery had been, and smoke wisps rose there as if even the souls of the dead were abandoning the charred valley for some more hospitable realm.

Pemberton and Serena followed Rough Fork Creek to Shanty Mountain, halfway up when they heard a shout behind them and saw Meeks coming their way. The accountant had never ridden a horse before coming to the camp, and he kept his back bowed and head close to the mare's neck. When he caught up with the Pembertons, Meeks lifted his head and spoke softly, no doubt fearful a raised voice might cause the horse to bolt.

"Galloway called," he said to Serena.

Serena turned to Pemberton.

"I'll catch up with you in just a minute."

"No," Pemberton said. "I'll wait."

Serena looked at Pemberton's face a few moments, as if searching for some feature in it that might counter his words. Satisfied, she nodded.

"Tell us," she said to Meeks.

"Galloway's traced 'them,' whoever 'them' are, to Knoxville and they didn't buy a ticket," Meeks said with some exasperation. "He also said to tell you no freight train left before he arrived, so 'they' are evidently still there."

Meeks slowly lifted himself higher in the saddle to retrieve a piece of paper from his pocket.

"He told me a telephone number and said you needed to tell him what to do next."

"Go call him," Serena said, ignoring the proffered paper. "Tell him I said they've probably got no one there to stay with and no money, so he should start looking around Knoxville."

"I didn't realize I was also a receptionist," Meeks grumbled, then began his halting descent back to camp.

Pemberton and Serena did not stop again until they were on the mountain top. Smoke dimmed the sun to the color of tarnished copper, the light around them transformed as well, tinted like a daguerreotype. Serena untethered the eagle, raised her arm and lifted it skyward. The bird rose, its great wings beating as if pushing away not only air but the very earth itself. It veered left, caught an updraft for a moment, then continued the ascent.

Pemberton looked back at the camp, the blackened absence where the house had been. The chimney had crumbled but the steps remained intact, looking not so much like the last remnant of a house but instead steps constructed for a gallows. The ladderback chair where McDowell had sat still faced the steps.

Serena reined her horse closer to Pemberton, her leg brushing against his. He reached out his hand and caressed Serena's upper leg. Serena placed her hand on his and pressed firmly, as if wishing Pemberton's hand to leave its impression on her flesh.

"What shall we do about our former sheriff?" she asked.

"Kill him," Pemberton said. "I can do it if you want me to."

"No, Galloway can do it," Serena said, "as soon as he gets back from Tennessee."

Pemberton looked up and saw the eagle's circle had tightened. It had spotted something.

"What will it hunt in South America?"

"A snake the natives call a fer de lance," Serena said. "It's far more deadly than a rattlesnake."

"As for my hunting, it doesn't seem I'll get my mountain lion," Pemberton mused, "but a jaguar will surely be an equal challenge."

"One even more worthy of you," Serena said.

Pemberton gazed into Serena's pewter-gray irises, the specks of gold within them, then the pupils themselves. How long, Pemberton wondered, since he'd looked there, had the courage to accept such clarity.

"You're more the man I married than you've been for quite a while," Serena said.

"The fire reminded me about what matters."

"And what is that?"

"Only you," Pemberton said.

The eagle's shadow passed over them, then the bird flung itself earthward, landing fifty yards below. The bird jousted with its prey, the snake's rattles buzzing furiously at first but soon intermittent.

"That's forty-two it's killed since early April," Serena said. "I should take it over to Jackson County, let it kill some there before cold weather drives the snakes into their dens."

Serena took the metal whistle from the saddle pocket and blew, then swung the lure overhead. The bird ascended and with two great wing flaps glided up the ridge to land next to the horses, the dust-colored rattlesnake set down like a piece of slash. Pemberton's horse neighed and cantered backward and he had to jerk the reins, but the Arabian was so used to the bird and its prey that it did not even turn its head. The snake twisted onto its belly, and Pemberton saw where the bird's beak had opened the snake's midsection, tugged free strands of purple guts. The snake's tail rattled feebly a few moments more, then was still.

IT was two afternoons later when Pemberton heard the sound of Galloway's car as it bumped and rattled into camp. He went to the office window and watched Galloway rise stiffly from the car, a plum-colored stain darkening the left side of his face. The left eye socket was blackened, the eye just a slit. Galloway walked into the slash and stumps and searched with his good eye until he saw Serena. She was riding toward camp, the day over. Galloway hobbled up the ridge to meet her. With his gone hand and damaged face, he appeared a man who'd fallen sideways into some dangerous machine.

Pemberton sat back down. He told himself not to think about what Galloway's face might betoken of the child's fate. He made himself think instead about the fire, those moments flames had enclosed him and Serena, and how he did not know if they would live or die, but nothing else mattered except they'd live or die together. In a few minutes Galloway's car started up and drove off out of the valley. Serena came into the office.

"Galloway's going to visit our ex-sheriff," she said, but offered no explanation of Galloway's injuries, nor did Pemberton ask.

Serena paused and looked at the boxes of files stacked in the corner for the coming move.

"We've done well here," Serena said.

Thirty-four

AT LEAST THERE ARE MOUNTAINS. THAT WAS what Rachel told herself as she and Jacob left the boarding house and walked up Madison Street. She stepped around a puddle. The rain that had fallen all day continued to fall as evening settled over the city. A gap in the buildings allowed Rachel a glimpse at the snow-capped peak of Mount Rainier. She lingered a few moments, took in the vista as she might a mouthful of cold spring water on a hot day.

She remembered the flat vastness of the midwest, particularly a depot in Kearney, Nebraska, where they'd waited two hours to change trains. She had taken Jacob for a walk down the town's one street. The houses quickly thinned out, then only fields of harvested wheat and corn beneath a wide sky. A landscape where no mountains rose to harbor you, give you shelter. She'd wondered how people could live in such a place. How could you not feel that everything, even your own heart, was laid bare?

Rachel walked toward the café where from five to midnight she was paid twenty cents an hour to wash dishes and clean off tables. Mr. and Mrs. Bjorkland let her lay Jacob on a quilt in the kitchen corner, and each night Mrs. Bjorkland gave Rachel big helpings of food to take home. Rachel passed enough destitute men and women on the streets every day to know how lucky she was to have a job, not to be hungry and in rags, especially after being in Seattle less than a month.

A car horn startled her, and she knew if she lived here the rest of her life she'd never get used to the busyness of town life, how something was always coming and going and whatever that something was always had a noise. Not soothing like the sound of a creek or rain on a tin roof or a mourning dove's call, but harsh and grating, no pattern to it, nothing to settle the mind upon. Except in the early morning, those moments before the city waked with all its grime and noise. She could look out the window at the mountains, and their stillness settled inside her like a healing balm.

Rachel crossed the street. On the other side, a policeman with a nightstick walked his beat. Farther down the block, a group of dispirited men lined up outside the Salvation Army building, waiting to go inside for a meal of beans and white bread, a soiled tick mattress to lay on the building's basement floor. A shock of curly red hair caught her eye at the front of the line. Rachel looked closer and saw the tall gangly body, no gray golf cap but the blue and black mackinaw coat. She hoisted Jacob in her arms and walked quickly down the street, but by the time she got there he was already inside. *If it was him,* because Rachel was already beginning to doubt what her eyes had seen, or thought they'd seen. She considered trying to get inside, but as she stepped closer to the entrance several of the men in line stared hard at her.

"The women's mission is over on Pike Street," a man with his front teeth missing said gruffly.

Rachel looked across the street at the theatre and checked the big clock at the center of the movie marquee, saw she had to leave or be late for work. As she walked back up the sidewalk toward the café, Rachel told herself she was just imagining things. Passing in front of the Esso station, she stepped over a puddle where gas and water swirled together to make an oily rainbow. The rain began to fall harder, and she quickened her pace, made it to the café door just as the bottom of the sky fell out and the rain came so hard she couldn't see the other side of the street.

"Let me hold Jacob for you so you can get your coat off," Mr. Bjorkland said as she came inside.

Mr. Bjorkland and his wife pronounced the child's name with an extra emphasis on the first syllable, as they did Rachel's own name. The names sounded gentler that way, and it seemed right to Rachel for the Bjorklands to speak in such a way, because it fit the kind of people they were.

"Here, to dry off with," Mrs. Bjorkland said, placing a towel on Rachel's shoulder.

Rachel went on into the kitchen and laid Jacob on the quilt. She opened her pocketbook and set the toy train engine beside the child. As she was about to snap shut her pocketbook, Rachel saw the folded piece of paper with a phone number and address. She opened the note and looked at the small precise handwriting you'd not expect from such a man. How much could you feel for someone you'd only spent six or seven hours with, she wondered. You couldn't call it love, but Rachel knew she felt something more than just gratitude. Rachel remembered the week she'd called the number night after night with no answer until, finally, the operator picked up and told Rachel the party she was trying to get in touch with was deceased. She held the note a moment longer and then placed it in a trashcan. She looked at Jacob. After I'm dead, she told herself, at least there'll be one other in the world who knows what Sheriff McDowell done for us.

She changed Jacob and gave him the warm bottle of milk she knew would soon slip from his mouth. Rachel took the cloth apron off the nail on the wall, tied it around her waist. For a moment she paused, feeling the kitchen's warmth, understanding something placid in it. A dry warm place on a cold rainy day and the smell of food and the slow soft breaths of a child drifting toward sleep. *A safe harbor,* Rachel told herself, and as she spoke those words to herself she remembered Miss Stephens describing Seattle while pointing to the far right side of the classroom's wide bright map.

Mr. Bjorkland came through the swinging doors.

"Get your dishwater ready," he said. "Saturday nights are the worst, so you'll earn your money this evening."

There was a clatter of pots and pans as Mr. Bjorkland readied the kitchen for the first order. Rachel glanced over at Jacob, his eyes already closed. He'd sleep soon, despite the din of pots and pans, the shouted orders and and all the other commotion.

Thirty-five

IT WAS SNIPES' CREW WHO CUT THE LAST TREE. When a thirty-foot hickory succumbed to Ross and Henryson's cross-cut saw, the valley and ridges resembled the skinned hide of some huge animal. The men gathered their saws and wedges, the blocks and axes and go-devils. They paused a moment, then walked a winding path down Shanty Mountain. It was late October, and the workers' multi-hued overalls appeared woven from the valley's last leaves.

Once on level ground, the men stopped to rest beside Rough Fork Creek before trudging the mile back to camp. Stewart kneeled beside the stream and raised a handful of water to his lips, spit it out.

"Tastes like mud."

"Used to be this creek held some of the sweetest water in these parts," Ross said. "The chestnut trees that was up at the spring head give it a taste near sweet as honey."

"Soon you won't find one chestnut in these mountains," Henryson noted, "and there'll be nary a drop of water that sweet again."

For a few moments no one spoke. A flock of goldfinches flew into view, their feathers bright against the valley's floor as they winged southward. They swooped low and the flock contracted, perhaps in memory. For a few seconds they appeared suspended there, then the flock expanded like gold cloth unraveling. They circled the valley once before disappearing over Shanty Mountain, their passage through the charred valley as ephemeral as a candle flame waved over an abyss.

"Sheriff McDowell, he was a good man," Stewart said.

Ross nodded. He took out his papers and tobacco and began rolling a cigarette.

"We'll likely not see one better."

"That's the God's truth," Snipes agreed. "He never gave quarter when near about any other man would of. He fought them to the end."

A bemused smile settled on Henryson's face. He nodded his head as he looked west toward Tennessee, spoke softly.

"And to think the only ones ever to get away from them was a eighteen-year-old girl and a child. That's the wonder of it."

Ross looked up from his cigarette.

"Makes you think God glances this way every once in a while."

"So they got away for sure?" Stewart asked.

"Galloway ain't gone back out after them," Henryson said. "The light's been on at his stringhouse for a week now, and I seen him my ownself yesterday evening at the commissary."

"He wasn't of a mind to explain the whyever of his face being tore up, was he?" Snipes asked.

"No, he wasn't, and folks wasn't lining up to ask him about it neither."

Henryson studied the silted stream for a few moments before turning to Ross.

"Used to be thick with trout too, this here stream. There was many a day you and me took our supper from it. Now you'd not catch a knottyhead."

"There was game too," Ross said, "deer and rabbit and coons."

"Squirrels and bear and beaver and bobcats," Henryson added.

"And panthers," Ross said. "I seen one ten year ago on this very creek, but I'll never see ever a one on it again."

Ross paused and lit his cigarette. He took a deep draw and let the smoke slowly wisp from his mouth.

"And I had my part in the doing of it."

"We had to feed our families," Henryson said.

"Yes, we did," Ross agreed. "What I'm wondering is how we'll feed them once all the trees is cut and the jobs leave."

"At least what critters are left have a place they can run to," Henryson said.

"The park, you mean?" Stewart asked.

"Yes sir. Trouble is they ain't going to let us stay in there with them."

"They told my uncle over on Horsetrough Ridge he's got to be off his land by next spring," Stewart said, "and he's farther on the North Carolina side than us standing right here."

"Running folks out so you can run the critters in," Ross said. "That's a hell of a thing."

Snipes, who'd listened attentively but without comment, put on his glasses and looked out over the valley.

"Looks like that land over in France once them in charge let us quit fighting. Got the same feeling about it too."

"What kind of feeling?" Henryson asked.

"Like there's been so much killed and destroyed it can't ever be alive again. Even for them that wasn't around when it happened, it'd lay heavy on them too. It'd be like trying to live in a graveyard."

Ross nodded. "I was just over there three months when it was winding down, but you're right. They's a feeling about a place where men died and the land died with them."

"I missed that one," Henryson said. "The war, I mean."

"Don't worry," Snipes said. "Another one's always coming down the pike. That's something all your historians and philosophers agree on.

A feller over in Germany looks to be ready to set a match to Europe soon enough, and quick as they snuff him out there'll be another to take his place."

"It's ever the way of it," Ross said.

Stewart looked at McIntyre.

"What do you think, Preacher?"

The others turned to McIntyre, not expecting him to reply but to see if any acknowledgment he'd been addressed crossed the man's face. McIntyre raised his eyes and contemplated the wasteland strewn out before him where not a single live thing rose. The other men also looked out on what was in part their handiwork and grew silent. When McIntyre spoke his voice had no stridency, only a solemnity so profound and humble all grew attentive.

"I think this is what the end of the world will be like," McIntyre said, and none among them raised his voice to disagree.

Thirty-six

THE FOLLOWING EVENING PEMBERTON AND SERENA dressed for Pemberton's thirtieth birthday party. Most of the furniture was gone now, packed and hauled off to Jackson County. As Pemberton walked across the room to the chifforobe, his steps reverberated through every room in the house. A dozen workers remained in the camp—Galloway, some kitchen staff, the men taking up rails to reuse in Jackson County. The valley exuded an almost audible silence.

"Where's Galloway been these last few mornings?" Pemberton asked.

"Working, but you can't know why or where."

Serena went to the chifforobe, took out the green dress she'd worn to the Cecil's dinner party.

Pemberton smiled. "I thought we had no secrets."

"We don't," Serena said. "All will be revealed this very night."

"At the party?"

"Yes."

Serena slipped the dress over her head, let the silk slowly ripple and then smooth over skin free of any undergarment. With a quick brush of Serena's hands, the material succumbed to the curves of her body.

Pemberton moved in front of the mirror and knotted his tie. As he examined his handiwork, he saw Serena's reflection in the glass. She stood behind him, just to the left, watching. He straightened the knot and walked over to the bureau to get his cufflinks. Serena stayed where she was, looking at herself, now alone inside the mirror's oval. Her hair had grown out in the last year, touching her shoulders, but tonight it was braided in tight coils set upon her head, revealing a stark whiteness on the back of her neck. Pemberton checked the clock and saw with regret that it was almost time to meet their guests. Later, he thought, and moved to stand behind her. He laid his left hand on Serena's waist, lips brushing the whiteness of her neck.

"Just two weeks before you have one," Pemberton said, "your thirtieth birthday, I mean. I've always liked our birthdays being so near."

Pemberton moved closer so he'd see both their faces in the mirror. The green cloth felt cool to his touch.

"Would you have wished we shared a birthday as well?" Serena said.

Pemberton smiled, raised his hand and cupped her right breast. They could be a few minutes late. It was, after all, his party.

"Why wish for anything more," Pemberton said. "Being with each other is enough."

"Is it, Pemberton?"

The words were spoken in a cool skeptical manner that surprised him. For a moment Serena seemed about to say something more, but she didn't. She slipped from his grasp, left him standing alone in front of the mirror.

"It's time to go and meet our guests," she said.

Pemberton drained his glass of bourbon and poured another drink, drank it in a single swallow. He set the empty glass on the bedside table, and they walked out into the early autumn evening. Farther up the tracks, men pulled spikes with crowbars, groaning and grunting as they paired off and lifted the three-hundred-and-fifty-pound rails onto a flat car. Pemberton looked past the men to where only wooden crossties remained, some blackened by the fire, others not. They blended so well into the landscape as to be barely discernable. Pemberton remembered helping lay the rails across these same crossties, and he had a sudden sensation he was watching time reverse itself. The world blurred, and it seemed possible that the crossties would leap onto stumps and become trees again, the slash whirl upward to become branches. Even a dark blizzard of ash paling back in time to become green leaves, gray and brown twigs.

"What's wrong?" Serena said as he swayed slightly.

She gripped Pemberton's arm and time righted itself, again ran in its proper current.

"I guess I drank that last whiskey too fast."

The train came over the ridge. He and Serena moved closer to the track and met their guests as they stepped down from the coach car. Kisses and handshakes were exchanged, and hosts and guests walked into the office. Among them was Mrs. Lowenstein, who'd not been expected. Pemberton noted her pallor and thinness, how her eyes receded deep inside the sockets, accentuating the skull blossoming beneath her taut skin. Ten chairs had been placed around the table. The Salvatores and De Mans sat across from the Lowensteins and Calhouns, Serena and Pemberton at opposite ends.

"What an impressive table," Mrs. Salvatore said. "It looks to be a single piece of wood. Is that possible?"

"Yes, a single piece of chestnut," Pemberton answered, "cut less than a mile from here."

"I wouldn't have thought such a large tree existed," Mrs. Salvatore said.

"Pemberton Lumber Company will find even bigger trees in Brazil," Serena said.

"So you've shown us," Calhoun agreed, spreading his arms to show he meant all at the table. "And I must say in a very convincing fashion."

"Indeed," Mr. Salvatore said. "I'm a cautious man, especially with this continuing depression, but your Brazil venture is the best investment I've found since Black Friday."

The camp's remaining kitchen workers came into the room, serving as bartenders as well as waiters. Their clothes were fresh laundered but no different from what they normally wore. Investors preferred money spent cutting wood, not finery for workers, Serena had reasoned. The supper fare was similarly austere, roast beef and potatoes, squash and bread. Pemberton had armed a crew with fishing poles that afternoon to catch trout for an hors d' oeuvre, but the men returned from the creeks fishless, claming no trout remained in the valley or nearby ridges to catch. Only the French Chardonnay and Glenlivet scotch bespoke wealth, that and a box of Casamontez cigars set at the table's center.

"We must have a birthday toast," Calhoun announced once the drinks had been poured.

"First a toast to our new partnerships," Pemberton said.

"Go ahead then, Pemberton," Calhoun said.

"I defer to my wife," Pemberton said. "Her eloquence surpasses mine."

Serena raised her wineglass.

"To partnerships, and all that's possible," Serena said. "The world is ripe, and we'll pluck it like an apple from a tree."

"Pure poetry," Calhoun exclaimed.

They ate. Pemberton had drunk in moderation the last few weeks, but tonight he wanted the heightened exuberance of alcohol. Besides the bourbon at the house, he'd drained seven tumblers of scotch by the time his birthday cake was placed before him, the thirty lit candles set in a four-layer chocolate cake that took two workers to carry. Pemberton was surprised at the extravagance of Serena's gesture. The kitchen workers set ten saucers and a cutting knife to the right of the cake. Serena dismissed both workers after the coffee was poured and the cigars passed around.

"A cake worthy of a king," Lowenstein said admiringly as the cake's flickering light suffused Pemberton's face in a golden glow.

"A wish before you blow out the candles," Calhoun demanded.

"I need no wish," Pemberton said. "I've nothing left to want."

He stared at the candles and the swaying motions of the flames gave his stomach a momentary queasiness. Pemberton inhaled deeply and blew, taking two more breaths before the last candle was snuffed.

"Another toast," Calhoun said, "to the man who has everything."

"Yes, a toast," Lowenstein said.

They all raised their glasses and drank, except Serena.

"I disagree," Serena said as the others set their glasses down. "There's one thing my husband doesn't have."

"What would that be?" Mrs. De Man asked.

"The panther he hoped to kill in these mountains."

"Ah, too late," Pemberton said, and looked at the expired candles in mock regret."

"Perhaps not," Serena said to Pemberton. "Galloway has been out scouting for your panther the last week, and he's found it."

Serena nodded toward the open office door, where Galloway had appeared.

"Right, Galloway."

The highlander nodded as Pemberton paused in his cutting of the cake.

"Where?" Pemberton asked.

"Ivy Gap," Serena said. "Galloway's baited a meadow just outside the park boundary with deer carcasses. Three evenings ago the panther came and fed on one. Tomorrow it should be hungry again, and this time you'll be waiting for it."

Serena turned to address Galloway. As she did, Pemberton saw that a diminutive figure in a black satin bonnet stood behind him in the foyer.

"Bring her in," Serena said.

As mother and son entered the room, the old woman's wrinkled hand clutched Galloway's left wrist, covering the nub as if to foster an illusion that the hand attached to her son's arm might be his instead of her own. Mrs. Galloway's cedar-wood shoes clacked hollowly on the puncheon floor. She wore the same black dress that Pemberton had seen her in two summers ago.

"Entertainment for our guests," Serena said.

All at the table turned to watch the old woman totter into the room. Serena placed a chair next to Pemberton and gestured at Galloway to seat her. Galloway helped his mother into the chair. She undid her bonnet and handed it to her son, who remained beside her. It was the first time Pemberton had clearly seen the old woman's face. It reminded him of a walnut hull with its deep wavy wrinkles, dry as a hull as well. Her eyes stared straight ahead, clouded the same milky-blue as before. Galloway, the satin bonnet in his hand, stepped back and leaned against the wall.

Calhoun, his face blushed by alcohol, finally broke the silence.

"What sort of entertainment? I see no dulcimer or banjo. An a cappella ballad from the old country? Perhaps a jack tale?"

Calhoun leaned over to his wife and whispered. They both looked at the old woman and laughed.

"She sees the future," Serena said.

"Marvelous," Lowenstein said, and turned to his spouse. "We won't need our stockbroker any more, dear."

Everyone at the table laughed except the old woman and Serena. As the laughter subsided, Mrs. Lowenstein raised a purple handkerchief to her lips.

"Mrs. Galloway's talents are of a more personal nature," Serena said.

"Look out, Lowenstein," Calhoun retorted. "She may predict you're going to prison for tax evasion."

Laughter again filled the room, but the old woman appeared impervious to the jesting. Galloway's mother clasped her hands and set them on the table. Blue veins webbed the loose skin, and the nails were cracked and yellowed, yet neatly trimmed. Pemberton smiled at the thought of Galloway bent over the old crone, carefully clipping each nail.

"Who wants to go first?" Serena said.

"Oh, me please," Mrs. Lowenstein said. "Do I need to hold out my palm or does she have a crystal ball."

"Ask your question," Serena said, her smile thinning.

"Very well. Will my daughter get married soon?"

The old woman turned in the direction of Mrs. Lowenstein's voice and slowly nodded.

"Wonderful," Mrs. Lowenstein said. "I'll get to be a mother of the bride after all. I so feared Hannah would wait until I was pushing up daisies."

Mrs. Galloway stared in Mrs. Lowenstein's direction a few moments longer, then spoke.

"All I said was she'd get married soon."

An uncomfortable silence descended over the table. Pemberton struggled for a quip to restore the levity, but the alcohol blurred his thinking. Serena met his eyes but offered no help. Finally it was Mr. De Man, who'd said little the whole evening, who attempted to lessen the disquietude.

"What about Pemberton. It's his birthday we're here to celebrate. He should have his fortune told."

"Yes," Serena said. "Pemberton should go next. I even have the perfect question for him."

"And what is that, my dear?" Pemberton asked.

"Ask her how you'll die."

Mrs. Salvatore let out a soft *oh*, her eyes shifting between her husband and the door, which she appeared ready to flee through. Lowenstein took his wife's hand, his brow furrowed. He seemed about to say something, but Serena spoke first.

"Go ahead, Pemberton. For our guests' amusement."

Salvatore rose in his seat.

"Perhaps it's time for us to take leave and return to Asheville," he said, but Pemberton raised his hand and gestured for him to sit down.

"Very well," Pemberton said, raising his tumbler and giving his guests a reassuring grin. "But I'll finish my dram of liquor first. A man should have a drink in his hand when he confronts his demise."

"Well put," Calhoun said, "a man who understands how to meet his fate, with a belly full of good scotch."

The others smiled at Calhoun's remark, including Salvatore, who eased back into his chair. Pemberton emptied his tumbler and set it down forcefully enough that Mrs. Salvatore flinched.

"So how will I die, Mrs. Galloway?" Pemberton asked, his words beginning to slur. "Will it be a gunshot? Perhaps a knife?"

Galloway, who'd been gazing out the window, now fixed his eyes on his mother.

"A rope's more likely for a scoundrel like you, Pemberton," Calhoun said, eliciting chuckles all around.

The old woman turned her head in Pemberton's direction.

"No gun nor knife," she answered. "Nor rope around your neck."

"That's a relief," Pemberton said.

Except for the Salvatores, the guests laughed politely.

"What killed my father was his liver," Pemberton said.

"It ain't to be your liver," Mrs. Galloway said.

"So what, pray tell, is the thing that will kill me?"

"They ain't one thing can kill a man like you," Mrs. Galloway answered, and pushed back her chair.

Galloway helped his mother to her feet, and at that moment Pemberton realized it was all a jape. The others realized also as Mrs. Galloway took her son's arm and made her slow clatter across the room and disappeared into the darkened hallway. Pemberton raised his tumbler toward Serena.

"Splendid answer, and the best any man could hope for," he said. "A toast to my wife, who can play a rusty with the best of them."

Pemberton looked down the table's length and smiled at Serena as the others laughed and clapped. The alcohol made everyone else in the room hazy to Pemberton, but somehow not Serena. If anything, she appeared brighter, the dress vivid and shimmering. *Evergreen.* The word came to him now though he could not say why. He remembered the touch of his lips on the pale bareness of her neck and wished the guests hours gone. If they were, he wouldn't wait but would lift Serena onto the table and undress her on the Chestnut's heartwood. For a few moments, he thought of doing it anyway and giving Mrs. Salvatore a real case of the vapors.

All raised their glasses and drank. Calhoun, who'd drunk almost as much as Pemberton, wiped a dribble of scotch from his chin before pouring himself another drink.

"I must admit," Mrs. Calhoun said, "that from the way she put on there were a few moments I almost believed the old woman *could* see the future."

"She played her role well," her husband agreed. "Never a hint of a smile the whole time."

Pemberton lifted his watch from his pocket and opened the case with no attempt to hide his purpose. The watch hands wavered like compass needles, causing Pemberton to raise the watch closer to his face.

"It's been a wonderful evening," he said, "but it's time for our revelry to end if you're to be at the station when the Asheville train leaves."

"But you must open your present first," Serena said. "Galloway can call the depot in Waynesville and have them hold the train."

Serena lifted a long cylinder-shaped cardboard box from under the table. She passed the box to Pemberton and he opened the flap, slowly removed a rifle. Pemberton placed his hands under the stock and set the weapon before him so the others could see.

"A Winchester 1895," Serena said, "albeit a more personalized one, as you can see from the wood and gold trigger and plating. And the scrollwork, of course. In the Rockies it's the weapon of choice for hunting mountain lions."

Pemberton picked up the rifle and ran his hand over the wood's glossed finish.

"I know about this gun," he said. "It's the one Roosevelt called 'Big Medicine.'"

"Too bad Teddy didn't use it on himself," Calhoun said.

"Yes, but who knows," Pemberton said, raising the rifle toward the window and feigning disappointment when he squeezed the trigger and there was only a click. "Perhaps that cousin of his will show up, and I'll take a shot at him."

Pemberton handed the rifle to Mr. Salvatore. The gift slowly circled the table, the women passing it with palms underneath as if a platter, except for Mrs. De Man, who like the men jostled the rifle in her hands, nodding appreciatively at the gun's heft and sturdiness.

"The scrollwork, Mrs. Pemberton," Mr. Lowenstein said. "It's beautifully done, but I don't recognize the depiction."

"The shield of Achilles."

"Such a gun would do good service in Quebec with our brown bears," Mrs. De Man noted as she passed the rifle to her husband.

Pemberton filled his tumbler again, sloshing scotch onto the table as he poured. When the rifle was passed back to him, he leaned it against the table.

"I'll kill my mountain lion first," Pemberton boasted, "then a jaguar."

"Brazil," Lowenstein mused. "What an adventure for the two of you."

"Indeed," Calhoun said. "Forests enough for a lifetime and plenty left over."

Pemberton raised his hand and waved it dismissively.

"Give us a lifetime and Mrs. Pemberton and I will cut down every tree, not just in Brazil but in the world."

The words inside Pemberton's head were luminous enough, but he knew that he'd tried to say too much. Vowels and consonants had dragged and halted like gears that wouldn't mesh, the words hopelessly slurred.

Salvatore nodded at his wife and stood.

"We should be going now. Our train back to Chicago leaves rather early in the morning."

The other guests rose and made their goodbyes, began leaving as well. Pemberton tried to rise from his chair, but as he did the room tilted. He sat back down, focused his eyes and saw Serena still sat opposite him, the table lengthening out between them.

"See them to the train?" Pemberton asked. "Not sure I can."

Serena looked at him steadily.

"They know the way, Pemberton," Serena said, watching him steadily.

The room slowly leaned back and forth, not as bad as when he'd stood up, but enough to make him grip the table's edge, feel the smooth waxed wood against his palms. He gripped the table harder. An image almost like a dream came to him of being alone on a vast sea and hanging onto a piece of wood as waves lapped against him, and then he let go.

Thirty-Seven

THE FOLLOWING MORNING PEMBERTON AWOKE with the worst hangover of his life. It was early, but what light filtered through the window stung his eyes. His tongue felt coated with a foul dust that had liquefied in his stomach. The previous evening returned in a series of blurry images that passed before him like boxcars come to unload freight he didn't want.

Serena still slept, so he turned on his side and closed his eyes but couldn't fall back asleep. He waited, not seeing but feeling the sun slowly brighten the room. After a while, Serena stirred beside him, her bare hip brushing against his. Pemberton could not remember if they'd coupled last night, or even how he'd gotten back to the house. He turned and looked at Serena through bleary eyes.

"I'm sorry," he said.

"Sorry about what?"

"Imbibing too much last night."

"It was your birthday, and you celebrated," Serena said. "There's no crime in that."

"But it may have cost us a couple of investors."

"I doubt it, Pemberton. Profits matter more than social graces."

Serena sat upright. The bed sheet fell away, and Pemberton saw her long slim back and the slight taper before the flare of her hips. She faced the window, and the morning sun fell lambent over her profile. Enough light to make his bloodshot eyes squint, but he did not turn away. How could anything else have ever mattered, Pemberton wondered. He reached out and held her wrist as Serena prepared to leave the bed.

"Not yet," he said softly.

Pemberton slid closer to wrap his other arm around Serena's waist. He pressed his face to the small of her back, closed his eyes and inhaled the smell of her.

"You need to get up," Serena said, freeing herself and leaving the bed.

"Why?" Pemberton asked, opening his eyes. "It's Sunday."

"Galloway said be ready by eleven," Serena replied, slipping on her breeches and riding jacket. "Your mountain lion awaits you."

"I'd forgotten," Pemberton said, and slowly sat up, the room leaning for a few moments then righting itself.

He rose, still groggy as he walked over to the chifforobe. He lifted his duckcloth pants and wool socks from the shelf, stripped his hunting jacket from a hanger. Pemberton tossed them on the bed, then retrieved his heavy lace-up hunting boots from the hall closet before sitting beside Serena, who was pulling on her jodhpurs. He closed his eyes, trying to stall the headache the morning light intensified.

"And you're fine here alone?" Pemberton said, his eyes still shut as he spoke.

"Yes, all I've got to do is make sure what's left in the kitchen and the commissary gets loaded on a railcar. But first I'll take the eagle out, a final hunt before we leave this place."

Serena rose, looking toward the door as she spoke.

"I have to go."

Pemberton reached for her hand, held it a moment.

"Thank you for the rifle, and the birthday party."

"You're welcome," Serena said, withdrawing her hand. "I hope you find your panther, Pemberton."

After Serena left, he contemplated going to the dining hall for breakfast, but his stomach argued against it. He dressed but for his boots, then lay back down on the bed and closed his eyes. For just a few minutes, he told himself, but Pemberton didn't wake until Galloway knocked on the door.

Pemberton yelled he'd be out in ten minutes and went to the bathroom. He filled the basin with cold water and plunged his whole head into it, kept it submerged as long as he could stand. He raised up and did the same thing again. The cold water helped. Pemberton toweled off and combed his hair so it lay sleek against his scalp, then he brushed his teeth as well to dim the nauseating smell of his own breath. He found the aspirin bottle on the medicine shelf and took out two, capped the bottle and put it in his pocket. As he was about to turn, he saw himself in the mirror. His eyes were bloodshot and his pallor could have been better, but his being up and about at all seemed a triumph considering how he'd felt earlier. Pemberton picked up his jacket from the bed and went into the front of the house where the new rifle lay on the fireboard. He couldn't remember setting it there last night, or being given the box of .35 caliber bullets beside it.

"Heard you had quite a evening of it," Galloway said as Pemberton stepped onto the porch, his face grimacing against the bright cloudless day.

Pemberton ignored Galloway's comment, focusing instead on Frizzell's truck parked beside the commissary. The photographer had set up his tripod on the railless track where the skidder boom had once sat, his camera aimed not at any worker living or the dead but the decimated valley itself. Frizzell hunched beneath his black shawl, oblivious to the fact that Serena, atop the gelding with the eagle on the pommel, rode toward him.

"What the hell is he doing?" Pemberton asked.

"No idea, but your missus looks to be going to find out," Galloway said and glanced skyward. "We need to be going. We got us a late start as it is."

"Go on to the car," Pemberton said, and handed the rifle and box of bullets to Galloway. "I'm going to find out what this is about."

Pemberton walked toward the commissary as Frizzell emerged from beneath the cloth, eyes blinking as if just awakened as he spoke with Serena. Pemberton passed the office, empty now, even the windows taken to the camp. The door was ajar, a few skittering leaves already wind-brushed inside.

"Secretary Albright's commissioned a photograph of the devastation we've wrecked upon the land," Serena said to Pemberton when he joined her. "A further way to justify his park."

"This land is still ours for another week," Pemberton said to Frizzell. "You're trespassing."

"But she just said I'm free to take all the photographs I wish," Frizzell objected.

"Why not, Pemberton," Serena said. "I'm pleased with what we've done here. Aren't you?"

"Yes, of course," Pemberton said, "but I do think Mr. Frizzell should compensate us with a photograph."

Frizzell's brow furrowed in surprise.

"Of this?" the photographer asked, his palm turned upward toward the valley.

"No, a photograph of us," Pemberton replied.

"I thought I made my views on such things clear at the Vanderbilt Estate," Serena said.

"Not a portrait, just a photograph."

Serena did not answer.

"Indulge me this one time," Pemberton said. "We have no photograph of us together. Think of it as a last birthday present."

For a few moments Serena did not respond. Then something in her countenance let go, not so much a softening as a yielding that Pemberton thought at first was resignation but then seemed more like sadness. He remembered the photographs she left in the Colorado house to burn, and wondered, for all her denying of the past, if some part of her yet dwelled on those photographs.

"All right, Pemberton."

Frizzell slid the negative plate from his last photograph into its protective metal sleeve and placed a new one in the camera.

"We'll need a less dreary backdrop, so I'll have to move my equipment," Frizzell said irritably.

"No," Pemberton said. "The backdrop is fine as it is. As Mrs. Pemberton says, we're pleased with what we've done here."

"Very well," Frizzell said, turning to Serena, "but surely you're not staying on your horse?"

"Yes," Serena said. "I am."

"Well," Frizzell said with utter exasperation, "if the photograph is blurred you'll only have yourselves to blame."

Frizzell disappeared under his shawl, and the photograph was taken. The photographer began packing his equipment as Galloway gave a long blast of his car horn.

"I'll have one of my men pick it up in Waynesville tomorrow," Pemberton said, lingering beside Serena.

"You need to go, Pemberton," Serena said.

She leaned in the saddle and pressed her hand against his face. Pemberton took her hand and pressed it to his lips a moment.

"I love you," he said.

Serena nodded and turned away. She rode off toward Noland Mountain, black puffs of lingering ash rising around the horse's hooves. Pemberton watched her a few moments and then walked to the car, but he paused before opening the passenger door.

"What is it?" Galloway asked.

"Just trying to think if there's anything else I may need."

"I got us food," Galloway said. "Got your hunting knife too. The Missus had me fetch it. It's in my tote sack."

As they left camp, Pemberton glanced up the ridge at Galloway's stringhouse, one of the few that hadn't yet been hauled to the new site. The old woman wasn't on the porch, was probably inside sitting at the table. Pemberton smiled as he thought of her prophecy, the way they'd all been taken in by her performance. They rode north, Galloway using his stub to guide the wheel when he shifted gears. Pemberton closed his eyes and waited for the aspirin to ease his headache.

After a while the Packard slowed and turned. Pemberton opened his eyes. Trees closed in around them. They bumped down into Ivy Gap, a swathe of private land just east of the park holdings. The car passed over a wooden plank bridge, and the automobile's vibration caused Pemberton's latent headache to return.

"Why don't you get a damn fender brace for this thing," Pemberton said, "that or slow down."

"Maybe it'll shake that hang over out of your head," Galloway said, swerving to avoid a washout.

They passed a harvested cornfield where a scarecrow rose, wide-armed as if forsaken. A pair of doves fluttered up amid the tatter of broken stalks and shucks, resettled. Pemberton knew men hunted them but could not imagine what satisfaction came from killing something hardly larger than the shell you shot with. The woods thickened until the road did not so much end as give up, surrendering to scrub oaks and broom sedge. Galloway stopped and jerked the handbrake.

"We'll have to hoof it the rest of the way."

They got out and Galloway took a tote sack from the back seat. Pemberton retrieved his rifle and opened the box of bullets, lifted out a handful and stuffed them in a jacket pocket. Galloway swung the tote sack over his shoulder.

"Anything else?" Pemberton asked.

"No," Galloway said, starting down the hint of road that remained. "All we need's in this tote sack."

"You have the car keys?"

"Got them," Galloway said, patting his right pants pocket.

"Give me my knife."

Galloway opened the tote sack and handed Pemberton the knife.

"Where's the sheath?"

"I reckon it's still in that drawer," Galloway said.

Pemberton cursed softly at Galloway's oversight, placed the hunting knife in the jacket's side pocket.

Pemberton and Galloway moved deeper into the gorge, crossing a spring bog and then a creek. They moved through a stand of tulip poplars whose yellow leaves shimmered the forest floor with new-fallen brightness. The land made a last steep drop, and they entered the meadow, tufts of broom sedge giving the open landscape a luster to rival the surrounding trees. A deer lay in the meadow's center, little left but rags of fur and bones. Galloway opened the tote sack and removed a dozen ears of corn, placed them in a full circle as if to enclose the carcass. Pemberton wondered if Galloway was enacting some primitive hunting ceremony, something learned from the Cherokee or done centuries ago in Albion, the kind of thing that had so fascinated Buchanan.

"That panther fed on this deer pretty good, didn't it," Galloway said.

"It appears so."

"I figured it would," Galloway said, taking a hawkbill knife from his right pocket.

Galloway walked over to the meadow edge where a bed sheet hung from a dogwood branch, its four corners knotted to hold something sagging within. He methodically freed the knife blade, then sliced open the bed sheet. A dead fawn spilled onto the ground. Galloway picked up a back leg and dragged the fawn to the meadow's center, set it beside the other carcass.

"This way even if the corn don't draw a deer, that cat will have something to gnaw on," Galloway said, and pointed halfway up the far ridge where a granite outcrop pushed out of the slantland like a huge fist. "There's a flat place on that biggest rock, even has a cave goes back in it a ways on the nigh end. You can set there and see this whole meadow, and it's high enough for that cat not to smell you. Some deer should show for them corn shucks come the shank of evening, and that panther won't be far behind."

Pemberton looked at the ridge dubiously. There was no discernable way up, nothing but mountain laurel and rock.

"Is there a path?"

"Not but the one we'll make getting there," Galloway said. "Mountain laurel covers up a place so fast you've barely got time to look behind and see your own footprints."

"There's not an easier way?"

"Not to my knowing," Galloway replied. "I'll haul that rifle in the crook of my arm if you want. Might make it easier for you."

"I'll carry my own damn gun," Pemberton said.

Galloway stepped into the mountain laurel. The plants quickly enveloped him up to the chest. Pemberton followed, gripping the rifle just below the trigger, the barrel held skyward so that only the stock brushed the plants. Galloway stepped through the tangles with no attempt to watch where his feet set down. The laurel soon became sparser as the land's angle increased. The sun was at their back, and its heat settled directly on the ridge. Pemberton's hunting outfit had not been uncomfortable in the woods, but here only a few stunted fir grew, nothing to give any shade. They moved around the barn-wide rock. The soil was loose, thinned by granite Pemberton now realized was the undersurface of the whole mountainside. Galloway gauged his steps, moving a few yards sideways to find where the foothold would be best. Pemberton's breath became labored. When he had to stop and rest, Galloway looked back.

"If you're not born to this skinny air a fellow will lose his breath easy up here."

They stood a minute in the outcrop's shadow. Galloway studied the jut of rock and pointed to his right.

"Seems last fall that I went around that side."

Galloway stepped edgewise and angled his way out of the rock's shadow, no soil beneath their feet, only granite. The last few yards Pemberton leaned forward and used his free hand to keep from slipping. The granite was hot to his touch. A thought crossed his mind that this could be another of Serena's japes. When they were almost level with the outcrop, Galloway veered a few steps more to the right and stopped where a spring flow created a natural basin. The older man sat by the pool and laid the tote sack beside him. Pemberton sat as well and tried to slow his panting. Below, the whole meadow unfurled, beyond it to the west Sterling Mountain that marked park land. Galloway pulled two sandwiches from the sack, unwrapped the butcher's paper and inspected one.

"This is turkey," he said, and offered Pemberton the other. "Your missus said you was partial to beef on your sandwiches. She had the cook slab it up good with mustard too."

Pemberton took the sandwich and ate. It wasn't particularly good, too much mustard and the bread tasted moldy, but despite the hangover he found the hike and bear crawl up the ridge had given him an appetite. He finished the sandwich and cupped his hand in the creek and drank, as much to wash the sandwich's taste from his mouth as thirst.

"That spring up top gives cold water even in the dog days," Galloway said. "You'll not find better water."

"It's damn sure better than that sandwich."

"A shame it's not to your liking," Galloway said, feigning disappointment, "especially after the missus made it up special for you."

Pemberton cupped his hand and drank more. The sandwich did not sit well on his stomach, and he hoped the cold water might help.

The sun was full upon them, and the granite gathered the midday heat and held it in the rock gaps. Pemberton yawned and might have napped a few minutes, but his guts began cramping and nausea followed. He thought of last night's drinking and wished again he'd been more moderate.

He checked his watch. Almost three o'clock. Galloway opened the tote sack and removed a plug of tobacco and the hawkbill, which he unlocked by setting his foot on the handle, using thumb and forefinger to free the blade. Then he set the plug on his knee, picked up the knife and slowly pressed the blade into the tobacco. Galloway placed the larger portion back into the sack, locked the knife and put it back as well. Each step was done with the solemnity and preciseness of ritual.

"Best go ahead and get up on that ledge," Galloway said.

Pemberton studied the outcrop.

"How do I get up there?"

"Stand on that smaller rock," Galloway said, pointing with his hand. "Then put your foot in that crack above it."

"Then what?"

"You got to hoist yourself the rest of the way. Grab hold of the ledge with your left hand, then drape your yonder leg up and hoist yourself over. It's flat as a skillet on top, so you ain't going to roll off."

Pemberton scanned the far edge of the meadow, searching for a glint of binoculars. He turned to Galloway, who examined the cut of tobacco as if searching for some flaw in it.

"If this is a rusty Mrs. Pemberton put you up to . . ."

Galloway met Pemberton's eyes. He lifted the black plug of tobacco to his mouth and used his index finger to tuck the wad behind his back molars. Only then did Galloway speak.

"It ain't no rusty."

Galloway brushed a few loose stems of the tobacco off his jeans but made no move to get up. He looked into the spring as if searching for something.

"I'd be of a mind to get on up there if I was you," Galloway said. "Won't be too long before the meadow starts to shadow up. Soon as it happens that panther will start making his way out of the park."

Galloway squirted a brown stream of tobacco juice into the spring and stood.

"When you get up there, I'll hand you your gun. It'll be easier that way."

Pemberton studied the outcrop, imagining foot and hand placements. There appeared to be no other way. He gave the rifle to Galloway and climbed up on the smaller rock, raised his left hand to grip the ledge top's surface. He put his full weight on the rock to make sure it was steady, then placed one boot toe in the crevice. As Pemberton lifted the other foot, he raised his right hand and placed it beside the left. Pemberton took a deep breath and kicked his right leg over the outcrop and rolled onto the ledge, arms spread outward so that he turned over only once, faced the sky.

A buzzing filled the air, and Pemberton first thought he'd disturbed a hornet's nest. He felt a stinging in his calf and raised his head to see a rattlesnake retracting into its coil. Three other snakes coiled less than a yard from where he lay, filling the air with their warnings. One of the snakes lunged and Pemberton felt its fangs strike his boot, snag a moment, and pull free. Then he was rolling off the ledge, hitting first the smaller rock and then the ground and then sliding and tumbling farther down the ridge. Pemberton stalled his descent a moment by clutching a sapling, but the roots jerked free from the thin soil and he continued tumbling downward until level land and mountain laurel stopped him.

Pemberton did not move as he waited for his body to tell him what damage had been done. His left ankle throbbed, and one glance at its odd angle told him the ankle was broken. Two, maybe three ribs were cracked as well. The hunting knife had opened a deep gash in his arm. Pemberton told himself he would be all right, but at that moment the venom that coursed through his veins announced itself, and not just in the leg. He could taste the poison in his mouth, though Pemberton couldn't understand how this was possible.

He stared upward, and for a moment Pemberton had the sensation that he was actually falling away from the earth and toward the sky. He closed his eyes. When he reopened them, he felt the earth solid beneath him. Pemberton raised his arm and saw the bleeding had not stopped. But at least not an artery, he told himself. Pemberton took a handkerchief from his back pocket and pressed it against the gash. The cloth quickly saturated, so he took a pair of wool socks from his jacket and pressed them against the wound. The socks were soon blood-soaked as well, but when he removed them the bleeding had lessened.

He touched his jacket pocket tentatively. The knife was still there, though its blade had cut hilt-deep through the lining. Pemberton placed his right hand inside the pocket, let his palm cover the elk-bone handle. He found the knife handle's solidity reassuring and did not loosen his grip.

A long time passed before Galloway made his way down the ridge and stood above him. The highlander seemed content to stand and gawk for the rest of the afternoon. Pemberton let go of the knife and pulled himself to a sitting position.

"You're about tore up as a fellow can get," Galloway said. "Lost a lot of blood too from the looks of it."

"Help me up," Pemberton said, and held out his arm.

Galloway lifted Pemberton to his feet, but once up the poisoned leg and broken ankle made it impossible for him to stand without help. Galloway put his arm around Pemberton's waist.

"Get me into the meadow."

Galloway helped him through the mountain laurel and onto the open ground, eased Pemberton into a sitting position amid the broom sedge.

"A rattlesnake bit me," Pemberton said.

He pulled up his right pant leg. Just above the boot, two small holes broke the skin, the flesh puffy and streaked red around the punctures. The taste of venom lingered in his mouth while sweat seemed to seep from every pore in his body. A tingling began in his fingers and toes, and Pemberton wondered if the bite caused this as well. Galloway squatted beside Pemberton and peered closely at the bite mark.

Pemberton took the hunting knife from his jacket and cut the pant leg from the thigh all the way through the cuff. The cloth fell away like a loose layer of skin.

"Won't do much good," Galloway said. "That poison has done got in your veins."

"I might get some of it out," Pemberton said, and pressed the blade tip on the bite mark.

Galloway placed his hand over Pemberton's.

"Let me cut. I done it before."

Pemberton released the knife and Galloway lifted the blade from the flesh. He studied the wound, then probed around it with the knife tip.

"Cut, damn it," Pemberton said.

Galloway methodically cut an X across the bite. He cut deep. Too deep, Pemberton suspected.

"That snake got you good," Galloway said as he raised the knife from Pemberton's flesh. "Sometimes they'll dry bite you, but this one's give you the full dose."

The two men stared at the leg as it continued to redden and swell. Pemberton remembered how Jenkins' leg had blackened and begun to stink. But he was a bigger man than Jenkins, and that would help dilute the poison. For the first time since he'd seen the snake on the ledge, Pemberton realized how dire the situation could have been. If he'd rolled onto several of the rattlesnakes or hadn't reached for the sapling, he could be dying, if not already dead. Pemberton felt a sudden heightened aliveness, the same as when he'd survived Harmon's bowie knife and the bear's teeth and claws. What he'd felt most of all that moment he and Serena held each other outside the burning house. Even the pain in his belly and leg and arm could not dim his euphoria.

Galloway wiped the blade on the tote sack. He laid the knife on the cloth and squatted. Pemberton knew some said you needed to suck the poison out, but he couldn't do it and damned if he'd let Galloway's rotten mouth try. Instead, Pemberton pressed the skin around the wound, squeezing out as much blood as possible. He stripped the leather bootlace from the eyelets and tied a tourniquet above the kneecap. Even without the lace, the right foot was so swollen that he had to turn and twist the boot to get it off. When Pemberton finally freed the boot from his foot, he peeled off the sock as well. He touched his foot, and the skin appeared ready to split open like fruit swollen past ripeness. His stomach felt as if he'd swallowed a bottle of lye. Galloway squatted nearby, his eyes on Pemberton, attentive.

"I won't be able to walk out of here," Pemberton said, and felt a wave of chills ripple through his body.

"And I couldn't haul you out even if I had a mind to," Galloway said.

Pemberton's temples ached as if gripped by metal tongs. The taste of the venom intensified and his stomach spasmed.

"Damn stomach," Pemberton gasped, then paused a moment. "I'd not think a snake bite would cause that."

"It don't," Galloway said. "I reckon that sandwich is what's bothering your guts."

Galloway didn't look at Pemberton as he spoke. He looked west toward the park land.

"You're gonna be in this meadow a while."

"Where's my rifle?"

"Guess I left it up there at the cliff rock," Galloway said.

Pemberton cursed.

"Take the car and go find a phone," Pemberton said, his voice tightening when a new wave of pain hit. "Call Bowden and tell him to fetch a doctor and get up here. Then go on to the camp and find Serena. She'll tell you what else to do."

Galloway did not reply at first. He instead stepped over to the tote sack and placed the hunting knife inside, used his fingers and thumb to slip the sack through his belt and make a knot. It was done so deftly as to appear one fluid motion.

"She already has," Galloway said, "told me what to do, I mean. Which is why I'll be leaving you here."

For a few moments Pemberton did not understand. His guts contracted with such force he grabbed his stomach, fingernails breaking the skin as if trying to dig out the pain's source. He shivered violently, and the pain lessened only to return again just as intensely. Pemberton felt lightheaded, almost ready to faint, and he wondered if that might be as much from the loss of blood as the venom.

"Must be that sandwich your Missus made special for you," Galloway said. "She mixed some rat poison into the mustard, then added some of that Paris Green to sweeten it. I asked her what if you tasted the poison, but she said men never noticed nothing that wasn't square in front of them. Guess she was right about that."

Galloway paused and wiped a dribble of tobacco juice from his chin. Pemberton felt blood inside his mouth and knew his gums bled. He spit out some of the blood so he could speak, but Galloway began talking again.

"She said to tell you she thought you the one man ever strong and pure enough to be her equaling, but you wanting that child alive showed the otherwise of that."

Pemberton closed his eyes a few moments and tried to focus through the pain. He tried to understand what Galloway was telling him, but it seemed too much. He tried to settle on one thing.

"How'd she find out?"

"Mama told her that day I was in Kingsport, but your missus didn't believe it. It was Sheriff McDowell set her straight. That day I went to visit him in the jail. He even told me the exact dollar amount you give him so she could check it against the ledgers and know he wasn't lying."

"Just you? He didn't tell Bowden?"

"Bowden run out the back door before I even got started good. He was out there vomiting. He didn't come back in till I was through."

"Telling about the child," Pemberton said. "McDowell thought it would save his life?"

"No," Galloway said, frowning slightly as he shook his head. "He knowed what the truth of it was the second I come in that cell. He knowed he was a dead man."

Pemberton looked into Galloway's eyes and knew he was seeing the same flat stare McDowell had seen.

"Did McDowell know where they are?"

"I believe he did," Galloway said, "at least where they went from Knoxville."

"But he didn't tell you?"

"I knowed McDowell wasn't going to offer up where they was. Oh, I whittled on him a good bit, enough to where any another man would have give up his own mama, but he wouldn't tell."

Galloway paused and scratched the end of his stump, became more reflective.

"He deserved better than he got, McDowell did. He lived and died by his own rights. If I had it to do over, I'd as lief have killed him quick."

Galloway took the wad of tobacco from his mouth and examined it a moment, threw it toward the mountain laurel. Pemberton squeezed his eyes shut. Words came harder now, the smooth glide of thought from brain to tongue ruptured. He formed a sentence and held it in his mind a few moments so it might clarify.

"Why'd he tell you about me helping him?"

"I'm of a mind he figured it'd be a way of getting at least one of you killed," Galloway said. "I reckon he was right about that."

Pemberton did not speak for a few moments. He thought of the child in the sheriff's office and tried to recall something besides the intense brown eyes. He remembered the child's hair. It hadn't been blonde but dark like his own.

"So the child's safe."

"Mama says he is, him and the Harmon girl both, but that's all Mama can tell me. They's got so far away she can't get them in her mind no more. That trail's went colder than a well digger's ass."

Galloway paused and his countenance appeared almost wistful. He raised his nub and brushed a bead of sweat from his forehead. Galloway stepped closer and kneeled next to Pemberton. He took the hawkbill knife from his pocket and freed the blade with the same slow deliberateness he might undo a bow. The blade clicked as it locked into place.

"Your missus said she didn't want you suffering any more than you had to," Galloway said, "but I can't kill you quick after the way I done the sheriff. It'd lay too heavy on my conscience."

The hawkbill slashed down, cutting open Pemberton's front pant pocket and freeing the twenty-dollar gold piece. Galloway picked up the coin.

"I will take this though," he said, placing it in his pocket. "I figured I earned it."

"Is there a panther?" Pemberton asked.

"You'll know the truth of that in a few hours," Galloway said, and nodded toward the park. "That cat will come across the ridge there and to the left of that cliff hang. It'll smell your blood and soon enough come on down and have a visit."

Galloway lifted the tote sack and swung it over his shoulder. He headed across the meadow, moving in the same shambling manner as before. I'll remember that slow saunter, Pemberton told himself, I'll remember it the very moment I kill him. Galloway stopped and turned.

"One other thing she wanted me to tell you. Your coffin, she said to tell you she's going to order it special from Birmingham. Your missus said she owed you that."

In a few minutes Galloway entered the woods. Pemberton caught glimpses of him through the trees and then a short while later as Galloway followed the trail over the rise. Then he was gone.

Pemberton reached for the gold chain on his pocket watch. He tugged until the watch emerged. When the gold shell opened, two half-moons of glass fell to the ground, but the watch still worked. The hands were on the three and six. Pemberton followed the almost imperceptible drag of the minute hand moving across the watch face toward the seven. He watched the minute hand as intently as possible, thinking if he could see time pass it would somehow make a difference.

But the pain was too much to concentrate more than a few seconds. His whole leg was now swollen, the pain constant all the way to the hip. The leg muscles began to spasm, as if the limb were frantically trying to shake out the venom. Pemberton's stomach heaved and he was glad since that might expel some of the poison, but when he looked at the ground he saw what had come forth was blood. His ribs and ankle hurt as well, but they were afterthoughts, as was his thirst. He'd have to wait the poison out a few hours, let it ease enough to limp out of the gorge.

Pemberton turned so he could face west. He tried to think of something besides the pain. He studied the Smokies as they unfolded into Tennessee. How many millions of board feet of timber were in those mountains, Pemberton wondered. The nausea returned, and more blood brightened the ground when he vomited. His mouth tasted of copper, and he thought of veins of copper and stream beds of jewels inside the Smokies. He thought especially of Cade's Cove, where old-growth yellow poplars yet remained. The tune the workers sang about the big rock candy mountain came into his head and lingered a few moments before dissipating.

Pemberton passed out, and when the pain woke him the day waned. The sun leaned its shoulder into the ridge, and shadows sortied out from the woods into the meadow. Pemberton could smell the leg, its skin now fiery red from kneecap to toes. The limb was dying, would soon enough be black and festering. Pemberton knew he'd lose it, but that would be all right. He could spend his working day on horseback, as Serena did.

His vision blurred and each breath came harder. Pemberton decided he had to start making his way across the meadow. He'd get as far up the trail as he could before full dark and then rest until dawn. They'd crossed a creek halfway down. He'd drink enough water there to get him the rest of the way.

Pemberton pressed both hands to the earth and dragged himself forward a few feet. The broken ankle announced itself anew, and he had to lay his head against the earth a minute. He tried to move again, and when he did the world gave way beneath him, as if trying to pull away. Pemberton clutched a hank of broom sedge and held tight. He remembered the afternoon he'd followed McDowell's police car out to the Deep Creek turnoff. How he'd sat there in the Packard with his hand on the hard rubber ball, and how, for a few moments, it had been like having the world in his grasp.

In half an hour, Pemberton was in the meadow's center. He rested and tried to gain up some strength. It was the only way, he told himself, not so much to survive as prove to Serena he was strong enough after all, worthy of her. If he could just make it back to camp, then everything could be again as it once was.

Shadows fell over him. The festering leg was like dragging a log, and Pemberton imagined the leg gone, how unburdened and free he'd be. If I had the knife I'd cut it off right now, Pemberton told himself, leave it and go on my way. Pemberton retched, but nothing rose into his throat. The world shuddered, tried again to tear free. He grabbed another fistful of broom sedge and held on.

When he regained consciousness, it was twilight. A cry like that of an infant came from the meadow's edge. Jacob, he thought, still safe, still alive. Pemberton raised his head toward the sound, but his vision had receded into some part of himself so deep no light could enter. A few minutes later he heard something brushing the broom sedge, moving resolutely toward him, and Pemberton suddenly knew, knew more surely than he'd ever known anything, that Serena had come for him. He remembered the evening in Boston when Mrs. Lowell had introduced them, and Serena had smiled and reached out her hand to take his. A new beginning, now as well as then. Pemberton could not see or speak, but he opened his hand and let go of the broom sedge, let go of the earth itself as he waited to feel Serena's firm calloused hand embrace his.

CODA

In the spring of 1975, an article appeared in Life *magazine about Serena Pemberton, describing her long career as a timber baroness in Brazil. Because of her age, the article had an elegiac tone, which the subject did not altogether discourage. She even volunteered that her lawyer had already been given specific plans for her burial (no funeral was mentioned), including internment in a lead coffin built in Birmingham, Alabama. Because it won't rot or rust, Mrs. Pemberton had answered when asked to explain such a choice.*

When the reporter wondered if there was anything she'd done in her life that she now regretted, Mrs. Pemberton said absolutely not, then turned the conversation to a tract of brazilwood in Pernambuco, which she hoped to purchase with the help of a West German tractor company. The magazine article's photographs were in color and contemporary except for one, a black-and-white picture that hung in the hacienda's living room. A nostalgic indulgence, she told her interviewer, quite out of character, but there it is. The photograph was of a young Serena Pemberton astride a huge white horse, an eagle on her right arm. Standing beside her was a tall powerfully built man. In the background lay a wasteland of stumps and downed limbs whose limits the frame could not encompass. The photograph's one flaw was Serena Pemberton's face, caught in motion and thus blurred to a gray featurelessness.

The article was read in September of the same year by a woman in a Seattle, Washington, hospital who awaited a heart operation that might or might not save her life. The Life *had been in a basket of magazines brought by a nurse so her patient might have something to read other than a tattered family Bible. The woman had carefully torn the article from the magazine and placed it in the Bible. She had visitors each day, including her husband, but it was the woman's son, who drove from Tacoma every evening after work to sit with her, that she showed the article to.*

A month later a man stepped onto the train platform *in Bertioga, Säo Paulo. He stayed in his hotel until midnight, then left his room to walk the town's cobbled streets. A thunderstorm had come in off the ocean earlier, and water pooled and eddied beside curbs and iron-grated gutters, but now the moon was out, giving enough light for him to make his way. Fifteen minutes later, he stepped quietly across the back lawn of Serena Pemberton's hacienda and onto the verandah. The man cut through a screen and stepped into a room bigger than any house he'd ever lived in. He pulled a flashlight from his back pocket, muting its light with his palm as he moved through the dwelling until he found the room he searched for. On the floor beside the bed, an old man snored softly on a pallet. He slept in his clothes, a pistol inches from his one hand. There had been a time when the man would have heard the slightest sound and awakened, but decades around machinery had deafened him to anything not written or shouted.*

He died first, the knife slashing his windpipe and then sawing across the vertebrae to make sure. The woman in the bed was not dispatched as easily. The town's doctor was also the coroner, and he found remnants of flesh under her nails on both hands.

She did not die in bed. A guard stationed at the front gate heard the huge brazilwood door open. The porch light had been dimmed for the night, but the moon was full, so the guard could clearly see the lady of the house taking slow but unwavering steps across the veranda. She paused at the end of the verandah and raised her left hand, tugged at the huge pearl-handled knife planted hilt-deep in her stomach. She was completely naked, though at first the guard thought she wore a dark silk slip. Her clipped white hair caught the full moon's light, and the guard, a man known for his superstitious nature, claimed later that for a few moments a garland of white fire flamed around her head.

She could not free the knife. According to the guard, she had looked down at the steps and moved one foot tentatively forward and then back as if testing the temperature of bathwater. It was then the guard saw the man behind her, his large figure framed by the doorway. He was so still the guard could not say if he had been there the whole while or appeared only at that moment. Then he was gone. Later that morning the police chief would ask for a description, and the guard would point to the photograph on the wall and swear that the man in the picture was the very man he'd seen. The police chief and the doctor dismissed the guard's words as another product of his credulousness.

But they did not dismiss the guard's testimony about what happened after he'd run up the walk and ascended the hacienda's wide steps. Serena had still been standing but the guard swore that she was already dead. Those among the townspeople who'd known her, including the police chief and the doctor, had no doubts at all as to the veracity of this aspect of the guard's account.

ACKNOWLEDGMENTS

The author wishes to thank the following for their help in researching this novel: George Frizzell, Charlotte Matthews, Phil Moore, Scott Simpson, and Ron Sullivan. Thanks also to my superb editor, Lee Boudreaux, my equally superb agent, Marly Rusoff, and Mihai Radulescu. Also Jennifer Barth, James Meader, Sam Rogers, my family, and the National Endowment for the Arts.

Although some of the characters in this novel actually existed historically, they are fictional representations.